TEHRAN MOONLIGHT

AZIN SAMETIPOUR

ISBN: 1491265191
ISBN 13: 9781491265192

For

Yasna and Arun

The penultimate moment in life is to look into the eyes that are wet, wet from the longing of love.

Sohrab Sepheri

One

Ya Fatemeh Zahra, please help me. Mahtab's pulse quickened. She opened her eyes and looked up from her plate at her family busily eating dinner before her. It was now or never. "Ostad Amini is holding a concert in May," Mahtab said, swallowing back the dryness in her throat. "It's for a charity."

Silence. Not even a look from her father who was soundlessly chewing, hunched over his plate at the head of the worn rectangular table, or from Pasha, her older brother, sitting across from her. Mahtab felt the seconds slide by like thick asphalt in the hot sun, the growing silence sucking the air out of the small room. The smell of fresh rice and *khoresht,* which usually made her mouth water, now made her faintly sick. Clearing her throat, she tried again. "He, I mean Ostad Amini, my music professor, has asked me to perform. He will pay me for it."

Mahtab knew she was taking a risk, a big risk actually, by bringing this up. Her family was religious, respected in the neighborhood as people who prayed five times a day, fed the poor from their meager means during Eid, and paid their respects to those who came back from the *hajj* in Saudi Arabia. Hers was a family whose daughters didn't date and instead covered themselves in honor with their scarves. How could she ask to play at a concert, where unrelated men and women could mingle behind the scenes? But this was different, Mahtab had told herself. This concert was sponsored by the Arman Foundation, an organization for the street children of Tehran. Kids who scratched a living off the smoke-clogged intersections of the city, selling candy or wiping the windshields of cars that drove by. In the past Mahtab would occasionally sneak out to do small concerts here and there, but this was different. It was being held at the Borj-e-Milad, the giant television tower that dominated the Tehran skyline. The ensemble would have to practice for at least three months together before the opening day and there would even be television crews, Ostad Amini had said.

"Who is singing? Can you get me and my friends free tickets?" Piped up Bahar, her baby sister, who was sitting next to her. A younger version of Mahtab without her slender figure, she had the same round feminine face, the big, liquid brown eyes that often caught the attention of the boys in the street. If only she would trim those eyebrows that threatened to unify across her forehead, but that would have to wait. Until she was in line to be married, that is. For now Bahar, barely eighteen, lived in the shadow of her older sister, content to let Mahtab do the talking for both of them.

"Don't even think about it. No concerts. You know better than to ask!" Pasha spoke up finally, a sneer on his lips.

"It's not a private concert. It's for charity! For the Arman Foundation. Think about those poor kids who'll benefit. Besides, Ostad Amini said it'd be good for my resume."

"To hell with Ostad Amini," Pasha spat between mouthfuls of rice. "All he does is teach stupid tunes to equally stupid students!"

For a moment Mahtab just stared at him. That he would cut her idea down was a given, but the insult, it hit her to the quick. 'Stupid students.' He was staring back at her now with those cold eyes of his, lighter than hers, set in a pale face with lips pulled shut. Then he suddenly smirked and turned away.

"No need to get yourself upset, Pasha," her father Rasool said calmly. A small man with silver-rimmed glasses perched upon his nose, he seemed to swell slightly in Mahtab's eyes, like a bird about to trill, as he spoke. "Mahtab, we have already talked about this more than a hundred times. You know it is not appropriate for our family, for you to go there. So there is no need to bring this up again."

"Baba please! When one of your children can actually make money, let them. God knows we need it. Pasha here can't even hold a job for more than two months," Mahtab snapped back. Her father should know. As a family

2

they never seemed to have enough money. A high school math teacher, he still worked all day for a small government salary like most teachers in the city, augmenting his meager income with private tuitions when he could.

"Shut up," Pasha thundered, slamming the table with his fists. *"Arr, arr nakon*! Don't bray, donkey! Baba said no. Besides, do you want my friends to talk behind my back and say Pasha's sister is a performer? A dancer?" He spat the last words out like it was a contagious disease.

"Dancer? What the hell are you talking about? I am a musician! I play the violin. I don't dance in front of people!" Mahtab cried.

"Shut up Mahtab! *Chashm* of course, she won't go, Pasha *joon*," her mother, Monir said stepping in. Hurriedly, she began pushing steaming white rice and *khoresht* onto Pasha's plate. "Do you want more? Is that enough, *pesaram*?" she said, hovering over him, spoon in hand.

Pasha grunted and scowled at her before getting back to his plate. Mahtab opened her mouth and then reconsidered. What was the use? She sighed inside. Her mom was the glue that held their dysfunctional family together. Short, with a bell cut of hair, Monir had filled out in her middle age. She still had the beautiful brown eyes her girls had inherited, but hers were almost always tired, worn by the constant vicissitudes of raising a family. Thin lips with age lines were now pressed in concentration as she continued with her task at hand.

"Pasha, please don't upset yourself," she implored.

Mahtab turned her face away. Her mother was always like that. Always pacifying, always holding things together. And forever living in fear of her husband and son, the masters of her universe.

Mahtab felt her grandmother's glare before she heard her speak. "Monir, why are you keeping her at home? Why isn't she married already? If she had a husband, she would be better behaved!" she croaked, her scrawny face twisted into a frown.

"I am not, Boji!" Monir exhaled, her right hand slapping the back of the left. "She doesn't want to get married. You are the witness to it all the time. Whoever comes forward to her *khastegari*, to seek our permission for her hand, she dismisses immediately. Look what happened to the downstairs neighbor's nephew!"

"Well," Boji said, clicking her tongue, "that's because you give her the chance to choose. I never gave my daughters a choice. Whoever we chose, they married. Just like that. Look at yourself. Your parents chose my Rasool for you, and you obeyed. Watch out, Monir!" she said wagging a finger, "Mahtab is twenty-three; she is getting old, and before you know it, you'll have a *torshideh*, a pickled girl in your home! Is that what you want her to be, a preserved spinster?" She pulled her scarf tighter around her henna-streaked hair.

"*Torshideh!*" Pasha laughed loudly, slapping the table with his right hand.

"Monir, I tell you, she needs to get married so this poor child," Boji said, pointing at Pasha, "doesn't have to deal with her anymore. He is tired of shepherding her." Boji sighed, her eyes resting on Mahtab. "She is like an untamed mule. But when she gets married, she won't be our problem anymore. Her husband will have to put her straight."

$$\curlyvee$$

Later on in the kitchen, Mahtab almost dropped the plate she was rinsing when her mother caught her arm from behind.

"Maman, you scared me!"

Maman quickly looked around and then whispered, "Mahtab, are you out of your mind? Why did you mention the concert in front of Pasha? You know he doesn't like you to do these things." Then she added quickly, "It's only because he wants to protect you. He says it for your own good."

Why did everyone think they knew what was good for her? Mahtab looked into the sink, its greasy water gurgling through the little hole in the center. Why did they think she needed protection from herself? But what really made her insides boil like molten metal was her own mother. The woman, who had brought her life, was supporting it all, explaining and rationalizing away every one of their dictates.

She put her hand on the faucet and turned to her mother. "*BeKhoda*! God! This is what musicians do, Maman. We play at concerts. That's how we share our talent with the world. My life is the violin, but here in my family, I am not allowed to play outside. I am not allowed to play inside. I am not even allowed to mention anything about my violin or my family will get mad! What can I do?"

"*Eyb nadareh*, it's OK. You play at school, don't you? What Pasha says is really for your own good. You know he means well." Maman paused and smiled. "After all, what will the neighbors say if they see you going to places that are not suitable for young girls? Who will marry you then, eh? Remember, like spilled water, once a girl's reputation is ruined, it will never come back!"

Mahtab looked into her mother's eyes and heaved a sigh. The expression in those large sad eyes, apparently open to light but closed to understanding, made her chest ache with sadness. There was no point arguing. Her mother would parrot whatever her father or Pasha said. She would never take her side.

She watched her mother's retreating figure through the door, running off to another perpetual chore. Even though Mahtab taught at the music institute six days a week, these occasional violin performances were good for her resume, not to mention the pay. And she wasn't going to miss them just because of her brother's stupid sensibilities. Besides, Mahtab really felt for those kids, and it would be great to help them in any way she could.

Her mobile phone buzzed. It was an SMS from Nasim, and the heaviness around her seemed to lift a little. She was Mahtab's best friend since they were five and her only window out of this suffocating place.

"Tomorrow I'll pick you up from work. *Basheh*, OK?"

She thumbed back, "OK, be there at six."

As she put her phone down, Bahar came in and stood next to her, her hands folded together like a pilgrim in supplication.

"Please get me tickets. Please."

"No one is singing. It's an orchestra!" Mahtab sighed. "That's if I can escape and actually go to the practices. I feel I can't breathe in here, in this home, in this family. Sometimes I feel like I should just get married to the first person who comes to my *khastegari* and leave this house!"

"Yeah, you do that, and make Boji happy. Seriously, come on, Mahtab, what's not to like here?" Bahar smiled mischievously, her hands moving around with a flourish. "I have to climb four stories to get to our apartment, which is fun, especially the nights that I have to take the garbage down. An elevator, forget it; the last time they talked about it was when they promised to put one in when they built this dump!"

Chuckling, Bahar continued. "Sometimes, when I come back from school, I just stop to enjoy the stone walls of our building. You know, covered with those torn advertisements and posters, looking for the latest addition, the newest plumber or candidate to fall for!"

Mahtab let out a small laugh.

"See, I got you to smile after all. I am right, *na*? It's so *chic*, just like a prison you see on TV. And most of all, we have our superstar, Pasha!"

Pasha's voice lifted from behind them, a yell that carried over the noise from the TV in the living room. "Bahar! Mahtab! Ayyy! Where's my tea?"

"Oh, see, that's what I came here for! To serve his highness," Bahar whispered before lifting the white china teapot off the *samovar*. The steaming tea poured into the cup like a small amber waterfall from the spout.

"Coming!" Bahar yelled back, holding Pasha's teacup and saucer.

"Make sure it's hot enough for him, or he'll send you right back," Mahtab said, touching the cup.

"It's hot enough to burn his tongue!" Bahar snorted before stepping out.

Two

It was time to make excuses. Mahtab's last student, Sanam, had just left. Mahtab's fingers poised for a moment over her phone before she punched in the numbers that she knew by heart. The mechanical ring over the receiver seemed to go on forever, each tightening the rubber band within her. Who would pick up on the other side?

"Bahar, it's you." Mahtab exhaled audibly. "Good. Tell Maman I am filling in for Raha again at the school and I'll be late."

"I wish I had a friend like Raha," said Bahar.

"You can." Mahtab chuckled. "You just have to make her up and slowly introduce her to the family! Just don't name her Raha though."

"OK, I'll name her Azadeh then!" Bahar laughed. "They both mean freedom, don't they? So where are you going?"

"I am going with Nasim to this photo gallery. It belongs to one of Sepehr's friends."

"Oh. OK, have fun." She heard the note in Bahar's voice, the loss of interest replacing vicarious hope. For although Mahtab knew Bahar would do almost anything to get out of the house, looking at "pictures," as she called it, was not one of them.

7

"You are late, Nasim," Mahtab said the moment she settled herself into her friend's car. Nasim looked perfect as usual, in a sky blue *manteau* that covered her slim, almost statuesque body. Only she could carry it off, Mahtab smiled. Make her *manteau*, the government mandated jacket of modesty into another fashion statement that made heads turn.

"Don't worry, *azizam*. We don't want to be there too early, or people will think we're desperate." Nasim laughed, clutching the thin, neoprene-wrapped steering wheel, weaving the little white Peugeot into a solid wall of snarling, coughing cars and trucks that occupied the road ahead.

"Nasim, I need to be home before eight."

"Relax, Mahtabi. You'll be fine. You'll have enough time," Nasim said with a laugh. As usual her *roosari*, headscarf was around her neck, thrown off her dyed blonde locks.

"Nasim, fix your scarf! I am not in the mood to get caught by the morality police."

Nasim narrowed her large doe eyes and parted her full lips slowly, "The only morality police that I have to deal with is you Mahtab *joon*, and that's because you are such a chicken! Loosen up, girl. No one is going to catch us!" Nasim sighed and then went on. "I wish you'd stop worrying so much and at least be a little more excited about the hot guys that are going to be there."

Mahtab let out a small laugh. "If any hot guy takes half a glance at my family, he'll run for his life."

"*Azizam*, you don't have to show him your family, do you?" Nasim smiled, her perfect teeth flashing as she turned her gold-rimmed Gucci glasses toward Mahtab.

"Then how am I going to marry him?"

"Not all relationships have to end in marriage, Mahtab *joon*."

It was easy for Nasim to say. Mahtab clutched the door handle as they suddenly lurched to avoid a blue Zamyad pickup, pouring out black smoke from its side. The smell of half-burnt diesel fuel filled the car.

"Are you driving or doing laundry?" The driver of a black car, a hatchet-faced youth they had cut off while passing the pickup truck, yelled from the side. Nasim leaned out of the window and yelled back, "Shut up, dickhead!"

"Nasim, shame on you," Mahtab said, shaking her head.

"What? You want me to just be quiet and let him get away with that? Laundry! His mother's doing his laundry, not me. I'll show him."

"I think you already did!" Mahtab said, suppressing a laugh.

Ever since Mahtab could remember, she and Nasim had been friends, from their first tea party to the cramps of their first periods and the crush on the long-haired boy who lived across the street. The girls had lived in the same building up until the sixth grade when Nasim's dad had struck it rich in the real estate boom that followed the war. With that money Nasim's family had moved to the swank Shahrak-Gharb neighborhood while Mahtab's was forced to move to Sabalan, but the distance never overshadowed the girls' friendship.

⌒◯

It was getting dark by the time they finally reached their destination. The Seyhoon Art Gallery was right off the sidewalk, an older gray stone building flanked by Doric columns. Mahtab looked at the large yellow banner that hung above. Written in *nostaligh*, curving, calligraphy lines of high Farsi, it proclaimed "Colorless Tehran" by Nima Rahimi, Winner of the Tehran Photography Contest 2006. Finalist in the Asian Documentary Series, Tokyo, 2007.

"Do you remember the picture that got him nearly in trouble?" Mahtab asked Nasim.

"Was it about the girl who was pregnant but had no ring on her finger or something?"

"Yes! That's the one. She had her left hand on her pregnant belly without a ring, and in her right was a rock. It was beautiful."

"I know you like art or whatever," Nasim said, raising her eyebrows just so to avoid destroying the layers of foundation that lay beneath, "but for once try to act normal. I want the hot guys here to take half a glance at you! So your left hand won't end up empty!" She smiled, working a piece of gum. "Wouldn't it be great, you know, if you had someone? Then we could all go out, me and Sepehr, you and your guy! Speaking of Sepehr, where is my boyfriend?"

"*Harfesh bood*, he heard you! There he is coming toward us," said Mahtab, tapping Nasim's arm.

"Salaam," said Sepehr. His warm brown eyes shone as soon as they fell on Nasim. They had met only three months ago but the two had really hit it off and were now inseparable.

"Your hair looks cute," Nasim said, touching his spiked hair. Sepehr smiled an easy smile.

"Are you alone?" Nasim asked, joining hands with Sepehr. Next to him she reached up to his shoulders.

"No, Ashkan is with me," he said.

"You managed to bring him?" Nasim said, looking at him with a pout. "Well, you are not taking care of him this time. You're with me now!" Nasim cooed, pulling Sepehr closer.

While Nasim and Sepehr peeled off, Mahtab found herself engrossed in a picture of a wizened farmer looking confused in a brand new Tehran metro station. But her moment in silence didn't last long. It was Nasim, "Mahtabi, *bia*! Come, let's go meet some guys!"

"All you think of is boys," Mahtab muttered as she walked across the cavernous hall. Cultured voices and their echoes filled the room as people clustered around large photographs with spotlights suspended above their frames.

They found Sepehr with a group of his friends, typical Tehrani fashionistas. The men dressed in black, dripping cologne, and the women's scarves down around their necks, sunglasses propped in their carefully coiffured hair. Mahtab's eyes were drawn to a guy standing next to Sepehr, even taller than him. He was silent, unsmiling, his arms crossed over his broad chest. In fact, in the few times she looked in his direction, he wasn't even looking anywhere close to where they were; his eyes drifting over the ceiling and the high walls above them.

"I don't know if you remember Ashkan, my *pesar amoo,* the son of my father's brother," Sepehr said to his friends, pointing to Mr. Serious next to him. "When we were in the tenth grade, he was in the ninth."

"Oh yeah, I remember," someone said. "He was in our school only for a little while before he left. At first we all thought he was your brother."

Ashkan smiled briefly but didn't speak. By now all the girls there were eyeing him. A young waiter came by, offering glasses of chilled sour cherry sherbet. Mahtab took one and left the circle. She knew if she stood there, she wouldn't get to see what she had come for, what she had lied to her family to do.

Mahtab found herself alone in a less-packed part of the exhibition. Suddenly she felt something. Turning around instinctively, Mahtab caught a looming figure next to her. It took her a split second to recognize him, but yes, there he was, Sepehr's cousin. Ashkan. His eyes, unlike most guys next to a girl, were not on her but intently focused in front. He was staring at the same picture she was looking at few seconds ago, a black-and-white photo of a small boy sharing his ice cream cone with a stray kitten.

"You like it?" he asked still looking ahead.

"Excuse me?" It took her a moment to understand him, that masculine voice. He had a definite accent, not from the countryside, but that of a *farangi*, a foreigner.

"Oh yes, it's beautiful," she said, swallowing back her surprise. "After all, he has won prizes."

"Really? What do you like about it?" he asked. She glanced at his face, but it was his eyes that made her glance back at him again. They were a striking green, with a splash of gold in the center that gave them an intensity that was a little unnerving.

She paused before answering, "Well, the lighting and the angles of the subjects really make them almost come alive."

"It's all about the right moment," he said, with the tone of a professor declaring a fact.

"Yes, but he also has a good eye for the right moment." What was he getting at? This was one of her favorite artists he was talking about.

"In my opinion, there is still a lot of room for improvement. He's still an amateur," Ashkan said slowly.

"Amateur, ha?" Mahtab said with a toss of her head. Her blood was boiling now! "Didn't you read the flier? He was a finalist in Tokyo. He was the winner of the 2006 Tehran Photography Contest. Didn't you see his picture of the pregnant girl in *Tasvir*? Amateur? Come on, give me a break! He has done a fantastic job."

He didn't reply, but his eyes stayed on her, and hers on his. She felt as though they were measuring her, but she would give no quarter back.

"There you are, Ashkan," said Sepehr, striding in and patting Ashkan on the shoulder.

Lucky for him Sepehr arrived, Mahtab fumed. Otherwise Ashkan would have been picking his eyeballs off the floor when she was done with him.

"What do you think of the exhibition?" Sepehr asked. How did he do that? Smile and talk at the same time. Mahtab wondered.

"I think for an amateur, it's OK," replied Ashkan.

"Are you a photographer yourself?" Mahtab asked, hardly containing the anger within her.

"No," he said evenly.

"Because the way you criticize it, I thought…"

Sepehr cut in. "Come on, Ashkan; it's not that bad."

"No, it's not," Ashkan said, looking at his watch. "I didn't say it was bad. I simply said there's room for improvement."

There it was again, that "room for improvement" thing.

"Like what?" Mahtab asked. "It's easy for people who haven't done anything to sit around and criticize other people's work. If you think you can do a better job, you should hold an exhibition yourself and let us tell you what better work is!"

"You are not getting the point. What was your name again?"

She now felt the full weight of his attention upon her. "Mahtab!" she spat out.

"OK, Mahtab, you misunderstood my point."

"What's your point? I think you made yourself pretty clear when you said these photos were not up to your standards. Isn't that true?"

He looked at Mahtab for a measured second and then said softly, "Like I said, you misunderstood me Mahtab." Then he turned and simply walked away.

Mahtab followed him with her eyes, a little confused. So that was the end of it? She felt a little cheated. Mahtab loved a good argument, and she was looking forward to a real victory over this jerk! Now it was like taking a bite out of thin air, shadowboxing into nothingness.

"Who died and made you the expert in photography?" she muttered at his retreating form.

⁓◌

Mahtab had known Sepehr from the day Nasim met him at an underground concert three months ago. He was fun, outgoing, and a fast talker who could keep them laughing in their seats. Nasim had confided that he was the best guy she had ever had, and she would know. How many had she gone through before him? But Sepehr's *pesar amoo*, this Ashkan. He seemed so different from his cousin, so cold, almost devoid of emotion that he could be from another planet.

On their way back in the car, Nasim grinned and said, "I'm going to drop you off and then go to Sepehr's apartment for a little post-show fun!"

She glanced at Mahtab and went on. "Don't look at me like that. I am not going to burn in hell. It's not a sin if I love him."

"It's a sin if you are not married. I have told you before. Anyway, I wasn't giving you a dirty look. I was thinking I could have gone home by myself and let you go for your sin, I mean, fun!"

"No, actually Sepehr is out for a little while too. He's dropping off his *pesar amoo.*"

"What was wrong with him?" Mahtab asked.

"Who, Sepehr?"

"No, that 'I am better than everybody in the world' guy. Ashkan."

A smile flashed across Nasim's face. "That's right you haven't met him before, have you? Don't worry about him. He is a foreigner." She let the words drop for effect, turning briefly to Mahtab. "Of course, none of our things are good enough for him."

"What kind of foreigner?" Mahtab's eyes widened.

"Didn't you see the 'Made in USA' label all over him? That accent? He only arrived from paradise three weeks ago."

"I noticed the accent," Mahtab admitted, "but 'Made in USA' or not, I don't like him."

"He's really good-looking though." Nasim winked. "But then again you don't like any boys, do you?"

"Oh Nasim. I do like boys, but the kind of boys I like my parents would never accept, and those they like I'd rather die than marry."

Mahtab looked out of the window at the moon just clearing the rooftops, bathing everything around in its silver light. She sighed, envying Nasim's freedom. For just like Mahtab's namesake, as the moonlight was beholden to the sun, she was beholden to her family's rules.

Three

The moon had risen to claim its place in the sky by the time Mahtab reached home. As she climbed the gray cinderblock stairs to her apartment, she muttered a silent prayer that Pasha wouldn't be home. Quickly, she wiped her lips to remove any trace of lipstick. Climbing the last flight of stairs as fast as she could, she peeked around the corner at the yellow pine door that led to her home. It seemed quiet, with only the faint smell of lamb stew in the air. Her heart sank. Next to her doorway, among the shoes neatly arranged to the side, were the black leather shoes she knew belonged to Pasha. But next to them were another pair. Definitely a man's, bigger than Pasha's. Pointed, black, and shiny, with toecaps that were punched and decorated, they looked like they had been used only a handful of times or belonged to a person who had a car. Who was this now?

She unlocked the door with her key and taking a deep breath, entered. The voice of the announcer was the first thing she heard, roaring the goal that Manchester United had scored. Down the corridor she could see the back of Pasha's head, thrown in relief by the flickering screen in front. As she edged forward, she saw another head next to him, long tapered, like a hatchet, with short black hair. Emad!

"Salaam," she said quickly as she hurried past.

"Sit, sit," she heard Pasha's voice and whirled around to see him looking at Emad, who had stood up.

"Salaam *aleikom*," Emad said softly. The first thing Mahtab noticed was his thick beard, clinging to his face like a dark carpet. And then his dark lidded eyes upon her, a small smile on his lips.

"Emad, please sit. You will miss the game!" Pasha said, patting the seat beside him. Emad ignored him. He looked like he had come straight from work, wearing gray pants and a white shirt still buttoned up all the way to his neck.

"Salaam," Mahtab returned.

"Where were you?" Pasha asked suddenly, his eyes narrowing.

"Work," Mahtab answered flatly. It was the only way to lessen his suspicion, to act like an automaton or an idiot. "I told Bahar. I had to take Raha's students. She couldn't be there today."

Nodding at them both curtly, Mahtab hurried to her room through the hallway.

"Pasha brought his boss here again?" Mahtab said, finding Bahar in their room, her eyes glued to her phone texting friends.

"Yes again," Bahar said, looking up from her phone. "When he came home with Emad, Pasha was actually upset you weren't back. He kept asking where you were. And his new boss even offered to go pick you up from work." Bahar chuckled. "Why was your phone off anyway?"

"I turned it off so they wouldn't catch me."

"I told Maman your battery died," Bahar said, leaning back against the wall.

"Is he going to stay for dinner?" Mahtab asked.

"Yes. Maman made lamb stew."

"*Vayyy*? Lamb stew? The prices went up again last week. And Pasha's so-called friend is here again? We don't run a charity to feed people here for free. Why can't Pasha go to his house for dinner once?"

Bahar shrugged. "I guess Pasha is trying to make Emad like him. Ever since he got the job last month."

"At least he has one now. Another month and it will be the longest he has ever had!" Mahtab replied, adjusting her scarf. There was a stranger in the house so she would have to keep it on. "I'll go help Maman set the table."

"We are so happy to have Pasha in our department," Emad said during dinner, sandwiched between Pasha and Baba. "He is a great asset, *mashallah!* I cannot be more pleased with his joining us."

"You are very kind, Mr. Emad," Baba whispered, sparks of happiness visibly lighting up his lined eyes.

"You know people said many times to my father that he must have gotten the job for me with his connections and all. But he didn't. I wanted to be my own man. I started working for the municipality as a clerk, and before I knew it, I was a manager in the transportation department. We do projects for the entire city."

"*Bah, bah*, Mr. Emad. That must take much intelligence!" Baba said, smiling.

"*Mashallah!*" Boji said, taking a sip of her *doogh*, yogurt soda.

"Then, thanks to God, I bought my new car. I tell Pasha too, *inshallah* give it six months in my department and you'll be able to buy a car and even have a down payment for a small apartment or something."

"*Inshallah*, God willing! Please have some more *khoresht*, Agha Emad," Monir said, adjusting her headscarf.

"Thank you, I've had so much already, Khanoom Sharifi," Emad said, touching his slight belly.

"How do you like your job, Pasha?" Emad asked.

"I like it very much," Pasha said with an unctuous smile. He seemed so different around Emad, his usual arrogance replaced with a slavishness bordering on sycophancy.

"You used to work in marketing before, right?"

"*Baleh.*"

"That's why you like my department better," he said and laughed. "Working on deals and money is way better than working with people."

Emad finally left after his second tea. When she heard the downstairs gate shut and then the muffled groan of a car starting, Mahtab tore off her head scarf, the scarf that she had been wearing all day at work and now at home. She felt the relief, the liberation of her hair as it fell around her shoulders.

Mahtab entered the living room to find Pasha on the edge of the sofa, leaning over a bowl of *tokhmeh*, sunflower seeds. He said, "You know this

Emad is so smart, he invested some money in the stock market and in six months he doubled it. Iran Khodro. The car company. What a genius! I should have bought too, but I had no money. This was while he was working on the city's new metro!"

"*Bah, bah! Mashallah!*" intoned Baba.

Then Pasha's voice dropped. "Do you know how much he makes a month?" He paused for effect before saying, "Two million toman!"

"*Inshallah,* you will too," Boji said. "*Inshallah* and soon you'll fetch a wife. I so long to see your little boys run around here."

"He won't be living with us, Boji. Once Pasha gets married, he'll move to his own home," Bahar said, her eyes glinting mischievously, "and then I can have his room!"

"You never know," Boji's voice was cracking now as she covered her eyes and sniffed, "*Inshallah,* his wife is a good girl and wants to live with us. Just like your mother, who lived with your grandfather and me when she got married."

"Where she is going to live? On my head? There is barely room for us as it is," mouthed Bahar silently behind Boji, looking at Mahtab.

Four

I t was three-thirty p.m. and Tara had not yet arrived. Tapping her fingers on the old wooden desk, Mahtab felt the weight of time on her, something she wasn't used to given the pace of her life recently. But to Mahtab, this was not work. She genuinely liked teaching her students, "her kids" as she called them. With Parmis canceling on her earlier, Farbod, a gangly fourteen-year-old boy would be her last student, but now it was Tara's turn. Mahtab opened the white door of the classroom and looked out. There was no one, only the sounds of a piano plinking distantly down the corridor. She shrugged. Tara was usually a few minutes late.

She sat back at her desk and gathered her papers. This room was where she had taught since the first year of college. How many years was that? Almost five years ago. Wow, that seemed like an eternity now. The Nava Music Institute had three other rooms that she could use, but she liked this one the best. The familiar shape of the large, white-framed mirror covered the adjacent wall, and a black Chinese made piano was up against the far corner. Framed pictures of various musicians, both foreigners and Iranians through history, hung on the ivory-colored walls. Her favorite was that of a man, his long face with sharp, dark eyes, crowned by a cascade of parted red hair. It was Antonio Vivaldi, *il preto rosso*, the red priest. With pieces like the *The Four Seasons*, Vivaldi was a composer in the baroque tradition to whom violinists the world over were indebted to. Or so Mahtab thought, for she was unabashedly a fan of his.

The rays of the afternoon sun were filling the classroom, painting it a warm orange. Mahtab glanced at the white-faced clock on the wall. Still no Tara, and it was already fifteen minutes into her lesson time. She picked up the worn study guide in front of her, the faded colors of an abstract European painting on the cover, and tossed it aside. She got up and walked to the window. Beneath the institute, on the fifth floor of their building, lay the street and the lighted signs of shops, the noise mercifully muted by the thick tinted glass.

Mahtab turned abruptly at the sound of a timid knock at the door. A second later, the door opened and the profile of a young chubby girl appeared.

"Salaam, Miss Mahtab," Tara said between labored breaths, tottering on unsteady legs.

"Oh good, you are here. Were you running again, Tara?"

"Sorry I am late," she said wringing her hands.

Tara was the picture of a mess, her scarf too short for her head and about to fall off; her socks, two different colors, settling around her brown schoolgirl shoes. "Where is your violin?" Mahtab asked, as she closed the door behind her.

Tara froze and turned her sad eyes to Mahtab's.

"I forgot," she whispered.

"Again? Then you have to go back. You know the policy. You have to bring your own violin or else you can't get lessons here."

"I know, Miss Mahtab," Tara said, her lip quivering, about to cry.

Mahtab sighed. "Where are your parents?"

"My dad dropped me off. He said when I am done, I should wait for him downstairs." She paused before bursting out, "Miss Mahtab, I am so sorry. My violin was left at my mom's place, and my dad said he wouldn't go to pick it up!"

Mahtab cleared her throat and said, "It's OK this time, Tara. Have you been practicing?"

The little girl dried her eyes and mumbled, "I have been with my dad since he picked me up on Friday."

"So no practice then," Mahtab murmured. "Well, let's see what you remember from last week. Obviously you don't have your book, do you?"

When Tara shook her head, Mahtab grabbed a book and a white violin from behind her desk.

"It's all right, leave it," she said, seeing Tara struggling with her scarf, trying to stuff her hair back into its tiny folds. "There is no man here, Tara. I'd rather you pay attention to me than worrying about your scarf."

For the first time, Tara let out a small smile.

"Come on then. You don't have much time left. Start from the beginning. Sit straight," Mahtab said, adjusting Tara's posture.

"Hold the violin like I showed you, chin on the chin rest, lightly. Let it be part of you, Tara."

With a small, shy nod, the little girl slowly brought up the bow.

"*Khoobeh.* That's it. Now remember the bow stays gently on the violin— on it, not into it, not over it. Here let me show you."

A little while later, a few hesitant notes began to flow, forming slowly, scratchily, the beginning of 'Happy Birthday to You.' Tara stopped and looked up at Mahtab. The little smile that touched her lips made Mahtab grin inside.

Before they knew it, the alarm clock went off, and Tara stopped, looking at Mahtab.

"It's OK, Tara. Finish the piece."

After she finished playing, Mahtab said, "Tara, you need to practice. You are doing great, but you just need to practice. Do you like to play the violin, or is it something your parents are forcing you to do?"

Tara's eyes fell. "I like it," she said, hesitating before looking up again. "I like it very much. But my mom and dad think it's a hassle for them to drop me off here every week."

Mahtab smiled and put her arm around Tara. "Let me tell you something about myself. My parents also hated for me to play the violin. They thought it was below me, my family's dignity, to be a musician. If they had their way, I was to learn to cook and be a doctor, all at the same time! But I chose the violin because I loved it. I loved it then and I love it now. So you should do what you love. If you love your violin, you should play it no matter what. *Basheh?* OK? Now, are you going to your mom's or your dad's home?"

"My dad's until tomorrow."

"Tell your dad to take you to your mom's house so you can pick up your violin. Tell him Miss Mahtab said it. OK?" she said, straightening her face in mock seriousness.

Tara let out a small tinkling laugh. *"Baleh! Chashm."*

"Good, I'll see you next Wednesday," Mahtab said opening the door and then walking Tara to the elevator.

When she came back, she called her next student, Farbod, who was already in the waiting room. A tall, skinny teenager with a thin fuzz of hair sprouting around his mouth, he was stooped over his silver cell phone, texting.

"Farbod, are you ready?"

"Oh," he grunted, looking up. "Salaam."

"Turn off your cell phone, Farbod," Mahtab said as she headed for her room.

"No, I can't," he returned.

"Yes, you can. I don't want what you did last time. You wasted half of the class texting. Remember, we only have forty five minutes."

Farbod muttered something under his breath. His eyes, half covered by a thick swath of hair, hid his expression, which was just as well, for Mahtab knew what mattered was what he did, not felt, if she was to teach him anything. But despite his mercurial moods, Mahtab was proud of him. He was sent by his parents, who had stumbled upon the music school in a newspaper ad. They were at their wits' end looking for something besides self-destructive time sinks for their son. What she had done was actually unlock a talent that even surprised the moody Farbod himself.

"Is it me, or do you look more beautiful every day?" he said once in the room.

Mahtab smiled and said, "Farbod, be serious."

"I am."

"Fine. Have you finished? OK, let's get started. Sit, get your violin ready."

"Chashm, my beautiful teacher," Farbod said, smiling. "What piece first?"

"Play Bijan Mortazavi's 'Dance of Fire.'"

Farbod let out a groan and shook back his hair. "I know that by heart!"

"Farbod, maybe so, but you haven't mastered it yet. Play it."

Mahtab turned toward the window as Farbod started playing; in the distance lay something that made a part of Mahtab's heart lift, felt herself rise above everything, every time she saw them: the Alborz Mountains.

Stately peaks of gray flecked by the white of snow, uninterrupted, shimmering in the distance. Something she had spent looking at since the first time she had been given that classroom years ago. Something she couldn't imagine seeing from home, from her window, which, even if it did admit a view like this, was always draped shut by thick brown curtains. Not to keep the sun out, but to shield the honor of the girls within from prying eyes.

After Farbod left, Mahtab took in a deep breath. She actually was glad she was done. Being her best student meant that Farbod also took a lot more from her, both from instruction and his attitude. But today, she had gotten him to focus, to concentrate on that one piece, to actually play better that he had played last time. He had moved beyond mere control of the violin to making it one with himself. Where he no longer thought of each stroke or how he held the fingerboard but let his thoughts and inhibitions yield to the music that flowed from the union between the violin and him. Slowly, she got up and headed for Mr. Javadi's office for her daily meeting.

Kamran Javadi was sitting at his desk. A short man in his late forties, Mr. Javadi's disarming looks hid a sharp intellect and musical talent that allowed him to play four different instruments: the piano, the tar, the violin, and the beautiful, sonorous guitar-like setar. With thick, black hair now peppered with gray, he seemed to never really leave the institute that he had founded over fifteen years ago. In fact, he was the soul of the Nava Music Institute and his enthusiasm and vision had built it into one of the best music schools in northern Tehran. He had married one of the piano instructors Maryam a few years back, and their little girls, though they weren't born in the institute, literally grew up there and were often found skipping through the various rooms. Now that would be a dream come true for Mahtab: to marry a guy in music. Someone she could relate to, share her love for music. Someone she didn't have to have to fight with just to validate her passion.

"Here are the student reports for today, Mr. Javadi," she said, placing several brown folders before him.

"Nazila still hasn't improved?" he said before he had even opened her folder.

"No, she doesn't want to play. Her parents are forcing her to do it."

He clicked his tongue. "OK, we'll give her till next week and then I'll talk to her parents. I have two more students, a sister and a brother, for you starting next week."

"I can't take more students. As it is my hours are full. Why don't you give them to Nooshin?"

Mr. Javadi shot her a smile. "They asked for you, Mahtab! You have a reputation here. You've been with us since when, you were what? Eighteen?"

"Yes, since the first year of college."

"And you are an excellent tutor! See, now parents call here and say we want Mahtab Sharifi to teach our kids. And many of these families, as you know, are well to do. Most of these kids have gone to other classes before coming here."

"I know. That's not the issue. You know I just have to be home by a certain time. It is getting difficult for me."

"Look, I know about your situation. Do you want me to call your parents? Oh, which reminds me, Ostad Amini called."

"He did?" Mahtab jumped at the mention of her mentor.

"Yes, and I think you should do it. The concert, I mean. It's big, Mahtab. It's the Tehran University Orchestra we are talking about. You do this and you could buy yourself a ticket to the Talar-e-Vahdat." Then he smiled. "And then you can get me and Maryam VIP seats!"

The thought that she could be in the running for the Talar-e-Vahdat. Oh, to be part of the National Philharmonic, even as an intern. That would be a dream come true.

"I'll change your kids' schedule. I'll put these two in because they specifically asked for you. But I'll make sure you have enough time to go to the practice. We'll remove Nazila. Does that work for you?"

Mahtab's phone beeped. "Yes, that works." And she got up. "I have to go now. I'll be late. And thank you for offering to call my parents. But please don't. I am afraid they will stop me from working all together if they found out about the concert."

Mr. Javadi paused, looking at her for a moment before shaking his head. "I would love it if I had a talented daughter like you. Getting a part in a concert this big without even auditioning! What's wrong with your parents?"

"Nothing. They are just worried about me."

"I understand. See you tomorrow. And don't forget to call Ostad Amini," Kamran said as Mahtab turned to leave.

Five

We are going to the movies. Azadi complex. You want to come? It was a text from Nasim.

Mahtab glanced at her watch, her mind already planning her next move. It was five pm. She could go to the movies, but she would have to lie again. Tell her mother that she was going to dinner at Nasim's house.

She took the bus, still debating whether she should have let Kamran call her home. But what other choice did she have? How would she get out of the house for those last-minute practices, for the three nights when they would actually perform? Ostad said if this concert went well those three nights in May, well, they could tour the country, maybe neighboring countries. And maybe even Europe. She sighed. Then what would she tell her parents? Pasha?

His name made her shudder. Pulling her mind together, she pushed the thought aside.

Didn't Kamran say this was her ticket to the Tehran orchestra?

To play in the Tehran National Philharmonic. It was Ostad Amini, her music professor in college, who had first encouraged that dream of hers, made it actually seem possible. She remembered it like it was yesterday. It was the first semester at Tehran University School of Music and she was going to drop out because she just couldn't afford the expenses associated with school, not to mention the constant badgering at home.

"Damn the evil," her father would say. "If only your Uncle Nader had not taken you to violin class when you were a child. We were foolish to let him encourage your stupidity, and now look what had happened? Every one of the neighbors' children wants to go to university to become a *doktor* or *mohandes*, an engineer. But our daughter goes to university to become an entertainer. You do not need schooling for that!"

Mahtab could picture it still, walking up those steps into the cavernous hall, past the male secretary who took her into Ostad's study. It was smaller than she had expected, the smell of old paper and rosin in the air. The walls were lined with open cabinets, filled with journals, books, and other detritus of a long career as a tenured professor. On the walls hung framed accomplishments, some in English, and in the far display case were musical instruments. Behind his desk, Ostad Amini had sat, a small man with curly silver hair, kindly gray eyes, and a long, flat Marx-like beard that bristled as he moved.

"Salaam. You are Mahtab Sharifi? First-year student playing the...violin?" He began in a querulous voice.

"*Baleh.*"

"So why are you leaving?" he said, holding up her letter of intent, his eyes on her over half-moon glasses.

She did not remember her exact words, but they did come like a torrent. Something in his tone had said that he meant his question. Minutes later, out of words and her cheeks wet, she heard him simply say. "Play for me."

"*Baleh?*" she said, sniffling.

"Take that violin from the case and play a piece you know from your heart. That's all."

And she did just that. The violin was old, the varnish on its edges and back cracked into lines. But it played like butter, mellow, the bow sliding over the strings like syrup, through a part of the *Moosighi Koochak-e Shab*, the *Eine kleine Nachtmusik* by Mozart, a favorite of hers.

When she put down her bow after the final note, his eyes were closed. Her pulse quickened. What had she done? Had she bored him so badly that she had put him to sleep?

"You have something very few others here possess," he said, opening his eyes. "Frankly, I didn't expect this given your exam reports, but from what you tell me about your problems, I now see why." He took in a breath. "You have true talent, Mahtab. In my years as a professor of music, I have only heard few other students play with so much potential." He allowed a little smile behind his mustache, "Usually this would be an occasion to celebrate. But given your situation, I'll try to get you help, Mahtab, starting with a recommendation to work for one of my old students. He has a music institute and needs help."

The loud squealing of the bus brakes, followed by the hiss of the air, jolted her out of her reverie. The bus was one stop before the Azadi movie theater, where she was to meet Nasim. It's not that hard, she told herself. All she had to do was lie, which she was used to. Lie to Pasha, Lie to Maman, lie to Baba, and lie to Boji. Tell her friends to lie for her. In that madhouse, if she wanted to survive, she had to lie. When opportunity rang at her door, she wouldn't miss it just because Pasha didn't approve of it. But deep down, she had a hard time believing herself, overcoming the doubt and fear that lingered within the dark recesses of her consciousness.

∽↺

Mahtab met Nasim a little after six in the evening, outside the Azadi movie theater. Their new favorite haunt, this large, square, glass-and-silver multiplex was brand new, having been built only last year from the ashes of an old theater that had burned down with people inside years ago. After they got their tickets, they waited in the busy, narrow glass atrium for Sepehr, scanning the crowd between snippets of gossip. Soon they spotted him, sauntering in with that slight swagger that Nasim raved about behind his back. Mahtab's heart sank. Why did *he* have to be here? She didn't lie to her family to get this. But there he was, a few feet from Sepehr. His *pesar amoo* and Mr. Know-It-All, Ashkan, in a pair of faded jeans and a blue sweatshirt. Waving, Sepehr bounded up, a big grin on his face. Ashkan nodded in their general direction. No handshakes, not even a salaam from him. He must think they were below his foreign standards. Not cool enough, she supposed.

"We have been waiting for you guys forever! My legs hurt now." Nasim complained to Sepehr, pointing at her high heels.

"*Akhey azizam.* I just came from work. It was really busy." Sepehr said. "When we go home, I'll massage your feet for you."

The pout on Nasim's face turned into a smile.

"Someone warned me, never date the only child. They are always spoiled and need lots of attention." Sepehr added with a chuckle.

"I am not spoiled."

"Maybe a little. But I like it. I like to spoil you *azizam*."

Nasim smiled and punched Sepehr in the arm.

Once inside the theater, they found their row of four empty seats. Sepehr went in first and then Nasim. So much for chivalry. Mahtab settled into her seat, craning toward Nasim as Ashkan took the last seat beside her. Why she was doomed to sit next to him?

The movie rolled on. Though next to each other, a stonewall could not have separated them better. She took pride in not looking at that arrogant ass. Although, she had to admit, she may have glanced a few times in his direction, catching him in her peripheral vision.

After the movie, outside the theater, Mahtab found it hard to repress a smile when Sepehr joked about the actor in the movie, but she could not help notice that her nemesis was unsmiling. Hands in his pockets, he watched Sepehr without changing his expression. It figured; not only did he irritate people with his lack of social grace but he also apparently didn't care for jokes either.

"Let's get something to eat. Anyone for Honey Pars?" Sepehr said hopefully.

They all agreed and headed out. Mahtab, still furious, found Nasim. "You guys are so mean, forcing me to sit next to this *borj-e zahremar!* This snake poison! You know, he is actually like a robot. Throughout the entire movie, not once did he even smile. Nothing! Had I known he was going to show up, I wouldn't have come."

"Well, you said it, *azizam!* He is a robot! He doesn't do well with us humans," Nasim said, laughing. Giving Mahtab a quick hug, she added, "Don't worry, I'll make sure Sepehr gets rid of him next time."

They walked up the stairs to the second floor where the restaurant's neon lights were flashing. The smell of fried oil and heavy perfume hung in the air. It took her eyes a second to adjust to the bright, almost garish red and yellow lights inside. The place was full, and the cacophony of voices melded into a monotone. It took Mahtab only a glance at the menu to know what she wanted; pizza.

The guys got hamburgers, but Nasim was a different matter. She couldn't make up her mind; was it pizza she was in the mood for today, or, no, was it hamburger, or was it fried chicken? Finally after some prompting from Sepehr, she settled for the pizza.

"Nasim, you and Mahtab go find a seat, and Ashkan and I will order and pay," Sepehr said, heading toward the counter.

Nasim turned back without even a second thought and headed towards the bright red tables and chairs.

"Please bring the receipt so I can pay my share," Mahtab interjected.

"What do you mean you pay your share? Mahtab *joon!*" Sepehr said. "Ashkan and I will take care of it. You both are our guests!"

"*Na, merci,* I would like to pay for myself," Mahtab persisted, clutching her purse. Everyone was looking at her now.

Sepehr sighed. "Listen, Mahtab, will you give me the honor to be my guest tonight, please?"

Mahtab hesitated for a moment and then finally agreed, with a pout. "But only as *your* guest. Not anyone else."

"Thanks!" Sepehr said, letting out a breath between pursed lips.

From under her eyes, Mahtab looked at the Robot. He was staring at her.

When they were all eating, Sepehr asked, "So how did you guys like the movie?"

Nasim and Mahtab said almost in unison, "It was nice but a sad ending."

"Mahtab, you must have liked it a lot. Considering she was playing the violin and all," Sepehr said before ripping into his hamburger.

"They should have asked you to play the violin part," Nasim said loudly.

Mahtab smiled. "Do you think I would pass as his daughter?"

Nasim winked. "More like a girlfriend."

"What exactly do you do?" It was Ashkan, sitting across the table, his eyes on her. She heard his accent before she heard him, the accent of a *farangi*.

"Pardon me?" A question from his highness. Mahtab hadn't expected this.

"Work? What do you do?"

"Work? I teach violin at a music institute, and sometimes I play at local concerts." She caught her fingers involuntarily adjusting her scarf under his gaze.

"Violin?" His eyebrows rose slightly.

"Yes, the violin." She stared back at him with a look that said, what did you expect? Sitting at home doing nothing?

"How long?"

She hesitated before answering. "Since childhood." Why was she even answering him?

"Interesting…did you study music in college?"

"Yes, I have my degree in music theory, and I teach and perform the violin. What about you?"

"I am an architect. I draft plans for houses, apartments, hotels."

Sepehr cut in, "Ashkan actually came to Iran this time to build a hotel for my father in Shiraz. It's amazing! You should see his blue prints. It's an oasis."

"It's a resort," Ashkan said flatly.

"Well, it's a big thing. My dad is investing a lot of money in it."

"He is not paying me much," Ashkan said and Mahtab could have sworn that she saw the ghost of a smile on his lips.

"Oh Sepehri, I hope your dad doesn't want you to go to Shiraz to manage it. I'll die without you," Nasim said throwing her arms around him. "He should send Sara."

Sepehr chuckled. "*Na azizam*. He needs me to manage his hotels here in Tehran. But if I go there, I'll take you with me."

"You should go for your honeymoon there," Ashkan said.

Sepehr put his hand around Nasim's shoulder and said, "So build it as fast as you can. Then it will be ready for our honeymoon."

"Are we getting married anytime soon?" Nasim asked, her eyes aglow with anticipation.

"Not right now. But we will *azizam*. I mean by the time it finishes, it will be like five years from now. Maybe we'll be ready by then."

"All right. Didn't you know? It's the new fashion now. People go on their honeymoon before they get married. So they can discover if they like each other!" Nasim said, her eyes dancing.

"Hey, I have no objection to that," Sepehr said. "Let's go to Monte Carlo."

"Do you have a bachelors or Masters?" Mahtab asked, turning to Ashkan, leaving Nasim and Sepehr to themselves.

"Masters," Ashkan said.

"So that's why you are so full of yourself!" It just slipped out of her mouth, but it felt so good.

"Excuse me?" he said with a start, his eyes widening.

"You seem very proud of what you have done," Mahtab said, trying to stay calm.

"Yes, I guess." Ashkan stiffened in his seat. He clearly had not seen this coming.

"That's what I thought," she said seeing her barb register in the pink that lit his sculpted cheeks.

"What do you mean? I worked damn hard for it. I went to one of the top schools in the States. Have you heard of MIT?"

"No," Mahtab admitted with a little hesitation. "What is it?"

"MIT is like Sharif University here for engineering. It's very prestigious," Sepehr said with a nervous smile.

"Which school did you go to?" Ashkan asked, leaning back in his chair.

"Tehran University," Mahtab snapped. "But it wasn't easy for me, like it was for you guys who study abroad. For you guys, you decide to go to college and boom, there you are. You have so much opportunity. For us it's so tough, it's like *kimia*, like alchemy. Not gold from metal, but from paper!"

Nasim interrupted, "At least you studied something you liked, Mahtab *joon*. My father, peace upon his soul, I miss him so much. He desperately wanted me to go to medical school. But I couldn't make it, so I decided to study nutrition. I mean, it's all right, I am happy, but sometimes I wish I could have studied fashion design. That was what I really loved!"

"*Akhey*, Nasim," Mahtab said, putting her hand on Nasim's.

"It's OK, *azizam*, I'm happy now."

"Well, I didn't listen to my parents, and I studied the violin. But it was hard, really hard. My parents hated the idea of me doing something as useless as music. My father was so disappointed that he couldn't tell his friends that his daughter was going to be a doctor or dentist. But it would have been harder for me to live with the regrets I would have had if I had not done it."

Sepehr, reaching for a French fry, said, "You did good, Mahtab *joon*. I remember we had a chemistry teacher in high school who always told us to forget about any interest in the subject you study. Do something that brings in cash! And I did just that. Business management from crappy Azad

University in Rodehen, and I've been managing my dad's hotels since then. Didn't like any of it. But I did it for my dad and of course the money."

"Of course it's easier for the ladies to pursue their desired field of study than for us men." It was Ashkan, looking intently at a cup that he was fiddling with.

Mahtab couldn't believe her ears. "Do you really think so?" she said, her voice shrill with anger.

Ashkan looked at her for a moment before going on. "Yes, of course. Girls get married, and then it's their husbands who usually look after them. So for girls it is easier to study whatever they like."

"*Na,* that's totally wrong! Don't give me that about girls nowadays waiting desperately to get married so they can have a scruffy man to take care of them. We girls here, everywhere in Tehran, want more than that! We want to be independent, be able to earn for ourselves. And we work really hard for what we earn."

Sepehr chuckled and looked away.

"No, I am serious, Sepehr!" Mahtab cried out. "Yes, even those girls on the street that you are thinking about. At least they make money themselves instead of living off somebody else. OK?"

Eating slowly until he finished, Ashkan then said, "But that's their choice! Women here are not obligated to work, but men are. They are *forced* to have jobs that pay to be able to provide for their families..."

Nasim cut him off. "He is right."

Mahtab's jaw dropped in disbelief while Ashkan turned to look at Nasim. What was she talking about?

Her hands on the table, Nasim craned forward. "If a guy goes to a *khastegari* for a girl, to ask for her hand from her parents, he'd better have a good job. Something important sounding, something big. Doctor, maybe? Engineer? Otherwise the girl's family will shoo him away like a fly. But we girls, you know, just have to be pretty and have no boyfriends. That is, none that are known about!" She winked. "So guys definitely are under more pressure to study and have higher-paying jobs in our society." She then took Sepehr's hand and said, "But don't worry, Sepehr, you'll be fine. My mom likes you!"

Mahtab sat up. "Yes, of course, because everyone likes to marry a girl who knows how to be a great housewife, a great cook, a baby maker. Who cares if she can read and write!"

She looked at Ashkan, her eyes challenging him. He paused and looked around the table. There it was again, the gold flash in those green eyes from the day of the art show. That unnerving fire. She jerked up as she realized he was already talking.

"…but that doesn't change the fact that the husband still has to provide for his family. In this society, that's the expectation."

"But Ashkan Agha, Iran has changed. I am sorry for you if you cannot handle it. If you need proof, go to Tehran University where you can find more women students than men!"

Ashkan went silent. The argument seemed over, and the tension in the room broke like a bubble.

The rest of that night Mahtab said nothing to Ashkan. Although she had clearly won, she had this sneaking feeling that it was only a partial victory, somehow made less by Ashkan's infuriating calmness. Come to think of it, he hadn't raised his voice at all; not even made fun of her words to make her look inferior.

It was cold when they stepped outside the restaurant. Silence fell, as the wisps of tension from the fight seemed to follow them into the crisp night.

Sepehr broke the silence. "Nasim, it's late. I'll give Mahtab a ride back to her home, then drop you off."

On the side street, a shiny red Mazda 3 bleeped as Sepehr unlocked it remotely. Nasim sat up front. Great! Mahtab had to sit with him again. In the evening light, Mahtab now got a chance to survey the arrogant ass. Thick, brown hair spiked with gel, an aquiline nose, a masculine jawline. Those green eyes with their flash of fire, still intense in the dim light. She now noticed the three white letters across his sweatshirt. MIT. Of course, he had to announce to everyone where he went to school. Too bad she hadn't known about this MIT of his. She smiled, remembering his reaction to her look at Honey Pars. He was built though, muscular, proportioned. Probably spent a lot of time at the gym. And it didn't hurt that his cologne smelled good too. No, it was really good actually, she admitted grudgingly, and he was quite cute, to the point that he could be a model. Nasim had been right after all. One thing was for sure, Mahtab was certain that with his looks he had the ability to steal any girl's heart. Any girl but her. She was just too mad at him and too principled to be seduced by his good looks.

They soon reached Mahtab's neighborhood in *Sabalan*. The familiar gray apartment buildings were now a spectral yellow in the glare of the streetlamps.

Mahtab saw Nasim turn to Sepehr in front and gently touch him. "Sepehr, remember to stop a little way back for Mahtab. We can't risk her family seeing you guys."

When Sepehr parked, Mahtab got out but not before Nasim gave her a quick hug. Without looking back, she started walking toward her home as the car made a quick U-turn and left the lane.

Six

The next week was very hectic. Mahtab took on the two new students Kamran had promised her, which, even with Nazila gone, added another half hour to her Monday's schedule. But the question that weighed on her mind was that of accepting Ostad Amini's offer to play in the upcoming concert. Yes, and after that who knows? She could even get a gig playing for famous singers, such as Payam Roosta and Mehdi Abari. And even the Aryan Band, the most famous group in Iran, at their concerts. But what if, yes, if she accepted and she couldn't? Forced out by her family who had already forbidden it at point-blank range. What had Pasha said? "No concerts! You know better than to ask!"

Of course he would say that. Her self-proclaimed boss that he was, she snorted. But deep inside her, she felt, no, she knew that if she didn't do this, her dream of playing in the Tehran symphony one day would be only just that, a dream. She would have to find a way.

⌒☉

By the time Mahtab got home that night, the evening call to prayer had long been sung from the neighborhood mosque, its sky blue dome now darkened by the receding light. Bahar was in the kitchen, knife in hand, peeling long, green Persian cucumbers for the salad. "Oh, thank God, you are home. What kept you so late? Boji was getting ready to cook your liver!"

Mahtab slipped by wordlessly, a finger to her mouth.

"Was that Mahtab, Bahar? Monir!" Mahtab overheard Boji as she retreated to her room. "That girl always comes back home late. I swear, if she were my daughter, she would not eat if she didn't help make dinner! That's why my daughters grew up so well mannered!"

Maman murmured something indistinctly, apologetically.

"Why don't you do something Monir? You are her mother for God's sake! Aren't you going to say something?"

Silence. The steady metallic ticking of the hallway clock seemed to dominate the silence as the seconds whipped along.

"A girl that stays out this late! What will people talk behind her back?" She heard Boji sigh wheezily. "It is best for her to get married as soon as possible."

Not a word from Maman. Just silence. Mahtab knew she could expect no more. It was just like her mother, never to stand up for her in front of others- Boji, Pasha, or even a guest from outside. Maman was the perfect doormat of the Sharifi house, to obey without question. And that was why everyone else expected the same from her girls.

Her fingers reached for the buzzing piece of plastic and metal that lay buried in her bag. It was Nasim. "Mahtab, you know Sara? Sepehr's younger sister? Her birthday is coming up, and Sepehr is throwing a birthday party for her at their hotel. He invited us too!"

"Us?" Mahtab's eyes narrowed. "No, he invited you, and because of you he invited me. You go. I don't feel like seeing the Robot again. Had I known he would show up last time, I wouldn't have gone in the first place."

"What do you mean you are not coming? I am not going anywhere without you. I need you there. Especially in a place where everyone will be Sepehr's family."

She kept silent.

"Mahtab! They'll tear me apart! Have you seen Sara? She's got 'I hate Nasim' written all over her face." Her voice was begging now and Mahtab felt her resolve failing.

"Come on, we'll go to the party and then you can spend the night at my home. That way you can tell your parents that you are at my home, not at the party. And...I promise to help you with your upcoming concert."

"Are you bribing me?" Mahtab asked, chuckling.

"Wait, it gets even better. If you decide that finally you want to date a guy, I'll back you up. I'll lie for you, I promise...Please, Mahtabi? Please?"

Mahtab laughed. "You promise to back me up with my concert?" she said, throwing herself back on her bed.

"Yes, I do!" Nasim said. "Anything to get you to come with me. I need you, Mahtabi. I really like Sepehr. I don't want to mess this up. I know you only love your violin, music and all that. But try to understand my situation. I'm actually trying to get married to a human!"

Mahtab smiled wryly. "Shut up, Nasim. The way you say things, people will believe you. What about your after-party fun at Sepehr's condo? If you take me, you'll miss it."

Nasim laughed. "He can take a rain check. I'd rather have you around when it's me against his family."

"Nasim, you know I'll do anything for you even if I have to face the Robot again. But stay with me."

"Thank you! Thank you! Mahtab *joonam*, if you were here, I would hug you so hard. OK, now what should I get her?"

"A head scarf. It's always needed, and if she doesn't like the style, she can give it to someone else as a gift."

"You had already thought it through then. I knew you were going to come!" Nasim laughed.

❦

Mahtab arrived at Nasim's house after work to get ready for Sara's birthday party. She breathed a small prayer of thanks. Nasim had remembered to get her mom, Simin, to call Mahtab's house after all. To get permission for Mahtab to stay the night. Unlike the last time they had tried to get away. But that was then, and she had tried hard to put that away from her mind.

"Mahtabi, thank God you are here! What do you think of this?" Nasim said, half naked, holding out a cream-colored *manteau*. "Is it too dull?"

"Wear something warm; it's so cold out there!" Mahtab said.

"I don't care about the cold; I need to look good," Nasim answered, searching in her closet.

"Of course it's your sister-in-law's birthday party; you should look good," Mahtab replied, laughing. "It looks great. But you'll be cold."

"Future sister-in-law…if she doesn't kill me first," Nasim said, her head still in the closet.

"She can't be that bad. She is Sepehr's sister after all."

Nasim pulled her head out of the closet and said, "You haven't met her. She hates me. She thinks I am below dirt, *dahati*, because I got Sepehr's attention and not one of her rich slutty friends." She sighed, looking down at the dress that was hugging her figure. "It's really the money though. I know it. Sepehr's family is so much richer than mine."

"Nasim! Who cares about Sara, or anyone else? You aren't dating her, are you? It's Sepehr you want, and I've seen the way he looks at you. He really likes you," Mahtab said grabbing her friend's shoulders, "Remember, this is your life here, not a dress or even your career. You have to fight for it."

By the time they left Nasim's room, scattered makeup covered the dresser, thrown around like confetti after a carnival, mute testament to their efforts.

"I'll clean up tomorrow," Nasim said as she turned off the light.

⤬

They waited for the *ajanse,* their private taxi outside Nasim's appartment. Nasim smiled, looking stunning in her cream ensemble and black knee-high boots. One of the many things Mahtab loved about Nasim was her wardrobe and the wonderful fashionable things she let Mahtab borrow. Things Mahtab would never be allowed to buy even if she had been able to afford them. Not everything though, like the miniskirts Nasim loved and often pressed her to wear or the sleeveless tops with their plunging necklines. No, that was too much, but there was so much more. Today she had taken Nasim's pale-blue *manteau* and her blue matching shawl, which she draped loosely over her luscious black hair.

The party was in the ballroom of Hotel Dariush, one of the hotels owned by Sepehr's father. The hotel, a modern glass rectangle jutting into the sky, was a clean oasis in the dust and heat of the heart of the city. Nasim would drive almost anywhere, except for downtown with its horrendous traffic. The *ajanse* wound its way past vendors and hawkers, finally driving into the covered driveway of the hotel.

Under the bright lights of the lobby, Mahtab saw about a dozen people, very well dressed, chatting in groups. Obviously close friends or relatives of Sepehr's. What was it that made them so obvious? Was it their confidence, always being rich, never having to worry about money, with means that were beyond her comprehension? Or was it simply their wealth that they wore with apparent ease just like Sepehr's Rolex?

Mahtab knew it was her before anyone said a word. It was *the* Sara. Standing next to a table in the ballroom, she was chatting with an impeccably dressed man whose jet-black hair was slicked back with enough gel to hold it against a hurricane. Almost as tall as Nasim, statuesque, she was in a formfitting black *manteau*. Mahtab smiled wryly at Sara's distinct nose job. Those cost money. And yet anyone who could afford them would get them in Tehran—a status symbol of pure discretionary display. Sara's face was beautiful though, a gorgeous oval framed by luxuriant dyed blond hair. But it was her eyebrows that got Mahtab's attention. Devil style. She had the famous shaved outer eyebrows with penciled-in slants that gave her the unmistakable faux angry expression of a kabuki mask. The rage in Tehran among the wealthy, it was outlandish, bordering on grotesque, in Mahtab's opinion. If her family ever saw her with one of those, she would...well, it was better left unsaid.

At that moment Sepehr arrived. With a grin, he pulled his sister toward them. "Sara, look, Nasim is here."

Mahtab and Nasim both smiled. A small tingle rose up Mahtab's spine as she felt those lidded eyes pass over her.

"My sister Sara," Sepehr said. "Sara, Nasim you know, of course, and this is Nasim's friend Mahtab."

"Hi, Nasim and Mahtab," she purred in a velvet voice that was cold as ice.

Mahtab handed Sara her birthday gift. *"Tavalodet Mobarak.* Happy birthday."

Without even giving it a second glance, she dropped it with two fingers onto a table piled high with other gifts. *"Merci,* you shouldn't have."

She smiled, her upper lip turned up baring shapely teeth. A mask for social graces. She was obviously just tolerating them for Sepehr.

"Let's go see Sepideh," Sepehr said, pulling Nasim with him. Mahtab followed them.

"Sepideh! Salaam," Nasim blurted out. "Mahtab, this is Sepideh, Sepehr's older sister."

Sepideh laughed. Her picture-perfect smile, just like Sara and Sepehr's, made it obvious that the three siblings had expensive dental work when they were younger. A large diamond wedding ring sparkled on her left hand.

"*Khoshamadi,* welcome, Nasim *joon.* It's been a long time."

"How's the baby?" Nasim asked her.

"Good. So far good," she said quickly, pushing back her bangs. "I hope this time...the baby will be ok."

Mahtab felt warmth radiating from her, genuine caring, almost maternal. They traded kisses on their cheeks. Ali, her husband, shook hands with a small murmured salaam. A little taller than Sepideh, his thin face was trimmed with a goatee.

The girls then took seats next to each other, with Sepehr pulling up a chair for Nasim. Mahtab's gaze fell upon a group of guys—young, hair slicked, eyes roving—making their way to the tables, their cologne practically announcing them before their arrival. The party boys here were making their move. Among them was a guy about Mahtab's height, with a pale, small frame and dopey eyes.

"Sepehr, will you introduce me to this beautiful girl you brought tonight?" he said, his eyes surveying Mahtab.

"Sure," Sepehr said, laughing as he grabbed him in a hug. "Well this is Mahtab, Nasim's best friend. Mahtab this is Babak. He's my *pesar ammeh,* my dad's younger sister's son."

Babak, who couldn't hide his grin, started off at Mahtab. "*Bah, bah*! It must be my lucky day! I am glad I made it tonight, so that I could get to see such a beauty!"

Mahtab smiled, her dimples showing. She was used to guys complementing her on her beauty, and he seemed vaguely interesting—in an entertaining sort of way, not a man of substance.

"Be careful with him," Nasim whispered in her ear. "He is a big player. He changes girlfriends like clothes."

Mahtab smiled and whispered back, "Don't worry, he's not my type anyway."

"Good," Nasim said turning to Babak, "See Babak, I told Mahtab all about you!"

"Thanks Nasim," he said, the smile dropping from his face, "Nothing too bad I hope. I don't bite Mahtab *joon*. Now if you'll excuse me, I'll be right back," Babak said, his eyes on her as he walked away.

"The Robot is not here," Mahtab said under her breath.

"I know. I wonder why?" Nasim said looking around.

"Probably they didn't invite him so he wouldn't wreck the party!" They both giggled.

Just as Babak returned to claim his place next to Mahtab, the food arrived. Great oval dishes of steaming saffron basmati rice, strips of sizzling kebab, *kabob koobideh,* and *kabob barg* with grilled tomatoes, bell pepper, and onions were wheeled in by waiters in pressed white uniforms. More soon followed carrying plates of *baba ghanooch*, thick creamy garlic yogurt, and mountains of fresh herbs that were dropped off at their table. As everyone began eating, Mahtab noticed him. He didn't bother with a greeting, but then that no longer shocked her. From the corner of her eye, Mahtab followed Ashkan's towering form into the room. He went straight to Sara and leaned over her. Then he kissed her on the cheek.

Mahtab heard him say something. Then a small box appeared in his hand, covered with purple wrapping, topped by a white satin bow.

Babak declared, laughing, "Ashkan, you made it for dinner. Did your girlfriend finally let you go?"

"Girlfriends, Babak! Say girlfriends!" said Ali, Sepideh's husband, with a wink.

Of course the guy has so many girlfriends. Let's see if he stays with any of them! Mahtab found herself thinking.

He swung over to Sepideh, and they traded kisses as well. Then some other girls that were standing nearby.

Mahtab gasped inside. Was he going to kiss every girl in this place? Had he no shame? As if they were his sisters. They were not *mahram*, not related to him. Why was he kissing these unrelated girls? Then she stopped. Of course, Sepehr and his family were western. Iranian in soul but as liberal in mores as people in France or Germany, and this guy Ashkan was made in the USA himself. This was nothing for them. But she couldn't help notice the under-lying affection that everyone here had for each other. They seemed so happy and free, so unlike her own family. In hers, the girls and boys, even cousins, stayed six feet away from each other, eyes averted, their greetings only dry salaams barely leaving their lips.

After dinner, two hotel staff wheeled out a large, glistening chocolate cake into the center of the hall. Camera flashes went off.

"Tavalod, tavalod, tavalodet mobarak," everyone burst out singing. Mahtab watched Sara soaking in the attention. She could never imagine her brother, Pasha, singing happy birthday to her, let alone holding a birthday party for her. The cameras never stopped clicking. Even the Robot was taking pictures. When it was time to open the gifts, Babak got up from next to Mahtab to get closer to Sara.

"Congratulations!" Mahtab smelled the Robot's cologne as she heard him speak.

"Baleh? Yes?" she said in surprise.

"Congratulations, they won today."

"Excuse me?" Mahtab felt something tighten within her chest. What was he talking about?

"Did Esteghlal win today?" he asked again quietly.

"Oh, soccer! I don't know. Did they have a match today?"

"I saw you wearing all blue, so I thought Esteghlal had won or some-thing." He was smiling faintly, his green eyes on her.

He was obviously teasing her. The fact that he looked so good with that smile only made Mahtab even more irritated. But instead of screaming at him like last time, she quietly said, "I don't follow soccer that closely."

"But you are wearing blue?" he persisted.

"This is sky-blue. Esteghlal's blue is darker," Mahtab said, now fixing her eyes on him.

"It doesn't matter; blue is blue, and down to the eye shadow you are wearing blue. Let me see your nails; did you paint them blue too?" he said, reaching for her hands.

"None of your business," she said, hiding her hands under the table.

Shooting her a smile, he got up and went over to talk to some girls. Some slutty-looking girls. Girls with faces made up like runway models. With

Devil style eyebrows just like Sara. Mahtab watched them gather around him, leaning forward, fixing their scarves, adjusting already adjusted hair-dos, laughing, tittering. One even held his hand to look at his silver thumb ring.

Stupid. They had nothing better to do than to define themselves by men like him. How much lower could they go? Living to please guys. Mahtab looked away, trying to ignore the spectacle he was making of them!

Sara took the purple box Ashkan had given her. She smiled at everyone as she tore open the wrapping paper with black polished nails. Inside was a thin, silver Gucci watch. Mahtab caught her breath. It was obvious that he had taken his time in choosing and buying this piece, not to mention the expensive brand name.

"*Merci*, Ashk!" Sara said in that velvet voice of hers. Then she glided toward Ashkan and ran her hands around his neck drawing herself close. Mahtab's mind whirred with possibilities. Buying such an expensive watch for his cousin? How much did he pay for it? Spending money seems to be no problem for him. Perhaps he is in love with her? That hug!

After the gifts were opened and every guest thanked, people slowly started leaving. "Sara, I want to drop Nasim home," Mahtab overheard Sepehr talking.

"Doesn't she have a car?" she asked, raising an eyebrow ever so slightly. Mahtab instinctively felt the ice in that honeyed voice again, a barb beneath muslin. Nasim had better be careful of her.

"She doesn't drive downtown."

"Is that so? But I need your car. You go with Ashkan," Sara said.

The last thing Mahtab wanted was to be in his car. First the movie theater, then Sepehr's car, and now this. Wasn't listening to his pronouncements on women the other day enough? But then it would cost her an arm and a leg to get a taxi to Nasim's home from here. So she surrendered with a promise to herself that she would just ignore him. Maybe she'd keep busy talking to Nasim. Maybe Nasim and Sepehr would keep talking. Or if worse came to worst, she would keep herself busy with her mobile.

Ashkan's car was parked just across the street. A gray metallic BMW 3 series. She would know, it was one of Pasha's dream cars and it looked like it had just come from the factory. The lights flashed as Ashkan unlocked the doors. As he got in front, Sepehr opened the front door for Mahtab.

"I'll sit in the back, Sepehr," she said.

"No, please. I want to sit with Nasim."

Khodaya, God! Now she had to sit upfront with him. But once inside, she had to admit; the seat was comfortable, almost cocooning her in its firm embrace. The scent of Ashkan's cologne hung in the car, mixed with the smell of fine leather. It was as if the cologne bottle had actually shattered in the car. Mahtab allowed herself another small sniff. It was so seductive, blurring her thoughts in a rush of scents.

"Have you fastened your seat belt?"

In astonishment, she looked at him. "Yes, of course…"

"Good."

"Anything else?" she asked, rolling her eyes.

"Not for now," he said looking away, the corners of his mouth twitching.

Mahtab turned to Sepehr and said, "Sepehr, we could have gone home ourselves. There was no need to trouble your cousin."

Before Sepehr could answer, Ashkan replied, "There is no trouble. But if you'd like to go home alone at this time of night, you are more than welcome to do so."

"Ashkan, please stop teasing. She might take it to heart," Sepehr said quickly, his hands on the back of the driver's seat.

Ashkan cut in. "I am not teasing. If she wants to leave, she can," he said, looking straight at her. Mahtab said nothing and looked away.

"It is true that Iranian girls are so high maintenance!" he finally said with a note of exasperation.

"What? I am not high maintenance. Maybe those girls at the party who were drooling all over you are, but not me," Mahtab retorted.

Ashkan chuckled dryly. "I guess if you are not getting out, then we'll start." The engine growled as Ashkan turned the key.

"Sepehr, can you give me directions?" he asked.

"First, take Hemmat Highway."

Then, after a pause, she heard Sepehr ask, "Ashkan, where were you? How come you were late?"

"I was with my Grandpa Jamshid. He finally bought the land."

"He did? And he wants you to build on it?"

"Yes."

"So then you have to go there," said Sepehr, a serious note creeping into his voice.

"Yes I do," Ashkan said flatly.

"But what about Shiraz?"

"Probably after that."

"What about your apartment building in Velenjak?"

"That's like ninety-five percent done. I had things settled the last time I was in Iran."

Ashkan then clicked on the stereo. Mahtab, who until that moment was looking outside the window with studied intent, reflexively turned around. She couldn't believe her ears.

"*Four Seasons* by Antonio Vivaldi!" She hated herself for having blurted it out. Why couldn't she just sit still and shut up?

"Yes. Do you know him?" His eyes didn't leave the road.

"Of course I know him! He composed wonderful violin pieces!"

"You play the violin right?"

"Yes I do, since I was nine."

Ashkan smiled. "Since nine? So how old are you now, like nineteen?"

"No, twenty-three!" Mahtab said, smiling. Was he praising her?

"Twenty-three? No! You act like a nineteen-year-old." The dart stung, burned through her chest like a hot ember. She cursed herself; she should have known better, coming from the Robot.

"Then how old are you if I may ask? Seventy?"

Ashkan chuckled. "Not even close. I'm twenty-seven!"

"Well, you look and act like a seventy-year-old," Mahtab hissed, looking the other way, her nose in the air.

Ashkan laughed out loud and said, "You are funny!"

"It wasn't meant to be funny."

Sepehr broke in from behind. "*Khoobi*, Ashkan? Everything OK?"

"Yes. Nasim's friend is hilarious!" He smiled as he shifted in his seat.

"Nasim's friend has a name," Mahtab spat out.

"Of course, Moonlight, right?" Ashkan said.

"Mahtab. Moonlight is the meaning of Mahtab." That was it. Any more from the Robot and she would slap him, ride or no ride.

"Mahtab," he said. "Well, Mahtab, if you want this CD, you can have it."

"*Na, merci.*" She turned away to her window.

"No, take it. I made it for you," said the Robot, ejecting it from the tape deck with a flick of his hand.

"For me!" Mahtab sat forward and pointed at herself.

"Yep for you," he said as he opened the throttle and accelerated onto the highway.

Mahtab looked away, out of the window. What was this now? He was just so unpredictable, so infuriating and yet…so unexpectedly sweet! This CD. He had made it for her! Mahtab tried to bring her scattered thoughts together. Why? Had he known that this was one of her favorite pieces? She had only told him that she played the violin, just once, and he had remembered.

When they reached Nasim's house, Ashkan said, "Hold on, I'll get the door for you." Then he got out of the car in one fluid motion and opened her door. Surprised, Mahtab, who hadn't expected this, instinctively took his outstretched hand. As she put her hand in his, their eyes fully met. In the light, his were gorgeous green, so riveting as they held hers, the hint of gold in the center hot, molten, smoldering. A small smile suddenly softened his face. Then, like a flash, he was gone, the car roaring away, leaving only Mahtab and Nasim together on the sidewalk.

"That was fantastic, wasn't it? Except for that bitch Sara!" Nasim said with venom in her voice.

"Yes," Mahtab said but her thoughts were elsewhere. What had just happened? She walked in the cold autumn air, a few steps behind Nasim, towards her friend's home. It seemed so unreal, almost a figment of her imagination, the choice of Vivaldi, his eyes, his hand, everything that had just happened. That is, until she felt the thin plastic disc that she was clutching tightly between her fingers.

Seven

That Saturday, after her last student had left, Mahtab stared at the dark screen of her Nokia before finally pressing the speed dial button. Ostad Amini. He had already called twice to confirm her for the concert, and each time she had procrastinated, put off the decision that she knew she had to make, because of her family.

"Salaam, *Ostad*," she said.

"Well, I thought you would never call," he replied in his gravelly voice.

"I said I would call one way or another."

"So now are you a lioness or a fox?"

Mahtab took a deep breath. "A lioness."

"Good. That's the attitude you must have on stage. Listen, practice starts next Wednesday at the University Amphitheater. Make sure you arrive on time."

"Of course."

"I will see you then," he said in an avuncular tone that she knew all too well. She smiled and then grabbed her bag to go home.

⌒⊘

It was dark when she got home and she was tired. When Mahtab pushed opened the front door, she stopped. What was going on? Everything seemed different. A big dish full of fresh fruits, carefully arranged, sat on the living room table. The white dust sheets, which normally covered the formal furniture, were gone. The smell of dinner that would tell her what was on the menu was barely there, and instead the sweet heavy scent of *esfand* hung in the air. This usually meant someone important was coming to visit, but she would have known that by now. Someone would have told her, wouldn't they?

"What is going on?" she asked Bahar.

Bahar winked at her. "We have guests..."

"Who? Tonight?"

Bahar smiled slyly. "Suitors. Yes, tonight."

"Suitors for whom?"

Maman burst into the room, panting, her face the color of beets, hair undone.

"Mahtab! Where were you?" she cried, throwing up her hands. "Never mind. Get ready. Put on the dress I ironed for you. It's in your closet!"

"What is going on, Maman? Bahar just said suitors!" Mahtab asked feeling a little sick, "Suitors for whom?"

"For me, Mahtab!" Maman shouted. "For whom do you think? Who is the oldest, unmarried girl in this house? You, Mahtab, for you! Hurry up and get ready. They are going to be here any minute!"

"Don't joke with me, Maman! You know very well that I am not planning on getting married anytime soon. I'm working extra hours just to get a hope, no, a hint of getting into the Tehran orchestra. I just don't have time to get married now."

Maman snapped back, "Stop this nonsense. There is no problem with you getting married. You can still work. You can get to your orchestra and still have your own house. Now hurry up, hurry up! They are on their way." Before Mahtab could reply, her mother was gone.

Bahar, who was still standing by the doorway, giggled. "Yah, just make sure you don't get pregnant on your wedding night, or you definitely won't get in the orchestra."

"Shut up, Bahar," Mahtab spat back.

As she started taking off her *manteau*, she asked, "Who is this guy anyway?"

"You won't believe it." Bahar smiled.

"Who?" Mahtab said, her voice rising as she tried to push aside the void that was taking over her stomach.

"It's your beloved Emad..."

Mahtab's jaw dropped, drawing a smile from Bahar, "Pasha's new boss. Isn't that amazing, ha?" her eyes were scanning Mahtab's face. "What misery. I would never want to be in your place!"

"What the hell? Where did he come from? What?? What in the world does Maman think, allowing him to come to my *khastegari*? He is not my type at all."

"Why not?" Bahar asked innocently.

"You know why! He is practically a mullah, the way he pronounces things. And that beard of his! And while he is complaining about the wrongs in the world, he is growing fat off the government."

Bahar agreed, "He is religious, isn't he? Every time he comes here, he asks Boji for the *janamaz*, the praying mat, and prays for like two hours."

Mahtab rolled her eyes. "Oh! As if that's my measure of a good match. *Akh*, this is the *ash*, the soup that Pasha cooked for me, isn't it?"

"I think so. *Bodo, bodo Mobarak bada!* Go on, go on, congratulations on your marriage!" Bahar sang the old wedding song that practically every Iranian girl knew from birth.

"Shut up Bahar! I am not going to marry Emad. How did this happen anyway?"

Mahtab wasn't sure if it was the anger in her tone or pity, but the silly smile on Bahar's face vanished. "This morning, Emad's mom called, asking to come for your *khastegari*. It seems like Emad has been interested in you since the first time Pasha brought him over." Then she leaned forward and whispered, "Mahtab, do you have a boyfriend?"

Mahtab, still reeling from the news, answered without thinking. "No... why?"

"No reason." Bahar shrugged, but her eyes never left Mahtab's face.

Mahtab gazed into the wall and whispered, "No, I don't have a boyfriend. I never had."

"Why aren't you ready yet?" It was Maman, arms akimbo. Then with a sigh, she deftly drew a lime-colored silk dress from her closet—a dress with a high neckline, conservative, for a good girl to be in, a present to be only unwrapped by the *khastegar's* eyes.

49

"Here, wear this. Come on, get going!" Maman said, waving her on. "They are here already. Here is your scarf. No hair out, Mahtab. You understand, no hair out. We don't want them saying that we have wild daughters here. And behave yourself." Maman was pleading now. "No smart comments like the last *khastegari*. Please be nice. He is Pasha's boss. Besides, you don't want to be a *torshideh*, do you?" Maman's face now was an inch from Mahtab's. Her lips were quivering. "You won't be young forever, Mahtab, and then good *cases,* you know, suitors will stop coming for you!"

Taking the dress from her mom reluctantly, Mahtab hurriedly changed. She only put on the most perfunctory lipstick, as she had no interest in making herself any more attractive for this new 'good *case*' and his family. When she looked into the mirror, she smiled, seeing her thick locks escaping from the back of her yellow scarf. She would leave it that way. They wouldn't control everything. From what Pasha said, Emad's family was conservative, but with money. The most dangerous kind, Mahtab thought, for their wealth and social standing only reinforced their hidebound beliefs and gave them the means to enforce their writ.

When Mahtab entered the living room, they all were already sitting. They slowly got up, smiling stiffly.

"Salaam, *dokhtaram!*" Emad's mother, Haj Khanoom Marziyeh, simpered. Her scarf was tied so tightly that Mahtab thought her face would pop. Heavy, yellow-gold bangles hung from her wrists, which clanged as she moved.

His father, who introduced himself as Haji Ghassem Dabiri, had a prominently displayed *tasbih*, prayer beads in his right hand, which he rhythmically moved as he kept count of his prayers. On his forehead he had a gray callous. A callous that came with hours of his head on the ground in prayer.

Emad was wearing a gray suit, his eyes on the ground. Of course he wouldn't dare be caught staring at her, not with everyone in the room.

"Salaam," he said from under his lips, eyes flitting to her face for a second. Pasha was slouched in his seat, next to Emad, a smug smile on his face.

Maman motioned Mahtab to the kitchen. She found Bahar already pouring tea into *estekan-e lab talayee,* Maman's most expensive, gold-rimmed tea set, reserved for occasions like this.

"Thank you so much, Bahar. Now please take the tea tray out so they think you are the bride, and leave me out of it!" Mahtab said with a thin smile.

"*Vayyy*, and take Mr. Emad Dabiri from you? Never," Bahar answered, and they both burst out laughing as Maman entered.

"Quiet down! What are you laughing at? *Khejalat bekesh!* Shame on you! What if they hear you? Hurry up, Mahtab. Take the tray out before the tea gets cold. Make sure you start with his mother first, and serve the groom last. Bring your hands low, so that it will be easy for them to pick up the cups. Wait for them to remove the cup completely before you move. And whatever you do, do not rush them," Maman clucked, her hands miming the entire sequence.

Mahtab rolled her eyes as she carried the tray. "I know, Maman, I know. This is not my first time having a *khastegari*."

"Yes, I know, but these people are different. Besides, you don't always listen, do you?"

"Or you can take the tray and dump it all on top of Emad's head. And he'll be the martyr of love," Bahar said, peeping around the kitchen door.

"Shut up," Maman snapped. She seemed like she was about to pop a blood vessel with the look she gave her daughter.

"These people are different!" Maman hissed. "They are very *kaleh gondeh*, important people. They dine with high officials of the government. Go now and behave," she said, giving Mahtab a slight push.

In the grand scheme of things, it was useless arguing with her mom, so Mahtab grabbed the famous Sharifi *khastegari* tray, polished to a lustrous gold, and headed out into the living room. She had done this many times before. She stood now, carefully presenting the tray to the seated guests, who murmured *taarofs* backed by fake smiles as they each took a steaming cup—flowery, useless statements such as merci, and lotf kardi, thank you, so nice of you. Pasha was the exception of course and took his tea without comment. At least he was consistent.

As Mahtab was about to turn for the kitchen, Emad's mother said, "Come here, dear bride; sit with us." On cue, Maman grabbed the tray from Mahtab's hand and whispered, "*Boro beshin.* Go on, sit."

Mahtab cringed, knowing this was coming. This was the last thing she wanted to do. She had nothing to tell them. Except that this was just a farce that had to be done, after which she would scream that Emad was not her match. She would have done that before, had she known that he was coming for *khastegari*, but somehow she had not been told. Every part of her being told her that what Bahar had said about Emad's mother suddenly calling was simply not true. Families like hers just didn't accept a call from a suitor's family and allow them to come the same day for a *khastegari*. Not any self-respecting family, that is. Mahtab fumed, biting her lip. That would mean that they had known. But whatever it was, she would play the part and then drop him. Then her family could not accuse her of destroying whatever little honor they had. She would fly above it all.

Emad's father stroked his white beard and began as she settled down on the cream-colored chair.

"So *dokhtaram*, my daughter, we have heard so much about you from Mr. Emad. By now it seems like we know your family very well. Agha Pasha, *mashallah*, is a very good man. Your family is a good religious family with morals and values like our own. We are very happy that you are going to join our family."

'Going to join our family!' They already think she is theirs. Mahtab stretched her lips upward and nodded.

Haj Khanoom Marziyeh, Emad's mother, took over, looking at her and then everyone else. "We have been wanting to fetch a wife for Agha Emad for a few years now, ever since he finished his military service and got a very good job. When he told us about your daughter, we decided to pull our sleeves up and come to her *khastegari*!"

Mahtab stared at the machine-made Persian carpet on the floor, its large red flowers locked in by flowery vines.

"*Mashallah*, she is such a modest girl," Haj Khanoom Marziyeh observed.

Mahtab sensed the woman's beady, black eyes never leaving her direction.

"She is not taking her eyes off the floor. *Mashallah*!" Haj Khanoom simpered on.

Haji Ghassem started again, his shiny baldhead catching the overhead light. "We heard you are working. Is this right?"

Mahtab said nothing, denying him an answer.

"Yes, she does," Pasha said in a dismissive voice. "She has a small job teaching violin to children. She really doesn't need to work. She does it to keep herself busy."

Doesn't need to work? Because Pasha has such a high-paying job to provide for them, Mahtab snorted silently.

"That's OK. Teaching is the job of the prophets, *mashallah*," Haji Ghassem genially continued. "It's a very valuable job, just like Mr. Sharifi's himself."

Baba shifted in his seat. "I am only a small man trying to do some good."

She had seen this done before. The art of deprecating himself in the eyes of others while trying to insinuate how pure and religious he was. It was said that to bring oneself closer to the ground was to reach higher to heaven. And no one she knew followed it more closely than her father.

"How old are the kids that you teach?" Emad's mom asked through her smile. Her eyes, however, were unsmiling. It reminded Mahtab of a predator evaluating its prey.

"Small kids. Primary school and all girls," Pasha answered for her.

"Very good." His mom nodded. "It's more comfortable for a woman to work with girls than boys."

A normal *khastegari* should have been the other way around; the girl's parents would be questioning the guy's credibility not letting their daughter be interrogated!

Haji Ghassem said, "So since Mr. Pasha knows Emad, and Emad has honorable interest in Miss Mahtab, this process should go very easily. We would not like our *aghd kardeh,* engaged future daughter-in-law, to stay in her father's house for long. *Alhamdolelah,* thanks to God, Emad and Mahtab will soon be living on the top floor of our home."

What? Mahtab's head began to spin. Live on the top floor of his parents' house! When did this happen? This was not how the other *khastegaris* had been. They talked as though they were taking her already, not asking for her. Her chest fell through the floor as a flood of cold fear surged through her. She had been ambushed! They had planned everything, her family and Emad's, way before this *khastegari*.

"That way they don't have to pay so much for the rent and can save money, so Mahtab *joon* does not need to work at all. She can take care of her husband and the children. And we can keep an eye on them as well," Haj Khanoom Marziyeh said, her eyes growing to slits as she smiled. She reminded Mahtab vaguely of a cat about to strike.

"*Alhamdolelah,* we have no objection," Baba answered. "Just give us a day or two and then we can plan for the engagement."

"Please let us know as soon as you comfortably can do, so we can let our family in Ahvaz know to come to Tehran for the engagement," said Haji Ghassem, his fat fingers carefully picking a *shirini,* a small round cookie covered in sugar from Monir's proffered plate.

This was not happening. Why would her parents sell her to Pasha's boss? Granted her parents were conservative, didn't allow her to see a boy until marriage. But she had done that willingly, knowing that she would be allowed to at least have a say in whom she was going to marry. Wasn't this what her mother and father had told her throughout her life? That marriage was the single most important decision in her life after God, and they would help her find the right man? Help her, not decide for her!

She thought back to the time she had asked Maman, dressed in a white *aroosi* dress that Uncle Nader, her favorite uncle had bought for her for Norooz, the Persian New Year. How old was she then? She must have been six, the first Norooz after the war. It was vivid, the memory. Heightened by the euphoria of peace, the markets were filled with fruit, sweets, and people; the air filled with the optimism that comes with the end of terrible deprivation.

"Who am I going to marry?" Mahtab had asked. She remembered her mother's face, a smile quickly replacing the look of surprise that passed across it. Maman used to smile a lot more in those days.

"Well, one day, *inshallah*, you will marry a good man with a good family."

"Will he be handsome? Like a prince?" she had asked.

"Of course, he will be so handsome. And a man of God that will be educated, like a *doctor* or *mohandes*." Her mother didn't use the word "love," even in those days. "But remember, marriage is the most important thing after God. He has to be a good man who cares for you and your family."

"But I'll choose him!" she had said impetuously.

"Of course, but with our approval."

Mahtab's mind wandered back. Shouldn't she at least be allowed to be happy with her match? What would she have in common to this man? His thick beard itself was a sign of how religious, how conservative, how stiff he was. Even the men in Mahtab's family didn't keep a beard this thick. And his family! Look at his mother, she barely showed her mouth through her black *hejab*, her face pressed by the tightly wrapped cloth, sweat darkening the edges. How did she stand it during the stifling summer heat? It must be like carrying around your own pressure cooker, and for additional steam, the black of the chador called to the sun for more heat! Yes, of course, Mahtab believed in Islam, and prayed, but this was lunacy. She wouldn't do it. Maybe that was it, she thought, smiling inside, a small lightening of the load within her. If they even got a hint of how she was, got to know her, they would withdraw. That was what the ultra-religious did, didn't they? Mahtab smiled inside till Emad's father took a long sip of his tea and said, "So now to more important things. The *mehriyeh*! The bride price that Emad *jan* here will owe Mahtab *khanoom*."

What? Before Mahtab could process what she had just heard, Baba spoke. "Please decide yourself. Whatever you say, we will accept."

"No, no, that's not going to work. Give us a figure." Haj Khanoom Marziyeh demurred loudly, her jewelry shaking as she laughed.

"You are more experienced than us," Baba said, throwing the ball back at them.

"Well, our first daughter-in-law's *mehriyeh* was a hundred gold coins..." Haji Ghassem began.

"But that was ten years ago," Emad chimed in. "Things have changed. The prices have gone up!" How gallant of him, Mahtab fumed.

"How about one hundred fifty *sekeh*, gold coins? Also a pilgrimage to Mecca that, *inshallah*, she and Emad can take together," Haj Khanoom Marziyeh said grandly, her eyes scanning the room before finally resting on Mahtab.

"What do you think, Mahtab *jan*?"

Mahtab didn't hear her; she didn't hear anyone. She saw mouths, lots of them, opening and closing at the same time, everyone looking at her. They were talking about her, her price. How much was she worth? One hundred *sekeh*, two hundred gold coins? How much was she really worth?

The room whirled around her. She wasn't going to price herself in this sick drama. Drawing herself up, she rose, her chair scraping noisily on the ground. The conversation died instantly, faster than an execution, and she felt the glare of all the eyes in the room on her. Mahtab fought the numbness that had grown inside her. Her head was spinning. No, she wouldn't show any signs of weakness to them.

She heard Haj Khanoom Marziyeh say, "Mahtab is so modest; that's why she must have left. She is such a wonderful girl."

"So it is agreeable? *Inshallah!*" Haji Ghassem added after a pause.

Mahtab's mind was now swimming with exhaustion and anger. How had things gotten so bad so quickly? This day, which had begun with so much promise, had now become pure hell. Just hours ago she had promised Ostad

Amini that she would perform; now she was getting arranged to marry someone she had never even dreamed possible.

Once in her room, she locked her door. Grabbing her phone, she called the only person she could talk to.

"Nasim. You don't know what they have done." Mahtab felt her eyes swim.

"What? What did they do to you again?" Nasim asked.

"They are marrying me to Emad!"

"Who the hell is Emad?" Nasim's voice was incredulous now.

"Pasha's new boss." Then she told Nasim everything. The ambush, the betrayal, and her family railroading her into a *khastegari* that was actually more like an engagement.

"Nasim, I am scared! I have a dreadful feeling that they are forcing me into a situation that I will not be able to live with. They have already decided the *mehriyeh!*"

"Mahtab, *chee migii?* What are you saying? You can't let them do it. It's your life! Be strong; you have to say no." Nasim was screaming now.

It was raining outside, the steady patter of drops everywhere. From the window of her room, she looked at the sleeping city, lights shimmering around her in a wide arc under the night sky.

The evening had thrown into stark relief what she had never paid much attention to before: Love. Marriage. Something she had wanted, of course, like any other girl. But she had never had the time for it. She had always been busy trying to carve out her little corner in life. Fighting with her family for things that other girls took for granted. Like studying what they wanted. Mahtab had to fight tooth and nail just to get into an undergraduate music school, while most of her friends at the institute had simply decided to do so. For her, well, Rostam of old would have found his demigod tests easier.

Absently playing with her hair, Mahtab sat on the windowsill, her mind grasping for something, anything, to take her away from this awful reality. Then it hit her. If Shirin Ebadi, her hero, a Nobel Prize winner and female lawyer who defended women in the courts of Iran, had given up when she faced adversity, where would she be? Another nobody, unremembered by history for what she has done. This *khastegari* was a challenge, and she would have to overcome it. She repeated it to herself. It was as though she could actually hear the air rush back into the void that had surrounded her. The feeling of fresh air, of hope within her, made her slightly vertiginous. She would fight even if it took every fiber in her to win. Nasim was right; she would not let them. After all, just because they came over and acted like they owned her already didn't mean that they actually did! Even if it took a couple of teacups on that Emad's head, she would get out of this like she had everything else before it.

Eight

*N*asim wasn't able to take the day off for the art show. Something about having used up all her vacation days and her boss giving her grief about it. This was even though Mahtab had told her about the exhibition weeks ago. Fine! She looked out the window of the blue bus as it ground its way to the north of the city. So now she would spend the afternoon at the gallery without distraction. Maybe this would work out after all. She loved Nasim but sometimes it was nice to go alone. To be able to appreciate a show for itself, not grade it by the number of hot guys who happened to be there.

She entered the gallery, past the sandy-colored desk and the green-scarfed woman who greeted her. Reaching the low-ceilinged hall, she paused. It was quiet, only the tap of heels and low murmurs floating across the room. The paintings were fascinating, vivid in a visceral sort of way under the crystal lights that illuminated them from above. Mahtab was drawn to one that looked like a body of water, deep blue on the right and sky blue on the left with a narrow splash of red in between, shimmering on the surface. In the middle was a picture of a sun, a brilliant orb of yellow and orange hues, under which lay a broken branch and a poem, floating in the sea below. She felt the urge to touch it. Instead she felt something on her shoulder, light but there for a flash. She spun around, half expecting nothing, and then gasped. The Robot! And next to him was a girl. She was young, not more than twelve or thirteen, and Mahtab could smell her lip gloss, a sweet strawberry scent. The girl was wearing a crisp navy-blue *manteau*. It looked like a school uniform but the grey crest embroidered on the right lapel told her it was probably private. Her *maghnaeh*, the black school scarf that was supposed to cover every strand of hair on her head was back all the way to her ears, revealing silky chestnut bangs. Just like so many other girls her age in Tehran these days that in their own way increasingly pushed at the boundaries that society had set them.

"Salaam," he said simply, almost as though he was expecting her. Maybe it was the light or how close he was, but Ashkan looked even better than her mind's eye had pictured him, in a pair of jeans and a black felt jacket.

"Oh, salaam...you? Here?" Then she stared at the girl next to him.

"This is Pardis...my sister."

Mahtab drew back as Ashkan came closer.

"Pardis, this is Mahtab, the one I told you about."

Pardis and Mahtab traded salaams. Mahtab's mind was whirring. He was smiling at her, his arm protectively around Pardis's shoulder. The fluttering in her chest grew, now mixed with something else. Shyness.

"Pardis, do you like art?" Mahtab asked, averting her eyes from Ashkan.

"Yeah!" she bubbled, "last night when my brother told me that there was an exhibition here, I was thrilled! So I told him as soon as school was over, I'd come."

Without thinking, Mahtab asked, "How old are you?"

"I'm thirteen."

"So you are in the middle school?"

"Yes, eighth grade." Her accent was less pronounced than her brother's, but it was there, that faint drawl.

They lapsed into silence, and the three of them turned toward the paintings. By now Mahtab could only feign interest in the gallery, her attention drawn, despite her best efforts, to the siblings beside her. Even more distracting was that Mahtab noticed Ashkan stealing glances at her from time to time as well. She tried to ignore him. She told herself that she was irritated with him. Not just for taking credit for telling his sister about the show, which in retrospect he had clearly only found out about from Nasim through Mahtab, but also something more. More than anything, Mahtab had to admit, she was cross with herself for letting him get to her.

"It was very nice meeting you. I have to go now," Mahtab said, trying to make a quick exit.

"Are you leaving? Already? Do you want to get a drink?"

She felt her jaw drop in surprise. The tone of his voice was still the same but almost imperceptibly softer, as though simply asking her for something. That "something" fell into her mind a second later. He was asking her to go out with him, and that sent a shower of cold and hot sparks through her.

"*Na merci*, I am going to be late. I have to go home."

Pardis said, "Why not? I know a coffee shop close by that's awesome." Then she turned to Ashkan, smiling in that unaffected way that only a care-free teenager could afford. "Do you know which one I am talking about? The one we went to with Mom."

Ashkan said, "Yes, I know. We can walk there." Then he turned to Mahtab and said, "Don't worry. I'll let you pay your share!" For a second she saw the hint of a smile on his lips.

"*Na merci*! Thank you, some other time." Mahtab felt herself reaching for the last reserves of her will to resist them.

Pardis said, "OK, sure. Maybe another time. It was nice meeting you."

Then Ashkan said something to her in English, and Pardis rolled her eyes and said in Farsi, "Oh yeah, you are right; this is Iran and you have to insist."

Ashkan looked at Mahtab and said, "Look, you are *tarofing*, aren't you? Iranians are so *tarof*! Always so over polite. Why don't you just say yes and come along? We are friends, right?"

Friends, when did that happen? Mahtab couldn't help smiling though as she sighed, "OK, fine. I'll come. Just for a little while."

They walked toward the coffee shop, Ashkan in the middle with Mahtab and Pardis on either side. Pardis was chattering away mostly in English, but now and then she would add some Farsi. He was listening to her patiently with the occasional, "Wow. Really? How funny." There was something different about him today. Adjusting her scarf, Mahtab walked on. No, not his face; no, it was his...eyes. It was his eyes, Mahtab finally decided. Yes, that was it. They were warm now, as though the icy intensity that she had sensed before had melted away.

The strong smell of fresh roasted coffee reached them long before she could see the large, plastic, brown coffee bean over the corner shop. The sign read Star Café.

"I've always wondered why they have the English sign so much larger than the Farsi one," Pardis said, looking at them.

"It's to tell people that it's western stuff. A slice of Europe or America. You know how people here love that," Ashkan explained.

"Really?" Mahtab asked.

"Do you see a *kababi* restaurant with its name in English? No, because they serve traditional Iranian food. Coffee is western though," he said, chuckling.

Entering the cafe revealed a small place with subdued lighting, filled with the aroma of coffee laced with cigarette smoke. White metal tables and chairs in front led to a lighted bar at the back, manned by a couple of young guys in crisp brown uniforms.

The neatly printed prices on the menu were exorbitant by Mahtab's standards. A coffee for three thousand toman or three dollars. A puff pastry for five thousand toman. Together, that would be a day's wages for a receptionist in an office. With the value of the toman where it was, for most in Tehran, the price of coffee here would land meat on the table for dinner in many homes.

"Pardis, Mahtab plays the violin. Professionally," Ashkan said after the waiter had left with their orders.

"Cool. That's great. One of my cousins is trying to learn. But she is always complaining that it's so hard." Pardis had perfect teeth just like her brother, but that was where the similarity ended. Pardis's eyes were hazel, unlike her brother's green.

"Well, learning the violin in the beginning is hard. It needs a lot of practice." Changing the subject, she asked, "What is the age difference between you and Pardis?"

"Fourteen years," Ashkan answered.

"Jeddi? For real? Fourteen years? That is a lot."

He said nothing and she knew better than to press on further.

The waiter arrived with their drinks. Mahtab carefully reached for her chocolate milk shake while Pardis got her pineapple glacé.

"Do you have any other siblings?"

This time Pardis answered, sipping on her drink, "No, just Ashkan and me."

"What about you? How many siblings do you have?" he asked.

"Us? We are three. Two sisters and one brother. I am in the middle."

Mahtab felt his gaze on her again. This time she felt him look right into her. Instant pangs of shyness welled up, and she looked down at her empty glass. Suddenly she could hear her heart beating and that curious warm feeling again rose in her chest, confusing her, flustering her. She could no longer stay there. "I have to go now. It's getting dark. I should get home."

"I'll drop you off," Ashkan said getting up, quietly leaving a few notes on the table.

A voice from the bottom of her heart yelled, "Yes, let him drop you home."

"It would be trouble..."

"Drop the formalities," he said firmly, holding open the café door for them.

The gallery in Qeitariyeh, as it turned out, was close to his parents' home in Farmaniyeh, and he decided to drop off Pardis first. She had piano lessons, he told her. Driving down the leafy boulevard, they turned into a steep, up sloping road. It had been freshly tarred. The houses on either side had high walls, mostly brick with large iron gates that announced each to the road. They finally stopped in front of a beautiful, old, red-tile-roofed house at the end of a cul-de-sac. Two stories high, it was probably at least fifty years old, a true survivor from the old times. Something rarely found these days in Tehran, with all of the tearing down and rebuilding in the city accompanying the torrid real estate boom. It had a high wall, and the wrought gate was decorated around the edges with floral designs. As Pardis got out, she smiled and said, "Mahtab, it was very nice to meet you, and thanks for telling Nasim about today's exhibition. It was too bad she couldn't make it. I love art and had a great time today!"

Mahtab smiled back, disarmed by her frankness. "I'm glad you did. It was nice meeting you too." So the Robot had given her credit after all. Her heart tugged inside her chest. She had judged him too early.

Pardis left through a small door next to the main gate, and for a moment Mahtab caught the flash of a lush green garden inside. Ashkan invited Mahtab to sit up front. The smell of coffee mixed with his cologne enveloped her.

"Your sister seems very mature for her age," Mahtab said, breaking the awkward silence that took over after Pardis had left.

"She has to be with all she has gone through," he said tersely before glancing away.

What had happened? It took all of Mahtab's will to resist asking more. How badly she wanted to know more about him now. But politeness first, she wouldn't be nosy. She would ask Nasim once she got home. But maybe just one question. It wouldn't hurt, would it?

"So you like to speak English?" she asked.

"It's easier for me. I lived in the United States, I mean, *Amrika*, almost all my life."

"So why did you move here?"

She felt him consider the question for a moment before he answered, "I came here two years ago after graduate school. First for a project that my grandfather needed me for. I finished it and then went back to the states. Then he gave me another project, and I found myself back here again. And now I have this Sheraz project." He was looking at her now. "I might go back after that or stay to take on something else. I'm not sure yet."

"It's Shiraz, not Sheraz. That's how you say it in Farsi," Mahtab said with a small smile.

"Oh," he said, a little taken aback. Then he chuckled, his smile brightening his face.

"Shee-raz. Say it."

"Shee-raz. You are right. My Farsi is very poor. Well, I have Sepehr to blame for that. He bails me out whenever I get into trouble."

"It's OK. You are learning. My English is not good at all."

Suddenly Mahtab realized there was something missing today. Something she had nursed almost from the day she had met him. Hate. She no longer hated him. Rather he was quite fascinating, in his own unique way. She looked away, a smile touching the corners of her lips.

His cell phone rang, cutting through the silence. Glancing at the screen, Ashkan said, "I'm sorry, it's my father. I should take this call."

"Of course, go ahead."

"Salaam, Kiumars," he said, cradling the black flip phone against his ear with his free hand, the other resting on the leather-wrapped steering wheel.

"I'm out. I just dropped Pardis at home. No, I can't make it. I'll leave tomorrow."

And then he broke into English again.

Kiumars? He calls his father by his first name? Not Baba? Not even Dad? Imagine how her father would react if she called him "Rasool." Blasphemy! Is this how Americans do it? What of the fourteen-year gap between him and his sister? Why would they want to have a kid after fourteen years? Perhaps Pardis was an "oops" baby. He was so hot…She blushed at the last thought that just slid into her head unannounced.

When he was done, Mahtab asked, "Both your parents are *Irani*. So how come your Farsi is so bad?"

Ashkan laughed, flicking his head up. "Well, my grandmother is American, and my mom spent most of her life in *Amrika* so she is practically American too."

"So that's where you got your green eyes."

"What? What did you say?"

"Nothing." Mahtab looked down at her hands. She was saying too much.

"Come on, tell me."

"Nothing. I just said that explains your green eyes."

"My eyes are green?" He was smiling again.

"You didn't know it?"

"No. No one had told me before. I thought my eyes were brown."

"Are you serious?" Mahtab asked in disbelief.

The corners of his mouth began to twitch. He was teasing her again.

Beemazeh. You are not that funny, you know," Mahtab said, half peeved. She wasn't used to being teased by a guy, especially a guy as hot as Ashkan.

"No, come on, you should have seen the look on your face. You actually believed me!" He was laughing now, a small chuckle that grew into a deep laugh, his beautiful features unlocked from his usual frown. She stared at him, not knowing whether to be cross at his teasing or happy to see him laugh.

"My mom is right. Boys can easily trick girls. Well, here is a living example," she said finally.

It was now drizzling outside. She heard his window open and the sound of rushing air filled the car.

"I love the smell of fresh rain," he said without looking at her.

"Me too," she said softly. Yes, she loved the smell of the first drops of rain as they patted onto the thirsty ground below. Filling the air with that indescribably earthy smell, truffle-like, that now mixed with the scent of musk and leather inside. It was the scent of winter in Tehran. The sounds of life, the cadence of the rain, now seemed even sweeter than before. Mahtab felt something special, something new within her, taking over every cell, every vein. A new, strange feeling that she had never experienced before, linked in some way to the man in the driver's seat beside her.

❦

Mahtab stepped into the corridor of her home and heard the TV. The dim outline of her father's head in front of the flickering picture made her stop. Slowly she tried to sneak by.

"When I was young, the man of the house always came home after dark, not the girls."

Cursing inside, Mahtab turned around. It was Boji, staring out of the kitchen. She was on the floor, her hands on a pile of green herbs strewn on an old newspaper.

"Mahtab, come here. I want to talk to you." She spun around, looking in the direction of her father.

"*Baleh*, Baba," she said with hesitation as she headed to the living room. Had he seen her in Ashkan's car?

Baba looked tentatively over his wire-framed glasses. "So, Mahtab, what do you think of Emad's proposal?"

Mahtab drew in a breath. "Nothing. I have told Maman before. I am not thinking of marriage at this moment. I really want to achieve my career goals first. I have so much to do." She didn't feel like meeting his eyes.

Her father leaned forward and said, "I know that, but this guy is a good guy. He is educated. You know he has studied computers. He is doing well. He is religious with values."

Her eyes fell on the large bouquet of flowers that Emad's family had brought the night of the *khastegari*; now slowly wilting in their crystal vase. Mahtab pulled herself together and looked up and said, "But, Baba, I want to fall in love with my future husband. I don't love Emad!"

Baba sighed, his hand rubbing the stubble on his chin.

"Falling in love is not everything about a marriage, Mahtab. Falling in love is just like a match to start the fire. Keeping that fire burning with your husband is much more important than that match. Love comes with time, after the marriage. Love grows between two people. Those so-called love marriages will end up in divorce." He paused, and she felt his eyes searching hers. "Now look at your aunt Mina. She was always a well-behaved girl. She never had any boyfriends. She waited until Agha Jamal came to her *khastegari*, and now look how happy she is. She is blessed with two sons!"

Blessed with two sons! What about Tannaz, Aunt Mina's daughter? Wasn't she a blessing too? Then her thoughts turned to her mother. Wasn't she a good girl before her marriage? Baba seemed to have divined her thoughts and added hastily, "Or your mom. Your mom and I didn't know each other till we got married, and see how happy we are? Our first-born was a boy. Now we have a good house..."

Mahtab didn't want to hear anything anymore. Her family had always thrust Pasha forward as their boy wonder ever since she could remember. But to have her father confirm it with his own words that daughters were nowhere as important as sons tore at her like a saw through her heart.

"I don't know, Baba; I have to think about it," Mahtab managed, trying not to scream and cry at the same time.

"That's OK; think about it." Baba's eyes relaxed, but he added almost as an afterthought, "But make sure the decision that you make is a sensible one. Think of your future. Remember looks and other childish factors are not good reasons for marriage. Besides, Emad has a good family, and they are like us. God fearing. And they have money. They can take care of you. What can be better than that?"

"Sure, Baba," she said, now desperately wanting him to let her go.

"Good girl," he said smiling, patting her hand. "Now go and help your mother with dinner."

Nine

Mahtab picked up the schedule on Wednesday morning as soon as she walked into the office. Glancing over it as she walked to her classroom, she noticed Farbod had been moved to Tara's time slot. As Kamran had promised, that freed up Mahtab's evening for her rehearsals. But where was Tara? She walked back to Kamran's office.

"Where is Tara? I don't see her on the schedule."

"Who?" Kamran said, looking up from his desk. He looked tired.

"Tara Yaghoobi, my three-thirty Wednesday student. She is not scheduled today. Did she change her day?"

"Oh, her. No, she is not coming back. Her dad called; I think it was yesterday, or was it the day before? Anyway, he said they couldn't make it."

"No! But she was so talented. I know the divorce was difficult on her, but this..."

Kamran sighed, resignation in his eyes. "Yes, it's sometimes like that. You have talented kids who can't come because of their parents, and you have kids who hate music but are forced by their parents to attend. That's life."

Over her lunch break, Mahtab called Tara's dad only to be told it was none of her business if he decided that music was a waste of time for his daughter. There was still hope though. Even though her father controlled her fate, Tara still lived part of the time with her mother. Maybe her mom would think differently.

By the time her lunch break was over, Mahtab had found the mother, Mojdeh Moghadam's phone number, in Tara's old music file in Kamran's office. She quickly jotted it down while Kamran was out. She knew what she was about to do was against the policy of the institute. But that girl had a lot of talent and, policy or not, Mahtab was not going to let it die just because of her parents' stupid decision.

                                                                      *

When Mahtab walked through the heavy wooden doors into the large cream-and-crimson-domed auditorium of the university, it was as though she was back in college. The same wonderful acoustics of the hall that carried the voices and notes across its vaulted ceilings, and the familiar smell of old textbooks and varnish that she had remembered since the day she had entered school. Could it really be already one year since her graduation? She took in a breath and smiled. The orchestra was getting ready on stage, and Ostad Amini was talking to another older man with a goatee, who had his hand on his chin as though pondering a musical conundrum. Mahtab walked onto the dimly lit stage.

"*Bah, bah*, look who lost her way to us," a girl with a glittery pink scarf said, smiling.

"Negar!" Mahtab cried before the two kissed each other's cheeks.

"How have you been, Mahtab *joon*? Too busy to remember us?" It was Taraneh, another friend from her year. Mahtab was home.

"You could call me," Mahtab returned with a laugh.

"Are you still single?"

"Thank God I am. How about you?"

"Me too. But Taraneh. She managed to catch that guy over there."

Mahtab looked at the stocky man with a head full of long black hair and cried, "No! Mehrdad Alavi? The one that all the girls had their eyes on?"

Taraneh threw up a finger with a slender gold band. "Yes, the Mehrdad Alavi."

"*Bah, bah*! Taraneh, well done. You scored high," Mahtab said.

"I know," Taraneh smirked.

"Girls, boys, stop stirring the gossip soup. It is time to practice now. Strings, bass, percussion, woodwinds to your places," Ostad Amini said, waving his hands toward them as though shepherding a flock.

They found their places, and sheaves of printed music were passed out. The sound of paper being turned and arranged on racks rose to a crescendo, and then silence. Mahtab picked up her violin, and as she placed it on her chin, she heard her phone beep. Putting the violin down, she looked at the screen. It was a text from her mom. Without opening the message, she clicked the phone to silent mode and tossed it back into her pocket. The next two hours needed her undivided attention, and she couldn't afford to have anything disturb it. Not when the Ostad was directing. Wonderfully warm and avuncular offstage, Ostad Amini morphed into a perfectionist on stage, expecting everyone to give as much as he did to the performance. Even his eyes behind their bushy brows seemed to sparkle with a strange glint when he conducted, throwing his arms above and below him in jabs and swings.

Mahtab had seen him summarily dismiss players from practice, and once even from the ensemble, when they were not giving it their all, and she didn't want to be one of them. Not now when she was so happy. So proud to be part of this orchestra, even though she was in the second violin group. One day she would be leading it, in the first. Perhaps even in the Tehran Symphony Orchestra.

⌒〜◯

When Mahtab got home that night, she was exhausted and cold. But before she changed, she took the note from her purse and called the number. It rang and rang till finally a hesitant voice answered.

"*Alo?*

"Salaam, Ms. Moghadam?"

"Yes? Who are you?"

"Salaam. I am Mahtab Sharifi, Tara's violin teacher."

"Oh." The voice paused. "Tara is not taking violin lessons anymore. Her dad can't take her."

"I know. I heard. I was wondering if you could bring her?"

"*Na, azizam.* I can't afford it." The voice sighed. "I live with my parents now. After the divorce my husband took everything. He didn't even pay back my *mehriyeh* in full. I had to give him half so I could have Tara every Thursday and Friday. Otherwise I would never have seen her again if my husband wanted it. That is what the court said."

Mahtab fiddled with the piece of paper in her hand and, swallowing hard, said, "Ms. Moghadam, I am so sorry. I called because your daughter really likes to play the violin. She has talent."

"My dear, I also liked a million things when I was a little girl. I didn't get any of them. Listen, our situation is different. We are not like you guys who have a lot of money and can do whatever you want to do. I have to work to earn a living now."

Mahtab sighed. If only Ms. Moghadam knew her situation. "Please, listen to me. I'll come to your home and I'll teach her every Thursday for free. Would that be OK?"

"What?"

"For free. I really believe that your daughter wants to learn the violin, learn music. And I want to help her. All I ask that you keep this a secret. If the institute finds out, I'll lose my job. And I'll have to pay a fine," she said in a low tone. "Please, do it for Tara. I can come tomorrow."

"Really?" Ms. Moghadam's voice hardened. "What's in it for you?"

"Tara. I want her to be able to play. She loves the violin. I have seen it in her eyes. She reminds me of myself when I wanted to learn music and everyone around me hated me for wanting it."

There was a long silence on the phone. Mahtab could feel Ms. Moghadam on the other side, deciding. Finally her voice came over, softer. "I see. I have to talk to my parents and Tara's dad."

Mahtab sighed. She felt so tired suddenly. "Sure, please remember that I am..."

"What's your name again?"

"Mahtab Sharifi."

"*Merci*. I'll get back to you next week. Good night," Ms. Moghadam said, her voice cracking over the phone.

⁓෨

That Friday afternoon was the quarterfinals of the Asian Cup between Iran and Qatar, being played in Doha and Sepehr was throwing a football party at his apartment. Iran had thrashed Qatar the few other times they had played before. Everyone knew Iran had the best football team in the Middle East. Mahtab smiled before letting her lips straighten again. But with their money, that tiny emirate Qatar was now buying all the talent it could lay its hands on. What if Qatar beat Iran? Mahtab's stomach turned. No Iran had to win. She looked up as Nasim's car slowed down. They were now on Jordan Street, that great boulevard of northern Tehran. Cars passed them blaring Persian pop music. That only meant one thing: they were close to Sepehr's bachelor pad.

This would be Mahtab's first time at Sepehr's apartment. Of course, Nasim had told her everything down to the size of the bed, but it was really quite different to actually be there. Even the area itself had a reputation in the city. Jordan Street, the trendiest street in all of Tehran. The unofficial party zone of the capital.

Sepehr's complex was like a lot of the newly built condos in the area. A rectangular whitewashed building of fourteen floors with large areas of blue reflective glass that looked more like a swank office block than a residence. Against the sun, it glimmered so unlike her gray home with its recessed windows hidden behind bars and tall balconies.

The inside was like a catalog from Europe, filled with cutting-edge décor and appliances, from the Bauhaus fridge trimmed in stainless steel to the massage chairs stuffed around a large wall of a flat screen TV that threatened to take over the room.

Mahtab recognized a handful of people from Sara's birthday party the other day. Of course Sara herself with her blond hair and Devil style eyebrows and Sepideh with her husband were there. There were others Mahtab didn't know, but was sure by the end of the day she would. Mahtab looked around for the one person she was expecting to see. Where was he? Surely Sepehr would invite him. Had he gone to Shiraz? His absence made something well up within her. Disappointment. Yes, maybe she was a bit disappointed; maybe she was hoping to see him. Until the bell rang.

It was Ashkan carrying a black plastic bag. The way it hung from his hand, it looked like it was heavy, swinging pendulously two and fro. Sepehr quickly took it from him at the door.

"*Merci, merci.*" He turned, yelling to the others, "Ashkan brought the goodies."

"*Saqqa*, the good Samaritan came and brought *happy water*," someone said, "We are saved."

Mahtab looked at Nasim, who grinned back. "*Mashroob,* vodka." And she laughed. "It's OK Mahtab. It's good. Ashkan knows where to get the really good stuff, not the usual *Aragh*, moonshine. But you don't have to drink it if you don't want to. I'm sure there will be others who will finish it for you!"

After a late lunch of pizza delivered from the Italiano Kitchen, everyone gathered in front of the TV. While Nasim and Mahtab were putting the dishes into the sink in the kitchen, Nasim said, "I am so glad this is an international game, and we're all fans of our national team. Otherwise it might have ended in a bloody war here if there were two of our teams playing."

Mahtab said, "how is that?'

"Oh, because Sepehr supports Esteghlal, and I am crazy about Persepolis, specially that gorgeous Fereidoon."

"Tell me about it. He is hot," Mahtab admitted, smiling. "He is *dorageh*, mixed, you know."

"That's why he is so drop-dead gorgeous. Oh yeah, if I hadn't found Sepehr, I would have married him," Nasim said, giggling, "If Sepehr finds out, he'll get so jealous…So, anyway, I told Sepehr I wanted to paint my half of the house red for Persepolis, and you know what he said? Then he'll paint the other half blue for Esteghlal!"

Mahtab imagined them perfectly capable of doing such a thing. "You two are crazy!"

She followed Nasim, who walked out of the kitchen with a big bowl full of toasted sunflower seeds. The quintessential Persian party snack, to*khmeh*. Nasim paused in front of the group until she got its undivided attention. Looking around, she squinted at everyone on the ground crowded around the TV.

"OK! Any Qataris here? Declare yourself or you will be tossed out…"

"I think he's Qatari; I heard him talking in a foreign language. I think it was Arabic!" Sepehr yelled, pointing at Ashkan. Ashkan deadpanned and raised his hands up in mock surrender. Everyone burst out laughing, drowning out the TV.

When the match started, the mood changed. Mahtab could feel the tension in the air, like electricity crackling with every kick, every attack.

"Ahhh! Piece of shit!!" The guys were yelling at the top of their voices now, cursing, oblivious to their surroundings.

The disappointment of fumbled kicks, strikes that ended in near misses and attacks, which safely passed Iran's goalposts, only added to the fire of the match.

Nasim took a handful of sunflower seeds and yelled, "Go, Fereidoon. Go!" As the player raced across the field, she looked at Mahtab and added, "Fereidoon *mard-e meydoon.* The man of the soccer field. Maybe you should marry him, Mahtab."

"*Chashm,* Nasim! I'll just go ask him. He's probably waiting for me right now," Mahtab said, laughing.

"Who is Fereidoon?" It was Ashkan. Nasim giggled and pointed out the rugged Iranian midfielder. "He is like you, Ashkan, half and half. His mom is German."

Mahtab saw him turn towards her and she felt her heart stop. "So you like mixed guys?"

"No, Nasim is just joking," Mahtab said quickly looking away, trying to control the thumping within her chest. What was he thinking? Even if she did, she would never admit it, especially in front of him!

By halftime, it was clear that the Iranian offense was wearing down the Qataris. It wasn't without a couple of yellow cards, but the Qatari star Mubarak bin Saeed now looked harried, arguing with the referee when the whistle blew.

"It's funny how quiet the stadium over there has become!" Sepehr chuckled at the screen.

"*Areh,* they have fallen under the spell of our team. Three to one, Sepehr. There is no hope for them now!" Babak laughed, flicking the ash off his cigarette.

The game went to overtime, but the score didn't change.

Everybody was discussing the match when Mahtab saw Ashkan get up and go toward the dining room. He was on his cell. She followed him with her eyes as he came back and leaned over Sepehr, who was finishing his drink. They spoke in English and Mahtab heard Sepehr saying, "OK, I'll call you tomorrow."

Then Ashkan announced to everyone and no one in particular, "Everyone excuse me, I have to leave."

Babak said, "Where in such a hurry?"

"I have to go to Mehrabad airport to pick up my grandfather."

"See, I knew he was Qatari. He is taking off. Making excuses when his team lost!"

Babak chimed in, "Don't go. We promise, we won't beat you up."

Mahtab looked at him and at her watch. Oh God! She needed to get home. She glanced at Nasim, sitting on the couch, her back in the curve of Sepehr's body, her eyes fixated on the screen. Smoke curled from a slim cigarette between her fingers.

Mahtab got her *manteau* and scarf. Nasim saw her and said, "You have to go?" But she didn't wait for an answer. Nodding, she got up. "OK, Sepehri, time for me to go."

"No," Sepehr replied and looked at Mahtab. "Can I get you an *ajanse*? Let my girlfriend stay."

"It's post football on Friday afternoon, Sepehr. You can't find an *ajanse*," Nasim said.

"I'll take you." It was Ashkan, throwing on a dark felt jacket. This time Mahtab didn't have the time to *taarof*. She had to get home, and she was simply out of time.

It was cold as they walked to Ashkan's car but Mahtab barely felt it. She wouldn't have minded it so much if she didn't feel so powerless inside, so mixed with emotion that her stomach threatened to drop through her legs. And if there was one thing Mahtab hated, it was to feel powerless before a man.

As soon as they got in to the BMW, Ashkan turned on the heat. "It'll warm up soon."

"Thanks for dropping me off. Again."

"You're welcome. I was leaving anyway."

Mahtab took in a deep breath. "Sometimes I hate it when I am so dependent on Nasim."

"Then maybe you should get your driver's license."

"I do have my driver's license. It's been collecting dust in my desk for the last four years."

"So you need a car then."

She did. But in a million years with her salary she could not afford buying one. Maybe one from the 1940s with the roof and doors missing, but even that would be a stretch.

"Where is your grandfather coming from?" Mahtab asked.

"From Kish Island. He purchased land there last month."

"So perhaps he wants you to build on it for him?"

"Not only that but he also wants me to become his partner."

"So when are you going to start?"

"I don't know. I haven't even started on the plans. He needs to first obtain a building permit, which will take a while here. Enough about me. How are things with you?"

"Me?" she said with genuine surprise.

"Yes, you. How's work?"

"Work is good," Mahtab said looking straight ahead.

"Tell me what it is that you do again?"

"I teach the violin to children of wealthy parents with high expectations."

He laughed. "Why did you have to put it that way?"

"Which way?"

"Wealthy parents with high expectations."

"Because that's the truth. I mean a kid can either play the violin or he can't. And you have to at least try help your kids learn! I can't do miracles if they can't or won't try to get them to practice. To even remember to bring their violins! To even come to class on time. But their parents expect them to be virtuosos after a couple of lessons with me or they quit."

"Sounds like you are having a hard time."

"Not always, I might have been exaggerating a little. The kids, though, they really make it worthwhile," she said, thinking of Tara and Farbod. "But yes, it is tough at times."

He chuckled and then asked, "Are you happy with your life?"

Mahtab felt the question hit her core, the very root of her being. Why had he asked such a question?

"Yes, I am quite happy with my life," she said, not a little defensively. She wasn't ready to confide in him. "I love it when my kids learn a new piece by heart. But my passion is something else."

"What is your passion?"

"You don't want to know." She looked at him.

"I do." He smiled at her as they raced along the road.

Mahtab smiled, eyes questioning. "Why would you want to know what I want in life? You barely know me."

"Well then, tell me so I can get to know you better."

She paused and looked at him, wondering if she should tell him. Then taking a breath, she said, "OK then, I want to become a member of Tehran's Symphony Orchestra. I want to be able to play the violin professionally."

"So why don't you?"

"First, it's not that easy to get into. I have applied many times without getting in. You have to have an impressive resume. Secondly, it doesn't pay as well as my current job." What she didn't tell him was that her family would never hear of something like this. But then again, she was trying to talk to him, not scare him.

"I see," he said, "Or you could marry a wealthy man and not worry about working again. Instead you could play the violin for him all day long," he said, glancing at Mahtab. She saw his green eyes on her, gauging her reaction.

"Very funny."

"It wasn't meant to be funny. I was just giving you my own opinion."

"I don't need a wealthy husband to be happy. I am quite happy as it is. Even if I am a penniless musician," she said, irritation creeping into her voice.

"But you just said you need money." His eyes twinkled.

"Well, I said that even if I get into the orchestra, I won't be getting paid much, but that doesn't mean I won't be happy. I would have gotten what I wanted. I never said anything about being happy or unhappy. You know, for a guy who claims to have lived all of his life abroad, you are pretty narrow-minded!"

"In what way?" Ashkan said casually, looking ahead as he turned onto Chamran Highway, which descended from the northern hills toward the south of the city.

Mahtab pushed her bangs inside her orange scarf reflexively. "It's the things you say. A woman should stay home and cook or clean all day. Only play for their rich husbands..."

"I never said that a woman should stay home and cook. I said women are freer to make a choice about what they want to do than men. A decision. Gosh, how hard it is for you to understand what I mean."

"Maybe because your Farsi is so poor!"

"I know it is."

Arrgh! He was so difficult to pin down, to get a satisfying reaction from. Just like the first day she met him at the photo exhibition.

"Or maybe you are acting like your Farsi is poor. You are acting as though you grew up elsewhere."

"OK, you don't believe me? Here, look at my birth certificate."

He leaned across to open the glove compartment. Mahtab felt his hand brush her thigh and instantly pulled away from him. It felt like electricity that touch, a discharge of warm and cold that ran up her body. Something in her chest stirred, but in the back of her mind she heard the ringing of warning bells. Her eyes were now on him, studying him. For any sign that this was planned, that this was a pass at her, a sign that he was trying to step inside her borders. If he had planned it, his face didn't show it. Her hackles dropped. Maybe she was wrong.

"Do you carry your birth certificate everywhere with you?" she continued, trying to recover.

"No, I don't. I was going to get married today, so I needed it," he said passing the booklet to Mahtab.

"Really? To whom?" Her eyes widened, her previous irritation now turning to frank confusion. He was getting married? Her face must have shown it for he laughed.

"Relax, I was kidding. No, I needed it for business a few days back. It's crazy here in this country. You need your birth documents for everything."

"They want to verify your legitimacy. That you had a father. It's very important here in Iran," she said, taking the booklet.

He sighed, "Don't I know that." Then he motioned to her with his hand. "Go ahead, take a look."

Mahtab took the familiar thin red booklet, the standard-issue Iranian birth certificate, and opened it. The first page held a picture of Ashkan, pasted onto cream-colored government paper. He was so young, probably no more than eighteen or nineteen, with long, chestnut hair that fell over his face. Her eyes fell on his name. *Ashkan Michael Piroozvand.*

"You have two first names?" she asked.

"Yes," he answered. "In America people often have first and middle names."

"Interesting." She then went on. "You are an Aries. Where is Boston exactly?"

"Northeast. Massachusetts."

Wherever that was, she thought. She knew about the big cities in Amrika, cities like Los Angeles, or Teherangeles as it was affectionately known by Iranians, where most *Iranis* went before and after the revolution. And where most Persian pop music was made. And New York, of course. But Boston was unknown to her.

She then saw his parents' names, typed, in separate columns: *"Kiumars Piroozvand*, born in Tehran. *Christina Julia Tabandeh*, born in Boston.

"Your mom's name is Christina?" she said, staring down at the page.

"Yes, but everyone calls her Tina."

She hesitated before turning the page. The next page would be the marriage information page—the names of any spouses, the date and place of marriage, and also information about his children, their names, birthdays, etc. As Mahtab turned the page, she heard him say, "Don't worry, it's empty."

"Oh no, I was just going to..." She felt herself blush. He was supposed to be driving, his eyes on the road. Not on her every move, especially one that betrayed any interest in knowing about him!

She shoved it back into the glove box and closed it shut with a thunk. "There, I put it back. Keep it safe; you will need to have your birth certificate to get married!"

A few moments later, curiosity got the better of her and she asked, "Why do you call your father by his first name?"

"I don't know. I have always called him Kiumars. Maybe because my mom called him Kiumars and I just copied her. Or maybe it's because I rarely saw him." His voice was distant now.

"So is it working for you, staying here in Iran?"

"So far, I guess. I am not sure how long I'll stay here though. I might go back after I finish my uncle's hotel, or I'll stay for the Kish project. It all depends. As you know my Farsi still is not that great. For me, it can be hard to follow, especially when it's spoken fast. Do you remember when we went to the movie?" Mahtab felt the inside of her chest tighten. Yes she did, to the last detail, and now apparently so had he. "I had a hard to time following the dialogue. Everyone else was laughing."

Mahtab remembered that well, all too well. How he had sat still in the cinema, not laughing or joining in. She had accused him of being dry, boring. *Borj e zahr-e-Mar*. A tower of snake poison. A Robot. Pangs of remorse sprang within her chest, catching in her throat like liquid heat, searing her conscience.

Ashkan's voice broke into her reverie. "What are you thinking of Mahtab? You seem awfully quiet."

She looked at him, his handsome face smiling at her. It just felt so nice, the sound of her name through his lips. Trying to pull herself together, she sat up in her seat.

"It was nothing," she said, not meeting his eyes.

The roads always got bumpier as they got closer to her home. No way to repair them was the common refrain in the street, and it was true. How was anyone going to block and repair a road here when they flowed endlessly with everything from people, cars, trucks and push carts? The buildings began to turn into an indistinct gray in the late afternoon sun, and the clogged roadsides began growing vendors like colorful toadstools. Melons piled high on old trucks, baby clothes hung in a stall, their recently discarded cartons with stamped Chinese characters lying on the side; and the ubiquitous flower sellers, often women fully dressed in the *hijab*, weaved through the traffic, carrying bouquets that miraculously still seemed fresh.

They were almost at the intersection to Mahtab's home, and she said, "You have to make a right in that street."

"I know the way to your house very well by now," he said, smiling. "It's freezing. I'll drop you off at your door. If anyone has a problem with that, tell them it was a taxi."

She couldn't hold back a laugh. "Who's going to believe a BMW taxi driver?"

He stopped the car. "Well, I really enjoyed talking to you. We should get together again, when I come back from Sheraz."

"Sure," she said without conviction. Not because she didn't want to, but because she knew she couldn't. It just seemed so impossible with her family, her situation. She quickly added, "I'll get out by myself."

Opening the door of the low-slung car, Mahtab looked around to make sure there were no familiar faces around. The car engine purred, and the chime of the door's open signal monotoned. He leaned over to her, his eyes fixed on her face, unwavering. She was about to turn away when he simply offered her his hand. She took it, and it was warm, as she had known it would be. Then he was gone. Mahtab followed his car with her eyes till it was lost in the darkness of the night. She stood for several minutes staring at the end of the street, a world full of hidden feelings in her heart. Mahtab finally raised her head and looked at the sky, and a single raindrop fell on her face. It then began to drizzle. In the midst of the cold rain that fell around her, she could hear Googoosh singing far away.

Love is the lullaby of rain at night. The sound of rain on the windows.
The minute that the dew meets the jasmine. It's the minute of birds flying free.
You are the love itself, and you are my half.
You scream my silence.

She didn't want to go home. She wanted to stay in the street under the rain and wait for that car with the man inside to return. She wished the road to her home from Sepehr's house had never ended. When she finally headed home, Mahtab barely felt the ground beneath her.

Ten

That following Saturday, the beginning of the working week in Iran, Mahtab made sure she was home early from work. Pasha had been asking questions about last Friday. Fortunately Nasim had covered for her with a tale about them going to friend's house to surprise her for her birthday, but she had to be careful; this couldn't happen every time. The moment she entered the kitchen, her mom, who was over the stove, turned around. Suddenly, she smiled and said, "Mahtab *joon*, Emad's family is going to choose a dress for you."

"For what?"

"For the engagement, of course. His mother said they are looking at sometime next week."

"Maman, I will not marry him. That's it!" Mahtab said quietly, looking straight into her mother's eyes.

"*Khafe sho,* Mahtab, shut up. Enough!" Maman yelled, throwing up her hands. "A good girl does not question her dad's decision. Emad is a good guy. Just because he is simple and not flashy like those guys you work with, doesn't mean that he is any less. No, he is better than all of them! Stop throwing a stone on your own good luck!"

"I wish the stone would work, Maman. I hate him! Even if you don't care about me, think about him. What about his life, being married to a girl who hates him?"

83

"What is the problem now?" It was Boji, who had toddled into the kitchen unseen.

Shaking her head in frustration, Mahtab knew this wasn't going anywhere. As she left the kitchen, she yelled back, "I am going to call Emad myself and tell him that this marriage is a mistake. It's my life we are talking about here!"

"*Kheily sarziadi*, you are way too brazen."

"No, Boji. I simply want to be happy. Is that too much to ask?"

Motioning Mahtab to stop with a gnarled hand, Boji lowered herself into a chair and then began. "When I was your age, I never dared to talk to my older people like this. I always obeyed what they decided for me, especially my father, brother, and my husband. The men know what is right when it comes to such things." She looked at Monir, then Mahtab and slowly raised an open hand with five scrawny fingers.

"I have five kids, *mashallah*; none of them were named by me. My father-in-law named all five of them. We couldn't argue or change his decision. He was older than us and our custodian." She sighed. "Now these youngsters, they have no respect for their elders. They want this freedom that will destroy them! This freedom that will lead to drugs, divorce, and *fesad*, ruin! Remember, without your elders, you are nothing, *dokhtar*!"

Mahtab felt her heart sink within her. Boji had never told her this before. She had not been able to name even one of her children. Not one! How terrible for a new mother. The way she was raised, the way people lived back then, controlling women like chattel. The worst part was that this oppressive system had been so well programmed into Boji that she was its staunchest defender.

Mahtab threw her hand around Boji and hugged her. She felt her stiffen, perhaps surprised at her granddaughter's affection.

"Oh, you poor Boji. You should have told the stupid man to mind his own business. That's horrible carrying a child for nine months and giving birth to it, tolerating all that pain but not being able to name the child. What a selfish jerk."

"Get away from me." Boji pushed Mahtab away from her. "Get away," she croaked. "Unlike you who have no shame, I respected my elders."

"I know you did. But now everything has changed, Boji, everything has changed! Just because I want to choose my own life doesn't mean that I disrespect my elders. There is a difference between respect and *zoor,* force. In your time, in order to control the girls, they told them if they rejected their parents' words, they were disrespecting them. We no longer live in the eighteenth century. Why don't you want to accept that? Nowadays, girls also have rights. They vote, Boji. They are the ones who are building the future. You should let go of the past. Let go!" She grabbed Boji's hands and held them. "Help us women, your daughters, be free. Say it: men don't own us. Come on, say it. Men...don't...own us."

Boji's eyes seemed to hesitate for a moment and then hardened. Slowly she withdrew her wrinkled hands and turned her face away. At that moment Mahtab knew she had lost her, whatever in Boji may have seen reason was gone.

Mahtab reached for the phone to call Emad, but Maman had already jumped up and grabbed the phone to her chest. "No, Mahtab! Please don't. He is a great *case.* Look how much they offered to pay for your *mehriyeh.* Who in our family has that much *mehriyeh* behind them?"

"I don't want the damn *mehriyeh,* Maman. I don't want to have a price tag. Why can't you understand that?"

Mahtab stared at her mother's face for a moment. It was fear now in her eyes, as Maman pleaded, "Your father will mind it. He will get mad. It will be a bad face for our family. How will Pasha then work for him? You owe your Baba and me that much. Give this guy a chance. I swear to God, he is not a bad guy. He has a car. His family has money."

"No, Maman. *Aslan!* I can't marry him. If I owe my life to you and Baba, then I owe love to my heart. Please let me marry someone I love. Someone I'll be happy with. If I am allowed to vote, then I should be allowed to choose my own husband."

"Mahtab, you don't know what you are saying. Don't destroy your life," her mother said, her *janamaz,* prayer mat now under her arm. It was time for her afternoon prayers.

～๑

Mahtab was washing the dishes from lunch in the kitchen when the front door slammed. There was yelling, Pasha's deep voice punctuated by the high-pitched entreaties of Monir. No, it couldn't be. She had just called a few minutes ago. Probably he fought at work. Her head whipped around as the kitchen door blew open, kicked in by her brother as he stumbled in, fuming. Mahtab looked down. It was best to avoid eye contact, she had learned long ago, when he was in one of his moods. When he would often be in an uncontrollable rage, looking to discharge his wrath on the first unfortunate thing that came in sight. He stopped. She felt his heat, the sound of his deep breathing as he just stood there. Even though she didn't look up, she knew he was staring at her.

"WHO THE HELL DO YOU THINK YOU ARE?"

Her eyes jerked up to his face.

"What do you mean?" she managed in the strongest voice she could muster.

"*Khafe sho*. Shut up! You know what I mean. Emad told me everything." His eyes were bloodshot, his face red, white spittle covering the corners of his mouth.

"Go, Pasha. Go, leave me alone. You can't make me marry him," she said, her voice weakening with the cold thread of fear spreading through her, catching at her throat.

He drew closer, his hands swinging. "I told you to shut up!"

"OK, I will shut up. You too shut…" She hadn't finished her sentence when she felt a sudden flash of pain. When he slapped her across her mouth.

"Pasha, don't! Look, she is bleeding!" Mahtab heard her mother's voice over the buzzing in her head as she tried to keep herself standing. She tasted the blood, the salty unpleasantness that was in her mouth.

She felt herself being shoved against the wall, smell his sweat as he screamed, "This *saliteh*, this bitch, called Emad and told him she's not marrying him. She has shamed us, me! This wasn't supposed to happen, Maman, and you know it. Stupid, worthless pig!!"

She heard Maman gasp. "I am sorry. You go. I'll talk to her. I'll make her call Emad and apologize to him."

"No, you are too soft on her! That's why she dared to call him in the first place! I'll make her do it myself," he roared back, jamming Mahtab further into the wall.

The jolt slammed through her, knocking her to the core. A hoarse scream rang in her ears; for a moment she wondered who it was until her mind registered it. It was she.

"I am not marrying him! What part of it you don't understand? This is crazy. This is a madhouse. I am not marrying a *dar-e pit* a low-life. This is not the age of Qajars, forcing girls to marrying someone they don't want." Her head snapped back as Pasha yanked her by her hair, drawing a sharp cry. He then began to rhythmically beat her head against the wall.

"Who is a *dar-e pit*?"

"No one, no one! Awww, let go of my hair! Oh, *Khoda!*" she cried.

"I am going to chop off your hair if you don't shut up. *BeKhoda*, I will shut you up. So help me God!"

"No, no, Maman!!..."

The pounding continued. Brilliant blue and green stars appeared in front of her eyes as the edges of things blurred. The floor came up toward her as she fell, as he let go of her. Pasha was yelling over her, "You will. You will." Then he reached for her thick, black hair, now a ruin, and dragged her like a dog. "Go call Emad. Now," Pasha snarled. Although panting from the exertion, Pasha was smiling now, a smile of wounded pride assuaged by her at his mercy.

Mahtab was now crying, begging, tears running across her beautiful cheeks. "Pasha, Pasha *joon elahi ghorbonet beram*, I die for you Pasha *joon*, please. I don't like him. I am your sister. Don't do this to me, Pasha, please. *Toro Khoda*. I will do whatever you say. I am your sister! Doesn't that mean anything to you?"

"Why should it?" he hissed. "You made me look like an idiot in front of Emad! You will pay for this."

He finally did let go, exhausted from the effort, and dropped into a chair. From the floor, Mahtab knew this was dangerous too. He would start probing her now that he was lucid.

"Why don't you want to marry him? Do you have anyone else under your pillow? Is there another guy?"

"*Na, beKhoda*; no, I swear to God. Here's my mobile phone." She held out her phone. "See if I have any guy's number or if anyone calls me. *Na, beKhoda.* You can monitor my life to see I am saying the truth."

Pasha snatched her little silver phone and started jabbing at the buttons.

"We'll get to that too." After a few minutes of pin-drop silence punctuated by the click-clicking of the phone, Pasha threw the phone back at her. He said, "You call him now, and you apologize to him. You will say you love him, and that you will marry him. You'll do that now, Mahtab."

Mahtab just sat there, weeping. "No I won't. I can't lie about this. I can't. I don't like him."

"Yes you will!" Pasha ordered. Mahtab flinched, waiting for the blow that was surely coming. There it was! Across her thigh. He had removed his belt. She tried to run to her bedroom, but he caught her in the middle of the passage. Then they came, one lash after the other. Maman was screaming, "Pasha *joon*, leave her alone please! If something happens to her, Emad will never marry her."

Pasha threw the belt down and, catching his sister's neck, dragged her to the family phone. "Now you will talk to him or I will break you!" he said, pushing the receiver into her face.

The front door key turned loudly. The door opened to reveal her father, Rasool, looking haggard, carrying his briefcase, his old gray jacket over his arm. One look at him told her all she needed to know. He was angry.

"What is going on here? I could hear you all from downstairs. What would the neighbors think of us?"

Jabbing at her violently with his finger, Pasha began, "Baba, do you know what this *khar* has done? She has called Emad and called off the engagement!"

"Is this true, Mahtab?" Baba drew himself up as he said it, his fingers growing white around the briefcase handle. She didn't answer, avoiding his gaze.

"Answer me! What did you do?" her father said, drawing in a deep breath. He looked very pale under the glare of the living room light. "Mahtab, don't you think of anything? Don't you think of us, our reputation? What will Emad's family think of us? The people around us will talk. I will not be able to face them in the street. Such a good family he has. Both his parents have been to *hajj*, to Mecca. Their older children are happily married and have kids. No divorce in their family. Pasha is working for him now. Do you want to jeopardize his job?" He paused, catching his breath. "And he has money. He is like gold. You should grab this proposal with both hands." Then he drew closer and asked, "Do you have someone already that you are so against this marriage? Well, do you?"

"If you do, I will spill his blood and yours too, Mahtab," growled Pasha.

"No," Mahtab said under her breath.

"*Na, nadareh*," her mother jumped in. "No, she doesn't. I know where she goes. She never spends more time than is needed outside."

"I don't have any boyfriend. I just do not like Emad," Mahtab said weakly. "You can beat me all you want, but I will never marry him. Never! Even if that causes me to take my own life! I won't marry him."

Baba sighed, rubbing his eyes with his fingers. "I don't know what sin I have committed that I am paying for it with this girl. She has no shame, no respect, no understanding. She just lives her life like a wild person. You are no longer a teenager, Mahtab. Wake up! This is not *Amrika* where you can do whatever you want."

She was down to the last ounce of her physical strength, "What have I done, that I am a shame? I have never had any boyfriends. I don't run around and sleep with boys. I don't steal. I don't smoke. I don't drink. I don't do drugs. Why am I a shame?"

She cried out when it came, the thud followed by splitting pain that left her ears ringing loudly. She didn't know if it was her father or Pasha who had slapped her. Instinctively her hand went to her face and she felt a warm trickle of blood start from her nose.

"Don't you ever dare talk to Baba like that! Shameless!" Pasha growled, cracking his knuckles.

"Leave her, Pasha. Call Emad," Baba said. "The poor guy must be devastated now."

"I want her to talk to him herself. She has to apologize!" cried Pasha, towering over Mahtab, flicking his nails at her. He looked like the devil to Mahtab, with his disheveled hair, his shirt stained with blood. Her blood.

"She will. Let me talk to him myself first," Baba said, his voice hardening.

"No I won't."

"You won't? Is that how you talk to your father? *Khoda ghahresh migireh.* God will get angry," Boji snapped from behind, carrying a tray with two glasses of red sherbet syrup. She handed one to Pasha. "Here son, drink. Your blood pressure must have fallen low with all this stress."

Mahtab watched Pasha take the glass and drain it. Baba took the other.

"I'm sorry," Mahtab sighed, looking at the floor. "I didn't answer him back. All I want is to fall in love with the man I marry. Why is it so hard for you to understand that? All of you!"

"Love? You want love, Mahtab?" It was her father, his face red. He grabbed Mahtab by her arm and dragged her to the front door, and as he opened it, he said, "You want love? Here! Get out of this house! Go find love outside, out of my home. I don't want to carry your shame."

The room was spinning now. Mahtab felt time slow down as she looked down the path ahead. Everything felt surreal, like it was not really her here but someone else, she just a spectator in a tragedy being played for another. She knew that families disowned girls for dishonoring them. That their fate was something worse than death, that of a *farari*—an outcast, a runaway. To live from park to park, shelter to shelter, and the home of random men to earn their keep. Or worse, being sold to those Emirati sheikhs. But now she knew it, knew that those words were not idle threats but real, that her family was no different from the others.

The thump of the closing door brought her back to reality like a current clearing away the mud. Revealing her naked fear. *Without your family you are nothing, without your family you are nothing!*

"No, please, Baba, please don't do this," Mahtab cried, banging on the pine door. "Please don't throw me out. I am so sorry. I will marry him; just don't kick me out. Open the door, please."

It was several minutes before the door finally opened.

A few moments later, as Baba rang Emad, Mahtab listened numbly, looking down at the floor. She wished she could just go to sleep, a deep sleep to be away from all of this. She could hear his tinny voice over the receiver.

"I am not upset with Mahtab *khanoom*, I understand her situation."

Her father mumbled his apologies.

"Not a problem, Agha," Emad went on, his voice like honey. "Agha Sharifi, it is understandable that Mahtab *khanoom* is nervous and has mixed feelings. It's not about me. It's about her. She just thinks she is not ready for marriage yet. She thinks she is not ready to live with her husband, but I think she is ready. It's not her fault. She is just scared. It is good that we will have a long engagement, and then she'll be comfortable."

"God bless you, son. You are perfect yourself," her father gushed, hunched over the receiver. He shifted in his chair and clearing his throat, asked, "I hope you haven't told your father about this little misunderstanding."

There was a pause. The tinny voice over the receiver laughed sweetly, reassuringly. "No, I didn't think to worry him for something as small as this. I only told Pasha so he could talk to Mahtab. You know, help clear her mind of any doubt she has about getting married. Agha Sharifi, I am very sorry about any trouble I may have caused you..."

"No, no, Emad *jan*! It is we who should apologize for this embarrassment."

"Please don't mention it. No embarrassment at all. Please send my best regards to Boji, Monir *khanoom*, and of course, Mahtab."

"Thank you, Emad *jan*. You are like a son to me. Give my deepest regards to your father, mother, and family."

Carefully Baba placed the old, white receiver back into its cradle. Running his hand through his hair, he looked at Mahtab.

"See what a good guy he is? *Tala*! Gold! You will thank us later."

Yes, what a good guy he is, Mahtab thought bitterly. But not for her. She had tried to break this horrible engagement only to have the steel claws of her family shut themselves even more tightly around her. And now, to add even more salt to her wound, Emad was a hero for gallantly saving Baba from family shame!

It was overcast now, the gray blanket of clouds announcing the coming of snow. As the snowflakes began to fall, one by one, cold, nameless, into a white haze outside, Mahtab felt her world growing dark. But it wasn't sadness she felt as much as utter helplessness. What could she do? She sighed. It was Emad and her family, or her alone. And alone she knew that, even, just supposing she survived being a *farari* and found a man—a man she loved worth something, with a head worth his neck—the first question out of his family's mouth would be "Who is her father? What does he do?" After all, who would they go *khastegari* to if her father wasn't there to represent her? There seemed to be no escaping her fate. On the misty window of her room, she let her finger trace a broken line. She was that line.

Eleven

On the day of Mahtab's engagement, the *namzadi*, it was decided that they would also perform the *sigheh*. How much she hated that word. *Sigheh*, the temporary marriage that needed only a prayer to legitimize it, a simple ceremony that brought an unmarried girl and boy into sanctioned physical closeness under religious law. It was supposed to make them taste the sweet anticipation of marriage, but for Mahtab it was a cage that locked Emad even more firmly in with her.

Everyone was still running around madly trying to shoehorn in the final preparations. In her bedroom Mahtab was sitting on her bed, her shapely legs drawn under her, her dark brown eyes brooding into space. Maman had been after her for the last hour to change, but Mahtab had refused. She shuddered. It was Emad or the street. And then what would she do? Mahtab had never felt so powerless in her life, her fate being decided before her very eyes with no way to stop it.

At about five in the evening, the guests started arriving. It was a very simple gathering, which was how her father had wanted it. No ostentation for the religious puritan that he was, and in any event with her *jahaz* to be bought, there was no money even if he had wanted more. Not even dinner was served, only tea and *shirini* sweets. The actual ceremony only took a few minutes as she and Emad sat on their chairs, facing Emad's father who read the prayers that made them *mahram* to each other, religiously allowed to each other. Mahtab didn't look up, didn't care to even acknowledge Emad's father. But with the bruise on her lip still fresh from the beating the other day, she said nothing.

That night Mahtab cried into her pillow silently until she fell into exhausted, broken sleep. Then came the nightmares, or were they flashbacks of the beating? Pasha's face, the face of her father, purple with rage, throwing her out of the house. The sickly yellow pine door in her face. The smell of varnish. The sun had risen by the time she woke up to the incessant ringing of her cell phone. It was Nasim. There had been at least nine calls since yesterday, not counting this one. Mahtab put the pillow on her head and squeezed her eyes shut. Her head hurt. But she had to get up and go to work.

~⊙

The walk from Mahtab's apartment to the metro station took at least 20 minutes on a good day, but the blanket of winter snow, now soggy with the rush of cars and people made it only longer. Just before she descended into the metro, she got her phone out. There was a missed call from Nasim of course, one from Kamran about a schedule change, and one from Ostad Amini about the rehearsal. But nothing from Tara's mom. It had been more than a week and nothing had happened. If only Mahtab had their address, she would go there herself without asking. Then the reception cut and it was time to get her train.

Thankfully there were still seats available in the compartment reserved for women. As she dropped into her seat, a girl not much younger than Mahtab with eyebrows as thick as rope passed by carrying a large black sack, which bumped and bounced off passengers as she pushed her way through. She must have decided that she was in a good position because with a quick shrug, she dropped the sack onto the floor and drew out a bunch of colorful bras.

"Only 2000 toman, my dear ladies, only 2000 for these *chic* bras. It will make you look and feel better!"

This line seemed to work for a few women extended their hands to examine these new wonder bras. Behind the bra seller, Mahtab spied another girl, about Pardis' age, hawking eye shadow from a brown carton and yet another selling sandwiches. They must have been here since morning, all inside this compartment of the Tehran metro.

Once out of the underground, Mahtab dialed Ms. Moghadam's number as the escalator bumped its way up to the bus stop. The ringing finally gave way to a beep followed by a high-pitched voice from Irancell that apologized for the missed connection. Mahtab let out her breath in frustration. Irancell, her mobile plan, didn't even let her leave a message. She clicked off her phone, but she wasn't going to give up. She would call back again.

On the way she stopped by a pharmacy and picked up a box of aspirin for the headache that was her near constant companion since Pasha's beating. How many days ago was that? She winced, touching the scab that had formed on her lip. Yes, seven days. Seven days that had showed her what her family was really capable of and what little choice she really had in her own life. But here, at work, she was herself again. At least she had resolved to try to be. That shouldn't be hard, since she left the ugly ring Emad's family had given her at home. She sighed, her hands around her head. She needed to talk to a sister. Not Bahar, she was too young, too immature, but Nasim. Though at times a flake, she was the one person that Mahtab knew shared a connection with her, a bond that connected their souls across genes. She would call her once the pounding in her head stopped and her lessons were over.

෴

Mahtab tried calling Ms. Moghadam after work, but she still didn't pick up. Once she got home, just seeing her family made her head throb even more. The people who forced her into this mess. She hadn't fully changed when the *i-fone*, the home screen intercom, buzzed.

"It's Emad," her father said, standing behind the door. "Hurry up! Clean this place up."

"Oh, poor guy, he must have missed you," her mother said as she ran by to change into more appropriate clothing.

For a few seconds, Mahtab stared at the figure standing outside, framed in the black-and-white intercom screen. In his jeans and a black jacket, Emad was standing, arms at his hips, his head at an angle. He looked up straight into the camera with the expression of confidence, no, supreme confidence.

Like a conquering hero in one of the old Iranian movies, arriving at the home of a supplicant.

"It has begun then. He'll be here every night from now on," Mahtab sighed to herself.

In the kitchen Maman was fretting. "I wish he had called before. What will I feed him? I didn't cook meat today! The poor *pesareh*. He must be tired after working all day!"

All along Mahtab watched as her mom hurriedly brewed tea and threw together some *shirini* and fruit for her *pesareh*. For her new son.

In the living room, Emad was already sitting now, talking to her father, when Mahtab brought in the steaming tea. He was different. Not physically, but his bearing, his expression. Gone was the expression she had seen in the intercom screen, replaced with modesty, eyes lowered deferentially in front of her father, his hands upon his lap.

"*Zahmat nakesh*. Please don't trouble yourself. I didn't come to bother you. Actually, Mr. Sharifi, with your permission I am here to take your daughter out to dinner."

He said the last part as though slightly embarrassed, shifting in his seat. Such an actor.

Her dad, his eyes widening behind his wire-rimmed glasses, smiled and said, "Oh, of course, of course. You are now both engaged."

And just like that, with Monir and Baba at the door, Mahtab was walking out with Emad. Outside Mahtab saw his car for the first time: a white Kia Sportage parked by the main gate. He stopped to light a cigarette before unlocking the car.

Inside, as she settled into the dull gray fabric seat, she said, "I didn't know you smoke."

"Oh." He smiled. "Yes, I am careful in front of the elders. You know how it is with them. They think it's not right." He winked, his eyes glittering in the waning evening light. "Even my parents don't know, and I want to keep it that way. So your parents shouldn't either." Then he turned toward her and threw out his hands in the air.

"I am going to take you out to a place you have never seen! This will not be your *khoresht* and rice at home, I promise you that, Mahtab *khanoom*."

Forcing a smile, Mahtab wondered how he knew what she ate, and moreover, did he think she was such a neophyte when it came to food?

Unfortunately, his visual transformation had not extended to his prattle, which remained as self-absorbed as before. As he started the car, he went on about how he climbed the ladder of success faster than anyone else in his family. Even faster than his older brother who owned an insurance agency.

"What about your sisters? Where do they work?" She couldn't help asking.

"They have no use for a job. They are all married with children!" He laughed. "They didn't need to work like you did." He stroked his beard with one hand as he drove, the other resting on the steering wheel, the cigarette between two fingers. "But your family must need the money..."

He turned to her, his eyes shining. "Mahtab *joon*, I want us to be able to go to the *hajj* together. After the wedding! We will look so good in the family." He paused, his eyes darting away. "Of course we can take my mom and dad, and I will pay for it all. It will impress my older brother so much!"

"I don't want to go to *hajj* now. I am too young."

"It doesn't matter if you are young or old. Have you been there? No, you haven't. They have such beautiful shopping malls. There are so many electronic shops you can't even decide which one to go to. And the restaurants, the restaurants are all American fast food."

"Have you been there?'

"No, but I have heard. But I have been abroad. I've been to Dubai. Trust me you'll enjoy your foreign trip. It'll be your first time abroad. You'll shine in your family."

"Yes, but you know, I prefer to see the beautiful cities of Iran. There are so many cities here that hold so much of the history of Iran."

"Ah, that's for people who have no money. People who have money, they travel abroad."

"But don't people usually go to *hajj* for the pilgrimage, for God, not shopping?"

He laughed. "We can multitask. We'll do both."

Emad parked the car close to a shiny fast-food restaurant, all glass and colored lights like a bloated telephone booth. The sign above read Boof. He stood by his car till Mahtab reached him.

"Did you lock your door?"

Mahtab nodded. They passed the street and entered the busy restaurant.

"Mahtab, you go sit. I'll order," he commanded.

"But you don't know what I want."

"Don't worry. I'll order something nice for both of us. You go. I know this place very well. It might be confusing for you. Go and sit."

"I want chicken nuggets." She persisted.

He looked at her for a moment with a frown of irritation before smiling again. "*Baleh,* Mahtab *khanoom.*"

She got the first available table, sat down and looked around.

He appeared after a few minutes, smiling, "Is this restaurant good? Are you happy? I got soda too."

Sitting down, he plopped the tall plastic cups on the bright yellow table. "They'll bring the food soon," he added hurriedly.

"Yes, I know. I have been to restaurants before."

"Oh yeah, but not this one, right? It's pretty expensive."

Mahtab had been in this very restaurant with her friends many times while in college. How else did she know what to order pat without any menu?

Emad then reached for her hand, but Mahtab pulled it back. Even though her family had forced him on her, she was not yet his to take. In her own way she would make sure of that.

He laughed, but his eyes didn't. "Are you still shy? Come on, don't be shy. I am your fiancé now. You have to be with me. Give me your hand."

He stared at her. She didn't budge but returned the stare evenly.

He gave up and said, "So it seems like we are stuck till your *jahaz,* dowry gets ready." Her studied silence prompted him further. "You know, for our wedding. No offence, but with your dad's salary..." He trailed off, shaking his head from side to side. "And having to feed six mouths, he will never have enough money to buy your *jahaz.* What should we do? You can't come to my home without a presentable *jahaz.*"

This jerk was insulting her family. And the ultimate irony was that this was the family that had forced her to be with him, called him "gold," called him her savior.

Before Mahtab could respond, the food arrived. Emad had ordered cheeseburgers for both of them, their gray patties extruding through the buns. Like squashed mushrooms, she thought, they always looked like squashed mushrooms. She hated them. She wanted chicken.

"Emad, I asked for chicken nuggets. That's what I usually or..."

"You need to start liking things that I like, otherwise our marriage will have problems," he said glibly.

"What? Are you serious?" Mahtab's jaw dropped.

"Yes I am," he said sharply.

She sighed and started to eat. Emad, with his mouth full of food, said, "Put this ketchup on. It'll taste better."

He shoved a handful of fries inside his mouth. "He can get a loan or something."

"Who?"

"Your father." Swallowing with a grunt, he continued, "He can get a loan to buy the *jahaz* for you. You know, I am a guy, Mahtab," he said, rolling his lidded eyes meaningfully. "I can't wait forever. You should have seen my sister Neda's dowry. She had so much stuff, a big silver fridge, TV, microwave, all LG, all foreign." He looked at her, waiting for her reaction. If he was hoping for something from her, he was sorely disappointed. Mahtab couldn't care less about how much they had.

Then he started talking again. "My parents really took good care of the whole situation. They gave her everything she wanted. Handmade Tabrizi rugs. Silk, you know. And they didn't have to wait to marry because by the time her husband came to her *khastegari,* she had everything ready."

"How old was she when she got married?"

Emad nearly choked on his burger. "What's that supposed to mean?"

"You know, how long did it take for an actual *khastegar* to come ask for her? Maybe your parents had plenty of time to get things ready for her," she said coolly.

"That's beside the point," he snapped, "My parents take good care of their children. They are offering us the apartment above their own home. So we can live there as long as we want rent free, worry free. Isn't that great?" His hands fiddled with the checked burger wrap that lay limply on the tray.

"Yes, it is great. Living above my in-laws is what I always dreamed of," Mahtab shot back.

"What do you mean?"

"Do you really think I want to live so close to the parents of the guy I marry?"

He looked blankly at her.

"No! Of course not. Living like that would be like going from one jail to another. My own parents' house to another. Do you understand, Emad?"

"No, not really. Don't you know anything about the housing market? With these outrageous prices, how we can afford buying a house of our own now? Unless we go south very close to the graveyard. Then we can buy something there. A shack perhaps. A two-square-meter room and a one-square-meter bathroom. You should be realistic."

"But I thought you were rich, Emad. What about all the money you are making?" Mahtab smiled innocently as his features darkened into a frown. It felt good to give back a little for all she had endured that evening.

The reply was sharp, stripped of its usual honeyed tone. "I'm putting all the money I make into the stock market. My parents are giving us a free house in such a good part of the city, Sa'adat Abad. Have you been to Sa'adat Abad? Some people say it's like *Shanzelizeh,* the Champs-Elysees of Tehran, and you should appreciate that, given where you are coming from. And do you know how big our appartment is? It's two hundred square meters. It's huge. Now it's up to your parents to fill it up and I hope not with cheap Chinese shit! They should get Korean or European stuff. Keep that in mind."

Emboldened by her silence, Emad leaned forward, his right fingers drumming on the tabletop.

"Anyway, the point is that I can't wait. I want to marry you tomorrow. I want you!"

"You don't even know me that well. Maybe you should take some time to get to know me." She paused and a slight smile crept onto her lips. "Maybe, hopefully, you'll change your mind about me."

He leaned back on the chair, one hand above his shoulder, the other on his belly. "What's there to know? You are beautiful, and I like you. Our families like each other, and I am your brother's friend. Actually boss, but I don't want to hurt his ego so I say friend! So what's the problem? Only your shyness is in the way." His lidded eyes were on her face, searching for her reaction. "Give me your hand."

"No."

"Come on, I want to see your ring." His voice had acquired an edge now.

Mahtab slowly extended her hand toward him, and he touched the tip of her fingers and then the ring. A big, yellow, shiny monstrosity, studded with stones at odd angles.

"Isn't this beautiful?" he said, looking up and smiling. "My mother chose it. Do you like it?" He didn't wait for her to answer. "It's very expensive. Take good care of it. It's more expensive than my older brother's wife's ring. Make sure to remove it when you are doing housework."

Mahtab chuckled. She wanted to tell him that she only wore it when he was around. But she kept quiet.

When they finally left the restaurant, it was late. Mahtab shuddered in the cold as she walked to his car, wisps of vapor coming from their breath. Inside they sat in silence. He tried to make small talk, but she put him off. She looked away, drifting into thought, as lights streaked across her window. She needed Nasim more than ever now to talk to, to at least have someone understand what she was going through. She sighed. She had not returned Nasim's calls since Thursday, the day before the *sigheh*.

Lilting notes of Vivaldi floated into her mind. For a moment she could almost smell the leather, the seductive scent of musk, feel his presence. She had tried to suppress him, ever since her father had thrown her out of her home. Tried hard each time he came into her mind, like someone clinging to driftwood as a huge wave drove her inexorably upward. He was not for her, she had told herself. He was different. It reminded her of an old Persian saying, a favorite of her mother's. That flashy boys were for the neighbor's daughters, not hers. For some time she had even convinced herself fully that it wouldn't work, by picking on every negative thing she could think of, like his alcohol, even his good looks. And even if they ever did get together, even if, what about her music? Wasn't that the most important thing in her life? To get into the Tehran Symphony Orchestra? But. Yes but. Her insides had begun to ache now, not a sharp fleeting pain but a deep ache, one that told her otherwise.

She thought of that gray car in which he had confused and then captivated her after the evening at Sepehr's place. That CD he had given her. She had played it every night in bed and then carefully put in her little wood lock box with her other treasures in the morning. She smiled. Yes, he could irritate her with his pronouncements, but they were delivered so honestly, so earnestly that she just couldn't hold it against him anymore. Unlike the toad next to her, his saccharine voice barely covering his arrogance and presumption. She shuddered as she glanced away from Emad's profile. He was smoking again and looking straight out onto the road, scowling, his cigarette hand over the steering wheel. Yet seeing him angry only gave her hope. Maybe he would let go of her after all and call off this cursed engagement.

Twelve

Sitting at the bus stop, a small glass house affair with a layer of dust on everything, Mahtab looked at her phone, the diesel fumes curling around her. It had buzzed like this for the last ten minutes, as though possessed, lit up by either her mother's calls or Emad's texts. Thank God for the silent mode.

Mahtab had finished rehearsals thirty minutes ago, but Nasim still hadn't shown up. Several minutes later, Nasim's white Peugeot hatchback finally appeared and screeched to a halt in front of her.

Mahtab grabbed her violin and got in the car. Nasim waited for her to put her violin in the backseat before reaching across and hugging her. Mahtab burst into tears. Nasim handed her a svelte, scented tissue box as she navigated her way out of the bus stop. "Let's get out of here before that *gonde* bus flattens us," she said, glancing at the hulking, faded green bus belching fumes behind her.

Once on the road, she turned around. "Honestly when I didn't hear from you for two days, after your engagement, I thought everything was OK. I didn't expect this."

"You have no idea how bad things are," Mahtab said, wiping the wetness from her eyes.

"I can't believe they are doing this do you." She looked at Mahtab for a brief second, and Mahtab caught her look, one of outrage, anger mixed with sadness.

"Are you hungry?" Nasim asked.

"A little," Mahtab admitted.

"Do you want to go to Hila?"

A small smile lit Mahtab's face. "You know I am always up for Hila."

In Mahtab's firm opinion, Hila had the best pizza in the city, and it was a favorite haunt of theirs. A place they had often hung out during their college years.

It didn't take long to reach the pizzeria, tucked away in the middle of Tehran.

They had just sat down, opposite each other at a faux wood table, when she noticed Nasim staring at her. "Mahtab, you are crying!"

In disbelief, she touched her face. It was wet.

Reaching for her hand, Nasim began, "Mahtab *azizam*, stop crying. You can't cry yourself all the way to the *sofreh aghd*, the marriage ceremony and do nothing. You have to find a way to get out of this stupid engagement!"

"What do you think I should do? My mom thinks he is the best thing that could ever happen to me! My father says Emad is 'gold,'" she said, mimicking his quavering voice. Mahtab sighed, "Nasim, at one time I thought I knew where I, my life was going. I was so sure. Now..." Her voice broke, "I am so confused. I can't see anything clearly. I only pray for a miracle!"

Nasim cursed under her breath. "Just leave and stay with me," she said, leaning in to face her. "My mom loves you, Mahtab. You know she says you are the sister I never had."

Mahtab paused, touched by her friend's generosity. She sighed and shook her head. "I can't. That's the first place they'll look for me, and Pasha will come yelling, and will drag me out of your home by my hair. Do you want such a scene in front of your neighbors?"

Nasim thought for a moment and then smiled. "My neighbors will probably throw him out first. But seriously, what about Sepehr's apartment then? We'll go there. I'll ask Sepehr to stay at his parent's house. I am sure he won't mind."

"*Na*, it won't look good. Especially in front of Ashkan. What would he think of me? A *farari*, a runaway girl? Plus I don't want him to..."

It was the expression on Nasim's face, one of shock that confirmed her slip. Mahtab felt her face heat up as she blushed.

"What?" Nasim had nearly choked on her Miranda drink. "What?? What did you say? What about the Robot?"

"Nothing. I didn't…"

"What don't you want him to know?"

"Nothing. I was just saying it won't look good for you in front of Sepehr and his family."

Nasim chuckled, shaking her head, her smile broadening. "No. No, that's not what you said. You didn't say anything about his family. You said it wouldn't look good in front of Ashkan!"

Mahtab couldn't hide her grin, her fingers now in her hair. "No, I'm just saying. What if he wants to go there and hang out with Sepehr? Or take his girlfriends there? It's not good for me to be there," she said hurriedly, before sipping her 7Up.

"Yes, of course," Nasim said grinning, her eyes dancing. "Yes. It has nothing to do with you wanting to keep up appearances in front of him."

"What? No!" Mahtab said, desperately pulling herself together. Despite her best efforts, her lips seemed to have gotten a life of their own, grinning giddily when she had firmly ordered them not to.

Nasim leaned forward, pushing the little pizza tray off to one side. "Well, first of all he is working in Shiraz, so most of the time he is there. Second, he has his own apartment complex. He doesn't need to bring his girlfriends over to Sepehr's. In fact he has one apartment for each one of his girlfriends."

Mahtab's face fell. Girlfriends. Apartments. The words resounded in her mind as her heart lurched forward.

Nasim was smiling again, but her voice was reproachful. "You know, my darling, I think you are hiding something from me, and you can't lie to save yourself. That's not what sisters do, Mahtab *joon*. I told you about the day I had my first kiss, the moment I lost my virginity. You can't do this to me. It's just not fair!"

"Come on, Nasim, it's not a big deal. I just don't want him to see me like that, you know, homeless, disowned by my family." She sighed. "I fought with him all the time. I don't want him to see me as a loser."

"Mahtab *joon*! I think someone here has a crush on Ashkan and is desperately trying to deny it! I wonder who that person is?"

Mahtab's face grew red as Nasim turned her head around, pretending to scan around the room looking for someone until her eyes landed back on her.

"It's you, my dear Mahtab. You have a crush on Ashkan!"

Nasim said it loud enough to have a couple of neighboring tables looking at them. Her face crimson now, Mahtab swallowed her reply.

"How long did you keep this from me?"

"I don't know, Nasim. It's no big deal. It'll go away. You see my situation; I am stuck with Emad now, and as you said, Ashkan has many girlfriends. What are my chances?"

Nasim carefully brought her manicured fingers together and laughed softly. "I was joking. He doesn't have anyone. He is kind of a workaholic, and when he is not working or at the gym, he is playing games on that stupid PlayStation with Sepehr. Like five-year-olds. You should see them; it's pathetic!"

Mahtab wasn't listening anymore. Ashkan didn't have anyone. She ran those words through her mind again, savoring each word like manna mixed with something new. Guilt. Guilt at thinking what she did. That even if she didn't have a chance at him, at least she could be happy that no other girl did!

"Come on, Nasim. Stop it! I'm engaged to Emad." She wished that she could laugh at Nasim's joke, be happy that finally her best friend had found out her secret; but no, she knew that she could not. The invisible chains of her family and what they had saddled her with, Emad, clung too heavily to her.

"You have to get out of it. There is no other way, Mahtab. Do you really want to live the rest of your life with that toad? Have his kids? You have to throw him out!"

"If it wasn't a sin, I swear I would have killed myself to get out of it!"

Reaching for her hand, Nasim's tone became serious. "Oh no! Don't do that. My kids need an aunt."

Mahtab smiled. "They will have two. Sepehr's sisters."

"Those two won't count. Especially Sara. She won't have time between her flirting and shopping to even look at them!" Nasim grimaced, wiping her hands daintily with a napkin. With a quick smile, she pulled out her cell phone. "Do you want to see some pictures of your love?"

The photos were small, almost postage sized, on the cell phone screen, but Mahtab could see enough. His chestnut hair, his perfect smile.

"We were at his grandfather's vacation home on Friday. He is something, isn't he? I heard he was a model while in college. Not just a small store model. For Abercrombie and A|X!" Nasim said, winking at her.

"Really?"

"Yes, Sara told me. She said that's how he paid his way through college."
As she began to click through the pictures, Nasim said softly, "Don't you
want to kiss those lips?"

Mahtab grinned. "Oh, Nasim, stop it." Then she got up.

"Where you going now?"

"Home. It's getting late."

"Sure, sure. With this curfew and all, how do you get out of the house for
your charity concert rehearsals?"

Mahtab smiled. "Every week is something different. Tonight I filled in
for Raha. Supposedly she is on vacation and I got all her students."

Nasim laughed. "I wonder what you would do if you didn't have this
made-up Raha?"

"She comes in handy all the time, especially if I need to get away. And
you know in the end, my family doesn't mind the extra money I bring in
from my tutoring," Mahtab said as she opened the door. As they stepped out
into the cold, Nasim stopped and whirled around. "I am going to help you
with Ashkan! I just wished you had told me sooner," she said, her hands on
Mahtab's shoulders.

⌒〇

"She has to be home; it's Friday," Mahtab whispered as she dialed Tara's
home once again. It rang three times and then a small voice spoke.

"*Alo.*"

"*Alo,* Tara?" Mahtab said, holding the receiver closer.

"*Baleh.* You?"

"I am Miss Mahtab. Your violin teacher."

"Oh hi Miss Mahtab." The little voice perked up on the other side.

"Tara, I've missed you. You are one of my good students."

"*Merci.*" The voice hesitated before continuing. "I can't come. My baba
says it's difficult for him. He has a new girlfriend now."

"How about your mom? Can she bring you?"

Silence. Then Tara spoke, "She said she can't afford it."

"Is she there?"

"She's in her room. She says she has a migraine headache. She has been
sleeping since morning."

107

"Is there anyone else I can talk to?" Mahtab said, her heart sinking. After all the effort, the phone calls, even her offer of free lessons, it looked like it wasn't going to make an ounce of difference.

"My grandma is here."

Over the phone there was the murmur of low voices, followed by an older voice that seemed animated, louder.

"Salaam. You are Tara's violin's teacher?"

"*Baleh.*"

"What can I do for you?"

Mahtab told her what she had told Tara's mother. "*Khanoom*, I can come to your home and teach the violin to Tara, if that would be acceptable to you."

"God gives you a long respectful life, *dokhtaram*. I would have brought Tara to her classes myself if it wasn't for my *artorooz* arthritis. Sometimes my joints hurt so bad in the morning, I can't even walk to the kitchen."

"I am sorry. I hope God gives back your health soon."

She sighed. "I don't know, my daughter. I'm getting old. Life is catching up with us oldies, and then we have so much to deal with. I worry about my Mojdeh; I worry about Tara. That *namard*, her ex-husband, didn't even give us Tara so I could take care of her. He's never around, and he leaves this young child at his home alone for hours. If she was here, I would take care of her."

"That is not fair, *khanoom*. But you know it's a man's world here in this country. Just because they have a deep voice and a face full of hair, they think they own us."

Mahtab heard the old lady. "What is there to say? God is the witness to it all. But thank you again. You are most kind to help this poor child. All right, I'll give you the address. When can you come?"

After Mahtab put the phone down, she grasped the piece of paper on which she had jotted Tara's address and leaned back, her hands over her face.

"*Khoda shokret*, thank God, at least this got solved," she whispered.

Suddenly what had been almost certain disappointment had been turned into a small miracle. Tara would get her lessons. She sighed deeply, thinking back to everything she had gone through—the *khastegari*, her family, Pasha's beating, her father's willingness to disown her. For Mahtab, lately miracles had indeed been in short supply.

Thirteen

It was Saturday afternoon and Mahtab was in her bedroom, the bow of her violin cradled in one hand, the box of rosin in the other. She rhythmically stroked the taut horsehairs till they looked like fine straw glazed by the morning dew. This was one of the favorite parts of Mahtab's day, a time to contemplate, meditate in peace. Framed by the small bedroom window, the rays of the sun now moved in, bathing the small room in an orange glow, throwing long shadows that formed surreal shapes against the walls.

Far away someone was calling her name. Mahtab ignored it until the voice grew louder and more insistent. It was her mother.

"Mahtab, Agha Emad is here." Mahtab got up from the bed and looked at the old white clock on her small dresser. It was four o'clock. What the hell was he doing here at this time? Without even looking at the mirror, without brushing her hair, without any makeup on, she entered the living room. Emad was sitting in front of the TV, a fresh brewed cup of tea and a plate of *shirini* already in front of him.

"Salaam," she said disinterestedly.

"Salaam," he said, surveying her up and down, his lips curling down, as she got closer. "Go get ready. We are going out."

"Where?"

"Somewhere nice."

"I am not feeling good, and my Maman needs me to get dinner ready."

"No I don't. I have Boji and Bahar to help. You go, *boro*," her mother said encouragingly.

Mahtab fumed inside. She wished for once her mother would leave her alone. But there was nothing she could do. She would go to his "nice" place, and hopefully this would keep him away from her for another week, like the last time they went to Boof.

☙

They had been driving steadily north. The choked roads of Sabalan and then central Tehran, with their throngs, jam-packed shops and grime, gave way to roads lined by tall trees and shops with English names. A freshly painted green sign announced *Sa'adat Abad*. The Fortunate City, one of the posh areas of northwest Tehran, where the new money lived. Emad's *Shanzelizeh*. He finally stopped the car by an old off-white apartment building with crenellated walls, looking a little like a castle from an amusement park.

"What is this?"

"My home," he answered.

"We are going to your home?" Mahtab asked, trying to keep calm.

"Yes."

"You said we were going somewhere nice."

"Yes, nice. Isn't my home somewhere nice?"

No, it was not. It was somewhere horrible. The look in Emad's eyes told her he had read her thoughts. He turned the key of the first-floor apartment and opened the door. Inside, it smelled of fried oil, onions, and spices, not unpleasant but strong. It looked empty except for the distant sounds of a TV inside.

"Come in," Emad demanded.

Reluctantly Mahtab removed her shoes and followed him inside.

"Where is your mom?" she asked.

"She is not home. She has gone to *jalaseh*."

"To do what? Pray?" Mahtab asked.

"How would I know? It's only for women, right? They eat dates, chitchat, and read the Koran, *na*? You should know that!" Emad said with a chuckle.

"I don't waste my time with such nonsense. I'd rather read the Koran daily by myself in silence than pretend to in front of others," she said with a wry smile. "For some of them, the *jalaseh* is the only time they touch the Koran!"

"Hey, watch it," Emad said, turning serious. "My maman and sisters love it. Besides, it is good for women to pray. It keeps them out of trouble." He paused, studying her, and then added, "Soon it will be my mom's turn to host one, and you should help her."

"Yes, sure," she answered flatly.

Mahtab looked around. To give him his due, Emad had not been exaggerating about their home. It was huge. The large formal living room was joined to the dining room, which then led to a family living room, all furnished with ornate cream furniture trimmed in gold paint, like something out of the presidential palace. Large woven red carpets covered the floors, wall to wall. Various pictures of different weddings sat in large unmatched frames here and there. But all the photographs had one thing in common. In each, the bride's head was covered with a white fabric, something between a hood and a scarf. Mahtab's attention was drawn to a big portrait of Emad's father in a gold frame above the main sofa in the living room. His face was impassive, except for a hint of a smile on his lips. But his eyes, they still had the same look as when she had first seen them at the *khastegari*—that of an absolute ruler, looking over his domain. Good God, he was going to be her father-in-law. How scary!

In the family room, Emad's brother Morteza had claimed the couch closest to the TV. Mahtab breathed a small sigh of relief. At least someone was home. Morteza, a younger, thinner version of Emad was thumbing his way through the satellite TV channels, music channels from Los Angeles, like greased lightning. He was in his pajamas, and a pile of sunflower kernels and cucumber peels sat in front of him next to an empty teacup.

"What are you watching?" Emad asked, a small undertone of disapproval in his voice.

"Nothing," he answered without even taking his eyes off the flickering screen.

"Salaam," Mahtab said.

He nodded briefly in Mahtab's direction before settling back in front of the TV.

"Let's go to my room," Emad said, putting his hand on her back, guiding her toward the hallway.

"Are we going to stay here at your home?" she asked.

"Yes, only till my mom comes back. Which will be soon," he said, smiling. "Come on, I want to show you my room. We have four bedrooms here. The apartment on the third floor, where we will be living, has three. It's smaller than this one because there are two apartments on that floor." As he walked down the corridor, waving his hands from side to side, he said, "This large one my parents built for themselves. The one above this is my older brother's." His lips drew tighter. "It's just as large as this one. But the two on the third floor will be for Morteza and me. We are younger, so we got the smaller ones."

Mahtab let out a small smile. Probably the first smile she had given Emad all day or for that matter since she had met him. Because she knew exactly what he was feeling. The eldest boy in an Iranian family always got the best of the family, be it affection, money, or the largest apartment.

"Anyway, they are on rent now," he said, walking on. "Morteza's and mine. Mine will be empty soon though, and I'll get it ready for us."

She let herself follow him to the end of the hallway where the bedrooms were. Once inside, he closed the door. The room was large by her standards, with a bed at the far corner, neatly made, and covered by a gray-striped bedcover. A birch-colored desk sat next to it, on top of which sat a large monitor. Several light brown files, some newer than others lay in front of it.

"See," he said, smiling, "unlike you, I don't share my bedroom with anyone. I have it all to myself."

"Sit." He motioned to the chair in front of the desk. "Remove your scarf... get yourself comfortable."

"Your room is really clean," Mahtab said, trying to lighten the tension that was rapidly gathering in that small space.

"Yes, my mom cleans it every day. I am not the kind of guy who cleans up after myself." He chuckled, before plopping onto the bed. "So how are you?"

Mahtab took a deep breath and said, "I could be better."

"Good," he said. His tone was soft as he smiled again at her. This time his eyes scarcely met hers before darting off, as though waiting for something to happen. The air in the room was electric, with nothing but the muffled sounds of the TV from other side of the house to mark the time. Finally, he sat up, pulling himself together, and moved closer to her.

"It's OK. You can remove your scarf, Mahtab." She could hear his breathing now in the stillness of the room.

He slowly brought his face closer to hers. She recoiled as his face, his lips, and his half-closed eyes drew toward her face. His eyes flicked open, and he grinned that repulsive smile that bared his uneven teeth. "Give me a kiss, Mahtab."

Those words shook her from her stupor. "No! What are you doing?"

"Come on, Mahtab. Just one kiss. We are engaged now."

"No, I can't kiss you. We are not married yet." She desperately jerked back, knowing how bad things looked for her. She was practically pressed back into her chair now, with nowhere to go. Desperate thoughts flashed through her. How could she have let this happen? What did he want from her? Was he going to take her virginity from her? They weren't even married.

"But we are *mahram* now, aren't we?" He was still grinning, only inches from her face.

"Yes, but that's different. We are *mahram* for the sake of being able to get to know each other. So that I can go out with you."

"What's the difference? We are engaged. We can kiss."

He put his lips on hers, his beard brushing her chin. Reflexively, she turned away. Her scarf fell on her shoulder; with her hands on his chest, she pushed him away. She saw that his hesitation was now gone, and his eyes were on fire. Diving in for the second time, he was more forceful. Pinning her in the chair, he pressed his half-open mouth on hers and pushed his tongue in, forcing her to open her lips. His breath smelled of cigarettes, making her want to gag. Gasping for air, she felt herself locked in by his hands around her head, her hair, feeling and grasping as he held her. He kissed her hard. She felt his hands loosen for a second before they were on her chest, touching, searching. She cried out a muffled scream. It was her breast. He had peeled her shirt up and grasped her nipple with such pent-up violence that she bucked. With strength she did not know she possessed, she heaved him off and pushed away, standing up, only the chair between her and him.

"I don't want to do this. Don't you understand?"

His breaths were coming in ragged bursts, and his eyes were on her but not her face.

"Come on, Mahtab," he said hoarsely, reaching for her. She pushed away.

"Make me come," he pleaded. Before her eyes, he unzipped his pants in one smooth movement. The white underwear was now incongruously showing through, bulging like a tent. Then he pulled it out. Mahtab instinctively averted her eyes, trying not to look at it.

"Come on, Mahtab, make me come...it's OK, you can look at it."

"Emad, please, let's not do this, not now," she pleaded, her face pale as chalk.

"Come on, Mahtab, I love you. I am not going to hurt you. It's just a quick suck. We'll leave the rest for the wedding night. Come on, give me your hand."

"No, no, I can't..." She tried to leave, but he was too fast for her. Grabbing her, he pulled her with a force she could not match. The bed was surprisingly hard as she hit it, forcing the breath out of her. "Do it. Make me come or I will force it inside you," he rasped, clutching her hand in a vicelike grip.

"I don't know how." She gave in, sitting up. At least he wasn't going to take her virginity.

"I'll show you," he said, standing up in front of her. Taking her hand, he thrust it on his thing. It was warm, throbbing. "Move it up and down," he commanded and then sighed heavily as she did.

"That's how you do it." He was already very hard.

As disgusted as Mahtab was, there was no escaping him now, his hands like a vice around her shoulders. She kept telling herself that at least he wasn't going to have sex with her. But it did not make it easier. She closed her eyes as she rhythmically pulled his thing. He was moaning now, low sounds at first that rose higher. Suddenly he held her hand.

"Eat it."

She must have looked dumbstruck for he said it again, huskily. "Eat it, Mahtab. I want to come!"

She shook her head wordlessly. Everything in her screamed at the thought of it, but she had no voice left to say anything. "No, please."

It was the last thing she managed before he pushed it in her mouth until she gagged on the salt, the thing, with its taint. She gasped, trying to breathe as she felt her head being rocked back and forth by his hands. "No teeth," he kept saying between guttural moans. "Good girl. No teeth." Then he came. She felt the force in her mouth as it flexed and pumped its heat into her throat. She drew back, throwing up on the floor, recoiling at the pale slime that dripped from her mouth, coated her hands as she desperately tried to get it out. All she could hear was his laughing over her, a silly high-pitched falsetto, as she retched onto the ground. When she finally looked up, he was buttoning his jeans.

"Go wash up," he commanded, looking at her with eyes that shone with naked triumph. She knew what he was thinking. He had tasted her.

She got up and went to the bathroom, which was at the end of the hallway.

When she came back, he was happily whistling to himself. "Get your *roosari*. I'll drop you off at your home."

"Where are you going?"

"Going out with my friends to eat. Hurry up! I am hungry."

He dropped her off at home with little said between them. At home, she washed her hands and mouth over and over again until they were raw. Until the taste and feel of him was replaced by the burn of soap on chafed skin. Looking up at the mirror, she saw her right arm. Five dull blue-red marks, the marks of his hand on her as he had grabbed her. Her nightmare had come true. She and Emad were *mahram*, and he could have her now. This was just the beginning.

Fourteen

The next afternoon Nasim showed up at Mahtab's house with news of Sepehr's sister, Sepideh. She had miscarried again.

Once in the safety of Mahtab's room, Nasim pleaded, "Can you please come with me? Sepehr wants me to go see her. He is trying to make his family like me. Not that they don't like me." She looked at her and paused. "But you know how it is. I have to show them I like them too. But I don't want to go alone..."

"Wouldn't they mind if I am there?" Mahtab asked.

"Of course not. They didn't mind at Sara's birthday, did they?"

"Would Ashkan be there?"

"I don't know. But Sepehr said to go to his place first. Sepideh is at her parents' house, resting after her miscarriage. Sepehr will take us."

"OK, let me ask my mother."

In the living room, Mahtab found her mother and Boji watching a rerun of *Jumong*, a Korean TV serial that was a hit in Iran. Ever since the embargo, a whole generation of Iranians had grown up on Japanese and then Korean serials dubbed in Farsi. That is those who couldn't afford satellite dishes.

"Who had a miscarriage?" Boji asked.

Mahtab went cold. How had she heard them through the walls? What else had she heard?

"My cousin," Nasim said without skipping a beat. Then, with an expression of what could only be described as true grief, she went on and on about how sick her cousin was, how the doctor thought they were going to lose her too, how much blood she had lost. Mahtab smiled inside as Maman's and even Boji's eyes moistened. Nasim was many things, but best of all she could spin a yarn longer than most.

On their way downstairs, they bumped into Pasha. He averted his eyes away from Nasim. Mahtab could almost hear what was going through his mind: *"Jendeh!* Slut!"

"Where are you going?" he snapped at Mahtab.

"To the hospital. My cousin had a miscarriage," Nasim chimed in.

"I am not talking to you," he said, his eyes still not meeting hers. "There is no need for Mahtab to go. Go back home."

"Pasha, Nasim's cousin is my friend too. Maman and Boji said I could go. I'll text Emad. He can pick me up after we are done."

"Are you wearing your ring?"

Mahtab silently lifted her hand to Pasha's face and then strode out of the front door.

"Getting you out of this house is like pulling teeth." Nasim chuckled as they made their way to her car.

They drove northwest, the afternoon sun a muted orange through the haze that perpetually hung over the city. The traffic slowed down to a crawl at the Resalat Bridge. Built only last year, it had fallen victim to the one thing that happened to every thoroughfare in the city, new or old. Gridlock. Their windows were now down in a hopeless attempt to fight the fumes that entered the car from everywhere. Nasim's favorite music was blaring, something about love and redemption, sung in a husky male voice to a low, thumping rhythm. Mahtab's neck prickled as she felt the gaze of eyes on her from cars separated by less than a mirror's width from hers. Eyes that were surveying her, judging her. She tried to keep her gaze forward, but it was only a matter of time before two guys in the white Hyundai next to her were leering and waving, their oversized black sunglasses giving them the vague appearance of detectives from a cheap movie. *"Khanoom bebakhshid*, excuse me, ma'am," the one next to her called out.

Nasim looked over and gave him a smile that made the silly grin on his face nearly split it in two.

"Don't encourage them!" Mahtab hissed, "or they'll follow you to your home. You know how they are. Just ignore them."

"Really? We could have so much fun," Nasim said, flicking her cigarette.

But after a few minutes, even Nasim tired of their attention. A few well-timed turns and Nasim had lost them in the morass of traffic. Mahtab looked up at the shadow that had cast itself across them. The tower that loomed above seemed to rise like a needle into the blue sky, red lights winking from the spire at the top. The Borj-e-Milad. They were getting closer.

༾

"OK, here we are. Hopefully we don't have to spend too much time with them. Is Emad really picking you up?" Nasim asked before pulling up the thin hand brake with a yank.

"No, I lied to Pasha."

"I feel bad for you, Mahtab."

"And I feel bad for Sepideh."

"Yes. She is a mess. The doctor had told her that she couldn't keep the babies. This was like her fourth or something. But she keeps trying."

Mahtab couldn't imagine it. Losing four of your own children. How Sepideh must feel, the focus of her motherly love lost again in the blood of her miscarriage. Mahtab, of course, had heard of miscarriages. But four consecutive losses!

Nasim rang the bell and the door opened. Wearing only a T-shirt and shorts, Sepehr gave them a subdued smile before showing them in.

"Sepehr, you are not ready yet?" Nasim snapped. "We need to get the flowers too."

"Come in for now. They are still at the doctor," Sepehr said quietly.

The sound of explosions punctuated by muffled yelling resounded down the hall.

"Who is it?" Mahtab's heart hammered.

"Sepehr, hurry up or you'll be dead!" That voice was unmistakable. Ashkan.

The girls removed their *manteaus* and *roosaris* and made their way to the living room as the synthetic sounds of war grew louder. Mahtab saw him first. Sitting on the edge of the black leather sofa, Ashkan was shirtless, only

119

in his jeans, framed by the large flickering flat screen in front, a Sony PS2 in hand. He was unshaven, and several Pepsi cans, Delester bottles, and an empty glass lay around him. A faint sweet smell that pinched the tip of her nose was in the air. Alcohol.

"Ashkan, get up! The girls are here," Sepehr yelled above the din.

"Already?" He flicked his head toward them, his eyes flashing. There was something visceral in them, alert like a boxer in a ring. It was clear that he had been deep into whatever he was playing. Mahtab heard him say something in English, which she was sure would have translated nicely to a Farsi swear word, before he paused the game. He stood up. Mahtab silently caught her breath. He was beautiful, his broad chest towering over a narrow waist, with arms that were bulging in all the right places. The only word she could find in her daze was a *zooleh*, muscles. In a flash, he was up searching for his shirt. She felt a nudge and turned to see Nasim grinning at her. Of course she would now, after all Mahtab had told her about him. It took all her strength to suppress a smile and wave Nasim into silence.

"Over there," Mahtab said, pointing to a T-shirt on the coffee table.

"Thanks," he said before putting it on in one smooth motion.

"What are you guys doing here? This place is a mess. Why aren't you ready to see Sepideh?" Nasim said, sitting on the couch between the cans and bags of snacks that lay around.

"They are not home yet. My mom said they are still at the doctor's office. I don't know why she keeps doing this to herself. Every time this happens, she becomes miserable for months. We were just hanging out now till they get back," Sepehr said.

"Playing games?" Nasim asked, her eyes narrowing.

"We are de-stressing. I was there last night when they brought her home from the hospital. I felt so bad I couldn't sleep. It was terrible. She and my mom cried all night."

"I've told her she should adopt," Ashkan said.

"She won't. You know that. She wants her own blood," Sepehr chimed in.

"She has a point. She can make the babies, but she just can't carry them," Nasim said.

"Maybe she can rent a uterus," Mahtab said softly. "That's an option, but it costs a lot."

"What do you mean rent a uterus?" Sepehr asked.

"Yes! The doctor, you know, takes the, umm, her thing and his things, and they mix them up and put it in someone else's *rahem*, uterus and she carries it for them. It's her blood but in someone else's body. They pay her, of course, for carrying the baby for them," Nasim explained.

"Wow!" Sepehr said, astonished. "I should tell her. That's a great idea."

Turning to Ashkan, Sepehr said, "Girls are amazing. When it comes to these things, they know everything!"

"I still think she should adopt instead of going through all this. She would do good by adopting," Ashkan said, his fingers on his chin.

"Well, it's her kid and she doesn't want to adopt. You can adopt if you want," Nasim said before turning around and throwing her hands out. "You are crazy! *BeKhoda*. Look at the mess around here. How long you've been playing?"

"It's an online tournament. We have been playing almost all morning!" Sepehr said brightly. "We're winning!"

Ashkan noisily opened a bottle of Delester. At least it wasn't alcohol. Then he smiled wickedly. "Maybe you'd like to play?"

"Hell no," Nasim said.

"OK," Ashkan said, smiling. "Then you won't mind if I do!"

He sat back and the screen roared to life as he unpaused the game. For Mahtab, it was impossible to ignore the fireworks on the TV screen. In olive-green fatigues, Ashkan's on-screen avatar was now running, leaping through a burned-out building. Jerking to a stop, he peered through a shattered window at something gray lumbering along the road. In a flash he lifted a big olive-green cylinder onto his shoulder.

Boom! The TV seemed to explode as the large gray tank was knocked out by Ashkan's bazooka, a trail of gray smoke connecting his gun tube to the burning hulk of metal. Wincing, Mahtab caught the smile of satisfaction that flew across his face at the unmitigated savagery of the shot. All that ran through her head was, what a child! He looked like a three-year-old with a new toy gun.

"Seriously, can you turn it off?" Nasim yelled. "I didn't drag my friend here to show her this barbaric action." Snapping her eyes at Sepehr, she asked impatiently, "Are we going or not?"

"My mom said she'd call when they get back. Have some patience," Sepehr said.

Mahtab was still trying to take it all in when she heard Nasim. "It's your phone, Mahtab." Looking at the screen, she shot a look at Nasim.

"Oh God, it's Emad," she whispered. Grabbing her bag, she rushed into the nearest room. Emad should not hear them, should not know where she was. She shuddered to think what he would do if he knew. Although she knew it was stupid, she couldn't shake off the fear, the dread of it. What if? What if Emad could trace her down by her phone? What if he could see that she was at Sepehr's house? She shook her head, trying to reassure herself that it wasn't him calling her to call her bluff. He couldn't know.

"Salaam, Mahtab." His voice honeyed over the phone.

She needn't have worried. He was at work and was just letting her know that he had met a Chinese delegation in the afternoon. For the new Tehran bus tender. The city was looking for new buses, and he and his friends in government—he couldn't tell her who they were of course—were looking at different companies. So he would be at work till late, but it was very important. Of course it was just like Emad. Besides the cursory 'how are things' in her direction, asking her what was she doing, it was all about him. She gritted her teeth in what seemed an eternity in that darkened bedroom until he finally hung up. Clicking her phone off, she leaned back. She was done with him for an hour at least before his next text. She could breathe that long.

Opening the door into the bright light of the living room, it was like someone had reported a plague. Everyone was standing, wordlessly, looking at her.

"Sorry about that," Mahtab said.

"Who was it?" Ashkan asked accusingly.

"My sister," she answered, not meeting his eyes.

"Your sister's name is Emad?" he deadpanned, fixing her with his eyes, those piercing green dots that threatened to bore right through her.

"What?" She recoiled back in shock. How did he know? She hadn't said anything in front of him. Looking around desperately, she saw Nasim furtively look away.

"Nasim?"

"I am sorry, Mahtab *joon*. It just slipped out. I am so sorry."

"And when exactly were you planning on telling us this?" Sepehr snapped.

"Yes, that you have a fiancé now?" Ashkan spat out the words, arms crossed over his chest. "All this time you were like, I don't want to marry and I hate men. I am this big feminist who likes to cut the balls off any guy who comes near me. And I don't have time for anything but my dreams, the violin, the orchestra. And all this while you were hiding that you were engaged?"

Staring at him, Mahtab felt the silence descending upon her, enveloping her. She wanted to counter, let him know how much she hated Emad, that he was forced upon her, that her family in their infinite wisdom had sold her to his family. That she wanted Ashkan. No, that she had chosen him in her dreams. But if she did, he would know. He would know everything about her. About how conservative her family was, how backward they were, what she came from. What she was from. A *dahati*. And he would run. She would never see him again. And in her mind, the one thing she was sure about was that his anger was preferable to his absence.

"I just knew it," Ashkan yelled, anger quivering through his body, his face turning red. "Iranian girls have double lives. All of them. You can write a book about it. The secret double lives of Iranian girls. Two-faced, two sided. But then again no one can blame them, can they? They are trained like this. Every time it's like 'I am late, I have to go home,' or 'don't drop me off by my home, drop me off one hundred yards away.' Now I get it! This was the reason. A fiancé. Not even a boyfriend. A fiancé!"

"Nasim," Mahtab said, tears falling down her face. "Nasim, I can't believe you did this to me. You dragged me here to go see Sepideh because you didn't want to face Sepehr's family alone. Because they b..." She stopped. She couldn't get herself to betray Nasim in front of Sepehr, to say what she had told her about them, in spite of what Nasim had done.

Turning around, Ashkan got up and grabbed his keys from the coffee table. "I'm out of here, Sepehr. Bye!"

"Wait up, Ashkan," Sepehr said. By now Ashkan had gotten his jacket and opened the front door. Sepehr ran after him but not before he managed to glare at the two girls. "You two. You are..." Then he was gone.

"I am so sorry, Mahtab. Listen. They were yelling, and I didn't want Emad to hear them. So I said to them, 'Hush. It's Emad.' Then Ashkan said, 'Who is Emad?' And at that moment I wasn't thinking. It just slipped out." Nasim started crying. "I am so sorry, Mahtab."

Mahtab grabbed her *manteau* and *roosari*. "I am leaving, Nasim."

"Mahtab, please," Nasim began, grabbing her bag.

"Don't worry. It's true I am engaged to an ass. So I'll just go deal with my own miserable life. Who am I kidding anyway?"

Bursting into the courtyard a few moments later, Mahtab found Ashkan pacing, arms crossed, head down, while Sepehr stood nearby talking, trying to reason with him. "Where are you going?" Sepehr called out to her.

"To her fiancé," Ashkan said sarcastically. "Didn't you know she has a fiancé?"

Mahtab turned back to Ashkan and snapped, "Will you shut up? Why do you care so much? It's none of your business anyway!"

She stopped. Ashkan was looking at her with an expression that could only be described as one of intense frustration, his brows knotted and his mouth a tense line.

"You...you just don't get it, do you?" he said between clenched teeth.

"Mahtab, wait! I am coming too," Nasim yelled from the top of the staircase, hurriedly throwing on her *manteau* and *roosari* as she spoke.

It was getting dark outside. "Let's just go back upstairs. All of us. Please," Sepehr pleaded. "OK, Ashkan? I mean, it's not the end of the world."

"I have to go," Mahtab said. "I am late."

"Mahtab, do you want to tell them anything? Explain yourself? Why you were hiding Emad?" Nasim said desperately, her eyes moving between the men and her friend.

"No thanks, Nasim. I think you have said enough. There is nothing left for me to say," she said and walked out.

Fifteen

That Thursday afternoon was cold and gray, with wind-driven drizzle that stung the face. Mahtab sighed. Even the weather seemed to mirror her fate. She had not slept well since her fight with Nasim and her embarrassment in front of Ashkan. Even remembering his name still singed something deep within her chest. But life went on, or more truthfully, it pulled her along. The bus groaned as it screeched to a halt at the bus stop. She looked outside in disbelief. She had actually arrived at Tara's grandmother's house on time, which itself was a tiny miracle. From the Nava Music Institute in the north of the city to Tara's home in Shahr-e-Ziba was about an hour if traffic held and the bus was on time, and today both had been in her favor. She rang the bell, noticing a small group of stickers arranged on the lower right side of the door. Several fairies and a blue-colored sticker that looked a little like Snow White. The fact that they were not dog-eared or faded told Mahtab that the owner had probably put them up recently. She smiled. Small footsteps were now approaching, and a moment later Tara opened the simple wooden door.

"Salaam, Tara. Are those your stickers on the door?"

"Salaam. *Baleh*, those are my friends."

"They are very pretty, Tara."

"*Merci*! I got them for *jayizeh*, as prizes. My grandma gives them to me when I do well at school. Sometimes I go outside and play with them, when my mom or Maman Zari are talking to someone at the door," Tara confided before running ahead.

The door opened right into the living room, which had two brown sofas. And waiting for them, hands together, was Tara's grandmother.

"Salaam, Mahtab *khanoom*. Thank you for coming. Please come in."

Maman Zari, Tara's grandmother, was a short, plump woman probably in her fifties with brown hair and a kind face. She quickly brought hot tea, which was a boon on that cold day. They were halfway through their lesson, with Tara playing "Happy Birthday," when the doorknob turned. A thin woman in a yellow silk *roosari* and dark blue *manteau* entered, her high-heeled shoes clacking on the tiled floor. Her face must have been beautiful at one time, still well-defined but now etched with lines leading to two shapely dark eyes. The look on Tara's face that of happiness mixed with fear told her this was her mother although Mahtab had never met Ms. Moghadam before.

Tara's mother took one look at them and quickly averted her eyes, like a schoolgirl who had cheated and was now caught by the teacher. Clenching her hands, she looked back at them and then said stiffly, "You must be Mahtab."

"*Baleh,* salaam."

"Maman," Ms. Moghadam yelled. The kitchen door swung open and Zari *khanoom* came out.

"*Chee shodeh?* What's wrong?"

"How much are you paying her?" Ms. Moghadam was now looking past them at her mother, her voice rising.

"Nothing. Go change first. Don't yell," Zari *khanoom* said firmly.

"I told you, Mahtab *khanoom*. I can't afford it," Ms. Moghadam said, slipping off her shoes.

"She is doing it for free. Calm down," Zari *khanoom* interjected, looking at Mahtab apologetically.

"Please, Maman, please," Tara begged. "She is teaching me for free."

Ms. Moghadam's tired eyes met Mahtab, and in those eyes Mahtab saw a world of grief and heaviness.

"I just don't have any money, don't you understand? I can't pay you," she said to Mahtab. "I can't pay you."

"I didn't ask for money. I don't want anything. Just let me teach Tara."

"Here drink some tea. You are tired. Just sit here and listen to your daughter play and all your tiredness will vanish. She plays wonderfully, thanks to Mahtab *joon*," her mother said, leading her daughter to one of the brown sofas as she placed a cup of hot tea in her hand. Sitting down, Ms. Moghadam removed her scarf, revealing highlighted hair that fell in every direction.

By the time Tara finished, there were tears streaming down her mother's face and Maman Zari's as well. Even Mahtab felt her eyes moisten, watching little Tara play for her mother, showing her what she had in her. And then her mother had Tara in her arms and was showering her with kisses. "My talented daughter. You are so wonderful. I am so sorry I didn't listen before. *Ghorboonesh besham.* My beautiful daughter. I love it. When *Baba bozorg,* grandfather comes home, play for him too."

Mahtab smiled and said, "Tara, your lesson for today is over. Now promise me you will practice every day for half an hour. Even when you go to your father's house."

"*Chashm.* I will, Miss Mahtab," Tara said, still in her mother's arms.

"*Dastet dard nakone,* I hope your hands do not hurt from this Mahtab *joon.* God give you a long life for what you have done today," Zari *khanoom* said softly as Mahtab put her things away. "God willing, one day, we can make it up to you," she said, pressing her hands around Mahtab's. "Do you live far away?"

"Not too far," Mahtab lied. These were proud people, and she didn't want to burden them with any of her own difficulties.

When Mahtab reached the front door, Ms. Moghadam called from behind, "Mahtab, wait."

Mahtab stopped and turned around.

"*Merci*, Mahtab *joon.* I hope you are not offended by my behavior," Ms. Moghadam said, looking into her eyes. "I just have a lot on my plate these days."

Mahtab forced a smiled, "No, not at all. It's OK." She fought back her own tears. If only Ms. Moghadam knew how much was on her own plate. "I am glad it all worked out. I'll be here next week. Just make sure no one from the institute knows. I mean, I don't want them to think that I am stealing a student from them. But still I don't..."

"Don't you worry! I won't say a word, not even to Tara's dad."

"Thank you. I gave my number to Zari *khanoom* in case something comes up and you have to reschedule..."

The sounds of Tara's violin filled the stairwell. Mahtab looked back and so did Ms. Moghadam, her face lit by a growing smile.

"I think she is practicing already!" Ms. Moghadam said. "She adores you, Mahtab *khanoom*. Sometimes I think after what happened to me, my divorce, that a part of me was so afraid that I would lose my only child. Not physically, you understand, but have her lose her happiness. She was so sad during our difficulties. But now, to think I nearly denied my child..." Her voice cracked.

Mahtab gently put her arm around her. "But you didn't."

Sixteen

The next week was warmer, signaling the approach of spring. The city was changing as well, like a great creature emerging from its winter slumber. Slowly, the annual ritual of spring-cleaning, *khooneh tekooni* began with newly washed rugs and curtains, splashes of woven color hanging out over the gray and brown square balconies of buildings all across Tehran. Like the flags of spring challenging the army of winter. The window cleaners now appeared, hanging precariously over walls with pails and cloths, swabbing, chattering, and climbing over windows now devoid of curtains. Naked, waiting for their washed drapes to return.

The streets were getting crowded now. The clothes stores, especially those for kids, were full of people, mingling and poking around, looking for the perfect deal. The many temporary bazaars, or *namayeshgah*, were popping up around the city to provide cheaper clothing and goods for those who couldn't afford to buy at the established stores. Pavement sellers were now everywhere. It was as though the streets of Tehran had become one big shopping mall. But to Mahtab, what did it matter? Her heart was blanketed by sadness. It was early evening, and her mother needed meat. Mahtab looked at her phone while walking to the little store across the street. She hadn't spoken to Nasim since that day of Sepideh's miscarriage. Nasim had often been careless and carefree, and just as often Mahtab had bailed her out, like the time she had warbled something in front of her own mother about how she got high with Sepehr.

But this time Nasim had cost her something a lot more, best friend or not. She had crushed her dream, her reputation, in front of the man she secretly adored.

Mahtab stood in line at Agha Hosseini's *qhasabii*, the neighborhood butcher. The small shop, with its greasy windows displaying whole carcasses of fresh goat and lamb, their heads arranged neatly at the bottom, was a point of pilgrimage for the neighborhood. The line was long, and the lone fan on the roof that lazily whirred around did little to move the thick air inside. A customer in front was arguing over the extra fat in her order when Mahtab heard a buzz. It was a text from Nasim.

"Mahtab please talk to me. I have very important news about Ashkan."

What could it be? What about Ashkan? Mahtab looked at her phone morosely. She had ignored Nasim's texts till now. Why should she answer now? What could possibly happen to change anything?

"What?" she punched in.

The text had barely left the phone before it rang.

"Yes?"

"I want to tell you something very important," Nasim said, her voice rushed.

"Go on. I don't have enough minutes on my phone plan to just chitchat."

"OK, I'll tell you. After you left that night, we went back upstairs, and you know when Ashkan gets mad, he drinks a lot."

"I didn't know that. So what?" she said, shifting her phone to her right hand.

"When he gets upset, he drinks a lot. And you know he gets into trouble. He was really upset with you."

"Why?"

"It's obvious, isn't it, Mahtabi? A guy doesn't get mad about a girl's life unless he cares about her! So I had to fix what I ruined."

"Oh. What did you say?" Mahtab said weakly.

"I told him the truth. That you didn't want anyone to know because you don't want this engagement. That your family forced you."

"Ahh! Nasim...*divooneh*. You're crazy! Now Ashkan thinks I come from shit!"

"You should have seen him. Someone had to save the poor guy!"

"So why didn't you tell me this earlier?" Mahtab said weakly, her stomach and heart trading places violently.

"Because you were such a bitch! You didn't answer my calls!" Nasim snapped back. "And I was really scared of you barking at me like this."

"What did he say then?"

"He said he wished you would have told him yourself. He would have understood."

"Yes, as if I could. Oh God, now what?" Mahtab cried, her head spinning.

"I haven't seen him since that night either. He was gone after that to Shiraz and then I think to Kish. It seems they bought a..."

"Yeah, I know about Kish." Mahtab could barely contain herself.

"OK, there you know more than I do about him. Anyway the reason I called now is that Ashkan's parents are throwing this big Charshanbeh Souri party." Nasim paused for effect. "At their home in Farmaniyeh and...Ashkan wants you to come too."

"Are you serious? He really said that?" Mahtab screamed giddily, ignoring the heavily wrapped woman in front of her now giving her a disapproving stare. "Nasim, beKhoda, he actually said that? You are not trying to cover up for your mess and hook me up with him?"

"No, I swear he said it." She laughed. "So I told him OK, but I am not sure if she can come. So then he said, 'Do you want me to invite her myself?'" Nasim said, feigning Ashkan's accent.

Mahtab could not repress a laugh. "It's true. He talks like that."

"So I said sure, and I gave him your phone number."

"Chee?" Her breath came out in a gasp, "You gave him my number?"

"Tell your mom and dad that you are with me."

"What about Emad? It's Charshanbeh Souri; he probably wants to be with me."

"Ditch him," Nasim countered sharply. "Come on, you can't miss this opportunity to meet your future in-laws! It's Ashkan's house, for God's sake. And slutty Elham won't be there because it's only family."

"Slutty Elham? Kiye? Who?" Mahtab asked, trying to keep her voice low.

"Hich kas. No one. Forget it."

"No, tell me, who is she?" Mahtab said, now almost screaming into the phone. Nasim could be so infuriating especially when time was short, Mahtab cursed, looking ahead. She had almost made it to the end of the line at the shop.

"OK, fine. There is this girl, Sara's friend, who's been desperately trying to stick herself to Ashkan. He is not into her though. Don't worry unless you don't come over. Seriously though, Mahtab, I don't care if you have to kill someone to get out of your home, you should come."

"*Basheh*, I'll come," she promised as she stuffed her phone into her jacket pocket and turned to face the smiling butcher. Agha Hosseini, the butcher, was a Shomali from the northern rim of land around the Caspian Sea. He limped, the result of a wound from the Iraq war, in which he had been a foot soldier.

"Salaam Agha Hosseini," Mahtab said.

"Salaam, *dokhtaram*. Your mother and father are good?"

"Yes, they say hello. One kilo of the *abogooshti* please. And one kilo *khoreshti*." Then she added, "Please, no fat."

"I always give the best cuts to your family," he said, nodding back to his son behind him. "So has your brother gotten married yet?"

"No, not yet."

"Inshallah soon," he said smiling.

"Merci Agha Hosseini. How much for everything?"

"For you nothing. *Ghabel nadareh*," The butcher *taarofed*. Then, he added with a practiced awkwardness, his eyes looking away, "12000 toman."

"Merci, thank you. My mother said to please put it on our account." Mahtab added.

"*Basheh*. Of course," Agha Hosseini said, taking out a blood stained brown leather notebook. Flipping to a page, he jotted down something with a black pen he grabbed from behind his ear.

She had just left the butcher's and passed a cluster of women at the vegetable shop next door, arguing loudly over the price of onions, when her phone rang.

Her eyebrows knotted when she looked down at the screen. An unknown number.

"*Baleh?*" she answered hesitantly.

"Mahtab?" Her heart nearly stopped at hearing that voice. That decidedly male voice, that accent. The way he pronounced her name.

"Yes?"

"It's Ashkan. Ashkan Piroozvand, Sepehr's cousin," he said. He needn't have.

"Yes, I know." It took everything out of her just to get the words out.

"Did Nasim talk to you?"

"About?"

"I am sorry, Mahtab, if I overreacted that night. It was a little hard to take. I mean, a lot hard to take," he said quickly.

"I see," she said, trying hard to keep her cool, which was nearly impossible between the thumping of her heart and the butterflies in her stomach.

"My parents are having a party the last Tuesday of the celebration of fire?"

It took her a moment to register what he was saying. Last Tuesday of the? Oh, Charshanbeh Souri, the last Tuesday before the Persian New Year, where, at night, everyone with a pulse jumps over bonfires all over town, even the little toddlers carried by their leaping parents. For a flash, she could actually see the yellow and red flames of the bonfires reflected off people jumping and laughing, united by the night.

Yes, you mean Charshanbeh Souri," she said slowly, smiling to herself. His Farsi was so childish. And so adorable.

"Yes! What you said," he said with relief. "Can you come?"

"I can't promise you. I have to see how things are." That was the truth, and she knew it.

"Will you let me know?" His voice was firm, like a hot knife through the butter of her heart.

"Yes. Thanks for the invitation. OK, bye now," she managed.

"OK then. It was nice talking to you, Mahtab."

And that was it. For a minute she just stood there, holding the phone to her ear. It had been so sudden, his call, and oh God, his invitation. She would have gladly settled for his voice but now this. A shiver ran through her as the meaning of his invitation sank in. Hesitantly, she thumbed the past caller numbers again just to make sure, to confirm that he had indeed called. Ashkan. His name brought a thrill, a wild racing to her heart.

This changed everything of course. She wended her way back along the worn path to her home, sidestepping the gully that ran through the middle. There was Ashkan to fight for; there was hope against the weight of her family, Pasha, and Emad. Oh, Emad, the thought of him now sent a shudder through her, down to her toes.

After dinner that night, Mahtab poured out a cup of tea and went to her father's room. He was at his desk, sheaves of lined paper bound by rubber bands surrounding him. End-of-the-term exams. She took a deep breath and began.

"Baba, I brought you tea," she said. "Do you need help with grading these papers? If you give me the key, I can grade them for you."

"*Na*, Mahtab. Leave the tea here and go. Go help your mom."

Mahtab hesitated, and for a few seconds she hung by the doorway, listening to the steady strokes of her father's pen against paper followed by the thunk of another exam hitting the pile on the floor. Then it all came out.

"Baba, I know how reputation and face is important to you. I don't want to do anything to hurt your reputation. But I can't possibly live with Emad, Baba. I don't like him. He controls me, he hurts me..."

He cut her off without even looking up. "I don't want to hear anything anymore."

"Please listen to me, Baba. *Toro Khoda*, I am your daughter! Don't you care about my happiness?"

"Happiness is a state of mind, Mahtab. It's not something that you can buy or sell or change. It doesn't come with husbands or clothes." He removed his glasses slowly and looked up. "Who do you think you are, Mahtab? You have way too many ideas. You are very *boland parvaz*! You try to fly higher than your station in life, above this family's means and our expectations. And this will lead you to falling below them and embarrassing us all!" he said it with such force that the pen in his hand snapped. "I know you want to follow the stupid movies you watch or the books you read about love. But you know what? I approved Emad for you. He is a real man and the one I trust. As long as you live in this house and my shadow is over your head, I make the decisions for you. I am your father. I am the one who tells you what to do," he said, his eyes on her, narrowing in anger. "I am tired of dealing with you. You didn't listen to me when you chose your college, your career path, and now this. You will listen to me this time and follow my directions. Now leave. I don't want to hear about this again."

"I hate him, Baba."

"Shut up," he shrieked, tossing aside the binder. "When are you going to stop being so spoiled and grow up? When?"

She didn't care about what she said anymore.

"Emad makes me do things that I don't like. He hurts me. What if I kill myself?"

The chair made a scraping sound as Rasool got up, his face a mask of fury. Grabbing Mahtab's arm with surprising violence, he dragged her through the corridor and threw open her door. She felt the bed hit her as she was pushed onto it, momentarily knocking the breath out of her.

"Are you threatening me? Your own father! You will never tell me what to do." He was screaming now, his face thunderous, almost purple. The veins around his temples were throbbing. Stunned, she stared at him, the sudden violence knocking her into silence. Where had this monster come from? Unlike Pasha, she had never seen her father like this before. Eyes bloodshot, he shook as he stuttered, "In this swamp of a city…this *lajan zar,* boys are either gay or doing drugs, smoking, drinking, stealing. Who can I trust? I know Emad and his family. He is a good man. He will not leave you alone with a child in your hands a few years from now. One day you will appreciate what I am doing for you! Now stay here until you realize that this is the best thing for you." With that he walked out and slammed the door. Tears ran down her face as she cried herself to sleep.

Seventeen

Ashkan's house, or rather his parent's home was in Farmaniyeh, one of the oldest and most beautiful parts of Northern Tehran, where people with old money lived. This was the neighborhood where the nobility used to live during the Shah's time. Even now, it was still one of the most desirable places to live in Tehran, for Tehranis as well as the foreign diplomatic corps, many of whom called it home.

It was spring, and the air from the heights was like a great cool stream in the middle of an arid desert. And with the air came the scent of flowers—roses, jasmine, and hyacinth.

"My violin is in the back of your car, *basheh?*" Mahtab said as they drove on.

"Don't forget to take it when you go home," Nasim said, gum between her teeth.

"I'll never forget my violin. It's my baby." Mahtab paused before saying, "Nasim, I still can't believe that I am here, with you, going to his house!"

"See, Nasim will always look out for you, Mahtab *joon*. See how I made up a story for your mom to believe and got you here?" Nasim said with a wink.

Mahtab laughed. "You are a good story maker, Nasim *joon*. What did my mother say?"

"Nothing about you coming to my home tonight. But she did tell me to tell you to be kind to your fiancé. Not to destroy your good fortune. Not to kick your good luck."

"What did you say?"

"I told her I'd pick you up from work and drop you off at your home on time."

"Not that. About kicking my good fortune," Mahtab said.

"I said I would, and I didn't lie. I'm telling you, Mahtab *joon*, if Ashkan goes for a kiss tonight, do not kick your good luck. Let the poor guy kiss you."

"Nasimmmmm." Mahtab could not stop grinning.

Outside the gray wall that led to the main wrought iron gates were a couple of late-model cars. Mahtab recognized Ashkan's gray BMW. Nasim screeched to a halt next to it at an angle, nearly scraping it. "I think I double-parked!" She let out as she yanked on the parking brake.

Mahtab stared at the house before her for a few moments. It was so beautiful. Just as Mahtab had remembered the day they dropped Pardis off. Not an apartment but a real house, with a red tiled roof, albeit fading with the slightest hint of green around the edges from years of moss. It was two stories high, with beige-colored walls and large windows with their own shutters that were tethered to the wall by small iron arms.

In the evening light, Mahtab saw Sepehr's tall form approach and open the gate. Hugging Nasim with one hand, he enquired with relief, "You made it OK?"

"Yes. Thank God we didn't see any police. Their random searches really suck." Nasim whined.

"Don't I know it? They are trying to catch anyone having even the slightest fun, especially tonight."

Mahtab recognized Babak and some of the other cousins. Down the street there were bonfires being lit. She could hear the hiss and crackle of fireworks everywhere, each set rising with a crescendo intermixed with the lone pops of single crackers. And everywhere the cool air smelled of wood smoke.

Sepehr whistled. "Babak, I'll be right back. When Sara comes, help her find a parking spot." Babak waved and smiled. The girls followed Sepehr through a smaller steel door into the courtyard.

"Ashkan! Ashkan," Sepehr called out.

A big German shepherd, deep glossy brown and black with a wolflike face, bounded into the courtyard. Its gray eyes were on them, tongue lolling over gleaming white teeth. Before Mahtab could turn for cover, he was on her, paws outstretched. Instinctively Mahtab screamed and jumped back, a half stumble, faster than she thought possible.

"Tiger! No boy." She heard the words, in that American drawl, and saw him walk into sight. Tiger? Who names an animal after another animal? Tiger immediately dropped his ears and began to wag his tail with a look of a naughty child who had been caught scaring the neighbor's baby.

"Ashkan! Your dog nearly knocked over Mahtab!" Nasim interjected playfully.

"Sorry. Actually my grandfather just brought him from his vacation home. He is so excited to be here."

"No kidding." Nasim stared at him.

"Are you all right Mahtab?" Ashkan asked his eyes on her, his hand on the dog's collar.

Mahtab nodded, her eyes still glued to the wolf in front of her.

"What's his name?" Nasim said gingerly patting the dog's head.

"Tiger."

"Like *babr*?"

"Yes."

Nasim rolled her eyes. "Interesting."

"You just arrived?" Ashkan asked.

"Yes," Mahtab managed to say.

"We'll go in to see the family first," Sepehr said, giving a meaningful look at Ashkan.

Scratching Tiger's ear, Ashkan said something in English that Mahtab didn't catch.

"You guys go; I'll join in a minute," Ashkan said, looking at Mahtab.

When they were out of earshot, Mahtab asked Sepehr, "Why is he not coming with us?"

"Ashkan is waiting for a special delivery. Crazy, I don't know why he didn't pick it up yesterday. It's risky tonight. If the guy comes here with a tail, the police I mean, Ashkan would be in trouble. We'll all be in trouble."

"What delivery?" Mahtab asked, glancing at Nasim.

"Mashroob. Alcohol for the party," Sepehr answered. "He is a good supplier, but tonight is very risky."

The courtyard sloped up to the house, which was set at the back of the garden. At the end of the yard, a set of granite steps led to the patio and then the main door. Mahtab could hear the sounds of people talking and laughing. A tingle of anticipation mixed with fear ran within her. She was about to enter his home and, much more importantly, see his parents for the first time. The foyer inside was in the shape of a half-moon, with two carved spiraling staircases on either end leading to the upper level. The house was old but magnificent, Mahtab thought, with pale marble floors and tall pillars holding up vaulted ceilings, from which hung chandeliers reflecting what seemed a thousand lights. People were everywhere, dressed wonderfully—women in shapely dresses, jewelry glinting, and men in well-fitting suits mixed with the more free-spirited in their jeans and designer shirts.

"My dad's family, aunts, and uncles," Sepehr said, nodding to the smiling people around them as he guided them through the house.

This was exactly how Mahtab had imagined Ashkan's family, glamorous, like the Shah's family of old.

They had reached the drawing room where Pardis, in jeans and a svelte, little red tank top, was playing the piano, her long, straight hair flowing over her back. A piece by Chopin, its characteristic mellifluous notes pouring out of the black satin grand. Mahtab smiled. Surrounding Pardis on the sofas were four people, two men and two women, silver–haired and immaculately dressed. Then Pardis's face broke into a smile and she waved and yelled. "Salaam Nasim, Mahtab."

"Sepehr, who are these beautiful girls?" It was one of the men from the sofa, a rotund old man in a dapper cream suit and Panama hat. He had rheumy eyes and a wide smile usually reserved for a favorite child. "Every time you come inside, you bring in more *hoories,* angels," he said, raising his cane, a twinkle in his eyes.

Sepehr laughed. "This is Nasim, Baba Pirooz. Don't tell me you don't know her."

Nasim waved her hand to the old man who touched his hat.

"And this is Mahtab, Nasim's friend," Sepehr added. "Mahtab, my grandfather Baba Pirooz. My dad's father."

"Salaam," Mahtab said shyly.

Then she heard a deep voice. "Mahtab? Ashkan has told me about you."

The tone of the voice wasn't that of a question, just a statement, an observation, flat without emotion. Mahtab turned to the man next to Baba Pirooz. Unsmiling, sitting ramrod straight in his seat despite his clearly advanced age, he had the air of command. Perhaps a former general, Mahtab thought. His steely, gray eyes were on Mahtab, unflinching, making her swallow. What had Ashkan told him about her? Most importantly, who was he?

She felt Sepehr's hand grab hers and lead her on. "We have to get going."

"Who was he?" Mahtab asked Sepehr once they were out of the room. "Oh, that's Amoo Jamshid, Tina's dad. Ashkan's Grandpa."

"He is scary. I nearly peed in my pants when he started talking to Mahtab. I thought he was going to put Mahtab in detention," Nasim said with a half-smile.

"What has he told him about me?" Mahtab asked, curiosity getting the better of her now.

"I don't know. Maybe you should ask Ashkan." Sepehr smiled with a raised eyebrow. "He is not scary. He is just very serious. Ashkan is very close to him. So I am sure he talks to him about everything."

"His grandmother is here too? The American one?" Mahtab asked.

"Edna? No. They are divorced. I think they divorced when Tina was very young. He is married to my dad's aunt now. She is there sitting next to Amoo Jamshid. That's how they actually met. Tina and my uncle." Then Sepehr asked, "Do you want anything to drink?"

Mahtab shook her head.

"Sure, what you got?" Nasim piped up quickly.

"Not you, Nasim! Please not tonight. No alcohol," Mahtab interjected, her face suddenly a mask of worry. "The police are everywhere tonight. Looking at everyone. If they stop us on our way home and find out you have been drinking, we'll be in deep shit. And I can't afford being in deep shit with you. Please."

"She won't drink much. She promises. Right, Nasim?" Sepehr said, his hand running around her waist.

Giggling, Nasim tossed her head back. "Big deal. I'll eat cucumber after like everybody else to get rid of the smell. It does work, Mahtabi."

But Mahtab knew that was just the beginning. Nasim would first have a drink and then smoke. Then someone, Sara, Babak, or Sepehr would offer her joint, and that was it. Nasim always claimed that they didn't do drugs when the *piro pataals*, the oldies, were around, but that was just a big lie. Sighing, Mahtab clutched her purse tighter. At least she had remembered to bring enough money for an *ajanse* if she needed it. But it would hurt. It would be all of last week's savings from her classes.

"Are you guys coming out or not?" Ashkan walked in, a black bag in each hand, Tiger in tow, nails clicking on the marble floor.

"We are. We are just going to get some *mazeh*," Sepehr said, reaching for the bag. "Let's see what you got."

"Do you drink?" Ashkan asked Mahtab.

"No. I don't." And then she said as an afterthought, "They are going to though."

"I thought so. Let them get their *mazeh*, their drink and snacks. We don't have to be here. Let's go out."

"You have a beautiful home," Mahtab said truthfully.

"Thanks. It's my parents'," he said, leading the way out to the foyer.

"Don't you live here?"

"No. I have my own place. It's up in Velenjak."

Mahtab had passed through there once before, long ago when the family was visiting the mountains after the war. "Oh, by the ski resort," she said brightly, without thinking. She felt his green peepers lighten.

"Yes, I can see it from my bedroom." He chuckled.

"It must be beautiful..." She trailed off, her eyes suddenly clouding with worry. "I should wait for Nasim. I want to make sure she doesn't take any drugs. She's driving back tonight and if anything should happen..."

He shrugged awkwardly. "Sure. But they will though. They always do in the end."

"And what about you?" she asked.

"What?" he said, blinking at her. "Oh, drugs? No! I'd never do that stuff. It messes up your body. But alcohol, well that's another story!" He laughed.

Mahtab looked at his gorgeous face. Suddenly his lips snapped tight with unseen resolution.

"Come on! Let's go," he said. As though on cue, Tiger barked.

"I didn't know you had such a huge dog," Mahtab said.

She saw the lines of his face soften as he looked down at his obedient companion padding next to him. "He is actually just a puppy," he said, stroking

Tiger's thick fur with his fingers. "He is only six months old! He's been with my grandfather since I travel a lot. But he is going to be with me for the next two weeks. He is a sweetheart. Aren't you, Tiger?" he said, petting Tiger's head. By now they were in the corridor that led to the yard. The faint smell of rich incense and candle wax hung in the air. Pictures of the family hung on the walls. Ashkan had lighter hair when he was a baby. There was a picture of him when he was in high school, with a skateboard; long, brown hair around his face; and his green-gold eyes serious, almost soulful. Even then, he was a heartbreaker.

Then there was another portrait of Ashkan. It was in black and white with very stark lighting that chiseled his features, making her tingle inside. Ashkan would have been twenty, twenty-one maybe. He was wearing a shirt on which was written Abercrombie & Fitch. It looked like it was from a magazine cover with his wild hair, wet, dripping. "This is a nice picture," Mahtab said.

He laughed. "Thanks. That was a long time ago. When I was in college."

"You look like a model there," Mahtab said, almost to herself.

Clearing his throat, Ashkan said quietly, "I was. I did modeling while in college."

"I should have known." Mahtab smiled.

Heading through the far door, she saw them. His parents. Besides the resemblance to Ashkan and Pardis, it was the slight stiffening, the look in Ashkan's face that gave them away. Just like that, there they were, coming from the adjoining room, laughing. Ashkan's mother looked to be in her early forties, almost too young to have a twenty-seven-year-old son. Ashkan's father, Kiumars, was handsome, almost rugged, but looked old. Not a natural old but age that came from things other than time.

"Mahtab, my parents," Ashkan said.

"Salaam," Mahtab said.

Tina smiled. "It's very nice to finally meet you, Mahtab," she said in accented Farsi. "Maybe you will play something for us. I hear you are a violin virtuoso." She had long, chestnut hair and the same green, sun-splashed eyes of her son.

"Thank you," Mahtab said, not knowing what to say. Who had been talking behind her back, was it him or Pardis? She glanced at Ashkan who seemed just as on edge as she was.

"Welcome to our home," Kiumars said with a smile. Tall, with gray cropped hair, he had hazel eyes that had same penetrating stare of his daughter. But Mahtab saw something else as well. In his jaw, his angular face. Ashkan.

"We were going outside," Ashkan said, moving toward the door.

"Yes, don't let us get in your way. Go out and have fun," said Tina, before twining her arm around Kiumars. Kiumars nodded and added, "Be careful out there."

Once outside, Mahtab's legs felt like jelly. She had been dreading meeting Ashkan's parents, but they seemed like nice people, without horns or tridents or spiked tails or other traits of the netherworld. But. Yes. But it was also well known that one of the great fears of any self-respecting Iranian girl was her in-laws. Not that she had actually thought of Ashkan and herself as married. She knew that there was the problem of Emad, her family, and everything else in between making that an obvious impossibility. But in her heart of hearts, she was certain that Ashkan was her dream, and dreams were worth being married to, even in one's imagination. And this dream had two parents that had scared the imaginary skin off her real body.

Outside the gates, fires were roaring in the street, music was pouring, and drunken guys were yelling and horsing around. Little kids were playing with firecrackers, and teenagers were shrieking and whooping as the larger rockets and fireworks whizzed and popped in the darkness.

"So this is the celebration of fire," Ashkan said, stroking Tiger's back, trying to calm him down after each burst.

"It is," Mahtab said.

"A bit primal, don't you think?"

"Not at all. It's beautiful. It's like the dance of fire."

"So you do this for Norooz?"

"Don't tell me you have never celebrated Norooz before," she said, turning to him in disbelief.

"Maybe once when I was like twelve or thirteen. I vaguely remember it," he said, looking into the distance.

"So what do you celebrate? Christmas and *Janviyeh*?"

He looked at her, a little puzzled.

"Well, I guess both. Christmas is the birth of Christ and *Janviyeh*, the New Year. So, yes we usually end up celebrating Christmas and *Janviyeh*." He smiled.

"So you are *Masihi*, Christian?" She persisted. He was so enigmatic, neither here nor there, Iranian but not quite.

"No...we are not. Not even my mom," he said thoughtfully as though remembering his past. "You know, Christmas for us is not about religion. It's about tradition. Like Norooz for you."

They barely could hear each other as a crescendo of firecrackers lit the road to more howls and whoops.

"Are you Muslim then?" Mahtab asked. She hoped he was.

"Umm, technically, I guess I am if you wanted to put it that way. I mean by heritage that is. My dad was born into a Muslim family, but he doesn't practice at all. My mom's father is Muslim though he doesn't practice either. My mom was raised by her mother, who is Christian, so she doesn't know much about Islam. My mom is spiritual though, in her own way. But Pardis and I don't have any real religion. We don't pray in any shape or form. How about you?" he asked, looking at his cousins jumping over the fire and laughing.

"I am Muslim. I don't pray five times a day, but I do believe in Islam and *Khoda* and Hazrat-e Mohammad. Every night I read one *sooreh,* a chapter from the Koran. It gives me hope and strength."

"That's good. See, I think people do need something to hang on to, to believe in, to make sense of the unknown. But I am not used to that. Even in desperation I can never get myself to pray to a higher power or source."

"Why not?"

"I was not raised like that, Mahtab. Had I been raised to believe in such things, yes, sure I might have prayed and stuff. But it's too late now to start believing in something that I don't know or feel."

"But do you believe in God?"

"I do believe that there is probably a higher power, but I don't believe in praying to it. I do believe in right and wrong, but as I said, I don't have any religion."

"So when you want to get married, in what religion are you going to marry?"

He chuckled. "Getting married seems like such a faraway thing to think of right now. But if and when, I guess it will be her choice, whatever she wants. I figure I'd just have to show up to the wedding."

"So what about your kids? What religion are you going to raise them? They need to have a religion, right?"

"Honestly, Mahtab, I haven't thought about this much. I am not sure if I even want to have kids." He chuckled dryly. "Come to think of it, I can't see myself ever having kids."

"Everyone gets married and everyone has kids," Mahtab said with quiet determination.

"Hey, guys, why don't you go and jump over the fire?" A voice called over. Mahtab made out the shape of Pardis wearing a wool cap and a thick jacket of some sort. What she saw next to her made her open her eyes in surprise. She was hand in hand with a cute, slim boy her own age, his spiked hair throwing shadows on the wall behind them.

"Salaam," the boy said plainly.

Ashkan nodded to him but addressed Pardis only. "Did you get to jump?"

"I did. Aryan helped me jump, and I nearly fell into the fire! I think my pant leg got singed. It's so much fun! You guys should do it," she said, giggling.

Aryan had thrown his hand around Pardis's waist, drawing her closer to him, almost protectively.

Trying not to stare, Mahtab couldn't help thinking that at thirteen if she had brought home a boyfriend, she might as well have brought her death certificate with her.

They walked toward the roaring bonfire in the middle of street. Guys were now whistling and clapping their hands as the girls were taking turns jumping over the fire, leaping in ones, twos, and threes over the yellow and red tongues that hissed and sent showers of sparks into the night. In the midst of it all, she heard someone chanting the ancient prayer of fire that was sung on this night since time immemorial.

Zardi man az to, sorkhi to az man. My sickness and unhappiness goes to you, O Fire, and let your energy and power comes to me instead.

It was perfect, that moment, the celebration, the place, and most importantly the man beside her. Unbelievable, she reflected, how she had made it here, against everything. She looked down for a moment to adjust her slipping scarf, and then she saw it. Her blood froze. It was unmistakable, the red flashing lights of a police car at the end of the street. She could almost imagine the two bearded officers in light green uniforms looking through the windshield, assessing their prey.

There was nowhere to run but inside, and she did just that. "Mahtab, Mahtab!" She heard Ashkan calling behind her, but all she could think of was not getting caught. Being caught by police, taken to the station. They would ask her who her father, her guardian, was and then the call. Her family would know, everyone would know where she was, what she was doing. She was supposed to be at Nasim's home, not some stranger's in north Tehran. Especially with alcohol flowing freely. Girls from her neighborhood did not go to north Tehran without a reason. Catching her breath, she sat on the cold steps in the courtyard, leading to the house.

"What's wrong?" one of his aunts asked from the door.

"Police," Mahtab managed to reply. "They just came..."

"Don't worry. The police here won't do anything. They know us, and we know them. We put twenty thousand toman in their hands, and they'll be on their way to collect money from another street. That way their Islam and our party are both saved!" She laughed dryly and then sighed. "You know, I miss the days when we could freely celebrate our culture without fear of punishment. During the Shah it was different. You weren't born then *azizam,* but it was so different."

⌁

Untended, the bonfire had now died down, only glowing embers left that someone soon put out with a splash of water. Mahtab heard the calls from inside the house, unfamiliar voices, and then Tina calling everyone in for dinner.

After dinner Mahtab desperately wanted to go home. Nasim unfortunately had other ideas. Mahtab found her in the living room, in the middle of a card game with Sepehr, Sara, Babak, and a few other young men, laughing and screaming as their cards flew into the pile in the center of the floor.

"Where is Nasim's friend? We want her to play for us." It was Baba Pirooz, Kiumars's father standing by, clutching his walking stick.

Voices died, and eyes rolled toward her direction. The weight of the stares in the room was almost too much to bear. From the grandparents, parents, aunts, and uncles, even the cousins, everyone seemed to be looking at her now.

"I don't have my violin," she managed weakly, shyness getting the better of her.

"It's in my car." She heard Nasim slur it out loudly from behind her.

God damn it, Nasim, could you shut up for at least one time in your life?

Sepehr said quickly, "I'll get it."

"I don't usually play at parties, Nasim," Mahtab said, looking around, searching for a way out.

"You play at concerts. What's the difference?"

"It's different," she said angrily. That was it! This time she was going to kill Nasim, friend or no friend. How could she not see that it was different? At concerts, she played for others as much as she played for herself. Here she knew she was playing for someone, someone who meant so much to her that she was scared. Scared of failing him in front of his whole family.

"Play something nice. An old piece that we elders can remember!" Baba Pirooz said, laughing, his rheumy eyes twinkling.

Sepehr brought her violin. As she took it out gently, Babak pulled up a stool for her.

The old man said, "Play *Elaheye Naz*. 'The Lovely Goddess.' Do you know how to play it?"

"*Baleh*," Mahtab said, trying to fake a smile.

Mahtab sat, nestling the belly of the instrument under her chin. She looked up to see Ashkan standing across the living room, smiling at her. She smiled back. Then closing her eyes, she drew in a deep breath and began to play.

The whole room went silent as the haunting notes poured from her violin, resonating within the room. Her fingers to the strings, the bow following in concert.

Someone started spontaneously singing. Mahtab opened her eyes. It was Babak's mom, *Ammeh* Fariba.

"*Baz Elaheye naz, ba dele man besaz*. Oh, the lovely goddess, be kind to my heart so this grief would leave me..." Others began to join in. When the song ended, the whole room filled with applause.

Then the requests poured in like a flood, voices everywhere in the room. *Ammeh* Fariba wanted her to play Googoosh. Another lady with a thin frame asked her to play Ahdiyeh. *"Na,"* Aunt Giti said, "play Delkash."

So she played not one but five more songs. Till she heard her phone buzz. It was Emad. It was time to leave.

While she was packing her violin back into its case, she heard Ashkan beside her whisper, "That was awesome. I have never seen them so worked up before."

"Merci. I am glad they liked it, but I really need to go home now. It's getting late. If only I can get Nasim to pick herself up."

Ashkan looked toward Nasim who was back in a corner dealing cards.

"It's fine," Mahtab said quietly. "I'll get a cab."

"No, of course I'll take you," Ashkan said without skipping a beat. "Let me get my jacket.

He was back a minute later, pulling on his black pilot jacket. No one would have noticed they were leaving together if Tiger had not barked so much after Ashkan.

"Where are you going?" Kiumars asked from near the French doors.

"I'm going to drop off Mahtab," Ashkan replied before kneeling down to grab Tiger. "I'll come get you tomorrow. You be a good boy. All right?" he said in English. Even the dog speaks English, Mahtab mused. She would have to improve hers too.

"You played beautifully, Mahtab," Tina said in her soft velvet drawl, her fingers around a long-stemmed glass.

"Ashkan, are you coming back?" his dad asked while holding back Tiger.

"No, Kiumars. I'll go to my apartment after I drop off Mahtab."

Halfway in the yard, Ashkan pulled out a mouth spray from his coat's pocket and sprayed his mouth. Seeing her stare, he grinned. "To get rid of the alcohol smell."

Outside, the smell of wood smoke hung in the air, creating a haze around the stars that studded the night sky.

"Thank you for dropping me off," Mahtab said finally.

"No problem. Let me get your door."

Once in the car, Mahtab said, "Pardis plays the piano very well. How long has she been playing?"

"Oh, I think since she was five or something. I am not sure. It's been awhile."

"Do you play the piano too?"

"No. Unlike some people, I am not musically gifted."

Mahtab saw his eyes rest on her for a moment. She just smiled.

"I do better with sports, physical stuff," he said. Then after a pause, he said softly, "Mahtab, I have never seen you play before. It was beautiful."

"Thank you. I'm glad you liked it," she said trying to keep her voice steady.

He cleared his throat and said, "Listen. I want to apologize again for my bad behavior the other day."

"It's OK."

"Don't you want to talk about it?" he asked, surprise in his voice.

"I'd rather not," she said, looking out of her window at the shadows and lights that whizzed past. What was there to say? He obviously meant Emad. And that name only brought her back to the reality that she was desperately trying to forget with Ashkan, here, in this bubble of escape.

"So just tell me one thing. About what Nasim said. Is it true?"

"I don't know what Nasim said." She turned to him.

"About that you…you…don't want him?"

"Pretty much."

"What does that mean?"

"I mean, look at me. I am engaged, right? Where is the ring on my hand?" she said, uncovering her left hand, the beautiful fingers curved, naked, unringed. "It's Charshanbeh Souri, the biggest night of the year. Every girl and boy who matters to each other wants to spend time together on this night. So who am I with, huh?"

"I didn't know you were forced into it. I would never have guessed that," he said, smiling softly, his eyes on the traffic ahead. "You, of all people. You eat men for breakfast!"

It was raining now and the after-party traffic was horrible, cars stuck in gridlock, the slanting sheets of rain slowing things to a crawl.

"Is there any way you can get out of it?"

"Yes, I could eat him." She smiled.

"You can't possibly marry someone you don't like."

"No. I can't."

She caught her breath as the flashing lights of a white-and-green police car from the opposite direction sped by. "Listen, if the police stops us and asks what our relationship is..."

"We'll say we are married."

She looked at him blankly for just a moment. It must have shown for the corners of his mouth twitched up ever so slightly even as he purposefully looked forward, his hands on the wheel.

"Don't joke. We'll say that I teach your sister violin, and since tonight is Charshanbeh Souri and no taxi was available, you are giving me a ride."

"Fine, but I like the first excuse better."

"Funny," she said, smiling.

"Do you work tomorrow?"

"No. I have the next three weeks off. Usually people are so busy before Norooz that they cancel their kids' classes for the last week of the year. So I get that week off and the next two weeks are Norooz vacation."

"Perfect. Then let's meet tomorrow for lunch and talk," he said, glancing at her.

Mahtab raised her eyebrows and said, "What about you? Don't you have to work?"

"No. I am done till after Norooz. Not by choice though. It's like no one else here wants to work during this Norooz thing. The whole country seems to shut down."

"No, not the whole country. Only the shops and factories. The government opens after the fifth day."

"That's crazy. But let's take advantage of it. Lunch tomorrow?"

"Sure, let's do it."

"But you have to let me pay for it!" he said, smiling.

Mahtab shook her head and let out a small smile.

"Do you want me to pick you up from your home?"

"No, not home." The vehemence was palpable in her voice, and he stared at her for a split second before going on.

"How about we meet at Mellat Park? It's just across from my office," he asked.

"That sounds better."

"I'll see you there at twelve thirty then?"

"Yes," Mahtab said, smiling. It was indescribable what she felt inside, like she was on a bed of bubbles that was lifting her, carrying her to the sky. "Please don't call or text if you have to cancel it before twelve o'clock. If for any reason I have to cancel, I'll text you early tomorrow morning, but please don't call me. OK?"

"OK," he said, looking at her.

When they reached her neighborhood, Mahtab grabbed the handle to open the door, but Ashkan asked quietly, "You haven't answered me, Mahtab. What are you going to do about it?"

"About what?"

"Your engagement."

"I don't know. I can't go forward, and I can't go back."

"Don't. Don't go forward like this. Break it off, get away!" He was imploring now with that same earnest intensity she had grown to love. She looked into his striking green eyes and sighed. "I am not going to marry him. I just need time to figure something out."

He nodded and said, "You promise?"

"I promise," she said, the heaviness in her chest growing. She knew that was a tough promise to make.

The silence was now oppressive, only broken by the steady patter of raindrops against the car. "I better go home," she said finally grabbing her violin, before opening the car door.

He turned to her and smiled. "I almost forgot your gift." He reached in the backseat and grabbed a box wrapped in gold paper. "For you."

"For me? What for?"

"Make-up gift."

"You shouldn't have," she averred.

"You've got to take it because it was special ordered, and I can't return it now."

"Thank you," she said, smiling.

She took the box, and after one glance at him, which could only be described as smoldering, she left the car. Purposefully she walked away from the car, not turning back toward the headlights that stayed in her direction for minutes. This was her street now, her area, and she couldn't risk it. As

Mahtab walked down the wet street, she shoved the square box inside her handbag, wiped her lips, and pushed her hair back inside her scarf.

The home was empty, except for Boji seated in front of the heater in the living room. She was rocking back and forth murmuring prayers, her prayer shawl wrapped around her.

"Where is everyone?" she asked Boji, who had gotten up to examine her. As she circled Mahtab, she looked like a guard dog sniffing a suspicious passerby.

"At your mother's sister's house."

"Why didn't you go?" she asked as she threw off her scarf and jacket.

"You know that I don't like anyone from your mother's side. Too loud, the people."

"Of course I forgot. You hate her side." Mahtab shrugged, making her way to the corridor to her room, trying to keep as calm as possible.

"Where were you?" That was the question she knew was coming.

"At Nasim's."

There was a pause, and then she heard Boji sigh. Not a small sigh but one that was meant to be heard.

"I don't think you should hang out with Nasim. It's not good for a girl with a fiancé to hang out with a single girl, especially that Nasim. She'll teach you bad stuff. *Az rah beh daret mikoneh.*"

Mahtab reached her room and closed the door. From her bag she fished the gift he had given her. It was a round box, about the size of a dessert plate, and covered in the most beautiful gold embossed paper, thick, rich to the touch. She lifted the lid of the box beneath. Her eyes widened as she saw the small, silver plate that sat nestled among the soft mauve tissue within the box. It looked so beautiful, so fragile. Picking it up gently, Mahtab examined it, afraid to breathe on it. It was one of those special decorative plates from Esfehan, light as a feather. The polished metal was intricately chased with designs of strutting peacocks and leaping deer around the edge, inlayed with metal of different hues. Her breath caught in her throat as her eyes fell on the center of the plate. For there, in beautiful curved *nastaligh* calligraphy was her name. "Mahtab."

Eighteen

The sun flooded the sky the following day, as though on cue for the upcoming season. The greenery, the trees, the bushes, the grass in the Park-e Mellat seemed so much more vivid in the brightness, making Mahtab squint behind her sunglasses.

Ashkan was already there, sitting on a bright blue bench facing the street under the shade of a *chenar* tree. His eyes were away from her direction, looking at an elderly couple side by side, balancing on rusty orange exercise bikes planted into the ground. One of many that had been set all over the city by the government to promote good health years ago. They were panting and laughing happily while they pedaled away, like great fat birds on pedestals.

Sitting there by himself, Ashkan looked so gorgeous, his thick chestnut hair slightly spiked up in front, dark sunglasses framing his masculine face. He had on only a simple navy-colored sweatshirt and jeans, but he made them look so good. Come to think of it, that's what models do; she smiled to herself, the dimples in her cheeks forming again. The anticipation of spending the day with him made her want to fly as she walked up to him.

"Salaam," she said softly, waving her hand.

"Salaam," he said, his eyes brightening as he got up. "Shall we go? There is an Italian restaurant in Vanak Square. Sepehr recommended it to me."

An old man who was sitting on the next bench was staring at them now.

"Yes, I know it. It's just a short walk from here," Mahtab said, glancing at the man and hoping he would stop staring, but he didn't. "Let's go."

Crossing the street, they started down the stone footpath toward the cluster of shops ahead. She checked herself instinctively in the mirrored glass pane of a shop window nearby. Her short black *manteau*, although a simple black, fit her slender form, giving it credit unlike the more billowing or over-tight cuts the other girls wore.

"You look good," he said quietly.

The restaurant, which was in the heart of Vanak Square, was packed. Getting the first available seats, they gave their orders to the waiter, who left almost before they could finish ordering.

"Now I know why this is their favorite place," Mahtab said once their food arrived. "I mean, Nasim and Sepehr."

"Why? Because the portions here are huge and Sepehr is a bear when it comes to food?"

Mahtab just smiled, her dimples showing in the mirrored pillar behind Ashkan.

"They are a cute couple, aren't they?" Ashkan said, his eyes on her.

"They are," she agreed.

Picking up a forkful of his meat-strewn pasta, he said, "This city is choking to death. Everywhere I go, it's so crowded. I couldn't even bring my car out today."

"That's because it's Norooz."

"It's crazy," he said a little exasperatedly.

"No, it's fun. Norooz is the greatest holiday in Iran. It's been around forever and even after the revolution, the new government still couldn't stop it. It wasn't Islamic enough for them, being part of our past before the Arabs invaded. You should cherish it."

"Cherish it?" he echoed her. "That sounds like something out of a book." She could see his eyes on her, their green made even more vivid by the sunburst of gold in the center. How could someone have such beautiful eyes?

"OK, love it then. You are Iranian after all!" she countered.

He chuckled.

Mahtab took a bite, her eyes dancing. "Actually you should look for the signs that come with it. Then the spirit of Norooz will make you happy. That's the magic of Norooz!"

He laughed unconvinced. "Signs of Norooz? Magic of Norooz? What are we, six years old now?"

"No...we are not six years old." Mahtab paused, raising an eyebrow in mock admonition, "Ashkan, the signs of Norooz are everywhere for everyone to see. It doesn't matter how old you are! It is in every corner of this city. From the flowers, the scent in the air, the laughter, even the extra crazy traffic. People are so excited! Look at the lines outside the pastry shops. People shopping for nuts, gifts, flowers. Even the fish market is busy selling smoked fish for the Norooz feast. Come on, Ashkan, you can't say you don't get excited by seeing all this."

Ashkan had by now polished off his food and was looking at her.

"Yes, I see it. But the truth is, I really don't feel it. You know I didn't grow up here Mahtab. I just feel so disconnected from all of this stuff."

She took in a breath and then just chanced what had been on her mind for the last half hour. "Do you want to go to Tajrish Square and see it all?"

"All what?" He looked surprised now.

"The signs of Norooz!" Mahtab smiled.

He studied her before asking, "Will that make you happy?"

"I am happy as it is. I just want you to see it too," she said, throwing a smile that she saw hit home in his eyes.

He looked back at her and finally, with a toss of his head, said, "Why not? Let's go."

For the short hop, they took a regular taxi to Tajrish. At first they both sat far from each other in the backseat of the old, puttering Peykan. But when the driver stopped for more passengers, Ashkan had to scoot over to her side. Now he was close to her, his left leg touching her leg, his arm touching hers. Mahtab closed her eyes for a second or so. She could be drunk by the smell of his cologne, be burned by the heat of his existence. Just as quickly, she felt a chill run within her. What was she doing with him, here? She was engaged. If anyone found out from her family or Emad's. What if? Involuntarily shuddering at the possibility, she opened her eyes.

"Tell me, what comes with Norooz?" Ashkan asked, his eyes on her.

"So many things, spring, new year, new life."

"New love?" he asked, with a hint of a chuckle.

She looked into his face and said, "Yes, that can come too."

Tajrish Square was always crowded, but today was extraordinary. There were people everywhere, and the noise was near deafening, a milieu of voices, horns, and rumbling buses trying to make their way through the choked roads here and there. The scent of saffron and rosewater, the hearty smell of freshly roasted *jigar*, liver, mixed with diesel fumes rose out of this frenetic scene.

"It gets busier each year," Mahtab said as they hurriedly made their way to the pedestrian path, avoiding the cars around them.

"It's crazy," Ashkan said as he jumped the big *joob*, gully and reached the other side.

"Careful of the motor bikes." Mahtab pointed to the helmeted rider trying to find his way through the busy pedestrian lane.

"Nowadays, things have changed and have become more commercialized. When I was growing up, they didn't sell colored eggs. We colored them ourselves. Now they sell pre-colored eggs."

"We colored eggs for Easter," he said.

"I thought you were not Christian."

"I'm not. I did it for fun, just like the other kids in my neighborhood."

"Do you still do it?"

"No, I did it when I was four."

Mahtab smiled and said, "I still color eggs for Norooz."

"Time to grow up," he deadpanned.

"You never grow out of tradition, especially tradition as old and as important as Norooz."

They stopped in front of one of the many open-air stalls, little more than a couple of old wooden boxes arranged stepwise onto which was thrown an old faded blue tarp. Even though she had seen this a thousand times, Mahtab always loved these kiosks not only for the treasures they held but also for their unabashed association with spring and the joy of Norooz. Glancing at Ashkan though, she couldn't tell if he was enjoying it, his expression somewhere between one of wide-eyed amazement and unease.

From the small stage of the stall overflowed everything you could possibly want for Norooz: Verdant *sabzeh*, freshly germinated wheat and lentils, in geometric shapes—rectangles, ovals, or traditional circles—neatly ringed by multicolored ribbons. Eggs of a million hues, some with painted-on designs vaguely reminiscent of those of Fabergè, stacked neatly in pyramids. On the side, *senjed,* dried wild olives with their brown, oily folded skins, and garlic lay visible in large, open, upright jute sacks. Behind them sat white buckets on the floor containing a myriad of tiny goldfish that darted this way and that to the hubbub around them.

"What do you want?" the seller asked them quickly, glancing at the crowd that had already formed behind them. He was a skinny man with a bushlike mustache who fidgeted with his hands.

Mahtab said, "We are just looking."

"Here," he said, taking two *senjeds* from the open bag. "Try this. I have the best in town. Don't buy it from anyone else." He had a thick *Azeri* Turkish accent.

A middle-aged woman stepped up to buy fish. "Which one?" the seller asked.

"That one. The red one. Not that red fish, the other red one!"

With a ladle, he expertly caught 'that' red fish, which the woman, after carefully giving it the once-over, agreed was the red one she was after. With a flick of his wrist, the flopping fingerling was in a clear plastic bag full of water and being handed to the woman who passed a crumpled bill in exchange.

"For us, fish, especially goldfish, signify the vitality of animals in our lives, so we put them in our *sofreh haftsin,* the Norooz display. They are beautiful, *na?*" Mahtab said, seeing the expression on his face.

"They're pretty," he said thoughtfully, before smiling, "What happens to all of them after Norooz?"

"People keep them as pets, if they make it," Mahtab said.

They walked on, making their way through throngs of people, to another shop, this one specializing in colorful candles.

"I take it candles are a sign of Norooz, right?" he asked, smiling.

"Yes!" Mahtab said. "It is for fire. Like yesterday when it was the day of fire."

"So what else comes with Norooz, Mahtab?" Ashkan asked. His voice was serious now.

"Happiness, love, lots of gift giving. Amoo Norooz, Haji Firooz."

"Go slow, too many names. I only picked up love and gift giving."

"I am amazed how little you know. You mean no one ever told you about Norooz?"

"Who would? I grew up with my mom and her side of family. And they celebrate Christmas."

"What about your father?"

He kept silent, his face hardening into a frown, and Mahtab knew better than to press on the subject again.

At this point she didn't care how long they would be together, or even about the danger of being seen with him that would bring her family's wrath on them or even worse: for an engaged woman, a sentence of stoning. It all seemed so trivial compared to his lack of knowledge, his lack of excitement at the single most important day of their heritage, of her world. But she would not give up. If there was even the slightest chance that he would be in her world, she would make him part of it.

They went inside the cavernous Tajrish mall. "Even the gold stores are full," Ashkan said, looking around.

"It's probably because all the good men are buying their wives *tala*, gold, as an *eidi*, gift."

He smiled. "Good men, ha?"

"That was a joke. But you should get something for your family."

"I did that on Christmas."

"Oh, come on. You should celebrate Norooz too. It is also part of your culture too, *na?*"

He paused a bit before unknotting his eyebrows. "Maybe you are right. I should get something for Pardis."

"Yes you should. What does she like?"

"She just had her ears pierced. Maybe I should get her earrings? Will you help me to choose something for her?"

"Sure. Let me talk. They'll hear your accent and raise the price."

Inside the *tala forooshi*, the jewelry store, they looked under the lighted glass display cases filled with glittering necklaces, rings, and bracelets. In a few moments, Mahtab was pointing out to something under the glass. It was a pair of small earrings, in gold, made into beautiful filigreed butterflies.

"Can we see that, please?" Mahtab said sweetly to the blue-suited man behind the counter. She knew too well that he was busy, he was probably tired, and she needed to show that she was interested in buying something, or he wouldn't bother with the effort.

She needn't have worried. The jeweler, a man probably in his forties with thinning back hair pulled the lapels of his suit together with his hands, before walking over. Mahtab wondered if he owned the shop or if this was his father's.

"Which one?" he asked.

"The butterfly earrings," Mahtab said pointing at a tray in the glass case.

He let out a broad smile and looked at Ashkan. "Looking for something for your fiancé?"

Mahtab's face went red, but Ashkan laughed and said, "No, it's not for her. This is for my sister's *Eidi*."

The man looked at him, obviously surprised by his accent, before laying out the earrings on a red velvet cloth.

The earrings came out to a hundred thousand toman. Ashkan took out a traveler's check from his pocket and scratched out the amount, bringing a grin to the man's face.

"What about your fiancé?" he said. "Don't you want to buy a gift for your lovely girl?"

Ashkan looked at Mahtab, mirroring the look of hesitation in her face. Suddenly he smiled and said, "Do you want something?"

"No, thanks," Mahtab said.

The jeweler shrugged and carefully dropped the earrings in a small blue-and-gold box and handed it to Ashkan.

"*Mobarak-e inshallah*," he said.

Ashkan put the box in his pocket and thanked him. Once outside, he laughed. "Are they always like that?"

Mahtab replied, "Most of the time. That's how they sell."

"That guy was funny. He thought we were engaged."

"They assume that once they see a girl and guy together."

Raising an eyebrow, Ashkan said, "Maybe this is another sign of Norooz?"

❧

As they stepped outside the mall, Mahtab felt her phone buzz within her handbag. She looked at the screen and her blood froze.

Where are you? It was Emad.

"It's him, isn't it?"

"Yes," she said curtly as she placed the phone back into her small handbag.

"And you need to go?"

She nodded wordlessly.

"Can I drop you off? I don't have my car, but I'll get a taxi for you. I'll come to your home and see you off there."

"No, it's crazy; then you have to take the taxi all the way home."

"Look, it's not a problem. I'd love to just to spend time with you. Can I please?"

"Fine," she said, smiling.

Ashkan flagged down a taxi, and the taxi driver grinned at the wad of bills he was offered. Once seated, Ashkan said, "So tell me about this Amoo Norooz."

"Oh!" She laughed. "Amoo Norooz is just like your *Baba Noel*, I guess."

"*Baba Noel*? Oh, you mean Santa Claus."

"Yes. He's also old and has a big white beard. He comes on the first day of spring to bring Norooz to the town."

"Norooz?"

"Yes, according to the story."

"What story?"

"Oh, it's just a childish story. It's for kids." Mahtab touched her scarf as she looked back at him.

"I would like to know."

"OK, if you insist. A long, long time ago, in a small village in Iran, there was a *pir-e-zan*, an old lady. Every year before spring arrived, she would dust and sweep her home and water the flowers outside. Then she would clean her balcony. She would cover it with beautiful handmade Persian rugs, and on top of that, she would lay her *sofreh haftsin*—you know, the Norooz display. The old lady would then make tea and prepare the *ghalyoon*, hookah. After all that hard work, she would have a bath and put on her new clothes. She would wear her special jewelry, put on makeup, and dab on fragrant rose perfume. Then she would sit on her balcony waiting for her Amoo Norooz. But she never did see him. She did this year after year. This spring though, something in her told her he would come, something she could not point to, but she knew it in her heart. He would come this time and see her."

"So did he?" Ashkan asked, his eyes on her.

"Hold on and I'll tell you!" She laughed.

"So this Norooz the *pir-e-zan* had worked extra hard, and she was very tired. She sat on the balcony waiting, but before she knew it, she fell sleep. Outside the little house in the village, the sun grew warmer, and something magical happened. The trees, one by one, began transforming, losing their winter brown for the wonderful green of spring. And beneath each one of the trees walked an old man with a golden cane. Tapping each tree with his cane, he chuckled quietly as though talking with them, which of course he was. Yes, it was Amoo Norooz. He had come and had brought spring with him. And yes, of course, he had come to see the old woman in her house that year. He found her still fast asleep on the balcony. Seeing her like that, he didn't have the heart to wake her. And so he put a flower in her ear and sat beside her on the carpet. He drank the wonderful tea she had prepared so painstakingly for him, ate some of the sweets from the *sofreh haftsin* and took a couple of puffs from the lit hookah. And then he left as quietly as he had arrived. When the old lady finally woke up and noticed the flower in her ear, the empty teacup, and smoked hookah, she looked out over her balcony and rubbed her eyes. The entire world had changed. It was spring! And she realized that Amoo Norooz had been there, and she had missed him. She felt so sad that she had to wait another whole year to see him. But she knew that although she had missed Amoo Norooz, the spring that he brought would remind her of him till the next time they met," she said with a small sigh.

"Nice story. Were they in love?" Ashkan asked with a twinkle in his eye.

"Who? The old lady and Amoo Norooz? No, I don't think so."

"Then why didn't he wake her up?" he asked.

"He couldn't. His heart was too soft to trouble her."

"I would have woken her up. Come to think of it, he should have woken her up," he said, his eyes on her.

"Well…he didn't," Mahtab replied. What was he talking about?

"Did he kiss her?"

"No!" she cried, looking at him incredulously.

The ends of his lips twitched. "I'm sure he did," he said, his eyes shining like a naughty child pulling a prank.

"But if he had kissed her, she would have woken up!"

He leaned forward, his eyes locked on her, until she could feel his breath. "Well, I think he kissed her lips! That's what lovers do."

Mahtab felt the heat rise in her cheeks. Ashkan was twisting the whole story. This was a fairy tale, not a love story! She had said it so well too, in her own opinion, pure, just like she had remembered it being told by her mother years ago. But now he was insinuating that Amoo Norooz and the old lady had feelings for each other.

"That's so inappropriate!" she said at last.

"I don't know about being inappropriate. It's clearly a love story," he said before shooting her that gorgeous smile. "And I love the way you told it."

What could she do with someone like this? She wondered. He knew which of her buttons to press to get her all worked up. But she couldn't be mad at him, not after that smile.

"Well, that's the story of Amoo Norooz," she said, looking away, trying desperately to fight the butterflies in her stomach.

Looking out, she realized the taxi had stopped moving. They were near *Pol-e-Said Khandan*, a neighborhood closer to her home now, at one of the intersections surrounded by rows of cars and trucks. Horns were blaring furiously as the traffic light up front aimlessly turned from red to green and back to red without anyone moving a single inch. Her watch showed six o'clock, and her heart missed a beat. Would she get home on time? She had only an hour before Pasha got home and now the traffic. But she would never have missed this for the world. She stole a glance at Ashkan who was looking out. Probably not used to the confusion around them. She slid back in her seat before suddenly sitting up again.

In the din and smoke, she spied a thin man. He was bobbing two and fro, almost dancing, winding his way between the cars. He was in red from head to toe with a face painted the darkest black. It was Haji Firooz tapping a yellow tambourine. He was singing in a nasal voice that Mahtab had known as long as she could remember.

"I am the Haji Firooz. I come once a year during Norooz," he sang loudly, his white teeth flashing in his blackened face. Suddenly he moved past them to deftly pick up a proffered bill from the car in front.

"I take it this is definitely another sign of Norooz?" Ashkan asked, leaning in to see better.

"Definitely! That's Haji Firooz. He makes people laugh and forget the sadness of winter."

"So like a clown?" he said.

"A clown?" She enunciated the word. "Can you explain what it means?"

"Do you know the circus? Where they have shows? With animals? And acrobats?"

"Yes, we say *seerk* for this."

"*Seerk*. Almost the same," he said. "OK, in the *seerk*, they have these men who dress in funny dresses and big shoes..."

"Oh! With the red noses." Mahtab grinned, her dimples appearing. "We say *dalghak*. Say it," she instructed, looking at him.

"*Dalkak*?" Ashkan said slowly, as though trying a strange dish.

"Close enough." She smiled. "No, he is not. Poor guy. In fact, in the old days, he was said to be the keeper of the fire. That's why his skin is so darkened and his clothes are burned."

"We should give him something," Ashkan said, taking a blue bill from his wallet.

Since the back doors had stubs for window openers, Mahtab gave the *eskenas,* the note to the driver to pass it to Haji Firooz.

Like a hawk, the man with the darkened face swooped to their car and took the note with an exaggerated bow.

"I am the Haji Firooz. I come once a year during Norooz," he sang, rolling his eyes and giving them a big toothy grin. Then he was off with his tambourine into the traffic ahead.

"He's funny," Ashkan said with a laugh.

"Kids like him." She smiled, looking up at him, "By the way, thanks again for the gift. It was really...special"

"Oh, you're welcome," he said, shifting back in his seat. "Did you see the back of it?"

"No, I didn't," Mahtab said, looking at him.

"Oh! You should see it. I hope you like it," he said quietly before looking at her. Not just a glance but a long, deep look with an intensity and, yes, longing that made something within her release and flutter. Then she saw his eyes fall on something. It was her hand resting on the vinyl seat. Her heart skipped a beat as he reached for it and took it into his own tanned fingers and held it. She looked up into those beautiful green eyes of his and said nothing. There was nothing to say but only to feel, to hold, to explore the physical spark of the man that sat beside her.

When Mahtab told the driver to stop, Ashkan, drawing her hand closer, said, "Mahtab, if I don't see you till after the holidays, have a wonderful Norooz."

"You also." And then she added softly, "Ashkan."

She saw his eyes light up. "Thank you so much for showing me a little of your Norooz. It really meant a lot to me."

"You're welcome. It's your New Year too, you know," she said, suddenly aware that the taxi driver was now staring at them. "I really had a good time."

"Me too. You are so much fun to hang out with," he said.

Her phone began to vibrate again. Oh God, would they leave her a moment of peace?

"I have to go. You don't have to get out of the car."

As she got out, he asked, "Mahtab, can I call you again?"

"No. No, please don't. I am sorry," she replied and walked away quickly. It felt like a part of her, actually a good part of her, including her heart, was left in that car, ripped away from her with a great tearing sound as she tottered along. What could she do? She kept asking herself. Here was the guy who she knew wanted her. For her, not what she could do for him, or for his family or her *jahaz*, but just her. Like a man looking at the woman of his dreams. Yes, that was the look in his eyes in that taxi. Like a lake looking up at the full moon in the sky. But. Yes but. That was when the warm feeling in her chest, that liquid pleasure, froze to ice again. There were Emad and her own family. She could see their faces, she could see his grin through his beard, hear his unctuous voice, smell his breath. Cold fear now ran through her. If they ever knew about Ashkan. She shivered inside. If they ever knew, they would kill her, or worse, disown her. Death either way. She was sure of that.

Gingerly sliding the key in, Mahtab opened the front door to see Pasha and Emad sitting in front of the TV. The voice from the TV was yelling about another missed goal. She heard Bahar's voice in the kitchen. Helping with the dinner preparations, of course.

Taking in a deep breath, she quickly threw out a "Salaam" and ducked through the hallway. Pasha didn't bother to answer her back, and for a moment Mahtab thought she had gotten past.

"Where have you been?" It was Emad. The tone may have been casual, but Mahtab felt a chill run down her spine. For the implied suspicion in the question was all too real.

"At work," she said, clearing her throat.

"Till now?"

"Yes, what's the problem?"

"Problem? Don't you think it's a bit late for a girl to stay out of the house till now?"

Mahtab looked at the clock; it was seven. "Well, it's almost Norooz and we were busy..."

"Busy? Busy with what? Are you working in a *shirini forooshi,* a sweet shop? Selling pastries for Norooz that you say you are busy? Ha?" Emad said with an empty laugh, his dark eyes on Mahtab. He reminded her of a snake in the zoo, eyeing a mouse in its cage.

"Well, with the traffic of Norooz..."

"Traffic?" His voice rose imperceptibly.

"Yes. I was waiting for a taxi in Emam Hossein Square for almost half an hour."

"Then why didn't you answer your cell phone, eh?" Now he was yelling.

"I didn't have reception. You know Irancell has problems."

Emad glanced at Pasha and then back at her. Finally, he said, between gritted teeth, "From now on I will come and pick you up from your work myself."

"I think that's a great idea," she said, smiling for the first time since she had arrived home.

As she walked away, she overheard Emad. "Your sister has a long tongue. She answers back all the time."

"I know." Pasha laughed. "But it's your problem now!"

She locked the door behind her and went straight to her drawer. Unlocking it, she gently took out the delicate, silver plate that Ashkan had given her from within the recesses of a pink folded towel. How thoughtless of her not to have looked behind it last night. But she would now, and she let out a small gasp at what she saw. On the back of the plate, in looping English script, it said:

To the Mahtab of music, to the Mahtab of dreams.
Ashkan
March 2009

She couldn't believe her eyes. There it was in silver, the essence, the proof of his feelings. She felt herself float, lift almost off the ground in her joy.

"Oh, *Khoda joon*. Dear God."

Suddenly there was a harsh knocking on her door.

"Mahtab…Mahtab…," Emad was yelling. Springing into action, she quickly buried the plate under the towel and slammed the drawer shut. Glancing at the mirror, she saw the mascara running from the wetness in her eyes and quickly dabbed them dry. Taking a deep breath, she threw open the door.

"What?"

"What are you doing?"

"If you let me, I would change my clothes."

Emad cocked his head and peered in her room, moving his head left to right as though trying to catch something. "Were you on the phone?"

"Do you see any phone in my hand?"

They stood there. She looked at him, refusing to budge from the doorway. Finally, with a dart of his tongue, he said, "I came early to pick you up and take you to my home. No one was at my home today. It was a missed opportunity," he said, dropping his gaze for a moment, his face a mask of disappointment. "There might not be any opportunity till the end of the Norooz holiday."

"Good, I can take a break then," she said, stepping back.

He came in and quickly bolted the door behind himself. "Unless you can do it quickly here," he said, his eyes wide, pulling her hand to his crotch.

"Are you crazy? My family is out there," Mahtab whispered, struggling to pull her hand away.

"They are busy. No one will know. Come on. It'll be quick. I am already hard."

She had no choice. Her hand in his, he rubbed it, pulling her like a rag doll. Till he released it on her hand and then on the floor.

"Oh God, I love you," he said, pulling up his zip.

He left without another word and Mahtab threw a towel down on the floor to cover his slime. Then she dropped on the floor, her back against the wall. She was exhausted but just as she closed her eyes, her phone began to buzz. It was Nasim.

"I'll call you later. I just got home," Mahtab said weakly.

"How was it?"

"It was good. I'll call you," she said with a sigh.

"When? What happened?" She heard the note of concern in Nasim's voice.

But Mahtab clicked the phone off. Her head hurt. Her hand stank of Emad. She hated it, hated him, hated herself for accepting the situation, and for the first time ever, she hated, actually hated with every fiber of her being, her parents for putting her in this mess. But at that moment, the words on Ashkan's gift echoed in her mind, pushing aside everything, her anger, frustration, even Emad. Sitting up straight, her clean thumb began to fly over the keyboard.

"Thank you! What you wrote was beautiful. I am sorry you can't call me."

Then she sent another text, a small smile appearing on her face. "But you can text me."

It only took him a minute to answer. "I am glad you liked it. Thanks for letting me text you."

Nineteen

The large white clock was ticking down toward zero on the TV screen. In front of it, an announcer, a man with a closely trimmed beard, sat propped up on his elbows, discussing the meaning of Norooz with his cohost, a petite woman in a cream, buttoned-down *manteau* and scarf.

"Would you say, then, that Norooz is an Iranian day, not a religious day?" the woman said, glancing at the clock.

"*Baleh. Baleh*! It may have been a religious day in the old times, but now it is only cultural. An important day, a proud day for all Iranians of this country. And the world!" he said proudly before adding quickly, "Of course, as long as our Islamic traditions are recognized and maintained through this day."

"*Inshallah*," the woman intoned.

"The Prophet Mohammad, peace be upon him, himself recognized Norooz and said the day that the world wakes up from winter slumber is like heaven on the earth. And God will bless the people. And for us, the Shia Muslims, Norooz is recognized through Islam, which makes it even more beautiful."

They both now looked at the large clock ticking away. In the next few minutes, the clock would ring out the exact time of Norooz, the *sal-e tahvil*, the spring solstice, to all of Iran. And when the clock struck zero, people in their homes, in the homes of families all over the country, most around a table like Mahtab's would cheer, share hugs, and make wishes.

"How many minutes?" Bahar asked from their room.

"Less than two minutes. Hurry up," Mahtab replied.

"I'm coming. Just one more finger to polish."

"Bahar! Hurry up," Monir yelled over the TV before grabbing the faded green prayer book that had been in the family as long as Mahtab could remember. Moments later, they were all together around the *sofreh*. Baba, Boji, Pasha, Maman, Bahar still panting from her run across the house, and Mahtab, all waiting for the year to change. It was so pleasurably familiar, like the chance to relive wonderful memories again. And it was the one time, the one consistent time, that she could remember her family being happy, truly happy all together, in the spirit of Norooz. Mahtab knew what would happen next like the back of her hand. In the next sixty seconds, each would make a wish or read a prayer. She looked at her family, at Baba. He was smiling, an arm around Maman's shoulder. So was Pasha, holding onto Boji, even when his eyes met Mahtab's.

The *sofreh haftsin*, the table setting welcoming Norooz since time imme-morial, looked wonderful, like out of a card in a shop. It had to be for Maman and Bahar had worked on it since early yesterday morning. They had cleaned the oval mirror ringed with cast-metal flowers, which now sat in the table's center, with vinegar and polish. Then the matching candlestick holders that sat atop the cream-colored tablecloth that covered the table. In front was the green Koran with a tear on the bottom edge, where the binding met the cover. Mahtab had seen it on the *sofreh* every year since she could remember. It was a gift her mother had gotten from her in-laws for her wedding. That was more than twenty-seven years ago, before she was born, a world away from her. A string of polished sky blue prayer beads sat next to the Koran surrounding the *mohr*, the clay pentagon that was used for *namaz,* praying. Sprouted lentils, all about ten days old, their stems and leaves like a green oval carpet, took the shape of the oval dish they were in. Eggs, hand painted by Bahar and Mahtab the day before, carefully chosen red apples, vinegar, a clove of garlic, coins, sumac, *samanoo*, and sweet pastries sat in crystal dishes around the center, like radial splashes of color around a central sun.

The TV began to roar. Mahtab looked at the screen. The announcers had gone, leaving the dark screen to sparkling exploding lights. Fireworks. To the blaring of trumpets, a voice, a man's voice, deep and slow announced, "The beginning of the year 1388."

"*Sale No Mobarak.*"

"*Eid Mobarak!*"

Everyone,—Maman, Pasha, even Baba—were now smiling and hugging. Boji, with her hands together, palms raised upwards, began praying wordlessly.

Soon guests started to arrive, aunts, uncles, and their children on both Rasool and Monir's sides, even distant ones that they only saw once or twice a year. Every time someone and their family arrived, tea and sweets and *ajeel*, nuts would appear on the table after the salaams and hugs died down.

∽᥍

While getting more tea for yet another set of guests, her phone buzzed and the screen lit up. A text populated the yellow rectangle. "*Eid-et-Mobarak. Now ditch Emad and come hang with us. We are going to be at Sepehr's parents' house tonight. We have the whole house to ourselves. Ashkan is there too. I'll pick you up at eight.*"

"In my dreams," she murmured as the steaming ochre liquid from the large teapot filled the rows of glass cups on the tray. Picking up the tray, she marched out.

It took all of her agility and then some to stop barreling into Emad past the door. Which may have been a good thing, she thought, but she didn't have time for that.

He smiled, his eyes on her. "*Chai, eh? Merci,* I'll take a cup. Then you'll have less to carry!" he chortled.

Giving him nothing more than a tight smile, Mahtab walked past him and began serving the tea in the living room. When she came to her mother, she whispered, "Can I go to Nasim's house tonight?"

Monir looked at her and then glanced at her husband who was talking to his brother across the room.

"For how long?"

"For dinner."

"Monir *khanoom.*" It was Emad who was still holding on to his tea. "With you and Mr. Rasool's permission, I would like to take Mahtab to my home."

173

"I don't think that's a good idea," Mahtab said quickly.

"Oh! Of course. Yes, you should go, Mahtab!" her mother interrupted.

Mahtab frowned. "But, Maman, you have a lot of work here."

"Oh, I am sure Bahar and your mother can pull your weight till you come back. You should come with me," Emad snapped. "You should come and pay your respects to my parents. Today is the first day of the year. It's customary."

"Of course she'll come. I was going to tell her to ask you to take her. I don't need help. Go, Mahtab. Emad *jan*, you finish your tea, so she can get ready."

Before Mahtab could say a word, Maman was up leading her to the kitchen.

"Mahtab, you have to go or else you will never hear the end of it when you get married. They'll be talking about this all your life. How you never came to pay your Norooz respects when you were engaged."

"But I don't care what they think, Maman."

"You say that now, but wait till you get married and whatever your in-laws say will matter. It always matters. Trust me on that. Now go get ready," she said before a small smile broke over her face. "Besides, you should go and get your Norooz gift. I am sure they must have some gold ready for you."

"Maman, no amount of gold can help me tolerate them."

༄

They hadn't driven far when Emad lit a cigarette. "I have to tell you something very important. I have been wanting to tell you this for some time now." He coughed and went on. "I do not like you to work. I don't want my wife to work. In fact, you really don't need to work anyway!"

"I am not your wife yet," she said, looking right back at him. She saw a flash of irritation ignite in his eyes.

"But you soon will be."

"When I am your wife, we'll talk about it."

"*Zaboon darovordi*, you are answering me back? You have become quite brazen!"

"This is not about being brazen. I just don't think you should order me around like this. Who are you anyway?"

"Your future husband. And as your future husband, I demand you not to work."

"Whatever. We'll see Emad," Mahtab said, looking out of the window.

"No…I know you need money…but it is your father's duty to give you money until you marry me. Once we are married, I'll provide you with everything. Everything you want, tell me, I'll buy it for you. But I don't want you to go back to work after the Norooz vacation is over. Is that understood?"

"Let's see if we are still engaged after Norooz," she muttered under her breath.

"What? What did you say?"

"Nothing," she replied, looking down at her nails.

"That's right, and if you don't listen, I'll tell Pasha." He smiled slowly, winking at Mahtab. "You know he is not so gentle as me…"

"Do you have to be so cruel? Please don't say such things, not on this day. Don't take my happiness away."

"If you listen to me, you'll be happy forever," he said softly. She felt his hand on her thigh, his fingers feeling her, pulling on her skin.

"We haven't been together for so long…I miss you."

Pushing his hand away, she looked outside the window. "It's been less than a week."

She heard him curse under his breath and then nothing. Only silence until they reached his house.

꒰ꭓ

By the time Emad dropped Mahtab off at her home, it was dusk, the sky a darkening gray bordered by the orange embers of the setting sun.

Before Mahtab entered her house, Nasim called. "I'll be there at eight; did you get permission?"

"I am tired. I worked all day at our home, and then Emad forced me to go to his home," Mahtab said, cradling the phone.

"So he managed to take you to his home?" Nasim tittered on the other side.

"*Areh*, yes, and this time I had the honor to help at his house too." Mahtab's voice cracked.

"So what did they give you as Norooz gift?" Nasim said.

"Work!"

Nasim drew in a breath. "Nothing? Stupid *khasis* stingy people."

"I don't want any shit from them. He just dropped me home. I'll text you if I get a chance to come with you."

Maman was furious when she heard what had happened.

"Did they at least give an excuse? That it was not ready? That they would keep the gift for later?" Monir asked, her mouth wide open.

"*Na.* It wasn't even mentioned."

"This is not how it works. It's customary to give a gift to a new bride. That watch we gave Emad was expensive. They should have given you something."

Mahtab wanted to tell her that she didn't want anything from them. That the last thing she wanted from Emad's family was a gift. But she didn't. Instead she saw an opportunity, an opportunity to do something that just a few minutes ago seemed quite impossible.

"Maman. It doesn't matter."

Her mother looked at her, surprise in her eyes. Mahtab knew what Maman was thinking. Instead of her, it was her daughter who was doing the right thing, taking the high road, forgiving Emad's family for their slight.

"*Dokhtaram*, you are right," her mother said with a small smile. "We should not make a big thing out of this. Maybe they are planning a bigger gift for you next time."

Mahtab cleared her throat. "Maman, can I ask something of you? This is the last year I am single. Next year, I'll be a married woman." She let it hang, the certainty that she would no longer be part of this family but Emad's, under their rules, under their regulations.

"What is it, Mahtab?" Maman asked.

"Can I go to Nasim's house?"

"I have to get permission from your father," said Monir, the smile dropping from her face.

"Please, Maman, please, this is the last time," Mahtab begged.

Maman sighed and finally said, "All right. You go. I'll let your father know."

Twenty

"Bah, bah. You made it!" Nasim said, lighting a cigarette as Mahtab slammed the car door shut.

Mahtab chuckled. "I can't believe it either. God answered my prayers."

"Whatever it was. Now smile and be happy. Let's get you to your love. He is waiting for you."

"I look awful," Mahtab said, looking at herself in the rearview mirror.

"We'll stop by my home and I'll give you a makeover."

"Where are Sepehr's parents vacationing?"

"Singapore. We have their whole house to ourselves. You've been to their home before, right?"

"No, I've only been to Ashkan's house. I mean his parent's home."

"Now that is a nice house. Old but still very *chic*," Nasim said as they parked in front of her apartment complex.

"I told Maman I'll spend the night at your place. But I have to go back early in the morning," said Mahtab.

꩜

Nasim turned and cocked her head to the side, looking up and down at her, as the elevator doors closed. "Your jeans are fine. You need a shirt though. Something hot!"

"What, this blue thing won't do?" Mahtab said, drawing her hands over her baggy top.

"At the *Emamzadeh Gholi,* the town with the most awful fashions, maybe. I hear the *dar-e pit,* the low-life guys who hang around there love baggy! Very sexy!"

"Ewww. How do you know? Did you date a *dar-e pit?*"

Making their way to the walk-in closet, Nasim threw back a black strapless top at Mahtab. "Here try this."

The top was too tight, too short, and too revealing, something a singer would wear at a concert in Los Angeles. "I am not wearing this. My breasts will fall out of this thing."

Rolling her eyes, Nasim blew out a mouth full of air.

"*Azizam,* you need to show him something!"

"I want him to like me for me. Not for this," she said, waving at her bust. She then drew out a long-sleeve white top. "I'll wear this. It's tasteful."

"Do you want to cover your head with a black *roosari* also?" Nasim pouted. "Let's get your makeup done first, and I'll find something hot and tasteful for you."

⌒⊙

They reached Sepehr's parents' house a little after nine. It was dark outside. The Alborz Mountains were now only shadows in the distance, dimly lit by the city below. They parked at the far end of the street and walked toward the house. Mahtab had never been here before, but it felt like déjà vu. Nasim had talked about his place often, describing every detail, in her first gush after meeting Sepehr. And who could blame her?

The house was a large white building, two stories high, crowned by a roof that in front extended out in a semicircle, supported by large columns, covering a huge porch.

Faint strands of music—slow, melodious, almost soulful—and then voices floated as Nasim opened the door. Soon she threw off her scarf and *manteau* and ordered Mahtab to do so as well. This was the first time Mahtab had ever been to such a party. It was as if she had grown wings and landed in America. This wasn't Tehran; these people were not the same people who walked in the streets of the city during the day. The French doors parted into a large hall that was dimly lit inside. The ceiling seemed to disappear into the dark, with only the crenellated white molding showing through. There was music, a low hypnotic beat, punctuated with tinny clangs pulsing in the background. Smoke hung in the air. The smell was overwhelming, cigarette smoke and perfume, sweet moonshine and something else. Sickly sweet, almost cloying, it lingered in the background, like smoldering damp incense.

"Nasim." Mahtab paused. "What's that smell?"

"What? Oh, the smell!" Nasim chuckled. "Oh that, it's ganja! Don't worry, it won't get you high, not yet anyway."

She could see people moving inside the living room, actually the shapes of people, talking, slow dancing, sprawling on sofas in the dim blue light, kissing. Everyone was everywhere.

"Nasim? Where were you?" a voice yelled out. It was Babak, looming in the dark.

"Babak, where is my Norooz gift?" Nasim shot back.

"I am your Norooz gift."

"Ha-ha! You are funny," Nasim said, pulling Mahtab away. "Let's get out of here or he'll be all over you like last time."

Making their way into the house, Mahtab spotted Ashkan coming out of the kitchen with a drink in his hand. Her feet froze as he came toward them and her heart almost stopped beating. "Nasim, he is here," Mahtab said.

"I know. Seriously, act normal. You are practically dating him, aren't you? Remember, you went out with him the other day. Don't be shy!"

"Hello." Ashkan gave Nasim a hug and kissed her right cheek. Mahtab moved back a little to avoid contact and settled for a "hi." What was wrong with her? She cursed herself under her breath, trying to fight the shyness that had suddenly appeared from nowhere.

"I brought Mahtab." Nasim winked. "I went to her home and practically dragged her out."

"Fantastic," he said. "Do you want a drink?"

"Yes, but let me find Sepehri first." Nasim looked at Mahtab. "You good here?"

"I am all right." Mahtab nodded quickly, trying to hide the thumping in her chest.

"OK. Let me find Sepehri, and then I'll be back," she said, disappearing into the gloom.

"Do you want a drink?" Ashkan asked, his eyes glancing on and then off Mahtab.

"*Na merci.*"

He cleared his throat. "So Happy Norooz. To you, I mean."

"Yes, same to you." Mahtab smiled. "Did you have a good first day of Norooz?"

"I did. I was here with Sepehr."

"Let me guess, playing PlayStation?"

He laughed.

"Everyone smokes here," she said.

"And most are probably high by now. Listen, do you want to go out? Get some fresh air?"

The air was crisp outside, with a gentle breeze rising from the Alborz Mountains. The moon was out, a silver disc hanging in the sky. They stood in the balcony overlooking the large yard, and in the center, a rectangular swimming pool held the reflection of the moon above.

"Do you want to take a walk?" he asked her.

"Sure." They walked toward the pool in silence, only the sounds of crickets accompanying them. Everything around them threw long shadows in the silver moonlight.

"It is a beautiful night," he said quietly.

"Yes, it is beautiful tonight," she said before turning to him. "It's the first day of Norooz and guess what? The magic of Norooz did work!"

"In what way?" he asked.

"I can't tell you, but it worked." Yes it had worked, for how else could she be here with him right now, against all odds on the first night of Norooz?

"Does it have to do anything with your fiancé?"

"No. Why? What do you mean by that?"

His face fell. "Your fiancé…well…you don't like him. So I thought…" He didn't finish his sentence. "Anyway, do you want to sit?" He pointed to the white swing set with printed flower cushions.

"Sure."

"I still can't believe you are engaged. It's like a nightmare becoming real," he said with sudden force, looking straight ahead, away from her. "You have to get out of it!"

"Don't you think I tried?" she blurted out.

He was looking at her now, his forehead pinched in a frown, thrown in relief by the moonlight above.

"My family thinks he is a good match because he is from a religious family. They trust his family. He has a college degree and works for the government."

"So?" he said simply.

"A job with the government means money, a house, a car. Besides, he is my brother's boss." She looked him in the eyes and went on. "Remember, even you said that a guy has to have something, be somebody, to provide for his family. Well, for my parents, Emad has."

Ashkan kept silent, leaning forward to kick at the ground with his foot. Finally he said, "I remember what I said. But I assumed the girl would like the guy. It's clear you don't want him. Doesn't that matter at all?"

"Have you heard of the phrase love comes after marriage? That's what my parents believe. They hope my love for him will grow after we are married. You must be laughing inside, thinking who thinks like that these days? Well, my parents do." Mahtab sighed. She wanted to tell him about her fear, why she had gone along so far. The fear of disownment. Of being a *farari* girl, a girl without a respectable family. She breathed out, almost to herself. "I am stuck between a society moving forward so fast and...and a family trying so hard to hold me back."

She stole a glance at him. His eyes were elsewhere now, his face furrowed with thought. Finally he spoke, his voice more distant than his eyes. "You don't have to marry him. Not him, not anyone you don't want. You are in Tehran. You work, right? You are twenty-three, right? You can leave. Start a new life. The way I see it, in the end, it's your choice Mahtab!"

They sat in silence. Thoughts whirled through Mahtab's mind. He was asking her to give up everything. Risk everything. It was easy for him to say it. He had money and a wonderful family! Of course she didn't want Emad, but what was the alternative? Didn't he know how bad the life of an unmarried girl could be, without family, without money? The sound of high heels descending stairs came from behind them, and then a figure stepped into the pale moonlight.

"There you are, Ashk. Come upstairs and join us." It was that slutty Elham. Mahtab had seen the pictures for Nasim had made sure of that. That voice, coming from a mouth slightly off to the left, in a permanent lipsticked smirk, her breasts pushing out of her tight tank top. Mahtab's eyes fell on her tight skirt riding way above her knees.

For a moment Ashkan looked at Mahtab. Then he turned toward that half-naked Elham with a smile, before turning back.

"We'll catch up later, Mahtab. I'm going to get a drink. Do you want anything?"

"No thanks," Mahtab managed. Her heart sank at the sight of slutty Elham's mouth opening ear to ear as she grabbed Ashkan's hand and walked away, stilettos echoing. A sound that sliced into Mahtab's being surer than a knife.

～ↄ

Back in the house, all she wanted now was to get out, get away. Where was Nasim? People were everywhere; a group was sitting in the living room, talking, laughing out loud, drinking. All of them had cigarettes in their hands; one girl was sitting on a guy's lap. But there was no sight of Nasim. Never a fan of house parties, even if she hadn't been to one, now everything about this house repulsed her. The drugs, the alcohol, the off-tune guitarist in his garish orange chapeau, shaking his head to that awful tune.

Finally, she found Nasim, Sepehr, Sara, and some of the other cousins in the kitchen. The air was rank, filed with the fumes of drugs, smoke, vodka, and food. Nasim was sitting over the kitchen island, her face in a folded piece of paper between her hands.

"Nasim?"

Nasim's face lifted off the sheet of paper, and Mahtab saw the white powder on her nose, like frosting after eating cake. Nasim sniffed and then, in a curiously nasal voice, yelled out, "Oh, Mahtabi, *Koja boodi*? I was looking everywhere for you."

"I have a headache."

"Come, take this. You'll feel better." It was Sara, sitting on a chair in the corner. In her outstretched hand was a thin cigar with the same curious, sticky sweet stink she had smelled before.

"No thanks."

"Can I get you anything?" Sepehr said, sliding up next to Nasim.

"Nasim, my head is really hurting!" Mahtab said, holding her head.

"If you want, you can go upstairs to my old bedroom and lie down. It's the third door to the left." Sepehr offered, looking concerned.

"Thanks, Sepehr. Nasim, text me when you are ready to leave."

"OK. I love you," Nasim said, laughing, her cigarette's ashes falling on the floor.

As Mahtab was leaving the kitchen, she heard Sepehr say, "Is she mad at us?"

"*Na*, her fiancé is shitting all over her. She is in a deep mess," Nasim answered, slurring her words.

Why did Nasim have to tell everyone everything? Mahtab cursed inside as she walked upstairs.

Despite the noise, Mahtab was sure she could hear muffled moaning and grunting from behind the closed doors as she passed. What if that was Ashkan? She shook her head, tears threatening to spill from her eyes. Sniffing, she pressed on.

She found Sepehr's bedroom and shut the door. Thankfully it was empty. She didn't remember how long she was sitting in the dark, on the floor, her back against the bed, when the door creaked open. She looked up to see the silhouette of Ashkan's frame in the doorway before he switched on the light. Mahtab sat up straight and put her hands through her hair.

"Mahtab? Nasim said you came upstairs. I've been looking all over for you."

"I have a headache," she said, looking away.

He closed the door and walked toward her. "Do you need something for it? Medicine?"

Placing a square-bottomed glass filled with amber liquid on the floor, he sat next to her.

She didn't want to think of what he had done with that half-naked girl.

"Why are you here?" she asked.

"I was looking for you. I told you," he said, settling next to her.

"Why? What about your friend? Don't you want to be with her?" She cried, fixing him with a glare.

"I have a lot of friends," he said slowly, his eyes still on her. "But I want to be with you now. Do you want a drink?"

"No. I don't want a drink! I don't drink! I don't smoke. I don't take drugs. I have never slept with any guys. I have a fucked-up life that I can't even take credit for destroying myself." She sniffled, trying to dry her face with her hand. Once she found her voice again, she continued.

"I envy every half-naked girl downstairs who has the freedom to do whatever she likes to do. I envy Nasim, and she is my best friend. I envy those girls who flirt with you and get to go home with you, even if they are cheap-looking sluts."

He stared at her. But before he could say anything, Mahtab went on. "You know who else I envy? Your sister, Pardis. That's right, Pardis! Do you know why? Because she gets to spend time with you. She gets to have you in her life. Me, I never know every time I leave you if I'm ever going to see you again!"

"No," he said, taking a gulp of his drink. "No. You don't know what you are saying. Leave Pardis out of this. You don't know..."

"Of course," Mahtab said. "Of course. She is your baby sister. You're protective of her." Then almost as an afterthought she added, "You are so much older than her. What, like you could be her uncle."

"I can't believe you said that," Ashkan said, looking at her angrily. "What's wrong with you?"

"What's wrong with me? I am not the one who smells of alcohol!"

"No, you smell of hatred, Mahtab!" he said, getting up. "And don't give me that magic of Norooz crap. It's obvious that you don't believe in any of that shit yourself. You are so angry inside that you see everyone the way you want them to be, not who they really are." He finished his drink. "Go take charge of your own life. And leave those who haven't done anything to you out of it!"

Tears rolled down her face as her mouth opened in a silent sob.

"Stop crying. OK, I'm sorry. Stop please. I didn't mean to hurt you," he said sitting down, trying to put an arm around her. But she shrugged it away.

"Everyone is mean to me. Pasha is mean. My parents are mean. Emad is mean. Now even you have become mean to me! There would have been magic if you..."

"What are you talking about, Mahtab? Would I have come looking for you if I didn't care about you?" She felt his eyes on her, but she couldn't look up.

"Listen, Mahtab. I am also frustrated. So frustrated. Just like you," he said at last. "But please leave Pardis out of it. She hasn't had an easy life, whatever you may think. There is a good reason for the age difference, all right?"

"What is it? Tell me." she asked.

"You don't want to know. Believe me, you don't," he said looking at the floor. "Why do you care anyway?"

"I don't care. I just want to know. You can tell me, or you can leave and go back to your girlfriend Elham!" she said, tossing her head up in the air, her arms now folded across her chest.

"She is not my girlfriend. God damn it!" he said clenching his teeth, his hands on his head.

"The way she was holding on to you, she looked like your girlfriend."

"There! You said it. She was holding on to me, not me holding on to her. You have a fiancé and I am biting my lip, not saying anything."

"What's that supposed to mean?"

"You very well know what that's supposed to mean." He took a deep breath and drank the melted ice in his glass. "I need another drink."

"No you don't. As it is you are half drunk." She grabbed his pants and pulled him down. "You go out and that half-naked girl will steal you again. Tell me, why are you so much older than Pardis?"

He settled down on the floor and looked up at the ceiling. Then after seconds that seemed like minutes, he said, "Because my father..."

"Did he have another wife?"

"Will you let me talk? He was captured in the war. The Iran-Iraq war." She gasped. "No?!"

"Yes," he said, nodding. "He was like eighteen. I wasn't even born yet." Ashkan got up. "Really, I need a drink."

"OK, fine. Go," she finally said. He got up and turned around. "I'll be back."

"Yes, sure. If she lets you."

Ashkan was smiling, and there was that glint in his eyes again. "You are so beautiful when you're jealous!" he said as he closed the door behind him.

Twenty-One

*C*lutching her head in her hands, Mahtab rested her chin on her knees and waited. The seconds ticked into a minute, and then the minute into more minutes. Her heart sank. He wasn't coming back. He was going to end up in bed with that Elham. Then all of a sudden the door opened. The dull pounding that she had tuned out in the back of her brain now crystallized into something between rap and techno music. Ashkan came in with a bottle in one hand, and a glass filled with clear liquid in the other. The music retreated to its dull thumping as the door closed behind him.

"And you're back."

"Here." He handed her the glass.

"I don't drink."

"It's water." Then he opened the palm of his hand. On it laid a small white pill. "Painkiller for your head. It took me some time to find it, but I did," he said, sitting beside her.

"Thanks." She smiled and took the pill.

When she was done, she felt his hand reach for hers. She didn't resist. "See, I managed to run away from that half-naked girl after all," he said with a small laugh.

"You can be funny when you want to! So, did you come back to tell me about your father?"

"You won't let it go, will you?" Ashkan said taking a sip from his bottle.

"No."

He chuckled. "My mom was expecting me when Kiumars was captured."

"Oh. They married so young."

"They weren't married."

"Are you serious?" She clutched her mouth with her hand before she stopped herself. She couldn't believe what she was hearing.

"Yes. They had met when my mom was visiting her father a few years before the revolution, before the war in Iran. My grandpa, Jamshid, had moved back to Iran after he and Grandma Edna divorced. He came here and married Soraya. Soraya happens to be Mon Parvin's sister."

"Mon Parvin is your father's mother, right?"

"Right. So my mom continued to visit her dad and Kuimars during the summers. She told me it was love at first sight. Then she got pregnant, but she didn't know until she was back in the States." He flashed her a naughty smile. "That September, the war broke out. Soon after, Kiumars was drafted. He was taken from school one day actually, just like that. Two army trucks drove up, and the soldiers called all the boys who looked old enough to the *hayat*, the yard. Then they loaded them in and trucked them to the front without anyone knowing. My father's family found out about him when one of the other parents called them later that day. Imagine the shock! But things were going very badly in the war at the time, you know, and things like this were happening all over the country. My father remembers the soldiers who had come to get them. They were little older than him, wearing green bands around their heads. They had volunteered to be *shaheeds*, martyrs, and they needed more to fill their place, I guess." A shadow fell across his face.

"What happened then?"

"He was injured at the front and then captured by the Iraqis."

"Ashkan. How come you never told me this?"

"Tell you what?" Ashkan barked. "Tell you so you can feel pity for me? I don't need that. I don't look for sympathy by telling people about my family's suffering. I never have!"

"No one would pity you. I feel sad for your father but not you. At least you escaped the war. Unlike us."

He chuckled dryly. "Easy for you to say. For the first eleven years of my life, I didn't have a father. For the first five, I didn't even know who he was. I was a child born out of wedlock, living in Boston with my mother. Then my mother married David. I had to live with a stepfather who it turned out cared little about anyone but himself. You see all those cousins of mine downstairs? They had a better childhood than I did even though they grew up here in Iran."

All of a sudden Mahtab felt so thirsty. She drained the rest of the water in her glass.

"I remember the day that they released the prisoners from Iraq. I was five years old," she said, looking at her glass.

"Yes, I remember it so well," Ashkan said, "August 1990. I was nine years old. We heard in the news that negotiations were finally done, and they were going to release the POWs. I remember when they started showing videos of the war, of Saddam, of Khomeini. My mom shut off the TV and said, 'OK, that's enough. Do you want to go biking?' I didn't want to go biking. I wanted to see my father."

He turned to look at Mahtab. "That's what I told her."

"What did she say?" Mahtab asked.

"She said she didn't know when he was actually going to be released. I knew she didn't. All she knew of were the Red Crescent letters sent sporadically to his parents. But I wanted to see him." He sighed. "I was nine years old. What did I know? I kept insisting, why can't we go see him? I'll never forget what she said next. I think it was the hardest thing she ever had to say to me." He paused to take a sip.

"What did she say?"

"She said that because she wasn't married to him, they wouldn't allow a child out of wedlock back into Iran. At the time I didn't understand what she was talking about. Just that I hated her for not letting me see my dad, my real dad because she was married to someone else. Things weren't the same after that. I watched every goddamned TV news bulletin to see if I could see my father's face in those dirty grey prisoner exchange buses. I had seen his pictures, in my mom's album, but I never did see him on TV. One day, when my mom was at work, I called my grandfather, my mom's father, Jamshid. I'd be lying if I said he wasn't surprised at my call, asking to go back to Iran. Things were still very difficult over there. But after listening patiently to me, he finally said he'd talk to Kiumars' family to see if I could go back. He did it though. They had to bribe a lot of people but they got it done.

189

"They made up a bunch of lies about Kiumars and Tina's relationship in order to get me a birth certificate. That they were engaged, a marriage date had been set, that the records were lost in an air raid. I think Kiumars being a POW, a hero there, helped. So I got my Iranian birth certificate and passport and came to Iran the following summer, against my mom's wish. I broke her heart, Mahtab. She never said anything to me, but I knew in a way she felt betrayed. She had raised me, but I left her for a man whom I had never seen."

"She couldn't come with you?" Mahtab asked softly.

"No. She was married at the time to my stepdad, David. She had no intention of getting back with Kiumars." He closed his eyes for a moment. "But I wanted to see my father. And for me, going back to Iran was actually exciting. I often imagined what my family, my cousins, would be like. I was so alone in Boston. Now I was going to see them all, even my grandparents on Kuimars' side, for the first time. And they were all so wonderful. So different but so nice. They all tried to teach me Farsi. When I stayed on after summer, I went to an international school for kids who were like me. Kids, who had grown up in another country and then moved back to Iran. I waited for my father, and finally in February 1992, he was released. Eleven years after his capture date in February 1981, imagine that! Kiumars came home, and I saw my father for the first time in my life. I was eleven years old. He was twenty-nine."

Mahtab wiped her face, wiping away the wetness that had gathered as he poured his heart out to her.

"I am so sorry. What did you do when you saw him?"

He snorted, "I was shocked! The hero that I had made up in my mind, my brave father? Well, it wasn't him. He was just a thin broken man, sick, bent, and tired. He was so skinny, like a starving refugee on TV. I had gone to school in Boston, telling all my friends that my father was a hero. He had fought in a big war. He was a soldier. I was proud of him, even when my friends thought otherwise. They were angry about the hostages and who could blame them?" He caught his breath and continued, "I loved a father whom I had never seen, never spoken to—an idealized figure, you know. When I saw him, his eyes were tired and there was no light in them. Worst of all, he didn't even seem to know me. Hell, he barely even smiled at me. I was crushed, of course. I didn't want to see that old-looking young man, who was far from the hero, the soldier I had made up in my mind. I even caught myself thinking terrible things. That it would have been better if he had died in the war and my image of him remained the same than seeing him like that, so sick and powerless. After all, he wasn't around for eleven years. All my hopes and wishes were gone. Like a glass that had slipped from my hand and hit the stone floor, shattered and lost. Nothing remained of him now. My imaginary father was gone," he said in a voice that she had never heard before. It was low, husky, filled with sadness.

"I am so sorry for you Ashkan. I didn't know," she said, trying to take it all in.

"It's all right...those days are over now. I eventually accepted him, but I could never call him my father. He too was very distant with me and in a certain way still is. He didn't feel like my dad so I started calling him Kiumars. He came to see me at Grandpa Jamshid's place after a few weeks. He was looking better, but his eyes were still tired and cold. With no love, no real love. He brought me a toy and his hat from the war, but no love..."

He sank back into quietness and then slumped slightly. She sat there as though tied down to that spot. Mahtab so badly wanted to put a hand on him, let her touch comfort him. Not as a girl wanting a boy, but as one human being to another.

"I really feel so bad for you, Ashkan," she said quietly.

"That's OK. I didn't tell you these things so you would feel sorry for me. In fact I didn't mean to tell you anything at all," he said with a wan smile.

"Of all the people I can think of, I would never ever have thought that the war would have affected you and your family, Ashkan," Mahtab said slowly.

Ashkan smiled. "Yes. You would think it would only have affected the religious and the poor who sent sons to the front and took missiles at home. Not a boy in Boston."

Silence fell. Mahtab couldn't say anything. There was very little in her past that could compare to the anguish that he and his seemingly perfect family had suffered.

He threw his head back and continued, looking at the ceiling. "My father suffered a lot in prison, but the worst were the emotional problems. Doctors could do very little with this. Try having a father who would yell and cry at night in his sleep. Or whose day started with a rainbow of medications, which he wouldn't always take. He would smoke all day, sitting by the window and looking outside, without a word to us, to me. I couldn't take it anymore," he said, pausing for a moment, his eyes closed as though recalling a dream. "Anyway, I went back to Boston after Norooz that year. But things were bad there too. My mom's marriage with David was falling apart."

"Oh no, why?"

"He wasn't a one-woman kinda guy. He was abusive and didn't work. My mom had to support him on a yoga instructor's salary. So I went to live with Granma Edna, my mom's mother for a little while. With all these things going on, Grandpa Jamshid came to our rescue. He got us to come to Iran. So we went, leaving behind David, the divorce and the financial disaster he had caused my mom.

"We came back, and to my surprise, Kiumars came to see me. He was much better now. He was working with his father at the bazaar, selling carpets. He was different now. More affectionate. He even hugged me when he saw me. He was living with his parents but asked me to stay with him instead of Grandpa and mom. Yet again I had to choose between him and my mom."

"And?" Mahtab asked, not able to help herself as he caught his breath.

"Well, I chose to live part-time with him and part-time with my mom. I guess it was my back-and-forth going that brought them together. I guess they both were hurt and found solitude in each other, or maybe their old love sparked again. I don't know. But in a small ceremony, they got married a few months later."

Mahtab caught herself smiling. "Oh, that's so sweet. I think they got together because of you."

"Maybe." He smiled and continued, "We stayed in Iran for a year. Then I was sent back to Boston to stay with Grandma Edna. My parents followed a few months later. Then Pardis was born. But things got bad in the States for my dad. He never really adjusted. He would get violent at times. His family blamed it on the imprisonment, on the trauma from being captured. He was the baby of the family, so they were all protective of him when he was in Iran. In the US he was alone most of the time. I was at school; Tina was at work."

He sighed. "Finally, two years later, he returned to Iran. And then my mom followed him. But I stayed on."

He leaned back and said, "So now you know why Pardis and I are so far apart in age."

Mahtab looked at him in the dim light of that room, sitting on the floor next to her. It was all so much to take in. All that pent-up sadness, anger, the reasons for his heartbreak.

"You know, you have the most amazing eyes, Mahtab," he said, smiling at her.

Her heart stopped in mid-beat as he came closer. He then put his hand on her cheek and gently brought her face to his. Then he kissed her. His lips were soft and sweet, so tender. All winter she had wanted him and now here she was kissing him. So close, so real, but so fragile. Like the thin layer of ice crystals on the grass on a cold winter day. It could break with a tip of a finger. So ephemeral. This couldn't last forever.

He finally said, his eyes still lidded with the afterglow of their kiss, "I wanted this for so long. From the moment I saw you in that gallery, I wanted to kiss you."

He kissed her again. When they finally let go, she reached for his wrist and turned it over. "What time is it?"

"Twelve thirty."

"Did you change the time?" she asked, trying to keep down her rising pulse.

"No. Not yet. The daylight saving starts tonight."

"Oh God, so it's actually one thirty in the morning!" She got up. "Where is Nasim? We have to go to her home. If my mom calls and no one is there..."

"Honestly, Mahtab, I don't think Nasim is in any condition to drive. I have a feeling she's going to end up passing out somewhere here tonight."

"Oh God. It's too late for me to get a cab and go home."

"Then don't go," he said, his voice unwavering, his eyes on her. "Stay. We can talk all night. Here." He got up. "I'll lock the door so no one else can bother us."

"If you lock the door, they'll make up stories," she said, pushing back her hair.

"Let them," he said. "Who cares? Do you really think those who make up stories have none of their own?"

"I have to go. I promised my parents I'd go back early in the morning."

"I'll drop you off," he said. His tone told her he wasn't taking no for an answer. "I know the drill. Near enough so you can walk. Far enough so they won't see you in my car. What time you have to be there?"

"Eight o'clock."

"Eight it is." He took his phone out and set the alarm. "Look, we'll wake at seven, OK? Satisfied. Now it's your turn to talk."

Although she was exhausted, Mahtab talked about her job, the upcoming concert, and then her dreams. She corrected his mispronounced words and told him how she had become interested in the violin, about Uncle Nader. It was as if she had known him her entire life, and yet she was telling him everything for the first time.

Finally, when their eyelids could stay open no longer, he got the extra pillow from the bed and lay down on the floor. "You take the bed. I'll sleep down here. Good night, Mahtab."

⁓𝄐

When Mahtab got home the next day, the memory of his kiss sent a thrill through her every time she thought of it. But something nagging came with it now, something that had risen in the morning with the sun. Her conscience.

"Oh God, I kissed him," she said under her breath. It wasn't right. It was a sin. That little voice inside now kept screaming at her. "You know kissing a guy who is not your husband is wrong. You will go to *jahanam,* to hell! He was not *mahram* to you."

On her bed, Mahtab drew her knees to her chest and took a deep breath. It was sin. Kissing a guy who wasn't betrothed to her was wrong in every way. Everyone knew that. It was *haram.* Forbidden. You would go to hell for that. And she was already engaged to Emad. If there was a double hell for that, she was sure she would be there. She sighed. Why did it feel so good, so right then? Did God feel bad for her because she had been ambushed, given to Emad, although she detested him and his family? Because she had tried to tell her father, only to be shoved out of the front door? Because Emad only used her when he needed her? Had he ever asked about her, her fears, her likes? No! But Ashkan had. Why was it wrong to want him then? Especially when it felt so right. It was love. It had to be. And love was good. Love was holy. Therefore, this sin must be holy; Mahtab grinned at her own audacity. She tried to suppress this grin that would not stop as she looked in the mirror on the wall of her room. Why else would Ashkan not have taken advantage of her? In that room on the first night of Norooz, alone together in the dark. Wasn't that the fate of girls who were with unrelated boys? Ashkan could have taken her, and no one would have known. But he had slept on the floor, and shared something far more important, a story from his life instead. The magic of Norooz had worked, and she knew it.

"Mahtab! Mahtab!" It was her mom calling. She got up, stretched her tired body and wrapped her thoughts away.

∽ⱺ

Mahtab was in the kitchen when Pasha came out of his bedroom yawning. He was in his pajamas.

"Where were you last night?" It was the first thing that came out of his mouth.

"At Nasim's house. Maman knows."

"Really?"

"Yes. Do you realize this is my last *eid* spending time with my friend before I get married?"

"Does this Nasim have a boyfriend?"

"No." Mahtab shook her head. "She has a suitor though who wants her so bad. But Nasim doesn't want to leave her mom. But then she is lucky because she gets to choose."

Pasha chuckled, opening and closing the lids of the pots on the stove, searching for something to eat. He said, "Someone needs to beat some sense into her then."

"Maman, look what he said," Mahtab cried.

"It's OK. He didn't say anything bad. He just said she should get married," Maman said as she put the glass of steaming tea in front of the *shazdeh*, his highness. "Do you like her? If you like her Pasha *joon*, we'll go to her *khastegari* for you."

"Hell no! She is a slut. Have you seen the way she dresses? I am sure she is used! Her expiration date has been over for some time," he snickered, sipping his tea.

"Stop it, Pasha. Stop it. She is not like that," Mahtab cried out.

"I think instead of worrying too much about that slut friend of yours, you should think of your own life, your own husband." His cold brown eyes were on her, a furrow between his brows. He had never looked uglier.

"I don't have a husband." Mahtab looked at her mother, who stared at them, her knuckles white around the handle of the spoon she was stirring with.

"You do! His name is Emad," Pasha barked.

"Is his name on my birth certificate?" Mahtab yelled. "He can call himself my husband the day his name is on there. Till then..."

"Stop it, please," Maman begged. "Yes, he is her husband. Of course he is, Pasha. *Bebin*, I made *ghorme sabzi* for lunch. Mahtab, call Emad to join us."

"I won't. I want to eat my lunch in peace."

"I'll call him then," Pasha said. "He said he wants to discuss a very important issue with us."

Mahtab felt the hair behind her neck stand up. What issue? Had Emad found out about last night? Had he followed them, spied on them? Oh God, he had, and he was going to kill her.

Twenty-Two

Mahtab's heart hammered in her chest as everyone gathered in the living room after lunch for Emad to make his speech. If this was about last night, well, there would be little left of her after they were done with her. Silence fell over the room as Emad cleared his throat and started. "Boji *jan*, Mr. Sharifi, Mrs. Monir, you don't know how flattered I am that you have accepted me as your son-in-law," Emad said, placing his right hand to his chest and bowing.

"And we are so lucky to have you as our son-in-law. Please eat something," Baba said pushing the fruit dish toward him.

"Thank you," Emad said, before looking at Mahtab. His eyes were inscrutable now, save showing that she was his intended target. "Mahtab, I only want to mention this in front of your family because I think they should know too. And I want to know their opinion." He paused before continuing, "Mahtab, I know you like your job and making money gives you a sense of independence, but I really don't want my future wife to work. Especially in this"—his upper lip curved up—"this music entertainment thing. You are with unrelated men. It's not right. I don't like that. Actually, it boils my blood to think of it."

Thank God. Mahtab breathed. It was not about last night, about the party, about Ashkan. Buoyed by the release of pent-up tension, she jumped up and cried.

"This is stupid, Emad. I teach little children."

"Yes, but what about the other teachers? Are they all women?" he said, his tone as innocent as a child's.

Before she could answer, Boji began, "He is right. If a husband is not happy with a wife who works, the money that she makes is *haram*, cursed, and she has to pay it as *kaffareh*, money to the poor,"

"Allow me, *Modar jan*," Baba cut in, nodding to Boji. "We understand. We are not happy with Mahtab being a musician either. She could have chosen other careers, like my brother's children, but anyway…what is done is done," he sighed.

"Baba *yani chee*, what does this mean?" Mahtab spoke. "Who is he to order me like that? I'm not even his wife yet!"

"Shut up," Pasha interjected.

"He is your husband. He has a right to tell you what to do," Boji said, shaking her head as Mahtab got up to leave.

"Sit down!" her father yelled. "And close that mouth of yours."

"That's not the only thing I have an issue with." Emad went on completely ignoring Mahtab. "She spends an awful a lot of time with her friend Nasim, when she could be spending it with my family and me. See, Mr. Sharifi, when my older brother got engaged, his fiancé literally moved in with my mom. She just didn't spend the nights, but she was there any time we needed her help. Like now, my mother has this *jalaseh* coming up soon. I have told Mahtab many times that she should help, but she doesn't take me seriously."

Mahtab looked at him in disgust and cried. "What the hell? It's none of my business to slave around for something so stupid. A whole bunch of women getting together to waste their time. Why should I work for it?"

"Shut up, Mahtab!" her mother, brother, father, and Boji all said in unison.

But Emad kept his calm. "I call at seven o'clock, you don't answer your phone. So then I text; then an hour later you text back, and you say you are still at work or you are with Nasim. Why are you avoiding me all the time?"

"Maybe if you had half a brain, you would know that I don't like you at all. I don't like to spend time with…"

The last word hadn't left her mouth when she felt the crack. Only a second after the force threw her head back, she felt the pain, the sting across her face as her ears began to ring. She looked to see Pasha's hand raised, his face crimson, a mask of rage. Something ran into her mouth, warm with the taste of salt and iron. The tissue she raised to her mouth returned a bright red stain on the white paper.

"It's OK," Emad said calmly. Not an inch of him seemed disturbed by the sight of her blood. "I didn't come here to fight. I am here to discuss Mahtab's work and her spending time with her friend."

"Your tea must be cold. Allow me to change it," Maman said leaning forward to grab his tea cup. She seemed to be cringing, her eyes away from the scene.

"No. It's good. I like it this way. I don't want to burn my esophagus."

He then sipped his tea slowly and said, "I want two things from you." He looked at Mahtab, her hand holding a napkin to her swollen lip.

"One, stop working. I don't know about now, but after you are married to me, you won't need any money. I will provide for you. Two, spend less time with your friend. Reduce it to maybe once or twice a month. Instead spend time with my family and me. Be a good daughter-in-law. Show my mother that you like her." He looked at Monir and then at Rasool meaningfully before continuing. "Call her every day and ask about her health. Go shopping with her. Help her; learn from her. You are no longer single. You need to take your responsibilities seriously."

"We'll talk to her," Baba said through clenched teeth.

"One more thing that I'd like to discuss, Mr. Sharifi. Mahtab and I have been engaged for a few months now. My family doesn't think a long engagement is a good idea," he said, looking at Mahtab and then at her father. "You know how it is. People will start talking behind our back. It's bad for my family's reputation. Our apartment is ready. We need to get moving with the *jahaz*."

"Her *jahaz* is almost ready," Maman said hurriedly. "Only a few items left to get."

"What's left?" Emad asked.

Maman hesitated and looked at Baba before answering, "The refrigerator, the stove, the washer and…"

"Here," he said, reaching down into his starched yellow shirt pocket. A white checkbook appeared in his hand.

Mahtab saw Baba's eyes widen in horror. "No, no, *Aslan*! Never, Emad *jan*."

Emad shook his head and smiled. "No, Mr. Sharifi, think of this as a loan. You can pay me back later. We all want to make this marriage come together. As soon as possible but with the way things look now, it will take forever…my parents accepted a longer engagement so you could get the jahaz ready but…"

Emad was insulting her father in this very room with everyone around him. Mahtab looked at her father and then at Maman. Nothing. Baba was silent, looking down at the fraying carpet below. Maman was looking at him, her face drawn. A bubble of rage welled up within Mahtab. Whatever her father had done to her, said to her, it still didn't make that right. Emad had no business insulting him. Insulting her family.

"Will you at least be ready by Emam Hasan Askari's birthday," Emad said, picking a tooth with his finger. "My father thinks this would be an auspicious day to have the wedding."

"That soon?" Maman asked.

"It's not that soon. It's about a month from now."

"Yes, we will. Don't worry yourself, *pesaram*. Please," Baba said, running a hand through his hair, his voice pleading.

Emad smiled that smile of his, before he reached out for a baby cucumber on the plate beside him.

Although the conversation drifted to other things, Mahtab could not help notice that the white rectangular piece of paper, that ugly check of Emad's, sat in front of his plate for all to see.

When Emad got up to leave, Mahtab said, "I'll walk you to the door."

He then turned toward the room, threw his palm across his chest, and bowed to everyone before heading out.

In the alcove outside the front door, Emad reached down to tie his shoes.

"Emad."

"Yes." He didn't look up at her.

"If you loved me, you wouldn't let Pasha hit me like that."

He kept looking down before finally answering, "Honestly, Mahtab, I think you deserved it. You are so difficult. You don't even listen to your own father!"

She closed the door after him, and her hand went to her lip. She drew her hand back sharply. It ached, even more than before, especially in the silence. Then the voices from the sitting room reached her ears.

"How are we going to buy all that *jahaz*? In three weeks?" her mother said. "How much did he give you?"

Mahtab let out her breath silently. So her father had taken the money after all. So much for family honor. Baba mumbled something in a low monotone.

"That won't even cover the kitchen set." Maman's voice had reached a falsetto now.

"We'll borrow," Baba said from what seemed like his throat. "We'll borrow from my sister and your brother. We are going to send her off, and then we'll be done with it."

"At least let her work until the wedding date so she can make some money for the *jahaz*."

"Didn't you hear what he said? He said he doesn't want her to work." It was Pasha.

"He doesn't have to know," Maman replied.

"Three weeks won't change anything," her father said finally.

"I wish you didn't take that check. They are going to put it on her head for the rest of her life. That they gave money for her own *jahaz*," Maman said sighing.

"No he won't. He is a good guy. He has good character," Baba said, reassuring her. How naive of him.

Mahtab walked into the sitting room at that moment. Maman and Baba were sitting on the main couch. Pasha was on love seat, and Boji next to him shelling pistachios noisily on a white cloth on her lap.

"Shame on you, Mahtab!" Boji cried.

"Yes, have you no shame?" Baba picked up where Boji left off. "Why did you talk to him like that?"

"You should be so grateful that he wants to marry you," Boji chimed in, her hands still shelling. "If I were in his position, I would have called off the engagement long ago. I wouldn't want to be the husband of such a shrew!"

"You mean the husband that I didn't want to begin with!" Mahtab said, recoiling from the shock of her own explosion. "Why don't you get it? I don't need a man to define myself. To be complete. I have so much to do in my life already."

She stepped back. Pasha was up now and everything flew out of her mind. Only survival remained. Dashing down the corridor, she dodged Pasha and slammed her door shut, drawing the deadbolt home.

∽᥈

It was the last day of the Norooz holidays and Mahtab was lying on her bed, listening to music, when her mother barged into her room. "Mahtab?"

"*Baleh* Maman?"

"What are you doing?"

"*Heechee*. Nothing. Just sitting here waiting for you all to decide my life for me."

"How much do you have?"

Mahtab stared at her. What was she saying? "What do you mean?"

"Money, how much do you have saved away?"

"I always give you whatever I make."

"In your savings account, under the pillow. Come on, you must have a few thousand toman tucked away somewhere." Her mother's eyes were on her now, searching her face.

"I don't. Do you want me to sell my kidney to get you some?"

"Don't start again," Maman sighed and dropped her shoulders. "I'll have to sell some gold. Maybe barter the carpet in the living room for the *jahaz*."

"Maman, you can't possibly be serious. I'm not going to marry him. Don't get yourself worked up!"

"*Khafe sho dige*. Enough!" Maman cried.

The one thing about Maman was that Mahtab could at least yell at her, argue with her without the certain fear of a beating. And today Mahtab felt like screaming. Taking it out on someone. Even though she knew her mother was just like her, a servant in her own home.

"Maman, I want to marry for love."

"Love?" Maman asked dryly. "Mahtab, open your eyes! Nowadays no one falls in love. No, I take that back. They fall in love with paper and metal. Money and cars. Rich boys marry rich girls. Maybe there was a time when a boy fell in love with the girl herself. But that time is gone. Now they measure how much she is worth by how many houses and how much land her father has!"

"But I don't care about money. I just want to be happy," Mahtab said.

"Think!" her mother said, pointing to Mahtab's head. "You say that now. Wait till you have to carry your belongings on your shoulders every six months looking for a new house to rent. Like what I did. When I married your father, he had nothing. Every six months we were moving to a new home. Because every time they raised the rent, every time the prices went up, we couldn't afford it. So each time we moved a little more south, to a slightly cheaper place. A little smaller, a little dirtier," she said the last sentence almost in a whisper as she rubbed her eyes.

"First it was war, then it was the inflation; I had a baby, a husband still in college, and our only income was from his weekend tutoring, which was next to zero. It was terrible. Some days I could not afford milk for you both."

"Oh, Maman. I die for you, what you had to put up with." Mahtab tried to hug her mother. But Monir quickly wiped her tears and gained her voice back. "Think, Mahtab, this guy is financially stable. I know I am repeating myself, but I am going to say it till it goes into your head."

Mahtab said nothing. She felt spent, so tired. What was the use of saying anything?

"I talked to your father." Maman looked at her now. "You can work till the end. So you can make some money for your *jahaz*."

Mahtab ignored the buzzing from the table beside her bed.

"Aren't you going to answer it?"

"What?"

"That's your phone ringing," Monir said, leaning in. "Take it. It's rude to let it go unanswered."

The voice on the other side was perfunctory, speaking before she could get a word in.

"Mahtab, I made an appointment for the tests on Monday. It's two days from now, but that's the best those stupid fools at the department could give me. We need to have the paperwork before the actual *aghd* ceremony."

"You know I won't pass. I have a disease," she smirked, glancing at her mother.

"Shut up," her mother said in the background, slapping her cheek. "He'll think you are serious."

Mahtab grinned and gestured for her mother to leave.

"Ha-ha, you are so funny," Emad said. "How could you have a disease when you are a virgin? Which if my family didn't need the cloth bloodied on our wedding night, you wouldn't be by now."

"No doubt about it…" She laughed dryly.

"I've got to go now." He cut her off. "I'll pick you up then."

Twenty-Three

"I've missed you," Ashkan said the moment Mahtab got into his car. "Two weeks was hard, way too hard not seeing you."

"I couldn't get out before," she replied, still trying to believe that she was here, with him, that same fragrance of leather and scent around her now.

"I know. But you are here now. That's what matters." Before he had finished talking, she felt his hand on hers, muscular and warm.

They headed north. It was midmorning of the first day after the Norooz holidays, and traffic was light. They drove past the new concrete bridges, their pillars sticking up like giant jagged teeth, and up the highway until it broke into a head of smaller roads at the foothills of the Alborz Mountains. It was a glorious April day, the sun still incandescent in the sky. The mulberry trees on either side of the street were blooming, and the city looked cleansed, beautiful, reborn. She felt the cool air of the Alborz Mountains touching her skin. Strangely it warmed her heart. The sweet smell of mulberry blossoms and the fresh cut grass. The feel of spring. The irresistible sense of feeling like fourteen again. Falling in love for the first time.

Mahtab felt good that she had called into work and got the day off. Actually, she hadn't worked at the Nava Music Institute for the last three weeks. One more day wouldn't hurt, she thought especially since she left home this morning with everyone thinking she had gone to work.

Ashkan slowed into a cul-de-sac, and she saw a magnificent cream building with wrought iron-enclosed balconies.

They entered the three-level underground parking garage, and Ashkan
pulled into the first parking space. The sign on the wall said *reserved*. He
swiped a card, and they walked the steps to the courtyard through the steel
door near his car. In the little patch inside the courtyard, red and yellow
tulips grew.

"This is beautiful," Mahtab said, looking up at the high-rise. It was at
least fifteen stories high. "Did you really make this yourself?"

He laughed. "It's not like I threw the bricks up one brick at the time.
But, yes, I planned and executed it myself."

"Where did you get the money to invest?" She hated herself for asking,
but she had to. This was a multi *milyard* toman building after all, at least a
few million dollars.

"My Grandpa Jamshid."

In the elevator, Ashkan put his key in a blue slot and pressed number
fifteen.

"Why the key?" she asked.

"You'll see."

The elevator opened onto a hallway, but it was nothing like anything
she had ever seen before, not even at Sepehr's. This was a private hallway,
richly carpeted, directly leading into an apartment with rooms lit by sunlight streaming in from large rectangular windows. Recessed lamps lit the
hallway, and the inside smelled of fresh paint and varnish.

"*Cheh ghashangeh*! So beautiful!" she said, looking around in awe.

"Do you like it?" Ashkan asked, looking at her, a hand rubbing the back
of his neck. "I haven't had a chance to put in much furniture yet."

"This is the most beautiful place I have ever seen."

She wasn't exaggerating. It was beautiful, like something out of a
European magazine. But empty, except for a couple of folding chairs; a small
plastic table in the living room; and two black things shaped like boomer-
angs that ran to a squat black box beneath the large flat screen TV. No furniture, but his PlayStation looked ready for action.

On the opposite wall hung a flag, more like a pennant, navy blue. On it
were two red socks with the words "Red Sox" next to them.

Ashkan nodded and smiled, following her gaze.

"That's my team, the Boston Red Sox. They are a great baseball team. The best in the States actually!" Ashkan said with a laugh.

Best team or not, Mahtab knew the meaning of that name from somewhere, perhaps her English class in school. That was it! *Jurab*, what you wear on your feet!

"They name a team after socks?" Mahtab asked.

A moment of confusion passed over his face before he said. "Well, it's better than naming a team *rah-ahan*, a railroad, like you guys have! Anyway, that's beside the point. They are awesome, and one day I'll take you to a game at the ballpark!"

Outside the huge tinted windows was a large stepped balcony with a small rectangular swimming pool, glistening aquamarine in the sun. It was actually filled with water, unlike most private pools in the city that had been drained after the revolution. In the distance a familiar pencil-thin form crowned by a scintillating orb rose from the orange-tinted sprawl. The Borj-e-Milad, the television tower that dominated the Tehran skyline, was shiny, new, almost out of place in the sea of gray and brown buildings that stood around it.

They walked upstairs, a set of French double doors opening into the oversized master bedroom with a walk-in closet and a Jacuzzi. A shower room with glass walls that could hold at least three people was in the corner, next to two stainless steel bowl sinks with matching brushed metal faucets hanging over them like swan necks over water.

"Where did you get all of these things, Ashkan?" Mahtab asked, running her hand over the door handle.

"Here in good old Tehran. Yeah, I was surprised too! You can find everything here. I wanted this house to be the most perfect home I could design." He smiled, shrugging his shoulders. "I figured while I am living in Iran, something should make up for it!"

"Living in Iran is not a sacrifice, Ashkan! It's an honor." Her voice trembled as she left the bathroom. He and his *farangi* attitude!

"Mahtab, please understand. I really have no attachment to this country."

"I know you don't. You are a stranger to this country, this culture, and these people. But there is more to this city than what you know. So don't disrespect it."

He looked at her, his eyes thoughtful. "I didn't mean to offend you."

Mahtab looked away, to a window near her. Beyond it the city skyline shimmered in the daylight, ringed by the Alborz Mountains, bald except for the dusting of snow on their peaks.

"Ashkan let me show you Tehran. The real Tehran!" Mahtab said, keeping her calm.

He laughed. "What's there to see? The pollution? The oppression? The women forced to wear scarves in summer till they faint in the heat? Which one do you want to show me? I mean, I can't even buy a drink here without the fear that if I'm caught, I'd be lashed!"

She wheeled away and faced the wall. "If Iran, if Tehran is so bad, then what the hell are you doing here? Ha?"

"Well, the truth is I really missed my family, my mom."

Turning around, she saw him look away. She sighed. Maybe she was being too hard on him. It had to be difficult for him, adjusting here in Iran. Having grown up so far away, in almost a different world in *Amrika* with its Christmas, its Red Sox, and its movies. Having grown up without even knowing Farsi properly. And after what he had told her at Sepehr's parents' house about his mother, his father, the war, and the separation, how could she expect him to have any happy memories from here?

"Ashkan, listen. There is more than that. You know, even you are a product of Tehran."

"How so?" he said, looking a little confused.

"You told me your mom got pregnant when she was visiting your dad here, remember?" she said, her eyes not leaving his.

Ashkan chuckled.

"See? So just give me your hand and come with me. I'll show you places you have never seen. Good places. Remember Norooz? That was beautiful, *na?*"

"Can I trust you?" he said raising his eyebrows.

"Of course," she said, smiling and giving his arm a punch. It was like punching a rock. "Of course you can trust me, and you won't be disappointed."

He smiled and said, "Well, I'll trust you if you trust me."

"I wouldn't be here if I didn't trust you," she said, smiling. "For a start, you should come to my concert. It's next month."

"I can't wait."

"I'll get you a free ticket then."

"Have a seat," Ashkan said, pointing to the bed.

He dropped down beside her, making the bed bounce. She stole a glance at him, and their eyes met. Then she looked away, shyness getting the better of her.

She felt his hand on her shoulder. He smiled, the full intensity of his green-gold eyes on her as his hand began to move up and down. He leaned forward and placed his lips on hers, his scent, leather and musk, flooding her. His kisses were soft and warm, gentle at first but growing more powerful, more wanting. When they separated, he stared, his eyes wide, a half smile on his face.

"Oh, I almost forgot." He shoved his right hand in his jeans pocket and drew out something small and silvery. Mahtab gasped. It was a chain on which hung a pendant. The shape was instantly recognizable. Recognizable from the time Mahtab had first laid eyes on a music score. That of a G clef, looped on itself in white gold, dangling before her.

"Your Norooz gift."

"No. It's too much," she said, trying to settle the storm within her.

"For you nothing is too much."

He raised his hands, the chain dangling between them like shimmering moonlight.

She pulled her hair up so he could fasten the chain around her neck. She could feel his hands lightly touching her as he worked the clip, leaving a delicious tingling behind. She put her hand on the pendant. The metal was cool yet seemed alive in her hand. Without saying a word, she leaned forward and kissed him. They kissed and kissed until their breathing got faster, heavier. He gently pushed her down. She felt his hand move toward her belly and then under her tank top. She did nothing, her desire overruling her limits. Then they were around her breasts. Instinctively her hands held his and pushed them away.

Something in her mind kept crying out in the background. A voice she hadn't heard since the day of her first kiss. Something that she strained to hear. He relented but then began kissing her neck, his lips, warm and soft, down toward her chest. Then he was above her, whispering in her ear, his breath hot, urgent.

"You are so beautiful, Mahtab."

It was the most wonderful thing she had ever heard. Then the fear that had built up beneath the fire within her rose as he yanked off his T-shirt and threw it across the room. Revealing his broad chest. His perfect six pack. He got her orange tank top and pulled it down. Leaving only her strapless black bra on. There it was; she could hear that voice now, thunderous, deafeningly clear. No, this is wrong. This is wrong. This is against God. And with it came a bubble of naked fear, like someone sinking into deep water, seeing the light fade above. She tried to push him away, but he didn't stop. Her bra was off now, only her hands between her and him.

Ashkan looked at her confused. "Why? What's wrong?"

"No," she said.

"I thought you were OK with this."

"No," she said again, trying to get up with her hands still around her chest. "I don't want you to see me naked."

"Why not? We like each other, for God's sake," Ashkan said staring at her.

"We are not husband and wife yet," Mahtab said, her eyes on his.

"So?"

"We are not married! It's not right to be this close. It's a sin, Ashkan, as clearly as it is written in the Koran."

"You are something, Mahtab." Ashkan shook his head and blew out a long breath. "Fine. Just let me kiss you then," he said, leaning in before slowly kissing her lips. Then he went down her neck. Mahtab felt her body melting under his soft kisses. Their breaths were now heavy, rhythmic. Then he was looking at her in surprise, at her hands now pushing against his chest. Mahtab sat up, her back pressed against the wooden bed frame, and looked away.

"Look," he said, running a hand through his dark brown hair, "Don't worry. I don't want to do anything that you don't want to."

Mahtab tried to pull her tank top up. He put his hand on hers and smiled. "Not everything, I guess. Leave it off. You need to get used to being naked around me." Then he laughed and shook his head.

"What Ashkan? What's so funny?" she said, her arms folded across her chest.

"You are mentally and physically a virgin, Mahtab. That's what. And don't you deny it!" he said, lying down next to her, crossing his arms under his head, staring at the ceiling. "This is a beautiful part of life between a man and woman. Between two lovers!"

"Yes, but only if they are married. Then it means everything. Otherwise, it is only sin."

He chuckled. "You're too cute. I have never met a girl like you. Never. That guy, your fiancé, has he never wanted to kiss you or do anything with you?"

Mahtab swallowed and saw his eyes grow wide, his lips part in realization.

"Don't tell me you haven't done anything. You must have kissed him. He must have…"

"Stop it. I don't want to talk about it," Mahtab said, trying to get up.

"What? You're not married to him either."

"That's different. I am to be married to him. We are *sigheh* to each other."

"Oh yes, of course, I forgot. You are in a pretend marriage with him, so he gets to do whatever he wants with you. Even if you hate him, he still gets to. But I don't. Honestly, Mahtab, *dokhtari*? Are you a virgin? Or is this all just an act?"

"What do you think? I am an Iranian girl with honor. I don't go sleep with guys before my wedding night."

"Oh yeah? All the Iranian girls I've met here are quite OK with sleeping with guys before their wedding night. Well, just look at your friend Nasim, for instance!"

"They are different. My family is different. Don't bring Nasim into this. She only lost her virginity to Sepehr."

"Yeah, I know about that," he said sullenly.

"How old were you when you first had sex?"

"Sixteen," Ashkan said without missing a beat.

"Sixteen," Mahtab repeated. That was twelve years ago. He had already experienced a whole different life before her, and not with just one girl. How many, she wondered?

"Mahtab," he said, tearing her apart from her thoughts.

"What?" she snapped.

"Look, I respect your decision of wanting to wait until your wedding night. I'll wait, OK?" His voice had lost its edge, the frustration it had had a couple of minutes ago.

"You'll wait?" She raised an eyebrow at him.

"Yes, I'll wait for you." He sighed. "I mean you never know, we might get married, right?"

"Right." She smiled. The possibility of him and her seemed so far away. Far away, even if she was with him right now. Just like the world he had shown her, so far from her own.

From the corner of her eye, she saw him shift toward her, felt his arms around her, pulling her down onto the pillow-soft bed until they both sank down, cupped together, Ashkan's body pressed behind her. She looked back to see him gazing at her, a hand propping up his head, his eyes shining. "Trust me. I promise," he whispered as his fingers began to play with her nipples, making them stand up on end. He then slowly moved his hand toward her jeans, and she felt the button unhook, then the zip fly open in one smooth motion. Everything in her was alive, tingling, her senses as taut as the horsehair of her violin's bow. His hand slid inside and went down farther. Mahtab opened her mouth to say something, anything, but Ashkan beat her to it.

"Shhh. Just enjoy," he whispered as he played with her silky wet body, playing with her until Mahtab forgot everything. Until she tasted the forbidden fruit.

That night, at home, after a long shower, Mahtab sat on her bed. She could feel the water dripping from her hair onto the purple towel around her shoulders. The beautiful necklace that he had given her shone around her neck. She held the silver plate from Esfehan. Her name, beautifully engraved in the center of the plate, sat surrounded by peacocks of various metallic hues interspersed between flowers, chased into the plate by hand. Mahtab turned it around, saw his name, and then hugged it to her chest. His name. It was incredible. Everything that had happened between her and Ashkan. Even she wouldn't have believed it, any of it, if she didn't have the plate in her hand or the necklace around her neck. She carefully put the plate into a shoebox and hid it deep inside her closet. Then the necklace followed, into another recess. The walls of her room, the same walls that had surrounded her for years, again seemed to close in around her. As though the magic, the protection of his gifts, of Ashkan by proxy, had gone with their stowage. She was back in her world now, she realized, the world of her upcoming wedding, her family, and Emad.

Twenty-Four

Monday morning brought the appointment for the government mandated premarital tests and classes.

"Everything is set," Emad said once they were on the road. "My father has booked the *salon*; the owner is my uncle, did you know? He gave us the date we wanted. The cards are ready too. We'll give you about fifty for your guests. We are paying for it, so I'll keep the rest."

Mahtab looked outside. In the background she could hear Emad droning on.

"Mahtab, Mahtab." He was shaking her left arm now.

"What?" she snapped at him. "What do you want?"

"Are you listening to me?"

"Yes. No...what did you say?" she finally said.

"I said my mom wants to see you in the wedding dress today," he said slowly, his eyes still on her.

"Sure," she said looking away.

◌

It was best not to mention Emad, Mahtab thought as she knocked on Mr. Javadi's door the next day. She couldn't even tell her friends at the institute that she was engaged. How would she explain that she was forced into it? They were different, her friends at the music institute. Almost all had family money or they wouldn't be there in the first place. Who could live on the paltry salary from the school in these times when the bus fare itself ate up a good amount each day? Only her. With her friends though, the affluence and family support came with something else: openness. Progressive families that thought arranged marriages were for *dahatis*, uneducated people from the country. Mahtab could almost hear them gossip behind her back, shaking their heads. "Did you hear about Mahtab? Poor girl. Nowadays no one forces girls into an unwanted marriage. That's barbaric!"

Best not to mention the fiancé, she decided. So it would have to be a lie then.

"Good morning," Mahtab said as she pushed open the door.

"Well, well, look who is here. Who wants to brighten my morning?" Kamran said, removing his glasses and placing them on the table.

Mahtab smiled back. She knew Kamran too well, and his innocent flirting was no surprise to her.

"What can I do for you?"

"I have bad news for you."

"Oh no. What's wrong? You are not leaving us, are you?" he said, sitting up.

"Not quite, but I can't work after two o'clock anymore."

"*Chera*? Why? Did you get a better job?"

"If you think looking after a sick grandma who can't even hold her pee in is a better job, then yes," she said, trying to sound sincere.

"What happened? What's wrong with Grandma?" Kamran's face had fallen, and she felt a twinge of regret. It was such a silly lie.

"She had a stroke over the Norooz holidays, and we just brought her home from the hospital. My mom can't take care of her alone. Till we find a proper nurse, I need to help."

"And when would that be?" Kamran said, flipping open the calendar sitting on his desk.

"I don't know. We are still waiting for the *behzisti*, the government health insurance, to approve her case. The office said it would take a few months."

"Hmm!" he said, biting on the end of his pen. "I can't do this to your students, especially those who have asked for you. You know you have a waiting list."

"Yes, I know," Mahtab said. She didn't have to try to look sorry now. She felt terrible. The way she was letting Kamran down, not to mention the kids she was teaching. But what could she do? She cleared her throat and said, "But my grandma is very sick. I really have to do this."

"OK, let me see what I can do for you. You'll have to come in early then," he said, thumbing through his calendar, pencil in mouth. After a few minutes, he looked up.

"All right, can you come at eight instead of ten in the morning? For the orf classes?"

"Orf?! The preschoolers? You want me to lead an orf class?"

"Yes, that's all I have. At least you'll get some hours though. I'll switch your hours with Sima."

She thought for a moment and then drew in her breath. "Thanks Mr. Javadi. I really do appreciate it."

"You're welcome. God give her health back to her," he called out as she left the room.

Mahtab sighed as she entered her classroom. Orf meant dealing with preschoolers. Teaching them the ABCs of music. She had done it before when she was in college—as a college student earning extra pocket money, not a graduate teacher. She exhaled and rubbed her eyes. The honest truth was she had no idea what was she doing anymore. Perhaps she was waiting for a miracle. But that miracle was nowhere to be found.

⁓↺

When Mahtab got home that afternoon, she heard her mother on the phone. The way she spoke, from her polite but effusive tittering to her apologies for everything, she immediately guessed it was Emad's mother.

"Sure, sure. Thank you so much for your understanding. Yes, it's almost ready. No, no, please don't. No, she too will have it. It is all ready, just the big items. *Chashm.* Thursday it is."

Mahtab got a glass of water, and the moment her mother put down the phone, she asked, "What is the *deev* demanding this time?"

"Stop being rude. She is your mother-in-law. Don't call her a monster. She has the *jalaseh*, the religious ceremony, on Thursday and wanted to know if your *jahaz* is ready so her guests can see it after the ceremony," Monir said reproachfully, a hurt expression on her face.

215

"Do they want me to wear dancing clothes and belly dance for them too?"

"Shut up. *Khejelat bekesh!* Shame on you!"

Mahtab went to her room. It was a beautiful spring day; Mahtab felt like getting her violin and playing, but in truth, the coming of spring, with its bright days, had brought no warmth to Mahtab's life. It had been a week since she had been with Ashkan, but it felt so much longer. It all seemed so distant now. Ashkan had gone to Shiraz, and at home things were no better. At home Baba was staying out later, pulling more shifts. On the rare occasion that he was actually home, he was calling everyone he knew to borrow money for the wedding. Maman, Pasha, Boji, the entire family was constantly talking, laughing, crying, and running around for the upcoming wedding, her wedding. She felt like the lone girl in a movie who sat crying while everyone else danced on.

༄

It was three in the afternoon that Wednesday, and Mahtab's rehearsal practice with Ostad Amini at the Tehran University was just two hours away. And with traffic, it would be at least an hour getting there on the bus. She walked to the kitchen and back three times before finally asking, "Maman, Mr. Javadi couldn't find a substitute for today's students."

"No, Mahtab, you know what Emad said," Maman said, shaking her head.

"Maman, I'll be home by eight. Please let me go. I've worked there for four years. It's not right. If Emad shows up, tell him I have gone to buy *jahaz* with Aunt Mina. I'll try to answer his calls so he won't get suspicious."

"What about your father? Pasha?"

"Oh, Maman, make up a lie. Tell them the same thing. I'll call Aunt Mina and ask her to lie for me. Please, just this one time."

"I don't know what to say, Mahtab. I wish you just would listen and be a good girl. There is so much to do here."

"What am I doing, Maman? I cut my hours in half. I am teaching orf now. Do you understand that I have gone backward? Orf is for college students to teach, not me. Please, Maman. This is only a one-time thing."

༄

"*Bache ha.* Good news. Good news," Ostad Amini said, clapping his hands as he walked on stage. He leaned over, his white silvery beard quivering, as he paused for effect.

"We got the date. The university confirmed it," he said, and the whole ensemble burst out clapping.

"Congratulations," someone yelled out.

"Yes, yes. That means we are now official. It's fixed for mid-Ordibehesht, early May. Three nights. Put it in your heads now." He smiled and wagged a finger.

"I don't want any excuses later on. I don't care if your Aunt Kokab is sick or about to give birth, or if you have a fever. You'll be on stage those three nights whatever happens. Tell your family and friends to come too."

Taraneh raised her hand. "Ostad?"

"Yes? Is your aunt Kokab sick?"

"No." She laughed, her face turning pink. "Do we get free tickets?"

Ostad laughed. "Why is it with my students that they are always looking for free tickets? Yes, of course. You get four free tickets, and you can choose the night. Any other questions?"

Mahtab raised her hand.

"Yes, Mahtab? You want to get a free ticket for your Aunt Kokab?"

Mahtab suppressed a laugh. "No. Are you going to advertise? Would our names be published?"

"TV, radio, fliers, Facebook...what's the other one, with the blue bird?"

A guy said, "Twitter."

"Yes that, CNN, Fars News, Al Jazeera, you name it. We need to make sure people will know. No, Mahtab, your name will not be published till the performance night. Don't worry, no guys will find out about you."

"What about Aunt Kokab?" said the guy who played the flute.

"Yes, bring her too!" Ostad said and everyone laughed.

"All right, if there are no further questions, let us begin our practice. People, to your places, please," Ostad Amini said with a wave of his hand, taking his place at the conductor's podium. The buzz in the auditorium fell.

⌒◦

It was almost eight when Mahtab finally stepped outside into the busy street. It was drizzling outside, which meant going back home was going to be hell. She sat at the bus station, looking at the cars sliding by, the lights reflecting off the wet asphalt. People walked by, umbrellas in hand. The city seemed to hum on even in the rain, only slower but not stopped. If only time could be slowed for her; she sighed as she settled down on the plastic blue seat in the bus station. Her wedding day was next week. She still had not tried on her wedding dress, and tomorrow was the much-anticipated *jalaseh*. Tomorrow also was the day that her parents were supposed to have her *jahaz* ready.

How happy she had been this evening. The news that the concert would indeed take place after the difficulties Ostad Amini had in securing the hall. The fact that she would finally be playing in a real concert. That her fellow musicians, some friends from before and others just names on paper in the beginning, were now together in body and spirit, playing as one for one cause. To help those street kids who couldn't help themselves. To use their music and passion for a good cause.

How happy she was to be away from her home, from Emad, from it all. At that moment, it hit her: the profound loss that would come to her life with Emad. She buried her face in her hands. There lay two simple choices before her, each worse than the other. Either run away into utter uncertainty, or go home and face the unthinkable. She sat up, grabbing a strand of hair in her fingers and twisted it until it finally broke. She felt so tired, as though drained of all her energy. Yes, in the end, it was her life she was talking about. And it was better to live in uncertainty as a *farari* than face the certainty of life under Emad's heel. The bus roared and then hissed as it arrived in front of the station.

$$\backsim\!\!\mathcal{O}$$

It was well past nine when Mahtab got home. Her mother was in the living room, kneeling over, her head on the floor. *Namaz* time. Mahtab tried to close the door behind her as quietly as possible.

"Good, Mahtab, you are home. Did you find the blender or not?" Maman said hurriedly, getting up and tilting her head slightly to the left. Left, toward the direction of the corridor.

"Did your aunt drop you off and just leave?" Boji's face appeared in the corridor. She must have been napping for her eyes were the red of sleep and her scarf looked barely pulled over.

This was not what Mahtab needed right now. Another Boji interrogation.

Before she could answer, Boji said, shaking her head, "It's just like your aunt. She should have at least come up to pay her respects."

"What's going on?" Mahtab asked. The living room was a mess, boxes and things strewn everywhere.

"Pasha and your father are taking your *jahaz* over tonight so it'll be ready for tomorrow. Poor guys, out in this rain. They haven't had dinner yet. When they come back, thank them properly. They are doing it for you," Monir said, the *tasbih* still in her hand.

She would thank them all right, Mahtab thought as she opened the door to her room. And screamed.

"Maman!!"

"*Cheteh?* What?"

"What have you done?" she cried, running around her room.

"I sent some of your things to your new home. Boji helped me pack," Maman said brightly. "Your dad had hired a *vanet*, a truck. I thought it best to send some of the stuff you didn't need any more with them. That'll save time and money."

Mixed feelings of rage and fatigue rippled through Mahtab as she looked at the emptied drawers. There was nothing she could do to change what had happened.

"My stuff, Maman, it was my stuff," she said weakly, settling on the floor, a hand on her forehead. "You shouldn't have touched it."

૮૭

That night she lay awake, her mind spinning wildly. After everything— after the ambush when Emad's family came to the *khastegari*, her father's threats, even Emad's "needs" as he called it—nothing hit home like the emptiness of her room. The emptiness of her shelves, the missing clothes, even her framed diploma, shouted that this was really happening. That, with certainty, she was getting married to Emad and going to his home. Unless she did something, that is. Something she had always been afraid to do, something she pushed away every time it sidled into her mind. Until now. She would no longer wait for a miracle. She would call Nasim and tell her she was going to run.

Twenty-Five

The house was empty when Mahtab got home from work the next day. The clock on the wall said three o'clock. Walking down the corridor, Mahtab's eyes fell on a piece of lined paper stuck to her bedroom door. It was a note from Maman.

We have gone to Emad's house to help set up your jahaz. Get ready and come as soon as you can. Wear something beautiful so you can shine.

This was it. She threw her handbag with its music books on the floor. Sitting on her bed, she took in a deep breath and steadied herself. It was either this or "shining" at Emad's home. She saw his mother Haj Khanoom Marziyeh's face wrapped in its *roosari* like a melon, her beady eyes over her simpering smile. But. Yes but. The unspoken question hung heavily in Mahtab's thoughts. Nasim was her best friend. Actually more like a sister in the truest sense of shared kinship of thought, rather than Bahar, who although she shared the same blood with, was always more of a baby in Mahtab's eyes. Nasim had been that someone she had shared almost everything with, from her first crush on the boy across the street to her struggle to learn the violin to her feelings for Ashkan. Mahtab knew she could lean on Nasim whenever she needed to. But what about Nasim's mother? Nasim had said once that her mother would welcome her to their home. But was that really true? What would she think about this, about Mahtab moving in with them, with no clear plan ahead?

With a prayer under her breath, Mahtab punched in the numbers to Nasim's phone. It rang three times before she heard the click, her heart drumming in the background.

"Nasim, they have moved my things to Emad's house. I can't do it, Nasim, I can't." She cried into the phone, words tumbling out. "It's the *jalaseh* today and they want me there. I am so desperate. I want to run away. Now! Can I stay with you? Just until I figure something out."

"Mahtabi! Of course you can come stay with me, *azizam*. I'll get Maman to get the guest room ready for you." Nasim sniffed and then said, "You know, after you got angry with me over telling Ashkan about Emad, I was scared to lose you. So I bit my tongue, even though I knew how unhappy you were with Emad. I just wasn't sure you were actually going to do this."

"*Merci*, Nasim *joonam*. But are you sure your mother will be OK with this?" Mahtab exhaled.

"Of course! Maman will be so happy to have you, I promise. Mahtabi, *zood bash* come quickly! I am still at work, but I'll tell Maman to expect you."

Mahtab heard the doorbell ring. "Someone is at the door. I'll see you soon. You don't know how happy you have made me Nasim. Thank you! *Boos.*"

Mahtab threw the silver phone on her bed and ran to the door. She looked through the peephole and let out a gasp. There was Emad! She debated what to do. She wanted to run back, leave him there, not answer the doorbell that rang again.

"Mahtab, open the door! I know you're there. Your shoes are out here. Come on, open it." He yelled.

He was going to get the neighbors worked up, and then everyone would be at her door. Busybodies that had nothing to do but watch each other and gossip. Oh forget it, Mahtab cursed herself, as she unlatched the door.

"Why aren't you ready?" He looked different, in a white silk shirt and grey pants that actually fit him, and his beard looked like it had recently been trimmed.

"I am not feeling well," she said, not moving from her place at the door.

"Go get ready. I'll wait for you here," he said drawing nearer, his eyes jumping from her to behind her and then all around.

"I am not coming, Emad," Mahtab said. "I can't. Please understand."

"You are not?" The fake smile dropped from his face.

Mahtab shook her head.

"Is it because of this?"

For a moment Mahtab just stared at the thing in front of her, grasped in Emad's thin fingers.

"Where did you get that?" she cried, trying to grab the silver plate from his hand.

"*Areh*? It is because of this, isn't it?" He pushed her inside and closed the door behind him, slamming the bolt.

"Answer me. Who gave this to you?" he said, his eyes narrowing.

"One of my students," she said quickly, moving back into the living room.

"Your students? I thought you only teach schoolgirls. Don't bullshit me, Mahtab! Who is this Ashkan?"

"Give it to me. It's none of your business," she said, retreating further back.

He sat down on the couch in the living room and dropped his feet on the coffee table with a thunk, his shoes still on his feet. In the silence that followed, Mahtab could hear her heart thumping, the vise tightening around her chest.

"I said who is this *sag,* this dog, Ashkan?" said Emad in a low growl.

"And I said how did you get this?" Mahtab said trying to keep her voice level.

He leered, his eyes rolling to the side before settling back on her. "It came with your *jahaz* boxes. A trophy." He laughed, waving the plate in her face.

"You went through my boxes, my stuff?"

"No! Do you think I am that *bikar*, nothing better to do? My sister Neda found it. And you know what she said? 'Oh how cute, Mahtab has a plate with her name on it.' An expensive engraved plate at that! Something we could actually display in our home, unlike the other stuff your family brought. But guess what, sweetheart? She turned it around and there was a poem. Not from Rumi! But a love poem. From a *pedar sag,* a son of a dog. How long, Mahtab?"

"How long what?"

"How long have you been seeing him?" he said knocking over a bowl of nuts that sat on the table with the flick of a foot.

What could she say? There was nothing she could say to convince him otherwise. And, perhaps, inside a part of her actually wanted this, wanted him to know. That none of this was what she wanted—the *jahaz*, his family, or him.

He lit a cigarette. "You know the reason I wanted to marry you? It was because I was so sure, almost naively so, that you were a pure girl. Something rare to find these days. I was so sure that you had never had a boyfriend. I got that impression from your family, from you, from Pasha. Why, Mahtab, why?"

"You were right, Emad, I never had a boyfriend." She didn't lie. She didn't when he came to her *khastegari*.

"Then who the hell is Ashkan?"

Before she could answer, he rambled on. "You know, you can't find anyone better than me. Really. Ever! In your situation, with the little money your father has, no one worth anything would marry you. Have you actually taken a look at your *jahaz*? It's like something out of a *semsari*, a flea market. Yes, you are beautiful, but you aren't a businessman's daughter. You should have been so happy to marry me, to be accepted by my family, but..."

His sucked on his cigarette, and his eyes narrowed. Then he asked again. "Are you still seeing him?"

Mahtab didn't answer this time. Honestly, she didn't care anymore. All she knew was that she wasn't going anywhere with him, whatever he believed, whatever he thought about her. All she wanted was freedom from him.

"You are. Aren't you?" he said, getting up, flicking the still smoking cigarette across the room. "I can't believe it." He paced back and forth, his voice rising with each word. "What a slut! You, you, you are my *sigheh, mahram*, engaged to me, and you have a boyfriend?"

She said nothing. There was nothing to say anymore.

He turned to her, his eyes suddenly lighting up. "All these times that you said you were with Nasim, you were with him, weren't you? With your boyfriend? A man who is not your *mahram*?"

Emad's phone buzzed. Frowning, he looked at it for a moment before looking up. He drew in a breath and with visible effort said, "Go get ready. My mom wants to show you and your embarrassing *jahaz* to her friends, and I don't want her to be disappointed. We'll deal with this later."

He then lowered himself onto the living room sofa and looked around before his eyes settled back on her.

"Why are you standing there staring at me like the *abolhol*, the Sphinx? Go get ready. Now!" He screamed.

"I won't. I am so sorry Emad. But I am not going with you," she said slowly, her eyes unwavering on his. "In these months, when did I ever give you the impression that I loved you? You and I are just so different. You want a life with your parents, a wife to tend your home, go to Mecca. I am not that girl."

"Go get dressed, Mahtab. Go. Don't be stupid." Mahtab now heard a slight tremor in his voice, something she hadn't heard before. She kept staring at him until his eyes broke away from her.

"I won't," she said, before breaking into tears. "I am sorry that I am hurting your feelings Emad. But it is better this way. Do your really want to be married to a girl who likes someone else?"

"So this is it then?" he said quietly.

"Yes. I am sorry." That was all she could say. Yes, a small part of her did feel sorry for him, but she had her dreams and he would never be part of them.

She heard her phone ringing in her room. It must be Nasim again. She had to leave, leave before Pasha came home.

"Mahtab." She heard him call behind her, but she rushed to her room. It wasn't Nasim. It was a missed call from her mother.

She wiped the tears. Sniffling, she pulled herself together. She had to get Emad out, leave before he let everyone know. Before her family returned to claim her. She turned around and froze. Emad was standing in the doorway.

"Who was it?" he said, closing the door slowly behind him.

"My mother," Mahtab said, reaching across to open the door. Emad didn't move aside; instead he leaned back on the door handle.

"To the Mahtab of music, to the Mahtab of dreams. Who writes such *koseh sher*, such shit anyway? Is he one of those faggots whose hair looks like a porcupine? Those who steal their dad's cars to impress girls?"

"Whatever he is, he at least likes my music. He actually loves it. When did you ever ask me to play the violin for you? When did you ever show any interest in my music, ha?"

He chuckled. "I didn't because I really don't care for your stupid screeching on that thing you call a violin."

Mahtab suddenly realized how little space was between them. She stepped back trying, but he only moved forward till she hit the cold wall behind her.

Touching Mahtab's hair, he slowly said, "So you want to break up with me?"

"Yes," Mahtab said, fighting the urge to run. But today she would stand her ground in front of this weakling, this man who used others like her brother to get what he wanted. She wiped her eyes and pushed forward until they were almost face-to-face.

"I have nothing in common with you. Go away Emad! Now!"

"What about him? What do you have in common with him?"

He was now so close to her that she could smell the nicotine on his breath. He put his hands on the wall, locking her in. Blocking her. Mahtab felt the room close around her.

"Tell me. Don't be afraid." His tone was husky. "What do you have in common with him? That son of a bitch! Does he also play violin like you? Is he a *raghaseh*? A dancer, just like yourself?"

Mahtab wriggled her way out and rushed toward the door. He ran after her and in one leap grabbed the scruff of her tank top from behind.

"*Vaysa! Koja miri?* Wait! Where are you going?" he laughed.

His eyes were now laced with red, wide open with something Mahtab had never seen before. Hate.

"You are mad Emad! You have to leave now or I'll call the police."

"Call the police on your own fiancé? What for?"

He drew closer until they were so close that his beard touched her face. "You know when my sister showed me the plate this morning, I couldn't believe my eyes. I told her what you told me; I think it's one of her students or maybe an old colleague. I defended you against my own family. In my wildest dreams, I didn't think it would be a boyfriend. But when I saw your expression, when I showed you that damn plate, it all became so clear!"

Mahtab shook her head. She was no longer crying.

"You don't know, Mahtab, how hurtful it is to find out that your girl has a boyfriend on the side. How humiliating it is! To find out the girl you want has been seeing another guy behind your back. You can't even imagine how angry I am." Emad cried, his bloodshot eyes boring through her.

"Just let me go, Emad," Mahtab said weakly. "Don't you see? I am not good for you. I am not the kind of girl you want. Why can't you find someone else?"

She felt his fingers dig into her arms as he shook her. "Do you know the *keifar*, the punishment for a married girl having relations with another man? Do you know? Obviously you don't. Otherwise you wouldn't cheat on me with him. Well, I'll tell you. It's *sangsar*. Stoning, Mahtab!"

Mahtab nodded without a word. Of course, she knew that very well.

"*Kardatet*? Has he fucked you?"

She couldn't breathe in that space, the overpowering smell of Emad around her, his face in hers, his arms around her.

"Answer me. Did you have sex with him?"

"None of your business," Mahtab said at last. "I have nothing to do with you anymore. We are no longer..."

She didn't even have time to brace herself before she felt his hand across her cheek. The slap, the momentary shock without pain that drew her breath away before the stinging began. Then the dizziness and the nausea before she fell down.

"*Khafe sho*, shut up!" He spat above her.

Holding her cheek, Mahtab tried to get up, but he kicked her down again.

"I want to know if he has fucked you."

"No! Never!" Mahtab got up. "What do you think I am? I have values. I am not a loose girl. Oh, Emad, I had my entire life planned. Until you came and destroyed everything for me. I never asked for you to marry me. I never wanted to marry you. Now please let me go. Just let me go!"

He grabbed her hair and shook her head. She could feel him, his heat, and his anger.

Mahtab struggled free and tried to slap him, but he caught her arm. Twisting it behind her, he dragged her to the floor and straddled her back with his legs, like a beast pulling down its kill.

"Let me go, you son of a bitch," she screamed.

Trapped beneath his weight, she heard the thunk, thunk of buttons popping.

"What are you doing?" Mahtab screamed.

She tried to hit him with her hands, but he held them with one of his and hissed, "Making you mine."

"No, Emad, please. Please, you are making a big mistake." Her voice was ragged now as she wriggled and bucked against him. Then she began screaming louder and louder, screams of pure terror that echoed unnaturally within the small room.

"Shut up." Mahtab heard him grunt from above, felt his hand close around her lips, her face, muzzling her. The smell of nicotine was overpowering. She bit down, feeling the bones of his hand between her teeth.

"Bitch," he snarled as he slapped her again.

She struggled, but there was no way she could break free. She cried out, "Leave me alone. This is not right. Don't you believe in God?...Please leave me alone, please...If my father finds out about this..."

"To hell with your father!"

He held her down with one hand and pulled at her pants with the other.

"Get away from me. Get off me!" She cried.

She felt him press himself tightly against her so she couldn't move, her hands trapped under his thighs. Then the unmistakable sound of a zipper being undone, then her underwear was yanked down. Pulling free an arm, Mahtab twisted up and felt the soft skin of his back under her fingers. She dug her nails in like a cat, so hard that she felt his skin bunch up under her fingernails. Then she cried out, a cry that seemed to take all the air from her lungs. As she felt a sharp, deep pain of something tearing, ripping inside her. She screamed wordlessly and tried to kick him with her legs, but pain stopped her struggling. The last thing she heard was the echo of her own voice, "*Kesafat!*"

She gave in. Her insides burning, she felt something warm running down her thighs and hot tears down her cheeks. She felt him jerk, and then he was done. Just like that. But she had ceased to feel anymore, feel anything anymore. Her virginity was gone. Her hymen broken.

"Why did you do this to me?" she cried as she felt him rise off her.

He laughed sardonically. "Because you deserved it, *jendeh*! You are used now. No one wants a secondhand girl. Let's see if that fuck of a boyfriend of yours wants you after this." He got up and his eyes fell on his torn, bleeding back in the mirror. "*Vahshi*, you're a savage."

Then he spoke slowly, as though enjoying every word, "I don't want a *harzeh*, a girl who runs around with other guys while she is engaged to me. Go see if he'll marry a *pass moondeh,* a nonvirgin girl."

Pulling his pants up over his pale, hairy legs, he began to dress. Mahtab rolled over on the ground, faint, her insides still burning. He had raped her in her own bedroom. She watched him light a cigarette and draw in a couple of times, eyes closing briefly before opening again.

It seemed to take every bit of strength left in her body, but she managed to sit up, to at least face him with some dignity. She felt something fall off her. It was her bra, pink, torn, lying at an odd angle in her lap. She looked up to see him staring at her, his grin growing at the last gasp of her pride, her *abaroo* falling off before her. Tears blurred ribbons of his face into watery streams. She wanted her mother, to cry in her arms. For being raped, for losing that which she had kept for her husband, for the one she loved, for her wedding night.

"Did you hear me?" he said, grabbing her chin in his hands. "You will tell no one about this, Mahtab. Or I will make a case against you and him, your *pedar sag.* And then it will be over for both of you." He laughed and winked at her. "Remember, Mahtab, it's *sangsar,* stoning."

Then he sighed. "You know, Mahtab, I can't believe how much I thought you were good for me. I actually thought you would make me happy."

She closed her eyes, and when she opened them, he was gone, and so was the silver plate.

She felt soiled, body and soul. With shaking hands she put her clothes back on and then leaned against her bed. She hugged her knees and sobbed, each sob shaking her to the core. Somewhere around her, she heard her phone buzz, and later the home phone ringing in the distance. She didn't move; she couldn't move even if she tried as she cried herself to sleep.

Twenty-Six

Mahtab opened her eyes to the sound of something slamming. A door maybe, she thought. Was she dreaming? She squeezed her eyes again and looked up to see the evening light outline her window. She had no idea how long she had been asleep. She must have passed out. The noise was coming from the living room. There were heavy footsteps, rushed thumping, doors being slammed. Someone was yelling now, and Mahtab heard heavy footsteps in the corridor.

The door exploded open, and there was Pasha in a crumpled navy shirt hanging over his dark jeans. It was his eyes that transfixed Mahtab. They were wet, red, as though he had just been crying.

"Mahtab!"

Behind him was Maman, her cream-colored scarf still around her head, pushing through the door.

"*Vay*, Mahtab, what have you done?" Monir was wailing, hitting her thighs with her hands. "*Vay, bichare shodim*! We are destroyed!"

Bahar was sandwiched between Pasha and her mother, pulling at him from the side, her head barely at the level of his chest. "Please, Pasha. Please."

Mahtab recoiled at the expression on his face, the look of disgust. And then her heart fell as she saw what was in his hand. It was the plate. Emad had done it.

"*Kesafat! kharab!*" Pasha yelled and lunged at her. Mahtab tried to evade him, but in that tiny room she had no chance of escape. She felt her breath knocked out of her as she hit the floor and looked up to see him standing over her, his leg on her stomach. Then pain, wrenching pain as he began to kick her. One, two, three more kicks. He grabbed her arm and pulled her up, then shook her and said, "What's this?"

Then she felt something hit her. It was the silver plate in his hand, slamming against her face, her head. "What is this? Who the hell is Ashkan? You whore! You have no shame."

"Pasha, please!" Bahar was crying, grabbing his sleeve, but she was punched aside.

"Who's Ashkan? Speak up," Pasha yelled.

She didn't have time to answer even if she had wanted to. The plate that had her name and his name engraved together was so hard against her face, her temple.

Her mother was crying now. Bahar screamed, "Leave her. Please stop it."

"I'll break this piece of junk on your face. Who the hell is Ashkan? Answer me!"

The shock of the pain, the dull interlude of aching before the next blow landed went on. Her nose was bleeding now or was it her lips or both? She didn't care anymore. It seemed as though she was no longer there in her body but beside it, watching her beating. She just had to be brave, like earlier. He would hit her, and eventually he would get tired. He had to stop sometime, and it would be over. A feeling of momentary lightness went through her, scotching the pain, the ache, the fear.

"I swear to God, I'll kill him." Pasha spat as he raised his hand again.

"Leave him out of this. Take it out on me," Mahtab heard herself saying.

She saw Pasha scream something, his face contorted in red. She felt him grab her hair. Then the sick jerk of her head, the moment of free fall before the muffled crunch against the wall, like a shelled coconut against stone. Then again and again. Mahtab lost count. It didn't matter. Her hair would grow. Her head would stop hurting. Somewhere above she could hear her mother's voice. It was hard to make out, but she finally got it. "Please stop it, Pasha. If she dies, you'll be in trouble."

She saw Bahar try to step between her and Pasha only to be shoved out of the way. Heard her sister cry as he slapped her across the head. Then it was back to Mahtab again. *"Mikoshamet, kesafat,* I'll kill you, you piece of shit. You whore! I'll kill you first, then I'll kill him!"

Warm blood ran down her face, down to her lips, her neck.

"Koshtish, koshtish, you killed her!!" Maman was screaming. Mahtab was no longer there. Someone had taken her from that miserable house, from all the unhappiness, from the beating. She was gone. Around her was water, warm, like the loving waters of the Persian Gulf. She was walking in the water now. There was music from everywhere. Someone was playing the violin. What was she doing there? What was she wearing? Was it a wedding gown? She saw Ashkan running towards her. He was running but did not seem to reach her. She entered the warm water; the water welcomed her in like a mermaid. The waves hugged her. Someone from far away was singing one of her favorite nursery rhymes, *"Aroosake man.* My Doll." Who was singing it? She was too old to sing that. Then she saw a little girl who sat in front of her. She looked hard at her, and realized that it was herself. She started to sing but her dried lips wouldn't open. Then she noticed something. The little girl's temple was broken under a dark red stain. On her hands she had bruises, many black-and-blue wounds marring that pale skin. Mahtab sang with her, but her lips weren't moving.

My beautiful doll has worn her red dress, and is sleeping on the velvet blue bed.

One day my maman went to the bazaar and bought it for me. No one has seen a more beautiful doll than mine.

But why did the doll have bruises? Why was she hurt?

Twenty-Seven

*H*er eyelids hurt. She felt them ache dully in the reddish glow that lay before her eyes. The light felt strange, diffuse and warm like emulsified sunlight without a source. Where was she? Mahtab tried to remember, but her mind was like clouded syrup. All she could feel was her eyelids. Was she dreaming? Her eyelids refused to budge, stuck tighter than glue. She could hear the arteries in her own head as she strained. Then suddenly there was light as they moved apart with the viscosity of honey. Warm, yellow light filled her eyes before her strength failed her. She heard a beep, high-pitched and incessant. Then footsteps and a curtain being drawn hurriedly nearby.

"Mahtab, do you hear us? Open your eyes. Mahtab, this is Dr. Farahani. Do you hear me?" Someone rude was trying to open her eyelids, and there was a sharp light, a man in white looking into her eyes. Mahtab tried to close them. Someone was yelling behind her, a woman's voice. "It's number twenty-eight. The girl in the coma. She moved her eyes!"

᨟

The next time Mahtab woke up, her eyelids were less heavy. At first everything was blurry, and the brightness stung her eyes. She closed them quickly and, after a few seconds, forced them open again. She desperately needed to rub them, but her hands were made of stone. Peering out, she saw a clear tube dive into the crease of her arm. She had seen that somewhere. Yes, it was an IV. Under the sterile fluorescent lights, she couldn't say if it was day or night. Her nose suddenly came alive, as though freed from its cocoon. Alive with the sweet smell of alcohol mixed with something else. The metallic smell of medicine. Scanning with only her eyes, she saw herself draped in a white sheet, lying on a white-painted bed that looked like a set of ladders thrown together. She tried to remember. She had seen this kind of bed somewhere before on TV.

A dirty blue curtain was hanging from ceiling. Across from her feet, which were covered, sat an older woman bent over in a metal chair. She looked familiar. Her eyes were closed, her lips parted, with only a steady clicking from the metal counter in her hand. She knew what that was. It was for keeping track of prayers.

Then the curtain moved, and a short, plump woman with a white scarf appeared. She seemed to have done this many times, the way she walked quickly, her eyes on the clear plastic bag that hung on a pole above her head.

"You are awake?" she said suddenly, her voice high with surprise. Mahtab could see her face now, pale with black eyes edged in crow's-feet, fill her vision as she bent over her.

"*Ya Fatemeh Zahra*, you heard my prayers. I die for you, Mahtab *joon*. Are you really awake? *Alhamdolelah*!" The woman with the counter had now pushed aside the other woman and was leaning over, her hands cupped over her face.

"Can we get some water for her? Look at her lips. They are so dry. The skin is peeling." The water helped her dry lips open, but Mahtab still couldn't talk. Even if she had wanted to, she couldn't, with that plastic tube jammed down her throat. Instead, she just lay staring up at the faces above her.

"Are you OK?" The woman's eyes were wet, her mouth quivering like a dam about to burst.

Everything was hurting all at once. It was as though Mahtab's entire body had woken up with a scream, trying to make up for lost time.

The woman took out her mobile phone and made a phone call. Soon a girl rushed in. They both were talking to her at the same time. A babble of voices that seemed so loud, so unnaturally loud.

"Leave her alone," the white-scarfed woman ordered. "Too much noise and excitement is not good for her. Remember this is a hospital!"

She had known that. This was a hospital. How did she get here? The new girl was now holding her hand, saying, "Mahtab *joon, elahi fadat sham*, I die for you. Are you OK?"

"You need to leave now. Let your mom take care of her! Out!" the woman with the white scarf said, leading the girl out of the room.

The older woman was now clutching the railing of the bed, crying, smiling. "Don't talk, *azizam*. Don't talk. Just rest. It's OK. You are alive. That is what's important. Everything is OK."

⌒♍

For the next few days, Mahtab didn't talk or eat anything, although she was now staying awake for longer periods of time. Someone had left the blue curtain open today. Mahtab stared at the gray marble floor receding to white walls with windows placed so high she barely could see outside. There were two other beds in the room—one closer to the door, one in the middle, and hers, next to the windows. She couldn't see the faces of the other women in the two beds; she could only hear snippets of conversations behind curtains and sometimes the muffled moan. Her waking hours were filled between occasional visits from the older woman and the girl who seemed to know her, and a tall, bald man with small kind eyes and a white coat, who introduced himself as Dr. Farahani. Sometimes he brought a whole lot of other men in white coats, who animatedly examined her and asked her questions to which she would nod until her strength gave out. The doctors used words that she did not understand, foreign words at times. "Seems to have difficulty recognizing her mother. Probable posttraumatic amnesia. Still hyperreflexic though. Do you think she would benefit from an MRI of the head?"

Mahtab slept and woke up. She lost count of the days and hours.

When the older woman visited, she would do things for her like change her scarf, wash her face with damp cloths, try to feed her.

⌒♍

One day the woman with the white coat and scarf, who called herself a *parastar*, a nurse, came in and said, "Looks like Dr. Farahani thinks you are doing well enough to remove the tube. Then you can eat," she said, fiddling with the tube in Mahtab's mouth before her eyes fell on her patient's face. "But you are still very weak. So rest as much as you can, OK? You have lost a lot of blood."

One afternoon the younger girl from before came in alone. Mahtab's dried and chapped lips opened up very faintly. "Excuse me."

"Mahtab *joonam. Azizam*, what do you need?"

"Why am I here?"

The girl was leaning over her, the expression in her almond-shaped eyes setting something off in the back of Mahtab's head, something just out of reach, like a phone that stops ringing just before it is picked up.

"I would die for you! Good that you don't remember. You have to rest now. I promise I'll tell you when you are better."

Mahtab felt her strength begin to slip away. But today she had to know, to ask what she had wanted to, ever since she had woken up.

"Who are you?"

"I am Bahar, your sister," the purple-scarfed girl said, sniffling. Her eyes were glistening.

"Bahar? Sister," Mahtab whispered. She had a sister?

Mahtab closed her eyes. "I want to see myself. Can you give me a mirror?"

She saw the girl claiming to be her sister stop and look away. "I don't have any mirror," she said dully.

Mahtab breathed heavily. "Ask that woman," she said, moving her eyes in the direction of the patient who was lying in the middle bed.

"She is so sick. She can't answer me."

Mahtab took in a deep breath and croaked. "Then go ask the *parastar.*"

She saw Bahar look at her for a moment and then sigh. "OK. I will, Mahtab *joon*. Please don't tell Maman though. She'll get mad."

Mahtab slowly took a hand and touched her face. It was like doing something she hadn't done in years. Feeling her eyes, her nose, her mouth. Everything was there. She touched her cheek, then moved up to her head and stopped. Stopped at something that felt like cloth, but coarse, bordered by thick tape. A dressing. That meant there was a wound there, her mind registered dully.

Something had happened to her right temple.

"They didn't have any," Bahar said, appearing at her bedside.

"What happened here?" Mahtab said weakly, her hand over her right temple.

"It's just a small scratch. It'll be fine."

"No, something happened to me, Bahar. I know it. I was thrown into the water. That was it, wasn't it? I couldn't swim, and I drowned. Right?"

Bahar said nothing and turned away. But not before Mahtab saw tears rolling down her cheeks.

She looked at her hand, then up her arm to the clear plastic IV sticking out of it. Then she saw them. Marks, purple, blue, some turning a livid yellow green. Her mind was so fuzzy.

"Which hospital is this?" Mahtab asked.

"Emam Hossein," Bahar answered, sniffling.

"Is it a good hospital? Do they take good care of patients here?"

"Yes they do, *azizam*. Look at you. You are almost better. You were in a coma for two weeks. But you came out of it." She repeated, "You came out of it."

"Are the doctors here cute? I hope they don't have a crush on me."

"Mahtab *azizam*, you need to rest," Bahar said, straightening her blanket.

"I had a child. She died. She was so beautiful. She had green eyes just like her dad. She drowned though." Mahtab sighed. "I cried for three days when she died. Then I took her body and..."

"OK, that's enough," Bahar said before rushing out of the room. Mahtab thought she could hear the sounds of sobbing from behind the door.

Mahtab whispered, "My beautiful doll was beaten and then died."

A few minutes later, Bahar came back with the nurse. The nurse said, "It looks like you can talk very well now." Bahar was blowing her nose into a tissue.

"Do you know why she is crying?" Mahtab asked the nurse. "Because of my child. My child and I were thrown into the water; I survived but she could...ahh!" It took the nurse a split second to push the needle into her arm, and then there was no more to remember.

When she opened her eyes again, she saw a young man in a dark green uniform too large for his frame. He had a beard. A *komiteh,* a policeman perhaps. She closed her eyes quickly as something tightened around her heart. His beard reminded her of someone—a man who had touched her.

When she opened her eyes, the man was gone. But now there was a strange wetness in her bed, between her legs. Quickly she removed the white bed-sheet from her legs. It was red, bright red. Her bed was overflowing with blood, dripping from the bed onto the floor. Mahtab screamed. Two nurses rushed in to the room, walking through the blood. Their white uniforms were now crimson.

"There is blood, blood, blood," Mahtab kept screaming.

"Calm down. Calm down. There is no blood." A third woman, faceless, said pressing a needle in her right arm.

⌒◯

The woman in the next bed was still. A white bedsheet covered her face. Mahtab didn't know how long she had been awake, but she didn't make any noise. They might give her another shot in the arm if she moved.

"Good morning, Mahtab. I brought you a new *roosari*. See how beautiful it is?" It was the older woman again, the one she had seen the first time she had opened her eyes. She was wearing a scarf with lots of color and flowers tightly around her face. She looked tired, like someone who hadn't slept for days. "It's green with gold designs. Do you want to wear it?"

"Who are you?" Mahtab asked.

She saw her face tighten, her eyes fall within their sockets. "I am your mother. I told you that already, yesterday and the day before. I am your mother!"

"Be careful, don't step on the blood," Mahtab said.

"No, see there is no blood anywhere. It's all clean here," said the woman who was supposed to be her mother.

"But the blood came from here." Mahtab sighed, weakly motioning towards the middle of her body.

"Let me brush your hair," her mother said softly, a brush in her hand.

"Please, sing me a song," Mahtab finally said, turning her head to her mother.

The woman smiled, revealing teeth that were still white except for the far right that was shiny, capped in silver. She had seen that somewhere before.

"Ye shab-e Mahtab, Maah miyad to khaab."

"One night, the moon will rise to my dream. It will take me to the meadow, where there is a fairy who slowly, unsurely put her foot in the brook to comb her hair."

Her voice was scratchy, off-key, but beautiful and warm in its familiarity. A memory from a past far, far away, like a lullaby sung to a baby years ago.

"*Ye shab-e Mahtab.*" Mahtab's lips were moving now, barely audible, but enough to wet her mother's eyes. Sniffling, she pulled herself together and leaned forward.

"There is a doctor here who has a crush on me," Mahtab said. "He said he wants to marry me. But I said no. I said I am still too young. How old am I? Fifteen, sixteen? He said if I don't marry him, he'd give me to the bearded policeman. Why are you crying?"

"I am just so happy that you are alive," her mother said, wiping her nose with a handkerchief.

～〇

One day, days later or was it weeks, the nurse came in followed by Dr. Farahani. They smiled, standing at the head of the bed.

"Doesn't she look beautiful with her new scarf?" the nurse said, touching the third, or was it the fourth, scarf that Maman had brought for her.

"She does. And I have good news for you, Mahtab," Dr. Farahani said, beaming. "You are leaving the hospital today. Isn't that great?"

Mahtab blinked. All she had known, seen, was here in this hospital. Dr. Farahani, the nurse who had been there the day Mahtab had opened her eyes. Her room, its familiar blue curtain. This was her only home.

"But this is not fixed yet," Mahtab said, touching her right temple, the dressing still wrapped around it.

"It'll be all fixed soon, but you don't need to stay in the hospital for that."

"Where am I going?"

"You are going to a special place for some time. It will help you to recover." Dr. Farahani smiled and patted Mahtab's arm before leaving the room.

The wheelchair ride was fun. Bahar carried Mahtab's belongings in a small bag behind her as her mother walked by her side, opening doors, fussing over her from time to time. Behind her, one of the white-coated hospital nurses, someone she didn't recognize, pushed her along. Outside, an old yellow paykan sat idling by the black-and-white concrete pavement. Everything seemed so bright, so new outside, and her eyes felt like the first time they had opened in the hospital. When they cried to be shut in the overwhelming brightness of everything. Even the heat seemed to have a life of its own, radiating, shimmering off the hot black asphalt. Everyone helped her get into the car, and it was just as well for her legs felt like stilts for the first time.

"Bahar, you sit up front," Maman said as she slid next to Mahtab in the back. Then with a smile, she unwrapped a lollypop and placed it in Mahtab's hand.

"Mahtab *joon*, eat this until we reach our destination, *basheh*? Don't talk. Just look outside. Look at the people."

Mahtab looked outside at the people. They all looked so very busy. Talking on their toy phones to each other, over each other.

The taxi stopped in front of what looked like a large park with a green lawn and trees that shaded what lay beyond. A tall fence made of sharp-tipped black metal rods separated the park from the road. The car entered the driveway and came to a stop in front of a large girded gate. Monir got out, and after a few words, a uniformed man from the small blue-colored kiosk opened the gate. Then around the corner, a tall, thin woman in a navy-blue *roosari* and *manteau* appeared with another wheelchair.

"Salaam, Mahtab *khanoom*. How are you today?" she said as she steadied Mahtab into the wheelchair. "You are going to be our guest here."

They wheeled her onto the concrete path that led to a set of low yellow buildings with repeating rectangular windows punctuated by the occasional door. The buildings from the outside looked like a school, even with their numbered gray doors.

"Am I going to university?" Mahtab asked, looking around to the nurse above her.

"Something like that," the woman said. "Here you'll recover from your injury. I guess you could say it is a school to get you back to your life. And that is the most important thing for you now, right? OK, let's get you to your room."

It obviously wasn't in the first building because the nurse kept pushing at a pace that left Maman and Bahar struggling to catch up. As they passed the lawn and the large trees above it, Mahtab saw many women come into view, scattered around, some sitting on the ground, others on benches, and the lawn. All of them were wearing white *roosaries* over their plain pink *manteaus* and pants, almost like schoolchildren. As they passed, Mahtab felt the full weight of their stares upon her.

They wheeled her to another building, separated from the first one, at the other side of the park. Inside, it took Mahtab a few minutes to adjust to the dimness, which revealed a long corridor lit by a single fluorescent light that hummed in the background. Here the women in pink uniforms were all over. Someone suddenly screamed from the end of the hallway. Not a blood curdling scream but one that seemed more like a scream mixed with a laugh. Mahtab shivered, circular bumps growing on her arms. It was hot inside, but beads of cold sweat appeared on her forehead. The happiness of the morning outside, the trip from the hospital to this park was now gone, replaced by a vague feeling. A feeling of dread. After passing a few doors, they entered a room with three neatly made beds, bordering the walls facing them. Two were on the other side of the window and the third across by the wall. All three were bolted to the floor.

"This is your room," the nurse said with the practiced manner of someone who had done this more than once.

"You'll have two roommates. That's Shima over there." Mahtab looked at the plump girl in pink sitting on the far bed. She didn't even move but kept staring out of the window. The window seemed to have a checked design that covered it. Looking closer, Mahtab realized that they were bars. She had seen something like that before. Somewhere unpleasant on TV. Where they kept bad people. But she could not remember the name. The nurse was saying something. "...and Akram, who is not here. She is outside. You'll like them. And that's your bed," the woman with the blue scarf said, turning her wheelchair to the nearest bed by the wall. "And this is where you put your stuff," she said, pointing to a metal dresser next to the door.

She smiled, a small thin smile that did little to settle Mahtab's mind.

"I'll leave you here to get comfortable. I'll see you in my office, Mrs. Sharifi, for the final paperwork. You said you have the power of attorney from Mahtab's father?"

"Yes. I have the permission slip as well as the power of attorney that he gave me."

"I'll take those now to prepare her files. And I need your birth certificate as well as your husband's and the patient's too."

Maman reached into her black vinyl bag and took out a large envelope. "All the paperwork from the hospital and the permission slips from her father are in here."

The woman grabbed the envelope and said, "I'll see you in my office."

When the woman left, Mahtab asked, "Where are you going to stay?"

"I can't stay. I have to go back home. But I'll come visit you whenever I can. You'll be safe here. No one will hurt you," Maman said, her eyes not meeting Mahtab's.

"I want you to stay."

"I can't," Maman said, wiping her eyes with her hand. "I have to go back."

"How long I am going to stay here?"

"I am not sure," her mother said. "Listen, Mahtab. No one knows you are here. Not even your father." Maman stopped, her eyes looking away as though reliving something. Then her eyes were back on Mahtab but not before she had seen the fleeting expression across her mother's face. That of pain.

"Look, Mahtab, here no one can lay their hands on you anymore. You were badly injured. You don't remember, but you were. It will take some time for you to recover. But you will, *inshallah,*"

"How long will I stay here?" Mahtab asked, her eyes blurring with tears.

"I don't know, maybe a month, maybe more. But I'll come back," she said, hugging Mahtab before turning to Bahar. "Did you put her stuff in her drawer?"

"Yes." Bahar nodded.

"Remember, your name is Mahtab. Make friends with these girls, OK? I'll come back."

Mahtab watched them leave and sat back on her bed, its flimsy springs creaking under her. She sat there looking at her hands while the girl across from her continued to stare outside. The red light that shone through the window from the setting sun slowly turned to gray. Mahtab had never felt so alone before.

The same woman came back. "You were so quiet I almost forgot you were here. Here, take your pill."

"Here hurts." Mahtab touched her right temple.

"I know. Don't touch it. Let it heal. Take your pill."

It was still dark when she suddenly woke up. She was sweating. The other two girls were sleeping, making noises. Then Mahtab saw him. A shape that slowly formed into a figure. A figure with dark fatigues that she knew would be green, with a beard that was thinly trimmed. The same bearded man in the green clothes from the hospital. He must have followed her here. Something thin glinted in his hand. A syringe with a needle that seemed ten times the size of a normal one. He slowly moved toward her and smiled.

"Time for your daily shot."

He removed the white bed sheet from her legs as she watched. Before her lay her naked body, pallid in the night. With slow deliberation, his lidded eyes on hers, he forced the needle into the middle of her body. At that point, the weight that had held back her tongue broke with the pain, and she screamed.

"No, no, no!" There was blood everywhere, on the bed, on the walls, welling from her like a great dark stain in the night. There was the sound of yelling, someone threw the door open. The two girls were awake now, huddled under their sheets. The tall woman quickly drew something from a small bottle into a syringe, and there was a flash of metal before Mahtab felt her shoulder sting.

"Calm down. Calm down! No one is here. There is no blood," she said as she rubbed Mahtab's throbbing shoulder. The strength within her was now slipping away, replaced with the fog from the hospital.

"He was here," Mahtab murmured as her eyes shut themselves.

Twenty-Eight

"You need to eat," the nurse said, nudging her, pointing to the cold plate of rice and vegetable *khoresht* before her. The *khoresht* always reminded her of vomit, but it didn't matter. She wasn't hungry. After the second night when the bearded man had visited her and she had screamed, she had been injected, sedated by the nurse, before she went to sleep. And it worked. Whatever they had injected her with had closed her throat. He would still come, but Mahtab couldn't scream anymore.

It took her mother almost a week before she came back.

"Did you make friends with those girls?"

Mahtab shook her head and lowered her voice. "A policeman with a beard comes every night and hurts me, Maman; I am scared. Take me home. Please take me home. I want my dolls."

Maman sighed and stroked her hair. "When he comes, tell him *Khoda* God is with you. Call God and he will help you."

Mahtab brought her lips close to her mother's ear and said, "One night he removed his pants and he pushed his thing into me. It hurt a lot. Even now it hurts down there, Maman."

With a gasp Monir turned away, and for several seconds she shook, her hands clapped to her face. When she finally turned around, her eyes were red and her face drawn. Hugging her with a force that made Mahtab jump,

247

her mother held her and rocked her, murmuring something that took a few moments for Mahtab to catch.

"My poor child. My poor daughter. You are so beautiful. Why did it have to happen? Why, *Khoda*, why?"

⌒〇

The following days were long, hot, and stifling under the summer sun. Mahtab was sitting on a faded green bench outside, under one of the old poplar trees. The smell of freshly soaked grass and soil surrounded her as the old gardener, who never spoke, methodically watered the garden under the hot sun. Someone had told her that he had moved here and never wanted to leave. Or was it that he had no one to claim him? He was lucky though, she thought. At least in this heat, which didn't even spare the shade, he got to drench his face from time to time with the garden hose. She looked down at the pink uniform that she had on, the same one she had seen the other girls wear the day she had been brought to the park. Her nurse, whose name she still did not know, had given her the uniform in a neatly pressed bundle the day she had moved in.

"These are your clothes now. They will be yours till you leave. Pack up your own for your mother. She will take them the next time she comes to the *asayeshgah. Basheh?*"

"*Asayeshgah*, sanatorium," she mumbled the word under her lips. Where had she heard that word before? Suddenly she felt a pair of hands slide over her eyes. Mahtab screamed, and the hands flew off her face.

"Look!" Bahar's smiling face appeared before her. "Look what I brought for you! Your favorite Mickey Mouse ice cream!" she said, holding an ice cream bar in the shape of a smiling mouse, its chocolate ears glistening in the sun.

"My favorite," Mahtab repeated.

They sat on the grass and ate their ice cream till the sticks were licked dry.

"I have so much to tell you," Bahar said, turning to Mahtab.

"Bahar, there is a guy who rapes me every night. I want him to stop."

"Oh, Mahtab, I die for you. It's not true! These are nightmares. You had them in the hospital too. Look, see what else I brought for you?" Bahar said, pulling a small CD player out of her bag, followed by a handful of discs. "You put the headset on your ears, and you can carry this and listen to music. Here, which one do you want to listen to first?"

Mahtab slowly looked through the pile without a word before finally settling on one. "This one. What does it say?"

"Vivaldi." Bahar smiled, turning it over. "You really liked it before... Well, anyway, listen to it after I am gone." Then Bahar leaned over and dropped her voice. "So I was going to tell you. I have been trying to get Nasim to come see you. I mean I don't have any number or anything to contact her. They took everything you had in your room, even your phone after you know, after the event. But I am trying."

"Nasim? I don't know any Nasim."

Bahar blinked. "Don't you remember Nasim? She was your best friend. She even made me jealous sometimes, how close you two were together."

Mahtab shook her head. "Maybe I did, but all my friends are dead now."

Bahar took a deep breath and held Mahtab's hand in hers. "Mahtab, try to get well soon. It tears my heart to see you here in this place. OK?"

"But I am trying to get my degree here. It takes times. My professor told me it," Mahtab said, patting Bahar's hand.

"Yes. Of course." Bahar sighed. "Speaking of which, Ostad Amini sent this," she said, searching in her bag. "This is the CD of the concert you were practicing for. He said it was a great performance. He called home many, many times, Mahtab. He had no idea what had happened to you. Kamran also called home. They told everyone that you were in a hit-and-run accident."

"Who did?" Mahtab asked.

"Baba, Pasha, even Maman. Everyone believed them. And now they are telling everyone you are in a *behzisti*, a government nursing home because you can't move your limbs. Everyone feels bad for them." Bahar was sobbing now, dabbing her face with a tissue. "Nothing, absolutely nothing happened to their precious Pasha. And that asshole..."

Mahtab was screaming now. Long and deep, hands over her head, screaming. She had to get away from that gristly ball of a memory that had appeared before her, bloody, indistinct, and torn, like something you knew was bad even before you had fully made it out. Something was now stuck to her head, sucking on it like a fat tick on a dog. She pulled on it, but it wouldn't come off. In desperation she tore at it with both hands, and suddenly it was off with a sharp ripping sensation. The relief. The relief was palpable, like the relief of extreme pain suddenly numbed even if only for a fraction of a second. Something red and warm now trickled down her face, her right eye. Then there was blood everywhere.

She heard the girl, whose name was Bahar, yelling, *"Komak! Komak! Help! Help!"* and then darkness.

ༀ

The beam of afternoon sunlight was now a bright square on the opposite wall of the room. Mahtab lay on her bed with her eyes closed, her black hair now long, almost down to her chest. Listening. Listening to the CD with English alphabets that she had played almost every day since Bahar had given it to her weeks ago. She was better, much better since that time, since she had ripped the bandage off her head. She still had difficulty remembering what had happened, but whatever it was had not returned. Even the bearded man didn't visit her every night. The music was beautiful. It reminded her of something warm and wonderful, but she couldn't remember what. Her life had become a series of somethings, things that sometimes tried to evoke memories but only found feelings instead. Things that caused her mind to strain and her heart to ache. Bahar had talked about Nasim. Who was Nasim?

ༀ

As Mahtab's strength returned, she settled down into the routine of the *asayeshgah*: the wake-up bell in the morning, the meals in the large hall two buildings away, the mornings in the park as she still called it, the evening medicines, the pills that almost everyone seemed to get and take. Even so, although she had gotten used to the place, there was a fine line between tolerating it and actually liking it, and she was under no illusion about what it was. A place only to recover, as the nurse had told her when she had first arrived. To recover. And then what?

She had to see Nasim. Perhaps Nasim would be her key out of this miserable place. At least to remembering her past. For that, she had to see Bahar, but Bahar had not returned after the incident in the park.

One day, before fall, as the sun was still warm, her mother came in for one of her visits. This time she brought *sholezard*, rice pudding made intensely yellow by the liberal addition of saffron. When Mahtab finished eating, her mother took a box from her bag and said, "I was going through your things yesterday and look what I found!"

Mahtab opened the box and inside was a beautiful silvery necklace. At the bottom dangled a thin thread of white gold, looped on itself.

"Where did you get it? Who bought this for you?" Maman asked expectantly as Mahtab took it, looked at it, felt it. Mahtab said nothing. She didn't remember, but she did feel something inside. Something warm, something she hadn't felt in a long time. A feeling of happiness.

"You never showed it to me before, Mahtab. Here let me help you wear it."

Mahtab flinched as the cold metal touched her neck. She had worn this before. Someone had helped her wear this once.

Mahtab put her hand on the pendent and felt it. Yes, that was it. A G clef. Mahtab savored the morsel of knowledge like a favorite sweet.

"Someone gave this to me," she said slowly. "Someone dear."

"Don't lose it, OK?"

"Maman, where is Nasim?" Mahtab asked, her hand still on the pendent.

"Do you remember Nasim?"

"Yes," Mahtab lied.

"Well, she's been asking about you." Maman sighed. "I guess all these things wouldn't have happened if she hadn't introduced you to that guy."

"Which guy?"

"No one," she said nervously.

"Can Nasim come to see me?"

"No, Mahtab. After all that happened, it's best for you not to see her again."

That night, Mahtab made a decision. She would get herself out of here no matter what, and to start, she would stop taking the one thing that seemed to keep her mind bound. Those pills, starting with tonight's.

The next morning when Mahtab was washing up in the small bathroom at the end of the hall, she stared at her face in the old black-spotted mirror in front. She looked terrible, her face ashen, her eyes red and puffy. Her head felt like someone had taken a hammer to it.

"What happened to you? Answer me, Mahtab. What happened to you?" she cried, looking into her reflection. Everything seemed brighter, more discordant, sharper as though over-focused. The room around the mirror seemed to be moving slowly, in small crazed circles, making Mahtab feel sick to her stomach. What had happened to her? Then it struck her. It was the pill that she had not taken the night before; it had to be. Nothing else had changed.

Someone, a girl, yelled behind the bolted door of the bathroom, something coarse about enjoying a dump.

Then she noticed the thing on her head. Really noticed it for the first time. There was no dressing now. When had that been removed? It wasn't as large as Mahtab had thought it would be, but it was there. A reddish pink welt, a shiny scar planted on the pale skin of her right temple. She ran her fingers over it, as though confirming what she already knew was true. In her mind, a bewildering array of emotions and thoughts were rising, as though someone had opened a door and let the world in. But in there she was sure of one thing. What the nurse had said was not true. She wasn't born with it. The scar was new, maybe a few months old.

The headache continued that night, but for the first time there was a new peace in the thoughts that flowed in her, that took up spaces in her that had been long forgotten. Thoughts as simple as what she would do tomorrow in the yard, the pleasure of knowing that her mother would be coming in a few days, something she had actually remembered earlier that day. Something she had never been able to do before. And then it struck her. The fog that had occupied her mind for so long was no longer there. In the color and noise of her mind, she had completely forgotten the one constant that had been her companion since the hospital. And she hadn't even missed it.

∽෮

The days came and went, and the light grew shorter with each day. Even Mahtab's two roommates became part of her life, although not so much as friends as familiar fixtures. Shima, the girl who stared out of the window, had hair as short as a boy. A woman came to see her only once during the time she had been there. The nurse had told them to behave on that day because this was the first time she had come to see her in two years. Apparently she was autistic, and her family had been told that her condition was bad luck and so committed her to the *asayeshgah*. Akram, the other girl, was so short, so small that she could be a mouse. She was apparently mute. But if someone teased her, she would get angry, pull out her hair, and make noises. Other girls would tease her just to see her get angry. This was especially true of Shima, who liked to tease her when she was in one of her moods.

Shima would say. "I don't need to go to the zoo to see the monkey. There's one right here! Look at her. Her mother must have been a monkey too!"

One day Shima began again, taking the one thing Akram treasured above all. Her *aroosak*. A nondescript cloth doll that had seen better days; it may have been a gift from someone who had long since stopped visiting her. That *aroosak* was her life. Before bedtime Akram would first comb her *aroosak's* hair, hug her, and put her to sleep, gently laying the threadbare sheet over her like a tiny mother over her pint-sized child. Then she would climb in next to it and snuggle down for the night.

This time Mahtab could take it no longer. Without a word, she grabbed the doll from behind Shima, who let out a yelp of surprise. Then, in a flash, Mahtab was on the floor, Shima above her, her hand raised in the air. The next few minutes were a blur: Mahtab bucking, Shima's fist glancing off her shoulder, Mahtab's palms thumping against her assailant's chest, throwing her off with a grunt. Then a punch that drew red from Shima's lips, its violence even surprising Mahtab. For a moment Shima looked dazed, disoriented, before her gaze went past Mahtab to something behind her. It was Parvaneh, their nurse, and she did not look pleased. Behind her were faces peering through the open door, trying to see what was going on, curiosity writ across their faces. But none of it mattered to Mahtab. For even though she and Shima missed dinner that night in punishment for the fight, even though Shima made faces at her behind her back for the rest of the week, she had done two things she was proud of. One was that a little mother got her child back, and the other was that Shima never tried to tease Akram in front of Mahtab again.

⤳

The days were getting colder, and the leaves on the great trees outside began to turn red and brown. With the coming chill, Mahtab tried to stay indoors as much as possible. Mahtab still suffered severe headaches and at times had to lie down and close her eyes to prevent the spinning room from taking her over. But there was something else, just as equally surprising in its presence. That of hope, of something to live for. For most people, hope came from what they were to get or achieve, but for Mahtab it was the chance to find herself again, rediscover who she was, locked, stored somewhere in the recesses of her mind. Even the shoals of her memory were coming back, like precious bits that began to color the gray within her. Yes, now she remembered going to Tehran University, performing at concerts, the smell and feel of her violin. She remembered teaching the little children at school.

◡◠

The next time her mother arrived, Monir looked so different from how Mahtab had remembered her. She looked so old. Haggard, bags under her eyes, her face deflated.

"Look what happened to me," she said, showing her temple. "Some shit did this to me."

"No, honey, you were born with that scar. And don't use bad words, Mahtab *joon*. I know this place has taught you things, but remember that you come from a good family."

"I had a dream, Maman."

"If it's bad dream, don't tell. It's not auspicious to tell it."

"What if it's good?"

"First tell it to the water."

"How?"

"I've told you before. You go and turn on the tap and let the water run for a few seconds, not too fast, just a trickle. Then go ahead and say this with your eyes on the flowing water, 'Ya Ali, ya Mohammad, I had a dream. Please interpret it well for me.' Then go ahead and tell your dream."

Maman smiled and put her hand on Mahtab's shoulder. "Listen, since I am here, why don't you tell me your dream first?"

"I had a dream that you and a man were drowning me in deep water. I was trying hard to come to surface, but you kept pushing me down, deeper. It was dark there. I was scared."

"Enough! Stop Mahtab! I told you if it's not a good dream, don't tell me."

"No, Maman, I haven't finished. Then suddenly you smiled and pulled me up. And as I am coughing and catching my breath, I see no one but you. The man was gone, Maman. You had made him disappear."

Her mom smiled bitterly and said, "Do you take your pills, Mahtab?"

"I don't like them."

"I know. But you need to take them. They help you," her mom said.

"Maman," Mahtab said, putting her hand on her mother's.

"Joonam?"

"The man had a beard. He was the one in my dreams from before," she said, looking at her mother whose mouth had dropped open. "His name was Emad."

Twenty-Nine

"Maman, I want to leave from here. Please. This place is awful. It stinks. They have bars on the windows, like a prison," Mahtab said, looking at her mom.

"Mahtab, please stop it. Look, everyone loves you here. Your nurses, your roommates."

"But they are not my family, Maman. I want to go home with you, to my family."

"Didn't you hear what I said, *dokhtaram*? Your father wouldn't even see you in hospital. It breaks my heart, but it was my own son, your brother, Pasha, who put you in the hospital, gave you that scar," she said, her voice breaking. Drawing a tissue from her bag, she blew her nose and continued. "There is no family left, Mahtab. You are better off here than at home. Now at least you don't have to lie to live your life. Here at least you have peace."

"Stop crying, Maman, please. Please help me save myself."

"The bearded man you told me about. You are right to fear him. Yes, his name is Emad. You were engaged to him, and he raped you."

"I knew it," Mahtab mumbled. "I knew it. It was in my room. I remember now." Mahtab cried, violently shuddering, as if to shake something out of her body. She was now bent over, hugging herself, rocking.

"Oh, Mahtab. Oh, my poor child. Many nights after that I wished his legs had been broken and he had never come to your *khastegari*."

"I want to see Nasim; can you ask her to come here?"

"Are you sure? Really sure?" Monir asked, shifting in her chair.

"Yes, Maman. I have thought about it, and if there is one thing about this place, it is that it gives you the time for it! I want to see my friend."

"I hid your cell phone when they came looking for it. Your father and Pasha. Everyone called when you were in the hospital. Nasim, Ostad Amini, Mr. Javadi, Farbod's mother, who was actually angry that you had quit on her son; poor lady, she had no idea what had happened to you. And little Tara... her mother called so many times trying to get you to start again. I felt so helpless listening to their messages. But what could I do? Your father had forbidden me to talk to any of them. It was as though he wanted to erase you, Mahtab," Maman sighed. "Even Ashkan called. Do you remember him?"

"I think he has been coming to my dreams. One time, in my dream, he gave me my necklace."

"Yes, he did," Maman said, her voice dropping.

"I wish I could see him again."

Maman sighed. "He has gone. He probably has found someone else by now. What does it matter anyway? It was just a fling. Let it go."

Mahtab bit her lower lip to stop herself from crying. She would let him go. He deserved to be happy with whomever he was with now.

"What happened to Emad?" she said, blinking away the tears that appeared anyway.

"When you were still in hospital, Emad came to our home," Maman said, looking down at her feet. "Oh, I still remember his ugly laugh. He came with a truck full of all your *jahaz*. He got out and threw the key to the *vanet* to your baba and said, 'Here are your flea market things. Take them along with your *pasmoondeh* girl.'"

Maman took in a breath and steadied herself. "I said, 'What do you mean *pasmoondeh*? My daughter never spent a night out with a man.' He laughed a hyena's laugh and said, 'I made sure that she would be a *pasmoondeh*. I made sure her *curtain* was torn apart so no one else would marry her. Little did I know that she would be a vegetable for the rest of her life. Anyway, serves her right. That *jendeh*. You should have seen her face when I was taking her. She didn't want to, of course. But I got it anyway. How much she pleaded with me. She even said you,' he said, pointing to your father, 'would be upset with me. I told her the man doesn't have any balls!'"

Maman was clutching Mahtab now, crying, "And your father stood there and watched him without a word. Just like that. Oh, Mahtab, you don't know how I felt at that moment. I had just left you lying near death in a hospital bed, and this jackal comes to me in my face, looks into my eyes, and says, 'I've raped your daughter,' as easy as if he had gone to the shop. My beautiful daughter, a flower bouquet, now wilted in front of my eyes."

"Did he ever come to hospital to see me?"

"No, we didn't see him after he brought back the *jahaz*. And I sold it back to pay for the hospital bills. I have no idea how he could live with himself after what he did to you." Maman sighed and said, "I talked to a lawyer to see if I could convict him for the rape. We had witnesses to his confession now."

"And?"

Maman shook her head. "No, the *vakil* said as long as he was *mahram*, engaged to you at the time, he would be considered your husband, and nothing could be done."

"Even if it was forced?"

"A woman is supposed to always be ready for her husband, no matter what. That is the law."

Mahtab sighed and whispered under her lips, "*Pasmoondeh*. What about Pasha? Did he get any conviction?"

"No, no, Mahtab, your father as your rightful guardian should have pressed charges against him, but he would never do that. He would never put our family's reputation in danger. And besides, Emad had fired Pasha soon after the incident so he was at home, angry and crying, blaming you for everything. But don't worry, he has found a good job now..." Maman paused, before continuing, "In the end, it didn't matter. Your Baba told everyone that you were in a hit-and-run accident. You were brain damaged. Paralyzed and now living in a *behzisti* home outside of Tehran. And slowly people stopped asking about you."

Maman drew in a deep breath, and looked at Mahtab for a moment before she said, "I never wanted to bring this up. But why, Mahtab? Why did you have a boyfriend?"

"I don't know. It just happened," she exhaled. Then, she whispered, so low she could barely hear herself, "My life is passing by before my very eyes. I am so lost."

"*Chee gofti*, what did you say *azizam?*"

"Maman, get me out of here. Please. I want my life back."

"Where to, Mahtab *joon*? It's not like I can rent an apartment for you. We don't have money. I am still paying back the money we borrowed for the *jahaz*. At least the insurance is paying for this place and you are safe."

"So I am homeless now? With nowhere to go? I put up with all the stuff that Baba and Pasha did to me, so I wouldn't be homeless. Now I have no home, no family, nothing," Mahtab said softly, her eyes flooding with tears. Soon it would snow, and then it would melt, and Norooz would arrive, her first Norooz here and many other springs to come.

"He came to our home," her mother said at last. Something in her mother's voice told Mahtab to listen.

"Who?"

"Your boyfriend, Ashkan. I didn't want to tell you because...well, I didn't want to upset you."

"When?" Mahtab asked, feeling the thumping in her chest growing.

"Early on. A few weeks after the incident. You were just out of your coma. Nasim had told him about you. I was home alone, but I let him in. I was shaking. But I thought of you. You would do such things. You would always take risks. So I let him in, even though I was afraid."

"What did he say?"

Her mother chuckled. "He wanted to see you. Even after I told him the same lie we told everyone else, he kept pleading with me to at least let him see you. He is just like you, Mahtab, so persistent. So I broke down. I finally told him the truth. Everything. Down to the part where you were raped," Maman said with a sigh. "He got up and pressed his head against the wall. I was stunned. He was shaking, crying silently. I've never seen a grown man sob like that before. He kept apologizing over and over. Kept saying it was his fault."

"What do you mean, his fault?" Mahtab interjected, almost shouting.

"Let me tell you, *dokhtaram*. He said that it was the plate that he had given you that caused all this trouble. But you know, Mahtab, I was crying with him too, saying that it was my fault. That I had blindly sent the plate the night before with your *jahaz*, selfishly, because I wanted you to be with Emad. That because of it, you were now in a hospital bed without even your memory. Then something happened that I would never have expected. He just held me. A strange man, Mahtab. He held me. After he let go of me, he said, he knew his first gift destroyed your life, but he had given you another. A necklace. He asked me to look for it, show you, ask you about it. He said, maybe, just maybe, it might bring your memory back. Bring you back." Maman stopped and blotted her eyes. "He said, 'Tell her to remember the magic of Norooz.'"

"Then why didn't he come to see me, Maman?" she asked, her forehead knotting into a frown.

"I never told him where you were. I was scared. I wasn't sure. I wanted you to be safe. Maybe I didn't want him to see you like this. Sick. Confused. He came back again a few weeks later, but this time he didn't come upstairs. He asked about you. He said he was leaving for *Amrika*. He asked if he could see you one last time before he left.

"And again I told him that you were still in no condition to see him. It took a lot out of me to tell him that, to stand the look on his face. But I thought of you, in your bed with tubes, and it gave me strength. I told him to take the memories of you with him. Not to destroy them with the bitterness of reality. Because in the end, reality always betrays you. But memories, they stay with you forever, beautiful, loyal, and pure."

Mahtab closed her eyes and touched her necklace. She could still not see his face, but somewhere in her mind, she felt a pair of eyes on her. Not malevolent but beautiful, the color of emeralds.

⤴

Mahtab's head ached. Everything her mother had said weighed upon her like an ingot of grey lead. How destiny had betrayed her, how her life had gone from bad to worse overnight. Ten months ago, she had a house, parents, a violin, and a lover. Now she had nothing but her mother's monthly visitations.

She closed her eyes and imagined herself playing the violin in a large hall, among many others. In an orchestra, she imagined. But almost immediately she opened them again to a noise coming from the hall. A few seconds later, the door abruptly opened.

She felt her jaw drop as she stared at the girl in the doorway.

"Nasim."

She didn't know how long they hugged, but when they finally let go, Mahtab saw Bahar behind them, smiling. "I brought her. I wanted to surprise you!"

Mahtab grabbed her sister and threw her arms around her and squeezed until she gasped. "Thank you, Bahar! I don't know what to say."

"Don't say anything then. Come on! We are busting you out of here," Bahar said, opening Mahtab's drawer, throwing her *manteau* and *roosari* at her.

"Where are we going?"

"Come on, hurry up."

Mahtab quickly changed and followed her sister and Nasim out. They ran down the barely lit hallway to the exit, Mahtab still trying to catch up with the figures ahead of her. She heard the door thunk open ahead of her, saw the rectangle of sunlight, brilliant yellow. Then darkness. She pushed on the handle. The door would not open. She called out, but no one was there. Then she heard a familiar voice, that of the nurse behind her, laughing.

"You can't get out of here, Mahtab; you belong here. You belong here, you belong here, you belong here!" The voice echoed down the long dim corridor.

Mahtab woke up from her own screams. She had no idea how long she had been sleeping, but what she did know was that she had to get out of this place. She didn't belong here; she belonged in the land of music and moonlight.

✧

It was the evening before Norooz. Mahtab, still wet from her shower, was brushing her hair by the window. Through the bars, the trees outside looked like great pillars, their twisted branches sprouting new leaves, tiny and green. They looked so innocent, like little children being carried by their great old grandparents.

She jumped as the door swung open to reveal the nurse's towering form.

"Why are you sitting there, moping? Tomorrow is Norooz. You should be happy."

Mahtab frowned. She had no interest in starting a conversation in her present state.

"Come on, get your stuff," the nurse said, pulling open Mahtab's closet. "It looks like you are going home tonight."

"Home? Is my mom here?" Mahtab got to her feet, scarcely believing the words she was hearing. She furtively pinched her arm, just to be sure she was awake.

"Yes, she is here. She is checking you out. Here you go," she said, tossing her the same bag that her clothes had gone in the first day she had been admitted. "Come on, change into your clothes."

Mahtab could barely contain herself, and thoughts flooded her mind. Could it be? Had her father forgiven her? Had he actually wanted her back? What about Pasha? Would he apologize for all that he had done? Why now? Maybe after all this time, maybe they did miss her. Or maybe it was the magic of Norooz, bringing with it new beginnings. But they would have to understand that things would be different now. Mahtab changed into her black *manteau* and the green with gold *roosari* that her mom had bought for her in the hospital. She hadn't worn these clothes for almost a year now. Then she followed the nurse holding open the door. They walked in silence, their steps ringing on the concrete floors. Many doors had to be opened and shut till they past the wards and reached the administration building at the far end of the institution.

The nurse finally opened the door to a yellow room with a peeling sign on the wall that read Waiting Room. Please Wait to Be Called. The grimy room was empty save for a man sitting on the couch at the far side, his arms folded and his legs spread apart. Mahtab gasped and took a step back, but her eyes never left him. She blinked and looked again, but he was still there, looking just as shocked as she was. Ashkan. She stood there as the memories, no, *their* memories gushed into her head—their first meeting, the fights, Norooz. Truly, this was the miracle of Norooz.

"Salaam," he said, getting up. He was so gorgeous, his sculpted face, his built frame, his green eyes with their splash of gold.

"I thought you went to *Amrika* for good," Mahtab managed, her throat growing dry.

"I came back." He smiled suddenly, his eyes on hers. "I came back for you, Mahtab."

"I got my memory back."

"Yes, I know. Your mother told me."

She felt him, his familiar warmth, the strength of his arms as they wrapped around her like a fortress. Her fortress.

At any other time in her life Mahtab would have pushed back reflexively. Even holding him, here in public, could land them both in jail. But Mahtab was past caring. She would not lose her present for anything.

The door to the administration office opened and her mother appeared. Ashkan released Mahtab gently.

"How are you, Mahtab? Are you ready to leave?" her mother said before giving Ashkan a small smile.

"I am good," she said softly. "I was waiting for you all day today. I thought you would never come."

"I had some work to do," Maman said, looking at Ashkan.

"Here, let me carry this," Ashkan said taking the bag from Mahtab.

Outside the streetlights were throwing long shadows, but the streets were packed as if it were still daytime. People were everywhere getting their last-minute shopping done before the big day. The sweet smell of Norooz, a mix of purple and pink hyacinth and fresh pastry, hung in the air. There was a yellow taxi waiting outside the gate. Ashkan opened the door as Maman climbed in. She looked at both of them and then at him.

"You take good care of my daughter."

"*Baleh*," Ashkan said.

"Maman, where are you going?" Mahtab asked.

Monir smiled, a smile that lit her entire face. "He wants you more than anyone else, Mahtab. He loves you, but you know that already! Go start a new life together." She held Mahtab's face in her hands and said, "I'll come see you soon. *Eidet mobarak.*"

"What about Baba?"

"Maybe one day he'll change his mind. But for now some things are best kept secret."

Mahtab hugged her mother and breathed. "Thank you. *Dooset daram.* I love you."

Then Ashkan closed the taxi's door. Mahtab felt his hand reaching for hers as she watched the taxi disappear into the night.

Thirty

*A*shkan opened the door to his apartment. It was dark. He turned on the light. It was just the way it was before, even the PlayStation under the TV on the far wall.

"Come inside," Ashkan said. "Please."

Mahtab stopped to remove her shoes.

"No, it's OK. Leave 'em on. Actually, wait here for a second," he said with a smile, before disappearing behind the glass doors to the balcony.

"OK, Mahtab, come in now," he said a moment later from behind the door.

"Ashkan, this is so beautiful," Mahtab said, with lips apart.

All over the balcony and around the swimming pool were burning candles, their flames reflected in the pool, shimmering, flickering in the night breeze. Below lay Tehran, a million sparkling lights blinking like stars on the earth.

"I knew you would like this," he said softly. They stood there, looking out, until time seemed to stop in the myriad lights around them.

Ashkan shifted a bit, cleared his throat and said, "I left Iran, after trying to see you so many times. After what your mom told me, to go and forget." He paused and said, "But I couldn't. I kept looking for the signs of Norooz, and I realized that there wouldn't be any magic without the one I love."

Mahtab looked at him. Ashkan was gazing out over the city. Then he turned to her and whispered, "I came back to Iran last week and went to your home. Hoping just hoping for your mom to at least let me see you. Just a visit. I went fully expecting to get thrown out, have the police come after me, but your mom told me to meet her later, at a park. I couldn't believe my ears when she said that she wanted to get you out. That you had gotten your memory back!" He put his hands in his pockets and blew out a deep breath. "It took her three days to get all the paperwork ready for your release. Those were crazy days, waiting, not knowing if it would come through, if your father or brother would do something to stop it. And all the while, I was cursing myself. If I had not given you that plate. I know, Mahtab, that this was my fault. That plate..."

Mahtab put a finger on his lips. "Hush, let's not talk about that anymore. It wasn't your fault. Or my mother's."

He nodded, caressing Mahtab's scar.

"Do you want to stay here with me? I mean, if you don't, you can live in one of the other apartments in the building. But honestly, I can't live without you. This past year was hell for me."

Then as if talking to himself, he said softly, "You helped me to see this country differently. You made me rejoin this culture, a part of me that I didn't know I had. You even made me like this *daran-dasht*, this crazy city! You are my moonlight, my Tehran moonlight. I love you. I've loved you since the day at that photo gallery."

Mahtab whispered, "I love you too, Ashkan." She then bit her lip. Her cheeks were wet with tears. She wiped them and said, "But I still say he was an excellent photographer."

"OK, if you say so." He laughed. Mahtab smiled and threw her arms around him.

He kissed the top of her head and said, "Mahtab...I want to wake up with you by my side every day for the rest of my life. I want us to go to Boston, my city, together." He paused and said, "And if you want...if...you really want, one day...we can even have a baby together."

Mahtab opened her mouth. Ashkan was now on his knees, a ring in his hand.

"Will you marry me, Mahtab? Will you be mine forever?" Mahtab wiped her eyes. She just nodded and then burst into tears. He got up and slid the ring onto her finger. Then they kissed for what seemed like forever.

After they had found their breath, Ashkan said, "Now we are engaged."

"This is not how Iranians get engaged," Mahtab averred.

"I know," he said, kissing her, "but this is how we got engaged." Then he kissed her again and she kissed him back.

Suddenly she withdrew, her eyes wet. "Why? What's wrong?" Ashkan asked.

"I wish Nasim was here. I wish I could tell her everything."

He chuckled, "I wanted to surprise you, but I guess I'll tell you now. She's coming to see you tomorrow!"

She kissed him. She now wanted him as much as he wanted her. Gently uncoiling the scarf from around her head, he said softly, "Your hair has grown."

Mahtab just nodded.

Soft moonbeams traveled through the naked windows, the seductive breeze of the Alborz Mountains wafting in. It was the passionate kisses, the moments of desire, the yearning for unity, and nothing more. For Mahtab, it was only Ashkan.

When they fell back on the carpet, their breaths slowing, she heard him say. "Did I hurt you?"

She shook her head.

He breathed deeply and smiled. "Did you like it…to be with me?"

She smiled. "More than anything."

Then she wrapped a sheet around her naked figure and went to the balcony. The diamond shone on her finger. Googoosh was singing in the distance.

> *Am I dreaming or am I awake? You are with me, with me. If this is only a dream, let me dream forever. Tell me that I am awake, tell me that I am not dreaming. Tell me that from now on we won't be separated again.*

The moon hung like a silver coin over the city of Tehran that night. Mahtab stood on the terrace of her new penthouse and looked at the city between the mountains and the desert. The city made of shapes, of colored lights, of cement and metal bars. A confusion of buses, cars and people. The city that never stopped. But on this night, there were only the city lights, the moonlight, and the breeze from the mountains. There had been many moonlights like this since that moonlight when she had first met Ashkan. But now they were together. Mahtab knew that wherever she was, this was her city. This was her moonlight.

Acknowledgments

This book would have not happened if it weren't for my cousins in Tehran, who opened their hearts and helped me in every possible way. Thank you for giving me a glimpse into your lives. A special thanks to Nina and Shabnam who gave sisterhood a new meaning.

I would like to acknowledge my first ESL teacher, Ms. Georgi Tomisato who taught me more than I could imagine about the English language.

I would like to recognize Valerie Fiovaranti, who was instrumental in introducing me to the craft of writing.

Thank you Govind for your unconditional love and support and for being there every step of the way.

Yasna and Arun, thank you for sharing me with your paper and pen sibling, and for your enthusiasm to see this story come to life. You both rock my world.

Finally, I would like to thank you, dear Reader for taking the time to read this book. Without you, this story would not be heard.

CPSIA information can be obtained at www.ICGtesting.com
Printed in the USA
LVOW11s1626130814

398968LV00004B/903/P